THE DREAMER OF
THE VINE

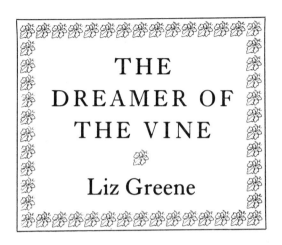

THE
DREAMER OF
THE VINE

Liz Greene

W·W·NORTON & COMPANY
New York   London

Thanks are due to Faber & Faber for permission to
quote the lines from 'Little Gidding'
by T. S. Eliot on page vi.

Copyright © 1980 by Liz Greene

Printed in the United States of America

All Rights Reserved

Library of Congress Cataloging in Publication Data

Greene, Liz.
The dreamer of the Vine.
1. Nostredame, Michel de, 1503–1566—Fiction.
I. Title.
PS3557.R384D7 1980   813′.54   80–21360
ISBN 0–393–01434–7

W. W. Norton & Company, Inc. 500 Fifth Avenue, New York, N.Y. 10110
W. W. Norton & Company Ltd. 25 New Street Square, London EC4A 3NT
1 2 3 4 5 6 7 8 9 0

To Lothar and Astrid
and to the ghosts who still haunt
the Château du Grand Jardin

And the end of all our exploring
Will be to arrive where we started
And know the place for the first time.

T. S. Eliot

Est unus deus et una dea. Sed sunt multa uti numina
ita et nomina . . . Sed haec cave enunties. Sunt enim
occulta silentio tamquam Eleusinarium dearum
mysteria. Utendum est fabulis atque enigmatum
integumentis in re sacra.

Mutianus Rufus

Part One

THE DREAMER
1503 – 1525

A child that goes to school and learns, when it arrives at years of discretion is ashamed of its childish work and destroys it. Thus shall it also happen to thee. For the time teacheth and giveth knowledge that not every pearl is a true pearl that is alleged to be so. Therefore a hand shall fall upon thee that will tear thee to shreds.

Paracelsus

I

I was five years old when the dream of the lady of the pool first came to me. It hung before my waking eyes in a tapestry of colours and shapes so much more vivid than the ordinary world in which I lived in St Rémy that all the next day I wandered about expectantly, waiting for my mother to tell me that we would soon undertake a journey.

It was not an auspicious time for such expectations. My father had been gone all the afternoon witnessing the purchase of a plot of land outside the town by one of the wealthier towns-folk. By the time he arrived home the cabbage had almost boiled away and the stew was a sodden mass.

'Of course he paid you well,' said my mother flatly, slopping the stew irritably into a wooden bowl for him as he sat wearily at the table.

'He will pay me two florins,' said my father into his beard, his mouth full of bread.

'Will?' my mother snapped sharply, whirling around so that the gravy flew from the big spoon and spattered the wall near my head. 'Do you mean to say that you have let another of these rich folk diddle you? Because you are too lily-livered to demand your fee? Because you are ashamed of being a Jew?'

'You know that I cannot badger a gentleman,' my father replied with a pale sigh. 'He will pay. They always pay.'

'Yes, in two weeks, in two months. We have food to buy, and taxes to pay, and Michel already too big for his shoes.'

It was the same quarrel as every other quarrel over every other meal. Two memories remain with me of my early child-hood. One was the alleyway outside our house which never received any sunlight and smelled perpetually of urine and boiled greens. The other was my parents' altercations. Each

9

evening became an opportunity for further insults. Although the meaning of these squabbles eluded me, the feeling underlying them was plain enough.

Seven years before, King Louis XII had passed an edict demanding that the Jews of Provence, under threat of torture and death, receive baptism and be welcomed into the sheltering arms of Holy Church. It had gnawed away at my father's soul ever since. He wrote a fine hand, and filed facts and numbers away in some mysterious cabinet of his mind so well organised and labelled that he never seemed to lose any of them. Because he was one of those men who are bound to form, God too occupied a little drawer in the cabinet in his head. Having misplaced the label for this drawer, he was given no peace. He feared that he would be punished by the Almighty, and saw in his humble and unstable notary's practice the visible signs of divine disfavour.

My mother saw in it alternatively laziness, cowardice, stupidity, lack of ambition, or the visible signs of my father's intent to punish her. She had been raised on tales of King René's golden court, with visions of wine and peacocks, sundrenched gardens of jasmine and lilac, tournaments and masques and Italian players strolling from the Campagne, orange groves jewelled with fruit. She was not inclined to accept with any grace the hovels and the frightened genuflecting and the endless clicking of rosary beads. Her bitterness fastened on matters of money, for the real failure cut too deep.

In the midst of this I could not ask about the pool, nor the lady with the rings, nor the mysterious abbey. After a few days I did not wait any more. Foolishly I thought it had been merely a dream.

I sit here now in the peace of my little attic study in this comfortable house in Salon, my arthritic old bones warmed by the fire, the dusty smell of my books about me. And I feel the familiar dull pain that has now made its permanent abode within my unwieldy body and will soon – if my calculations are correct – usher it to that threshold of which, unlike most men, I have never been afraid. And I look upon the advent of the dream and marvel that even then all was known, all was planned.

In my lifetime I have seen the beginnings of a new world

born amidst the pain of torture and the smell of charred bodies, amidst the stench of plague, the tragic farce of useless wars, the unseemly jockeyings of popes and kings around the revolving marriage beds of Europe – a world where the great rock of the Church no longer stands firm as the sole gateway to God. A new continent has been discovered where once it was thought the flat world ended in the vast void of space. Men weave cloth on great machines instead of with their hands. There are printed books and clocks instead of sundials to tell the time. And it was all foreseen. I have at one time or another been slandered, reviled, laughed at, feared, called charlatan and sorcerer and heretic and saint and prophet. None of these things makes any difference in the unfolding of the pattern.

The only true art that I possess, which cannot be taught to other men, is this thing of dreams. The mysteries of the heavens, the pathways and meanings of the wandering stars, the wisdom of centuries of human life and death distilled from Greek and Arab and Egyptian and Jew – all these can be taught. But it would seem that no one can be taught to dream as I do.

Other men have dreams, and I have many times been asked to explain to them the secret meanings of their nocturnal journeys. These journeys are so often banal, or puerile, full of pathos, seamed with the dark frustrations of the blood. The dreams of kings and queens, of which I have heard not a few, are the same as those of other men, and equally sordid. One cannot tell them this, any more than one can whisper in their ears the length of the thread that spans a life. I am alive, and live in wealth and comfort. For I have learned to be a cautious man, and have learned a golden tongue about other men's dreams.

But my dreams have always been clear and full of portents; and I have never understood from whence they issue. Once they visited me only in the night, and I did not comprehend them, but carried them like heavy embryos in the womb of my fear. Now, since I was taught, I can see them in the fire, and in still water. They span centuries, and only seem to roost in me like strange birds which perch briefly on some comfortable rooftop before the next stage of their unknown journey. I think that when I awaken free of this swollen and pain-burdened body which, physician that I am, I can no longer heal, I shall find that I have dreamed Michel de Notredame, and that in the welcome and inhuman light of that morning, this dream too will seem as though it had always been planned.

At first there was only the stream cascading gently over mossy rocks until it flowed, exhausted by its own frivolity, into a small pool. I could see the thick undergrowth, and trees which I did not recognise, drooping like weeping old women. An unknown landscape coalesced which bore no resemblance to the friendly hills of Provence. The sky lowered over me like a cocoon, grey and disinterested and cold. Undisturbed by wind or bird or insect, the heavy silence upholstered the world like cotton wadding, impenetrable. A peculiar light shone on the pool, giving it an opaque, greenish cast. I was aware of fear, and of a waiting, as though the pool concealed something unspeakable, yet not evil. I do not know what this fear is called, but I have felt it many times in sacred places – although not those which are sacred to Christendom. And there, in the dream, to my child's eyes, it was as though something holy yet terrifying were about to show its face to me; and I was afraid.

I know now who she is, or was, for it is five centuries since her body walked beneath the sun. She glided to the edge of the pool, making no sound, and leaned over to contemplate the reflection of her face. I could see the soft nap of the russet velvet of her robe, and the smooth draping of the linen wimple over her head, with a glint of gold underneath. She bent with a languorous pose, but I saw her twist her rings on her fingers, back and forth, one by one taking a ring off, twisting it, replacing it. Every finger on her very white hands glittered with gold.

Even in the dream, I thought she had a face pregnant with secrets. What those secrets were, I know now. Sometimes their awful burden still makes me shake and tremble for this devout Christian world, so sure of its faith and its pure and unsullied Saviour. I have never spoken these things aloud save with those who know, for I bear the blood of my race and am fond of survival. But in the dream, there was only a beautiful and regal woman, with some secret sorrow written across her white brow, and a face full of hidden things, playing with her rings.

One gold ring, in which a massive ruby mimicked a great gout of blood, slipped from her fingers and fell with a soft plop into the pool. The heavy atmosphere clung to my forehead like a damp fog. I thought I would choke. Something had claimed an offering. I wanted to cry out, but I was as frightened of the woman as I was of the pool. The nacreous wan light had begun to fade, and the pool looked black as obsidian. The woman sat very still, and I saw that she was praying, her white hands folded across her breast, eyes closed. She prayed for a long time. And then something broke the still blank surface of the pool, some unknown thing which rose and splashed and raised a great froth of bubbles as it clawed its way from the depths. In terror I covered my eyes with my hands and turned away.

When I looked up, it had grown dark. The woman had gone, and the pool was a silent black eye. I turned and looked over my shoulder. I saw the gentle hill rising above me with its darkened tangle of young ivy oaks and brambles and coarse grasses. At the top of the long incline stood the dim outline of an abbey. No light shone there. It seemed to have grown out of the earth, built in the squat and ugly manner of five hundred years past, humped like a crouching beast full of its own arcane secrets – a holy place, yet somehow unholy.

In the distance a line of men moved slowly, one by one, up the winding ribbon of the dirt track climbing the hillside between the ancient and pitted stone pillars that marked the structure's gate. They were cowled and robed, and I could not see the face of any of them, although the leader held a lantern muffled in the folds of his robe. They walked slowly and noiselessly, as though incorporeal. The dim light from the concealed lantern shone palely on the path and on what was hidden among the rocks and brambles.

Half-obscured by the undergrowth were the faint phantom corollas of golden crowns, and skulls with staring eyes, and the jewelled hilts of swords. Here was a half-buried shield, there a mace, bright bits of silk banners, golden coins. Before me flickered the rise and fall of a thousand years, and the dark vegetation slowly devouring all. There were crosses broken and splintered, images and holy relics, the worn icons of sad-eyed saints intermingled with the obscene couplings of gilded animals and naked women carved of stone.

I had only a brief glimpse, as the lantern cast its pool of thin light, and then darkness. Soon the somnambulistic cortège had passed, and vanished in shadows among the shadows of the abbey. The silence was absolute and teemed with presences. I heard the single sad note of a bell; and then I awoke. But I knew, a child shivering beneath the heaped furs and coarse woollen covers of my little cupboard bed, that the bell had called to me.

I I

I was sent to my grandfather Jean de St Rémy, my mother's father, when I was six years old. My mother explained to me that he was very learned, and could teach me better than she could do; and she spoke of my brother, who was only a baby, and of the responsibilities which lay heavily upon her. The house was terribly crowded, for my father's father lived with us too. No matter where I escaped, seeking some place of my own in which to play, I was always under someone's feet.

I learned later that my grandfather had insistently asked for me. Much later I learned this was because of the horoscope he had cast for me on the day of my birth. I do not remember feeling sadness at the going.

The woman who served my grandfather was called Madeleine, and she was deaf. It gave her an odd look, because when anyone spoke she peered intently at the moving lips. But she was large and benign, and led me kindly into the little parlour where my grandfather Jean awaited us.

'You will take care of him?' said my mother. But she was not really worried. The relief was obvious in her face.

'Well, boy,' said my grandfather, and put his big raw hands on my shoulders. He had been a physician of such skill and learning, it was said, that he had earned the patronage of *le bon roi* René. That beloved master was now twenty-nine years dead, stripped of his lands and his wealth, his only son poisoned, his daughter moribund of slow disease and imprisoned.

But my grandfather's bearing and mien still reflected his elegant past, spent travelling with his master through far-flung domains amidst the idyllic Arcadian lushness of the royal court. Jean de St Rémy was also an astrologer and a kabbalist. I did not, of course, understand this then. Nor did I know, or learn until thirty years had elapsed, who that mysterious and deeply mourned royal master truly was – King René, Duc d'Anjou, Bar and Maine, Comte de Provence and Piedmont, Duc de Lorraine, kingdomless King of Naples and Jerusalem and Sicily. Nor what secrets he held. Nor how the threads of his house's destiny intertwined like vines with my own.

I only saw that my grandfather Jean had the style of a court gentleman. Although his clothes were shabby now, they were nevertheless, in my six-year-old eyes, a most attractive thing, and vastly preferable to the style of a notary.

'What can you do?' my grandfather asked me. 'Can you count?'

'Yes, sir. And read, and write a little.'

'Well.' There was a faint surprise in his eyes, not because of these poor accomplishments, but because he had glimpsed something in my look. Some message passed between us, and I knew all at once that it would be well living with him. It was like hearing two notes played in harmony on the lute.

'We will teach you how to make your way in the world, boy. What do you think of that?'

'Very good, sir. And I would like to be a court gentleman.'

He let out a great booming laugh, and his beard bounced up and down on his chest. He still wore the black *houppelarde* of the Jew, though it was mocked now by the little gold crucifix threaded on a thin chain about his neck. Despite his age, he was well-made and tall and straight.

'Never fear, little Michel. One day you will have your heart's desire.'

Of course he spoke the truth. But I did not know then the cost, nor what strange path of dreams and visions would one day lead me there, nor to what mysterious line of royal blood I would, in the end, make obeisance.

15

I settled myself quietly before the fire, and he and my mother chatted for a while. They spoke of King Louis' vain wars in Italy, and of the precious gold that drained away like blood from a wound under the hot Peninsular sun. A new tax was sure to be levied soon to fill the empty coffers. It was not to be borne, my mother said. Had we not suffered indignity enough from this house of Valois? She rambled on about the furrier's wife, and the price of cabbages, and the pain in her back, and the sorry attack of rheum which had afflicted my brother Jean. Then she kissed me and was gone.

For a long time we merely sat there, I a child of six, he with his flowing grey and white beard and gnarled rough hands, with white streaks in his black hair, with hard lines carved across his forehead and along his eagle's nose. We stared at each other.

'You seem a healthy enough lad,' he observed, no doubt referring to my perpetually red cheeks and my rather stout frame, already a source of embarrassment to me. As a child I resembled a rosy dumpling.

'There will be plenty of work to do,' he sniffed. 'Supper will be soon.' And mysteriously the servant Madeleine appeared – although how she knew our conversation had ended, being deaf, I could not understand – and took me to my room. My father had brought my bag earlier in the day, and I found my clothes neatly hung on pegs, and a candle lit by the bedside, for it was already growing dark. I felt weary. An ending had come, and a beginning. The husk of my other life peeled away as easily as the chrysalis from an emerging butterfly, pausing to dry its wings before flight. I lay down on the bed and fell into a dreamless sleep, until Madeleine came to summon me for supper.

I have fame now, and the ignorant people of this town of Salon tell strange tales of me: that I made a pact with the Devil for my powers, or that I have been chosen as the mouthpiece of God. But the truth is that what I later became my grandfather Jean first shaped. He moulded the clay as it formed on the wheel, with a wisdom and kindness and patience that could only have derived from full knowledge of what I could eventually be and to whom I ultimately belonged. All I learned of the stars has been built upon the foundations which my grandfather first taught me; and all I have learned of healing, too, began with him. Where he acquired his wisdom, I could not then imagine. It was only later, when I became a student at Avignon, that I realised how much deeper it was than that of others.

To him I brought my one raw gift. I have always known the inside of people, on first meeting. As far back as I can remember, I could see a man's secret self peeping from behind his face, as clearly as the shape of his body protruding through the clothes which cover it. But that alone would never have sufficed to take me where I have gone. Another kind of illumination was necessary, something more vibrant and elusive, a species of inner flame. This flame, which has burned sometimes to bring blinding light and sometimes has scorched and tormented me, was first kindled by that gentle old man.

Because he was so interested in everything around him, he found a way to make it interesting to me. We walked through the streets of St Rémy, past the old crenellated walls and through the gate into the countryside. He told me of the history of each thing we passed. He showed me the ruined Roman arch and the ancient tombs, now mouldering beyond the walls where the hot barren fields began. He loved the past, and quickened it for me. He taught me the names of flowers and trees and herbs, and what their properties were. Nature was of a oneness to him, and he was full of old legends and strange tales and songs of chivalry and love and noble death. And gradually I began to sense the strata of the centuries in this little town sleeping beneath the burning Provençal sun, with the vibrant memories still pulsing secretly beneath the hum of the cicadas among the ruined stones.

We travelled one day by mule to Tarascon to see the great château which towers above the Rhône where King René spent his declining years. Now the King's governor of Provence lived there. But I could imagine it as it once was, the pennants waving gaily from the ramparts, while King René's noble Knights of the Order of the Crescent pranced across the ancient drawbridge on their great warhorses caparisoned in crimson and gold.

17

He taught me mathematics and Greek and Latin and Hebrew. As fast as my eager mind could process these things, he offered me the jewels of past wisdom: Aristotle, Plato, Tacitus, Homer, Virgil. And he never allowed me to forget my lineage.

'The children of Israel are ruled by Saturn,' he would often say to me, and frown, and look at his hands. 'We are the Chosen, the Scapegoat. Man must always have somewhere to cast his shadow, lest he discover that it is attached to his own feet. We have already suffered time out of mind, and we will suffer more. For Saturn is *Rex Mundi*, the Lord of the World; and we are his children.'

He would smile then, to cover his seriousness, and put his hands on my shoulders.

'If you are wise, Michel, you will go through this world with a mass each morning and a crucifix at your breast. Invocations to the saints must be ready on your lips, and a devout and humble look in your eyes as you approach the altars and the dignitaries of Holy Church. For that is the price Saturn demands of his children – to pass in disguise, so that the inner world's domains may be at your feet, while men never know your secret self.'

My grandfather too had become a Christian after King Louis' edict. But his conversion sat lightly on him, for he was not bound to the forms in which deity is worshipped. He did not feel he had betrayed his God or his ancestors by the baptism, or the prayers, or the little altar containing the statue of the golden-haired Madonna with inlaid lapis eyes which stood smiling serenely in the parlour.

'One name for God is as good as another,' he would tell me, for his mind traversed those spheres where it no longer mattered. I marvelled at this man who had lost everything, yet seemed to have lost nothing.

Although I saw my parents each Sunday for dinner and each morning in church, soon I forgot that I had any other father. The love between my grandfather and myself deepened and radiated outward, so that I was happy, and laughed, and experienced – for a time – a childhood like that of other human beings. I did not know that it would be so short. But perhaps, for its purpose, it was long enough.

When I was ten, he showed me his astrolabe. I thought it the most beautiful thing I had ever seen. It was made of brass and shone like gold because he polished it lovingly to keep it bright. He showed me the ecliptic, the path of the sun, and the poles and the equator of the earth, which he told me was round; and the circle by which, if I peered through it up into the heavens, I could measure the positions of the moon and stars. At the beginning, it was a toy. Later, as I learned, it became the most precious thing I knew.

We would walk out into the blinding haze of sunlight, and he would talk to me of the sun, the Great Light, and the secret sun within the heart of each man. He would talk of the moon, the Lesser Light, and her mysteries, the hidden ebb and flow of fluids – blood and lymph and semen – coursing secretly within the silent corridors of the body. Each wandering star, he told me, was a god, and each god was also manifest as a colour, and a musical note, and a metal, and a jewel, and a flowering plant. I learned to look into the faces of neighbours and passers-by and see there the marks of the choleric children of Mars, the sanguine children of Mercury and Venus, the melancholic children of Saturn, the phlegmatic children of the moon.

Once he said to me, 'I will tell you a secret, Michel. The crystalline spheres, fixed in the ether which men say surround our earth in space, are nothing but fantasy. Men are arrogant, and wish to believe that the universe has no other purpose but their own development. But in truth the earth circles in space, as do the other planets; and the centre and heart of all the universe is the sun.'

This seemed reasonable enough to me; for the sun, as anybody could see, was the greatest thing in heaven. When I went to Avignon, I found that no one had thought of such a thing. They believed me mad to contemplate it. If the earth went round the sun, they asked me, what kept it from falling away and rolling off into a black void? Many years later, I heard that a man named Copernicus had made a great discovery about this phenomenon. But I first heard it from my grandfather when I was eleven.

Although he no longer practised as physician to the rich, I

19

helped him to prepare his balms and unguents and potions and powders, which he dispensed freely to the poor of the town. I learned to set a broken bone, and stitch a gaping wound closed with the finest silken thread, and make a poultice of mouldy bread and spiders' webs to drain the pus from a reeking sore.

Later he spoke to me of the Zohar, and of the Celestial Spirits before the Throne of God, and of the elemental kingdoms of nature, and the Tree of Life. I felt dazzled by all this mystery. I did not think I could contain so much richness. I devoured, and grew, and became famished again, and devoured yet more. I begged him to tell me tales of King René's court. But most of all I loved the stars, and I loved his hands that could ease pain or mend the broken wing of a bird with such delicacy that no embroideress could move so nimbly, nor with such skill.

Sometimes I accompanied him to the houses of the sick. We would be greeted with civility, and I would be given a cake or a piece of marchpane while I sat and watched him tend his patients. We would then return home and he would take out his books and his astrolabe and calculate the horoscope of the sick man. Sometimes he would wait until the propitious moment to administer treatment. At other times he would shake his head sadly, and I would know it was that man's time to die. It may seem a strange childhood, with an old man for companion and such subjects for daily food, instead of the wonted activities that boys pursue. Yet I would not have chosen any other.

He unrolled my horoscope for me one day with great ceremony, as though it were a birthday gift. He had drawn it with care on the day of my birth, on a piece of parchment as fine as linen, and wrapped it round with a red ribbon. I looked with eager fascination at the strange markings. He shook his head and stared at me, not with unkindness, but with a kind of awe suffused by sadness.

'You will go further than I ever could,' he said. 'You will rise very high, little Michel, very high indeed. Look. This circle with the point at the centre is the sun, the Great Light. It stands overhead at the midheaven in the sign of Capricorn the Goat. That gives you caution and steadfastness and subtlety. And ambition that will bring you fame and honour. And a name that will live after you.'

That pleased me, but I could feel the unhappiness oppressing him. 'And this?' I asked, pointing to the crescent that marked the moon.

At first he would not answer. 'You will learn, in due time, how to read it.'

'What do you see, *grandpère*? Tell me. I am not afraid.'

He gave me that peculiar look again. 'A life of honour. But I fear that you will know much loneliness. And death dogs you. Here is the moon in the sign of Scorpio, in the House of Death, in quadrature to Venus. It is the death of those you love that dogs you. Death and secret sorrow. Learn to keep silence, Michel.'

He would tell me nothing more. I did not feel frightened. But I was afflicted by his sadness.

'I will not be alone with you,' I said foolishly. He only shook his head and turned away. He knew, of course, what time we had left.

When I had been with my grandfather Jean for six years, King Louis XII died, and his nephew the Duc d'Angoulême mounted the throne of France as King François. I, of course, did not much care, for at twelve years old one king is much the same as another, save for the pageants and festivities and pleasant things to eat and drink which accompany such changes in the great world.

Within a few months of the new King's accession he declared war on the Emperor Maximilian and invaded Italy. And a visitor came secretly to St Rémy and paid call to my grandfather very late in the night, and left as secretly as he had come.

I had gone to bed early that night, for my grandfather and I had been out walking, and I had eaten a heavy supper. It was not the sound of the hoofbeats outside the window which woke me, but the gentle rapping at the door. When I peered from my little casement window I could see a black horse tied to a post before the house.

There was nothing really strange in this, for my grandfather often had visitors among the wealthy, who were connections from his days at court, or who wanted some of his potions and ointments. But for some reason the sight of that black horse made me uneasy. I had a queer feeling, and crept from my room to the top of the stairs, not understanding why I should slink about my grandfather's house in this way, but obeying some deep instinct that warned me I was not meant to know of this visitor. I could not tell what hour it was. I had not heard the church bell. But it was very dark outside, and I felt as though I had been asleep for a long time.

I heard the murmur of voices in the parlour downstairs, and leaned quietly over the stair rail, listening. The staircase was pooled in shadow, and the yellow light from the tapers cast a ragged shifting circle on the parlour floor. Just within my range of vision I saw the visitor seated in one of the chairs before the fire. He was young, and wore a black cloak thrown across his shoulders, which was spattered with dust and stained with the marks of hard travel through boggy roads. It was cut of rich cloth, and matched the velvet cap on his dark head.

I reasoned that it must be some wealthy merchant or traveller whose family were taken sick and needed my grandfather's services. But their voices were kept low, almost in a whisper, and I heard the rustle of parchment that I knew to be the rolls of horoscopes which my grandfather kept locked in his bureau. Once again I had the feeling that secrets were being exchanged of which I was meant to know nothing.

I heard the dull clink of cups. My grandfather was pouring wine. The stranger's voice rose, and I caught the final words of his speech.

'. . . invade the Milanese,' he was saying. 'If you are certain he will live . . .' I saw him hold up his cup and make the sign of a toast. His voice came to me clearly.

'To M. le Comte,' he said, and drank deeply. I saw the blazon on his arm as he raised his goblet: three silver *ailerons* on a diagonal bar of crimson, against a field of gold. He leaned forward, and his voice dropped, and the murmuring conversation continued. And then, after some fifteen minutes, he rose and wrapped his cloak about him – he was clothed all in black – and grasped hands with my grandfather and made to go. I saw them walk to the door together.

'Do not fear,' my grandfather said. 'He will only be wounded in Italy. Great honour will come of it.'

'And the boy?' the stranger said. 'Will you tell him, then?'

'No,' my grandfather replied. 'He must find out in his own way, when the time is right. I will be long dead then. But he cannot be led. He is deep and secretive and stubborn. He must come to it of his own will.'

The stranger departed, and I heard the hoofbeats receding into the night. I crept back to my bed, and lay there until dawn staring at the black gnarled beams in the ceiling, and wondering. My grandfather never mentioned the visitor to me; and I, prompted by some obligatory reticence, never asked him. Now that I know, I see the magnitude of his wisdom. For I had indeed to come to it of my own will, if there is truly such a thing as will at all.

In my grandfather's house I dreamed of the pool only once. I was fifteen years old. I had been to the early morning mass with my mother, and my thoughts had drifted away on the clouds of incense and the droning of Latin until I felt as though I had floated out of my body and through the nave of the little church of St Pierre and frolicked among the clouds with the sylphs and devas of the air. My mother poked her elbow into my side, and I returned with a jolt to find the priest glaring at me. But he went on with the service, and I kept my eyes studiously on the ground as we rose to take our leave.

That night I had the dream. I remembered the place at once. The heavy cocoon of silence enfolded me, and the sense of some awful presence. But I was older now, and found myself wondering, in the dream, what it was that lived here and made its abode in the recesses of this still dark pool. I waited for the woman with the rings, but she never appeared. I waited alone while the light disintegrated into gloom and the pool turned black as obsidian in the dimness.

I turned and saw the abbey. It was the same, shrouded in shadows, lightless and brooding. I heard the bell, but it did not ring once this time. It tolled seven times, and I knew that there had been a death, and that the bell signalled the soul's passage.

At the crest of the hill, illuminated by no light that I could see, one of the monks stood, robed and cowled, as still as the black stone of the abbey behind him, a shadow against a backdrop of darker shadows. I stared and felt that I knew him. Although I could not see his face, his eyes glowed brilliant blue in the gloom like ghostly pale sapphires, fixed inexorably upon me.

I awoke with an acrid mouth and spasms of pain in my head and a sick sense of fear. I must have been delirious, for I can remember nothing of the morning nor the following day. Madeleine brought me hot possets, and looked tired and worn and sorrowful, and drifted in and out like a wan ghost. But I could not speak, for along with the headache had come a terrible burning in my throat, and my skin was hot and dry to touch. Later I learned that I lay ill for two days, muttering in the delirium of some unknown fever that they would come for me soon. And when I finally awoke and could see clearly and no longer felt the pain, my mother entered weeping, with dark blue bruises beneath her dark eyes, wearing a gown of black stuff, to tell me that my grandfather was dead.

III

My mother returned with me to the rue de Barri, and I was installed once more in my little attic room, now crammed with the books and manuscripts which my grandfather had bequeathed to me.

Nothing had changed during my absence. My father still droned on incessantly about tracts of land and florins and documents and the price of grain. I was a wild bird trapped in a fowler's net. Living with my grandfather, I had flown through the clear transparent spaces of the air and glimpsed the distant suns and stars of other universes. This grey world of earth, with no aperture for my spirit to escape, suffocated me until I withdrew completely into myself, burying my face in the books and manuscripts which were all I had left of him. I snatched the silent hours after the household had retired. All night, I would bend over my guttering candle, trying to claw my way by sheer force of will through the heavy clay encasing me in order to breathe once more.

'We must do something about the boy's education,' my mother said to my father not three weeks after my return. 'He cannot immure himself in that room all day and night as he does. It will give him an unhealthy outlook.'

There began a series of discussions, quarrels and debates over my preference for dead books to a live family and friends. My father took the problem to his father, Pierre de Notredame. My grandfather Pierre had been a close friend of my grandfather Jean since their youth. He was also an eminently practical man, having once been a grain-dealer. He offered the wisdom of age and experience.

'Send the boy to study at Avignon,' he said.

Thus I was sent, at the age of fifteen, to the City of the Popes. I envisioned it as a fantastic and foreign domain, a place of escape and refuge, a gilded city full of magical castles and hidden treasure. So desperate was I in my need for flight that I did not foresee the exchange of one prison for another.

I resided at the home of my father's sister Marguerite and her husband Thibaut de Mirecour; I attended the College of Liberal Arts in the Place des Études each day with my cousin Jaume. I had come to hate Avignon almost instantly. The dreams of a magical refuge shattered into infinitesimal fragments and were trod underfoot in the dust. It was a noisy and filthy city, perpetually churning like a vast bowl of foul soup, streaked with violent colour and sound – and the vulgar gaudiness of the perpetual processions, visiting prelates filing into the great papal palace which overshadowed the narrow streets. Cardinal de Clermont, the papal Legate, ruled Avignon as a petty king, all day parading his Swiss Guard like garish mannequins through the streets to remind the citizens that the power of God was not confined to prayer and good works. In grim counterpoint to the splendour of holiness, the bankrupts and criminals kept state in the shadowy and insalubrious alleyways of the town. Here were assembled refugees from every part of France, come to Avignon because it offered sanctuary beyond the bounds of the throne's jurisdiction.

I retired still further into my books. I quickly acquired a

reputation as a brilliant but peculiar fellow. Brilliant because feats of memory were no challenge to me, and I was said to possess a remarkable understanding of classical philosophy and astrology. Peculiar because I was a solitary and seemed to possess secrets.

My aunt Marguerite was a quiet and subtle woman. She seemed meek and humble, and glided about noiselessly with her dark head bowed and modestly covered by a spotless matron's cap, pouring wine and serving food and playing with the crucifix which hung suspended between her breasts. She had borne no other living children besides Jaume. There had been four miscarriages; and after that, Jaume told me, she and her husband slept apart and did not attempt to make a child again, lest she die of it. Jaume implied that it was his mother who had decided this.

My cousin and I maintained a tepid and colourless relationship, mild as watered milk. I tried to teach him astrology, which he thought to be nonsense at best and sorcery at worst. I spoke to him of my grandfather's belief that the earth was a ball which circled the sun. He shook his head and smirked, and offered instead his much more practical knowledge of the little kitchen maid who would be only too willing to introduce me to the delights of manhood.

'You are too old to mope about like a virgin priest,' he said, giving me a conspiratorial grin. 'A pair of white breasts under your hands and I will wager you will forget all about whether it is the earth or the sun or your own head which is revolving in space.'

After this I kept my thoughts to myself. It earned me the profound suspicion of my cousin, who began to eye me with a very speculative look, and took pains to prevent his body coming into contact with mine. It amused me that he thought me a sodomite, and it spared me the necessity of discussing the fantasies which had begun to plague my sleep. My tastes, it seemed, were normal enough. But I wanted more forbidden fruit than plump blonde Alys of the kitchens.

One evening Jaume accompanied his father to visit another cousin across the city. They were to stay until morning. I finished my dinner hurriedly and retreated frantically to my room, tormented by the fear that my dreams had in some magical way brought to pass that which I had secretly longed for. I tried to find refuge in Galen and Hippocrates and the humours of the blood.

Someone at school that afternoon had asked the professor whether more might be learned about the nature of man by dissecting cadavers than by philosophising abstractions about the body. The professor had responded with a white face and a thunderous shout that if such a terrible heresy were ever mentioned again, he would report it to the authorities. My head had been full of it all the way home. Images pursued me – of dark cloaked figures sifting into silent graveyards, carrying in a sack the shovels and the picks, exhuming and examining the freshly buried corpses by smoking candlelight in some dark and hidden room, poring over the forbidden mysteries of bones, blood, vital organs. I sat staring at my open books while bizarre figments chased each other frenziedly through my head – Marguerite, gently removing her fine woollen gown and her scented linen, the corpse laid out on the table in the yellow candlelight, Marguerite the corpse, the living body rising up white and glistening from a freshly dug grave . . .

The candle flickered in a draught, as I sat paralysed in a kind of trance while the black visions filled my mind and my body. When the delicate scratching at the door at last tickled the silence, I could only wait in terrified mute passivity.

I tried to look realistically at it. Why not? No one would have to know. Since her husband had repudiated her, her amusements outside the marriage were no one's affair but her own. But at the thought of a child I grew cold again, and relapsed into terror. This dark illicit entanglement could only end in some dreadful punishment for me, and a violent quarrel between the two families. It was impossible. Tomorrow I would seek out Alys of the kitchens, and shut my eyes and pretend that the yellow hair was as black as the blackness of my fantasies, that the vapid blue eyes were as dark and obscure as the still depths of an obsidian pool . . . But the door opened and Marguerite stood framed against the blackness outside, a shadow against shadows, with a single taper in her hand. Very gently, very delicately, she touched with her fingertips the

27

sensitive skin of my cheek and neck, as if it were one of the stable cats she stroked with her long sensuous fingers. As I looked into her shadowed eyes where the pinpoint reflection of the taper danced, I saw with mingled horror and fascination that she knew, she knew my dreams, she knew my darkness, she knew how to draw the *daemon* out of me; and she was without mercy. When she parted her lips in a smile the smile was mocking and hungry and full of power, and as I opened my mouth to whisper a protest, to beg her to leave me in peace, she reached up for me and closed my lips with her own.

In the morning I lay for a long time in twisted reveries, while the sun spilled through the window like molten gold. I had, of course, known the mechanics of the sexual act. One does not reach the ripe age of fifteen without gleaning, from bits and pieces of gossip and the whispering of classmates behind their hands, what it was about. In theory, it was no mystery to me.

The mystery and the terror resided in the emotions which had exploded within me, the obsessive, uncontrollable hunger that brought me to weeping and to savagery. There was something caged secretly within me which had broken violently free in the night and mocked me with its unknown face. The delicate sentiments of love which entwined the troubadours' songs had nothing in common with this hunger. It was neither tender nor solicitous, but violent and reeking of death. And she had toyed with it, laughed at it, tantalised and teased me, aroused and thwarted me over and over until I could have torn her eyes and her laughing lips from her body and drunk her blood. I had plunged into blackness in her embrace like some swimmer vanishing into murky waters where pain and pleasure were indistinguishable and fused in a horrible dance. When I emerged shuddering I did not know where I had gone.

Yet despite the fear and the self-disgust, despite my hatred of her who had called this thing out of me, I knew that I must go back again.

I V

One fine spring morning I walked to the Place des Études with my cousin Jaume, my books in a sack thrown over my shoulder, my eyes heavy and aching. I had indulged in one of my nocturnal meetings, and had snatched only an hour or two of sleep before dawn. Before my mind flickered continually the disturbing images of the night. I hardly listened to Jaume's ubiquitous babble as we moved through the narrow alleyways. The streets were full of people, for one of the great processions was weaving its noisy way through the town toward the papal palace. All the townsfolk had left their shops and houses to get a glimpse of some prince of the Church, bedecked in crimson and gold and borne aloft on his litter toward the vast and ancient monument of stone.

I had not the slightest interest in these processions of visiting prelates, for they seemed to reek with a stench of hypocrisy. The magnificent trappings of wealth displayed with such ostentation to a wondering and superstitious populace could have fed the poor of the town for a year, and not left a trace in the bursting coffers of the Church. I hated the papal palace too, for I thought it a cruel and oppressive place with its ornamented towers like twin horns piercing the sky. There was a dark feeling around it, as though the stones held the smell of blood from older days – days when the long-dead Pope Clément V, in unholy union with Philippe le Bel, had tortured and burned at the stake five thousand of the Knights of the Temple, while the smoke and the stench of charred bodies rose to heaven and the Order's last Grand Master, the aged Jacques de Molay, pronounced his fatal curse on Pope and King and on the royal line of France.

But Jaume loved a pageant, just as he loved his serving girls.

Because on that morning we had time to spare before the bell of St Didier rang to summon us to our books, he insisted that we walk toward the palace to see the procession. We were immediately caught up in the crowd, pushed and bumped and knocked about and carried along like flotsam on a great river, until we saw, at the front of the parade, the little group of heralds clad in shining silver tabards and brandishing cornets. With gleaming halberds the Swiss Guards tramped along behind them in red and blue and brilliant orange livery, and men-at-arms on great chargers, and a retinue of pages bearing torches and white tapers and swinging smoking censers, and the gentlemen of the bedchamber and the household clad in satin and silk. And at last we saw the litter covered in crimson velvet and cloth-of-gold.

Jaume nudged me in the ribs. 'Look at that!' he shouted in my ear, nearly deafening me.

We fought our way to the front of the crowd. Carried before the litter, supported by two pages in snow-white silken tunics, was a great golden cross, studded with jewels. It was half the height of a man, and must have cost thousands of écus. Behind it marched another pair of pages with another great cross. But this one was of solid silver with double arms, deeply engraved with mysterious symbols. At the feet of the crucified Christ a serpent coiled in sinuous spirals about an egg. At the tips of his outstretched hands were carved the faces of Sol and Luna, sun and moon. Above his head the hand of God pointed with second and third fingers in the sign of a blessing I did not recognise.

'What emblem is that?' I asked Jaume, beginning to be interested at last, for it was exquisitely beautiful and carried a strangeness.

He shrugged. A man beside me, hearing my question, turned toward me.

'The cross of the Kingdom of Jerusalem,' he shouted over the din of the cornets and the crowd. 'This is the procession of the new Cardinal, Jean de Lorraine. He is only twenty. Look, there, in the litter.'

I looked. I could only see in the distance a very young man gowned in scarlet silk whose golden hair and fair fineboned face seemed far too handsome for a priest's. He was borne along smiling and bowing, as though for all the world he were a king, while he held his white hand, sparkling with jewelled rings, in the sign of blessing to the curious and admiring people. I began to lose interest again. Here was some spoiled scion of a great house, the political importance of whose family had merited him such honour when he was scarce out of boyhood. I pulled at Jaume's coat to make him come away.

Then I caught sight of the embroidered banners held aloft by the retinue that followed in the wake of the litter like seagulls in the wake of some great ship. I saw quartered lilies, gold against blue, and crimson bars on a ground of silver, and again that strange double-armed cross, gold on a field of white like a sunbeam across a drift of snow. And at last I saw three silver eaglets barred on crimson against a carpet of purest gold.

I stood very still while the crowd heaved and jostled and shouted around me. The litter was going to pass directly where I stood, but I was not watching it; I was deep in thought. Well, I reasoned, here is a little mystery solved. What did it matter? It had nothing to do with me. Lorraine was not even a French house.

I tapped the shoulder of the man who had spoken to me. 'Who is this new Cardinal?' I asked him.

My informant was pleased to display his latest acquisition of gossip, and leaned close to me. Even at this early hour of the morning, he reeked of wine.

'Jean de Lorraine, brother to Antoine, Duc de Lorraine, and to Claude, Comte de Guise. The Comte de Guise fought heroically with King François at the battle of Marignano, and received twenty-two wounds, and almost died, and was miraculously healed. He is very close to the King. Great honours have been given to his house.'

A feeling of uneasiness pervaded me. I grasped Jaume by the shoulder and pulled him toward me. But at that moment the litter rocked by, and the crowd pressed flat against the houses to let the procession pass. A great sighing and murmuring rose up from the women, for Jean de Lorraine's youth and beauty and grace were worthy of a fairy tale. This Cardinal, I thought wryly, is not likely to pass his life in celibacy.

The men-at-arms rode by almost over my feet, and the smoke from the censers blurred my vision, and the golden tassels of the pages' banners brushed my arms. I stared at the young man who reclined easily amidst a pile of velvet cushions, still bowing and smiling. He turned, and for a brief moment his gaze brushed mine. I felt an intense recognition, as though I had known this face before, in some dream, some distant past. My heart gave a great thump, though the Cardinal merely moved his eyes, which were as blue as cornflowers, along to other faces, and the litter moved on. I hurried away, dragging Jaume protesting behind me. By the time we had reached the Place des Études I had a tight knot in my stomach, for something had frightened me which I could not understand.

But when I arrived home that night, there was Marguerite waiting for me. And all memory of the day – of the quartered lilies of Anjou and Sicily, the crimson bars of Hungary, the double cross of Jerusalem and the silver eaglets of Lorraine – all was banished from my mind by the dark cloud of her hair and the white silken skin of her neck and breasts.

It would seem now, after living these many years here in Salon, that apart from my peculiar talents I am as much a pillar of society as any man. I am titled Physician-in-Ordinary to the King of France; I give gold écus to abbeys and to the poor. I have helped Adam de Craponne build his canal to water the towns of the desert of Craux. My wife is a woman of property, my sons strong and healthy. This house, although not ostentatious, is comfortable and admirably suited to the needs of an old man in declining health.

But I did not learn until late this art of blending with the civilised world, like a grey stone among other stones. And then I was taught it, for it was required of me. In my heart, beneath the thin veneer of my Christian prayers and my solid household, I have always been a wanderer and an outcast. During my lonely years in the bustling town of Avignon, I recognised that no force on earth or in heaven could shape me in the mould of my fellow men.

The world during this time was slowly preparing to split itself open like a great pomegranate. The chief engineers in this work of demolition had only just appeared on the stage. Every-where brooded the terrible fear of the torments of Hell, equal-led only by the fear of the torments of Holy Church that awaited the heretic. A monk named Luther had just laid at the door of the cathedral of Wittenberg the egg which would hatch such bloody violence across the whole of Europe. But it seemed I could hear the ominous rumblings underground long before. The Emperor Maximilian died, and into the subtle and crafty hands of his grandson Charles fell the vast Habsburg domains of Spain, Holland, Belgium, Austria and Burgundy. And despite extravagant efforts and immense expenditure of money by King François, it was not long before the young Habsburg scion had slid into the empty and beckoning throne of the Holy Roman Empire. France stood poised between Spain and the Netherlands and the Germanies like a great nut waiting to be cracked. Suleiman the Magnificent mounted the throne of the Empire of the Turks and invaded the Balkans. One could hear on any street corner in Avignon that the world was ending and that the reign of Antichrist would soon be at hand.

The town astrologers peered nervously at their calculations, watching with dread the advent of the great conjunction – six heavenly bodies in the sign of the Fishes three years hence, in the Year of Our Lord 1524. I had my own opinions about the fate of France. King François was a fair king, gallant, gra-cious, chivalrous, handsome, patron of arts, collector of old masters and young mistresses. The glow of his golden court cast a romantic patina over the whole of Christendom. But there was a rot, a sickness, a despair that gnawed cracks through the gaiety and disclosed the sewage beneath.

The people of Avignon became noisier, and the streets became filthier. What can a man do when Hell yawns on his left and the paralysing salvation of Holy Church waits to eat his soul on the right? What becomes of his faith, his moral convic-tions, when those who are meant to be his spiritual shepherds are themselves submerged beneath their own sheep's dung? One can do what my cousin Jaume did: eschew the problems of theology, sink oneself into the soft bodies of willing women, drink, sing, and damn damnation. One can do what my aunt Marguerite eventually did: become obsessed with salvation in

33

God, which is a suitable surrogate for obsession with the flesh, and is perhaps in some paradoxical way the same. One can do what Calvin and Luther did: attempt to redress one's own shadow by redressing the shadow of the Church which one has oneself helped to build. And, in the process, never recognising that the problem does not lie in the nature of man's dogmas, but in the nature of man himself.

Or one can do what I did in my eighteenth year in the great papal conclave of Avignon. One can follow the lonely road within, wondering whence it will lead, keeping silence, brooding over the hints and omens that come in dreams which portend now some dark abyss, now some glorious salvation. One can weep in the nocturnal silence from the bitterness of one's isolation, yet sometimes wax scornfully proud of that which marks the outcast. One can sit for hours pondering over the mysterious familiarity of a pair of cornflower-blue eyes, and a gold banner embroidered with three silver eaglets on a bar of crimson, and a black horse, and a magical pool like an obsidian eye, and a woman with a golden ring set with a ruby like a gout of blood, and a dim abbey in the shadows of one's own darkness. And one can wait, and wait, for some message, some voice, some omen which will illumine the road, never knowing that one is already upon it, and that even if one tries to evade it, one cannot escape meeting oneself.

V

One night Marguerite crept to my room white-faced, clenching and unclenching her slender hands, her forehead filmed with damp.

'I have missed my monthly courses,' she whispered.

In the end it was only an indisposition. But during that night I died many times – died first in her arms and then again with each desperate scheme to find some road of escape from this nightmare. We spoke of medicines that would cause the gravid womb to spew forth its burden with unseemly haste, and I died in the maw of guilt. We spoke of her naming an unknown lover – some servant, some wealthy merchant who had passed through Avignon – and I died in the fear of inevitable discovery when the child was born. We spoke of her going away for a time, and I died in the leaden knowledge that somewhere in the world there would be a living thing born of this incestuous union which would dog my steps for the rest of my life.

We decided upon the first choice. But when she consulted the old woman who lived on the outskirts of the town, beyond the fortified walls, it seemed Marguerite suffered only from some illness that had infected her womb. The old woman gave her medicines, and her courses began again. Our liaison did not. I was not prepared to take such a risk again. I withdrew into celibacy and returned to my books. I decided to become a physician like my grandfather.

I wrote to my father to tell him of this decision. His first reply was angry and enumerated the costs required to send me to one of the great schools of medicine. But I knew that my grandfather Pierre would support me in my desire. A second letter arrived, a week after the first. My grandfather had offered to provide fees to send me to the University of Montpellier, where I would study to become a doctor.

I was nineteen when I arrived at Montpellier. I had learned three things: patience, secrecy, and fear of women. I spent three years at my studies there, attempting to render my life as cool, as pure, and as untouched as snow on a distant mountaintop. I still awaited a sign.

In the Year of Our Lord 1522, His Most Christian Majesty King François, having become bored with his women and his poets and his painters, decided to declare war on the Emperor Charles. Having tasted the forbidden fruits of Italy at the beginning of his reign, he wished to make a whole meal of them. Treaties formed and dissolved and reformed like bubbles on the surface of a stagnant pool. France allied with the Swiss against Venice, Spain, England and the Pope. France and England allied with the Pope against Venice, Spain and the Emperor. France allied with the Emperor against the Turks. And so it evolved, like the stately steps of some elephantine *saltarello* where the partners shift and shuffle and one never sees the same two dancers together twice.

In the following year a new rumour flowered in the gossips' mouths, and this one was hot and tasty, for it concerned the scandals of the court. It seemed that some shameful débâcle had broken out about the person of Charles, Duc de Bourbon and Constable of the Armies of France. No one in Montpellier even knew what Charles de Bourbon looked like. But the townsfolk spoke of him as though he were a local butcher who had been discovered in some forbidden bed.

Being young and dashing and proud and immensely wealthy, and a Prince of the Blood as well, he had caught the lustful eye of the ageing Queen-mother, Louise de Savoie. For a time they had become lovers. But this great lady had, to everyone's misfortune, made a clumsy overture of marriage to the arrogant young duke before his own ailing wife was even cold in her grave. He, in his high-handed fashion, refused her. She retaliated by obtaining the King's consent to seize his lands and his possessions, and drove him from his family seat at Moulins where he had reigned over his duchy of Bourboness with the splendour of a monarch.

Charles de Bourbon had retaliated in his turn, against both King and Queen-mother, by treating with the Emperor Charles. He was said to be wandering in disguise, pursued by the King's men, making his way through Auvergne, Burgundy, Beaujolais, Vienness, Languedoc and Dauphiny, moving in slow serpentine spirals to elude his pursuers, drifting downward toward Italy where his new master the Emperor would receive him. When King François invaded Italy, he would be met not by some German or Spanish general, but by an Imperial army led against him by the greatest soldier in France.

A few citizens of Montpellier quietly questioned the behaviour of the King and his mother. Most, however, were personally outraged that a Prince of the Blood should turn traitor and fugitive. They were quick to heap upon the young duke every vilifying epithet they could find. For was not the King God's anointed representative on earth, accorded sacred charge of the secular life of his people, as the Pope exercised charge of the spiritual?

Charles de Bourbon became known as the Great Heretic. It was the favourite pastime of an evening for the townsfolk to gather together and discuss possible means of torture and death for this man who, it seemed to me, had done the only thing possible in the face of unjust and humiliating ruin. Had I been in his place, I reasoned, I would have done the same. But when a man cuts himself from the herd for good or evil reasons, and performs actions that any man would perform if he were not protected by circumstances and his own self-righteousness, it is the fashion to make him the scapegoat. Thus one can avoid facing one's own complicity.

I remembered my grandfather Jean telling me that the Jews were ruled by Saturn, and were thus the Scapegoat for the darkness of other men. I wondered if the Connêtable de Bourbon too was ruled by Saturn. I never stopped to ask myself why my sympathies flowed so naturally in a direction which any Frenchman would consider treasonable.

In the core of the splitting pomegranate, I followed my studies with quiet obsessiveness, eschewing the usual pursuits of my fellow students – the street riots, the abductions and seductions of the local merchants' wives and daughters, the smashed windows and stolen shop goods, the drunken parties and the incessant patronage of the local drabs. I still waited for the unknown omen.

Occasionally I joined my comrades in their cups at a little tavern near my lodgings. It was called *les Joies du Paradis*, though its wine more often brought loose bowels and headache than visions of the angelic host. But sometimes even I had to burst the self-imposed fetters of my harsh solitude, and once in every few weeks I would get drunk with the rest of them. The women of the tavern I avoided, for I had a deadly horror of the pox.

It was at *les Joies du Paradis* that I met M. Plantard, as he called himself – for he never told me his real name. The tavern was habitually dark and crowded and reeking of the stench of sweat. On this evening when I left my books and accompanied my fellows there, it was particularly thick and fusty. Patrons had swarmed to hear the minstrel from Carcassonne. It was

37

said he knew all the old troubadour songs, as well as the popular *chansons* of des Près and Janequin; and he could improvise an *estampie* with such skill that it left the listener breathless.

The patrons and the serving girls had pressed themselves along the sides of the cluttered little room, shoving the tables and benches out of the way to leave space for the player. When I arrived he was already tuning his lute, his head bowed low so that I could not see his face. He wore an old tattered doublet that had once been rich. Now, however, the velvet was worn away in great patches, like the coat of a mangy dog. Nevertheless, it was threaded with what remained of a galaxy of seed pearls which now hung, albeit sadly thinned, along the breast and the sleeves slashed with faded satin. He had draped his short cloak over a bench and knelt on it as though it were a dais. The usual babble of voices and singsong had sunk to a low murmur as the audience, many of them already drunk, strained to hear the delicate plucking of the fragile strings.

Keeping his head bowed, he played first an old *estampie* of two centuries past, and one or two pieces from des Près, and then an antique motet whose haunting atonal cascades were like the wailing voice of some earthbound spirit longing for freedom. His voice scaled depths and heights as easily as a bird soaring and dipping in the air. I sat openmouthed in silence, feeling myself twisted into unknown patterns by the sweet and sorrowful ebb of his magical hands.

After a time he stopped to refresh himself with beer. For the first time, as he lifted his dark ragged head, I saw plainly his young-old face, for he looked across that dark body-thick room directly at me and gave me a bittersweet smile. I caught my breath in a hiss. I was flooded by the same sense of incomprehensible recognition that had once jolted me three years ago when I met the eyes of the young Jean, Cardinal de Lorraine, in procession at Avignon.

Here were eyes of the same intense blue, ingenuous eyes open as flowers, set in a proud, sensitive, sorrow-haunted face. He looked to be not more than thirty-five, but he might have been much younger, or much older. Gentleness and refinement and despair were stamped on all his features. It was apparent to me that he had seen much of the face of love, and most of it unhappy.

My loneliness reached out to touch his. I stood up and bought him a mug of beer, for I had an overwhelming urge to speak with him. I tried to reason with myself, knowing the gossip my gesture would produce among my fellow students. But I could not help it. Something about this isolated soul made me feel he was a brother, and I longed to offer him greeting before we passed on our separate journeys. I had never had a friend with whom I could share the frightening burden of my dreams and my presentiments and my fears. I had a wild idea that with this man I might.

He accepted the drink graciously, and although a number of people tried to ply him with conversation, he removed himself with tact and joined me at my table. I could see out of the corner of my eye the looks exchanged among my fellows. I knew I would be known as a sodomite at Montpellier from now on. But I did not care. This proud and gentle man who carried his sadness about him like a shroud was terribly, incomprehensibly, compulsively important to me.

'Where do you come from?' I asked him.

'I have been at Carcassonne, playing for the Bishop,' he said, dexterously avoiding my question and giving me his melancholy smile again. 'I have also been in Arcadia.'

I saw that his eyes, seemingly ingenuous, were full of veils, layers of veils like the translucent wings of butterflies, or the delicate gauzes that shroud the faces of Eastern women.

'And where do you travel after Montpellier?'

'Wherever my stars and my fate take me.' There was a long silence. 'Or perhaps,' he said, 'I will go where the war takes me, for war will come soon to these peaceful and sunny lands of Languedoc and Provence.'

I thought this absurd, but did not say so. The King and the Emperor might dance their ridiculous dance across the Italian peninsula; but I could not imagine war coming to the south of France.

'But surely a minstrel is not subject to the call of war,' I said. 'His task is to sing of love, not to bring death.'

He smiled at me again. 'Sometimes they are complementary.

With whom do I have the honour of speaking?'

'I am Michel de Notredame. I am a student at the university.'

'Ah, yes, the rowdy young physicians-to-be. But you do not seem to be cut of the same cloth, Michel de Notredame.'

'I rarely come to this tavern. But had I not bothered tonight, I might have missed your music.'

'Do you like my playing, then?' he said with complete ingenuousness.

'I think it exceedingly beautiful.'

'Ah, then I am not, after all, such a failure.' He bowed his head in courteous acceptance of the compliment. 'I am called Plantard. I have chosen that name because the growth of love is like the growth of the vine. All things begin with the seed, and develop into the mature plant. But they must be nurtured and protected. And sometimes a stronger stock must be grafted on, so that when the grape is picked, and the wine drunk, one sees and tastes in it the soul of the seed, which is the soul of God.'

I listened to this speech in perplexity. But then, he was a minstrel, and no doubt was used to speaking in parables.

He looked at me for a moment with his enigmatic eyes. 'If my instincts do not deceive me, you too dabble in the mysteries.'

'Is my solitude so obvious?'

'Yes,' he said with perfect frankness. 'As is my own.'

'I study the celestial science.'

'Ah. Perhaps one day I will ask you to look at the horoscope of a poor wandering minstrel who, having lost his honour, has only his lute and his fate.' The veiled eyes inspected me again. 'Because you are kind enough to flatter my humble music,' said M. Plantard with his bittersweet smile, 'I shall dedicate the next tune I play to you. But you must listen carefully, for the words hide secrets.'

I might have discerned then that the sign I awaited resided here. But I had not yet learned that kind of wisdom; I thought his remark innocent, and watched with pleasurable anticipation as he returned to his place in the centre of the room and retuned his instrument. He was built strong and straight, and carried himself more like a soldier than a minstrel. The din of conversation and the clink of mugs and bottles quieted again, while the elusive elastic voice plashed like water sliding over mossy rocks.

> 'Fruit de la nature
> De très noble naissance,
> Ida règnera
> Dans la justice et la sainteté.
>
> 'À la légitime comtesse de Bologne,
> Avec un encens brûlant,
> Chantons de purs chants,
> Et aussi au Duc de Lorraine,
> Le fondateur de la dynastie,
> La Fleur de l'esprit chevaleresque,
> Godefroi, l'honneur du coeur.'

Secrets indeed, I thought uneasily. Who was this man who tossed at me, like a gentle bouquet of flowers, the name of that house which dogged me, a misty shadow laden with intimations of foreboding? I remembered the vivid blue eyes of the Cardinal de Lorraine; I looked into the veiled blue eyes of M. Plantard as his resonant voice rose in the ripples of the ancient motet.

> 'Eustache était le premier,
> Le second, le noble Godefroi,
> Puis vint, comme nous le lisons, Bauduin.
> Ils traversèrent la mer
> Pour soumettre les païens,
> Pour trouver
> Le sépulchre de Dieu
> Et libérer Jérusalem.'

From time to time, as he sang, he shifted his obscure gaze to me. I reminded myself that it was I who had approached him. If I had not come to the tavern, if I had not bought him a mug of beer, would he have come to me? I could make no sense of it. It must, I thought, it must be chance. It is one of those strange chances that only the superstitious see riddled with the signature of fate. It cannot mean anything. It cannot.

> 'Enterrés dans des tombes voisines,

Recouvertes de plantes forissantes,
Ils peuvent être vus par beaucoup.
Ils conquerent une vie
Eternelle, paisible et pleine de grâce.

'Puissions-nous, séparés
Par la prison de la chair affaible,
Être enlevés de ce monde
Dans la gloire du ciel
Et les joies du paradis.'

There was a burst of loud applause and a showering of coins on the floor beside him, both for the beauty of the singing and the ingenious way in which he offered tribute to the tavern. I recognised something in the ending other than Church sentiments. It exuded a breath of the Albigensian heresy, which had been stamped out three centuries ago. I reminded myself that the old troubadours of the Languedoc were inevitably Cathar. This was one of their songs.

M. Plantard played for a while longer, then took another rest and came to sit beside me again at my table. For a time I watched him silently, trying to penetrate the veils which shrouded his sad, strange eyes.

I teetered on the verge of revealing my fears to him, but drew back.

'Why did you play that song for me?' I said abruptly.

'Did you not like it? It is an old motet to St Ida, written by Gilles de Pusieux a century and a half ago. I think it a beautiful piece.'

'But why to me?'

'You are very inquisitive, Michel de Notredame. I played it because it wished to be played. Did you not know that songs have souls and seek to be born in flesh, in the human voice and through human hands? They too long for their brief moment in the light before dissolving into the void.'

He reached over and gently fingered the little silver crucifix which I wore, for the sake of convention, about my neck.

'Do not place too much importance on this,' he said quietly with his melancholy smile, 'for it is too young. Michel of Our Lady,' he continued, *'in the beginning and the end was Notre*

Dame . . . She existed before the mountains and the seas came into being, or any living thing . . . Perhaps one day I will make that into a song.'

I shook my head. The man was half mad. Fair enough, I thought, for he plays beautiful music and his hands are like the hands of an angel. Perhaps one must be half mad to possess such a gift.

M. Plantard returned to his lute. Keeping his strange gaze upon me, he began a Florentine frottola.

> 'Io son l'occello che non pò volare,
> Non me essendo rimasto piuma alcuna;
> Io son quel segno dove a saltare
> Ve sforzano le stelle aduna aduna;
> Io son stancho nochier in alto mare
> Tempestato dal ciel e da fortuna;
> Io son con lui che più de nulla cura,
> Poi che dal ciel ogni uno ha sua ventura.'

> 'I am a bird without flight,
> at the mercy of the stars;
> I am a seaswept mariner
> buffeted by the gods and by fortune;
> Careless am I of my destiny,
> since heaven alone rules that of each one of us.'

An unaccountable sadness and weariness enveloped me like a damp mist. I rose and removed all the money I had in my pouch – a week's florins for my food and drink – and placed it on the floor beside him. I felt his veiled eyes on my back as I left the tavern and walked slowly towards my little room. Some chord had been struck within me, whether by the man or the music or his mysterious conversation I did not know. I felt suddenly that my isolation was unbearable, as though some fate, something dark and fierce and ancient, had called to me, pulling at me with delicate fingers. All that night I tossed on my bed, sleepless. I asked myself why I had turned back at the last moment from sharing with him that which I felt pressing to escape my lips like a trapped bird. But I could find no answer.

I rose later and peered through the little narrow window of

my room. Outside, the moon poured bright gilded pools over the rooftops of the town. The church bell tolled the early morning hour. Although I could not fathom why, I wanted to weep, for some unknown sorrow ate at me like acid. Who am I, I thought blindly, and whither am I going? The sad bright eyes of the minstrel seemed to haunt me, mirroring secrets, but I could not understand them. I wondered whether I might not, in truth, be what they whispered me to be. But I knew, with some profound certainty, that it was a different compulsion which had brought me to his side.

I felt as though my heart would break. I dressed and walked out into the empty dark streets. The only thing that might release my misery was a woman; but where would I find a woman at this hour of the night? I began to walk toward the poor quarter of the town, for here I would find someone, anyone, with whom to spend the remaining hours of darkness. And no matter how sordid or sad the coupling, it would somehow be more bearable than this terrible yearning invoked by the delicate strings of a lute.

I did not return to *les Joies du Paradis*. I heard a day or two later that the travelling player, M. Plantard, had moved on, headed toward Toulouse. I settled back into my studies with even greater intensity, for the time of the examinations was near. I knew I must pass through this rigorous testing to demonstrate to myself, if to no one else, that I could make my way through the world with honour like other men. In the hollow empty space deep within me, where isolation had stifled all seeds of human relationship, ambition had begun to grow.

I met the challenge of the examinations with little difficulty and received my licence with great ceremony in the church of Notre Dame des Tables, in the Chapel of St Michel. It seemed a good omen. I was now permitted to practise the art in which my grandfather had earned his livelihood. If I chose to stay at Montpellier and take the doctor's degree, the door was open to me. I resolved that I would remain for another three years at the university, in order that I might become a fully qualified physician. If I wished to obtain a teaching post here, it would be easy enough. Yet I had a strange, dim awareness that I was

44

postponing something, as though a future awaited me that I dared not contemplate.

That year arrived at last which the astrologers had predicted would bring the advent of the Antichrist. So far as anybody knew, no Antichrist appeared, nor was there a great deluge as some had anticipated. But the townsfolk were quick to attach the epithet of the Prince of Darkness to the Constable, the Duc de Bourbon, who had managed at last to slip out of France to Italy. Or to the Emperor Charles, who, apparently taking advantage of the curious configuration of the planets, sent an army through Lorraine to invade Champagne. It had been hurled back into Lorraine, we heard, and routed beneath the walls of Neufchâtel by the King's brilliant young general, Claude de Lorraine, Comte de Guise.

In retaliation for the Emperor's insult, King François again dispatched an army to invade the Milanese. It was mercilessly torn to pieces by Imperial troops, led by the dashing, the courageous, the poetic, the treacherous Charles, Connêtable de Bourbon. It crossed my mind briefly that the King had been foolish not to send the Comte de Guise against the Duc de Bourbon. But for some reason, Claude de Guise was not sent into Italy.

And in July, we heard that Charles de Bourbon, at the head of an enormous force of eighteen thousand men, had invaded Provence. He was now carving his way toward the Rhône, as though the south of France were a piece of meat on his table. The impossible had happened.

I was at once alarmed about my family. Although I felt no deep bonds, I would have been sorrowed had they become casualties of this absurd war – a contest more like a tennis match among irritated nobility than a serious conflict between nations. Eventually, however, the Duc de Bourbon was driven back into Italy by King François. The people of Montpellier burned effigies of the duke in the streets, and shouted that the Devil had been vanquished. I felt the same horror as any Frenchman that the country should have been laid open to the ravages of the enemy, and I applauded the success of the King's army. Yet I could not but feel a secret admiration for this noble

45

man who, a hunted and penniless fugitive just a few months before, had managed with such a bold stroke to humiliate the King.

King François underestimated his enemy. The French army, led by the *roi chevalier* himself, at last met the Imperial army, under the Connêtable de Bourbon, on the field outside Pavia, north of Bologna. The defeat was crushing. Half the *noblesse* of France lay dead beneath the scorching Italian sun. Charles de Bourbon – rash, romantic, high-handed and bold – took the King prisoner, trussed him up like a partridge, and handed him to the Emperor as a birthday gift. It seemed that the Antichrist, though he made no visible appearance, nevertheless hovered unseen, dicing with the future of France. For all at once, the country was without a king.

Amidst the confusion of frantic treaties and negotiations for the ransom of His Most Christian Majesty, another blow descended. And this new horror, more terrible than any war, was heralded for me by the dream.

I stood once again at the foot of that thickly wooded and shrouded hillside, peering down at the dark pool which lay silently, like a black jewel, in the ebbing light. The air hummed about me with some faint barbaric music, as though the pool itself were singing a voiceless, tuneless song. I felt tight-strung, I myself seeming to be the instrument upon which it played. The oaks and the coarse grasses were still; the surface of the water was like onyx; and then I saw, all at once, that a shadowy figure knelt at its edge, peering into the depths as if to fathom its secret.

I did not recognise his shape at first, for the light was very dim, and he was only a shadow against a backdrop of shadows. But he suddenly turned, as though abruptly sensing my presence, and I recognised the face of the strange troubadour of Carcassonne, M. Plantard. He was clothed all in black damask, while a black velvet cap seeded with pearls perched on his dark head and a black cloak cut of rich cloth hung from his shoulders. On his right hand he wore a great gold ring with a ruby like a gout of blood.

In these sumptuous garments he was no longer a poor minstrel, but was transformed into a noble lord. All the sadness and pathos had slid away, and he stood strong and courageous and proud. Yet he smiled that same bittersweet smile at me, his veiled cornflower eyes open wide and staring into mine. Then he looked beyond me, up the hill, and the smile slowly drained from his lips. I turned to see what he saw, and gazed upon the dark abbey rooted at the hilltop like some ancient animal, silent, shadowy, humming too with that strange unbearable tension which had made a tight knot of my stomach and sent a throbbing through my head and eyes.

M. Plantard and I stood and watched as a shape approached us from the shadows. But it was not the mysterious monk who had come to me when my grandfather Jean died, nor did it issue, like that apparition, from the abbey. Far more terrible, it was a faceless, shapeless thing, a noxious cloud, black, shimmering, volatile, like the reflection of some dark beast in the fractured surface of a disturbed pool, the materialised spawn of the nightmares which haunt both air and earth. I began to shake in terror, for I knew that this was Thanatos, come to claim an offering.

The abbey bell began to toll violently, and the clangour shattered the dome of the sky. The pool erupted in turbulent frothing and bubbling, while the trees shivered and convulsed and twisted as the misty dark shape swept past with a great wind at its back and vanished into the black distance.

Trembling, I looked into the face of the minstrel, and asked him with my eyes what it hunted.

The answer came back to me on the wind and the churning ripples of the pool, voiceless as the broken string of a lute. *It is hunting men.*

I awoke slimed with sweat, confused and bewildered, shuddering in my bed. I did not understand until the cathedral bell began to ring out madly an hour after dawn, and I heard the shouting and the wailing and the hurrying footsteps, and smelled the reek of fear in the streets below. It was not long before Guillaume, who slept across the hall from me, was pounding on my door to tell me the news. Twenty people had already dropped in the streets in convulsions, and dozens were wandering about dizzy with fever, vomiting black blood.

The plague had swooped upon Montpellier.

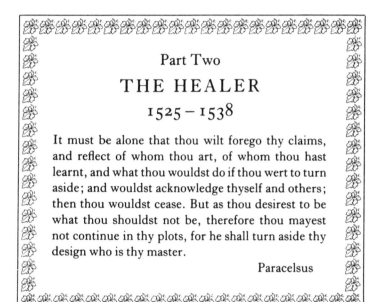

Part Two

THE HEALER
1525 – 1538

It must be alone that thou wilt forego thy claims, and reflect of whom thou art, of whom thou hast learnt, and what thou wouldst do if thou wert to turn aside; and wouldst acknowledge thyself and others; then thou wouldst cease. But as thou desirest to be what thou shouldst not be, therefore thou mayest not continue in thy plots, for he shall turn aside thy design who is thy master.

Paracelsus

VI

An epidemic of plague struck Provence in the Year of Our Lord 1525. Far more widespread and more terrible was the epidemic of fear. Fear saturated the streets, the houses, the churches, the shops, the whorehouses. Fear, hideous and cancerous, drove the townsfolk mad. Fear transformed hitherto sane, stable and sensible citizens into gibbering idiots who hurled themselves from the parapets of the city walls, who sewed themselves gleefully in their own winding sheets to await death, who with rictus grins stretched tight across their pale faces danced naked in the filth of the gutters, shaking their fists at heaven and defying all the devils of hell to claim them.

My learned professors at the university, only a short while ago, had discussed the profound theories of Galen. They had spoken with the greatest acumen and a superb confidence born of their august and unimpeachable knowledge. They had neatly sewn up the miracle of the human body in a series of geometric formulae that would have bewildered even Pythagoras, formulae whereby any illness might be appropriately categorised and dispensed with. Now they were stricken dumb. Galen's theories, however ingenious, could not explain away the fever, the convulsions, the coughing and spitting of blood, the boils, the agonising pain in chest and stomach and groin.

These august men, charged with the cultivation of the physicians of the future, fled the town in droves, carrying their robes and their sacks of money and their silver plate and their household belongings. They pelted madly toward the countryside, toward other towns, toward anywhere at all that might provide refuge from the miasma which they believed had fallen like a rotten maggot-filled fruit from the hand of God. Fallen, some said, to punish the Lutheran heresy which had begun to taint men's spirits. Alternatively, depending upon one's viewpoint, it was blamed on the corruption and avarice of Holy Church. Either way, it killed.

Montpellier began to resemble those visions of the world of the damned which glare from the nightmare canvases of the Fleming Adamite heretic, Bosch. Like a sausage skin, every church was jammed to bursting with people on their knees, on their faces, arms outstretched and clawing the air for the protective touch of some holy image. The air reeked with the smoke of tapers, the clouds of burning incense, the wailing and moaning and chanting and beseeching of hundreds of terrified voices. I saw entire families rushing through the streets, swarming and kicking and biting and scratching their way through the press for the sight of the statues and sacred relics, or the healing benediction of some priest or abbot. Prelates were besieged with offers of gold and jewels and cattle and even women, in exchange for intercession that might afford some deterrent against the ignominious and agonising death.

They prayed. Their prayers failed them. And bred by fear, like some hideous whelp from a bestial mother, there emerged from this hysteria which had seized the town the first beginnings of a great fissure in the solid and polished rock St Peter had built. For it did not escape the notice of their flock that priests and abbots too lay dying in the ordure of the gutters; and God had not reached down His hand to save them.

My grandfather had taught me simple methods of healing, and had instilled in me a deep belief that what derived from nature could be cured by nature. I avoided indiscriminate blood-letting, magical pomanders, incessant prayers, sacred talismans – thereby earning the profound suspicion of my colleagues. I worked with the herbs my grandfather had taught me to pick under the proper phases of the moon, hoping to test my rudimentary student's knowledge against the terrifying foe.

Most of the doctors in the town had fled. Those that remained began to shun me. The townsfolk soon heard that there was one healer left who did not seem to be afraid; and suddenly I was beleaguered with pleas to visit the sick. I began to envision myself as a hero, a saviour who would defeat the dreaded Scourge when the most sophisticated science of the day had failed. I imagined myself vindicating my humble origins, my strangeness, my isolation.

I found, however, that I could scarcely even reach the bedsides of my patients, so thickly surrounded were they by swarms of priests, murmurings of litanies and prayers, suffocating smoke of tapers and incense. And by the time the sick man had made his confession, and been persuaded that his sins had brought this terrible fate upon him, it was too late for me to help him.

The astrologers of Montpellier pronounced utter doom, and sat back and offered each other warm congratulations. Had they not predicted this coming of a terrible retribution for the heresy which poisoned the secret souls of the townsfolk? Municipal officials were in utter consternation, for a once orderly city had fallen into frenzied chaos. In their mindless madness, civilised people had broken loose and robbed and raped and pillaged and killed, because there was no longer anything to hold in check the beast within. Most of the magistrates quit the city hurriedly. Those that remained gave way to the abandonment. I had always envisioned the graceful spires of a gothic cathedral, the beauty of a painting, the sweetness of a song, as embodiments of the glory of which the human soul was capable. Now I saw the opposite of these things – men stripped of the outer husk of social conscience and aspiration to goodness. It was fortunate that I had no religion to lose.

The dead accumulated in the streets amidst the offal and the rotting garbage. I saw babies abandoned and prone women wailing upon some stinking corpse. And over all, the great cathedral bell tolled and tolled, a macabre counterpoint to the gentle silvery bell of the death cart that wended through streets and alleys. The bodies, some still alive and twitching, were trundled to great pits outside the town, where they were thrown haphazardly into nameless graves.

It was horrible watching men die like helpless insects at the hand of this unconquerable foe. Equally horrific was the shattering loss of belief that brought people teetering to the brink of madness. Church doctrines were part of the very fabric of their blood and bones; and those doctrines had proven useless. I reflected on the precarious balance of an edifice that made God

53

responsible for everything. I knew that this pestilence, terrible as it was, was a natural phenomenon, perhaps precipitated by the astrological configurations, but nevertheless natural. And I knew that somewhere, somehow, there must be a natural cure.

I experimented with burning aromatic substances – calamint, aloes, storax, amber, juniper, ash. I mixed sulphur and antimony and arsenic. I pounded coral and emeralds and lapis lazuli and rose petals. And I realised, as I tried every remedy I had ever been taught, that my youthful naïvety was utterly gone. For I saw only too clearly that men were completely ignorant of the substance of which they were made.

At last I could bear it no longer. I could not learn in Montpellier. The fear and clumsy efforts of my fellow physicians made it impossible for me to reach a sick man before he had been killed if not by the disease itself, then by human ignorance. Through my mind there resonated like a silent and incessant drumbeat the conviction that it was the filth that carried it, the filth that bred it, the filth swarming with flies and rats that gave it a home and nurtured it until it was strong enough to annihilate a town. My fellow healers thought me a fool, and laughed, and pronounced learned theories. I could not scour the offal from the streets of Provence with my own hands.

I packed my bag and took the road out into the countryside, following the Garonne to villages where I could tend the sick without interruption or censure. The people of the countryside learned to recognise me, for my name began to travel ahead of me. I was the young medical student who was not afraid of death, not deterred from the bedside of the sick and the dying, who did not shroud himself in grotesque garments, who did not endlessly pray.

I followed the course of the rivers through the villages of Provence and Languedoc, for the disease too followed the rivers, as though floating along the waters like some gossamer dragonfly as it continued its hunt. In fact, the polluted corpses carried it from town to town. Each day as I travelled on my mule along the riverbanks, I would see the white faces, the hair streaming like seaweed, the rigid limbs swept gently along by the sweet currents.

I knew from my horoscope that I would not be struck down.

It gives a man the appearance of courage to know when he is going to die. He can go where others will not dare, in full awareness that he is protected by his fate. The village people, of course, did not know this. They thought I possessed some magic power, because I was not frightened of touching them, examining them, cleansing them, nursing them, breathing the foul air of the sickroom. I found that the healing of fear was often accompanied by the healing of the disease. I found that keeping a sick man scrupulously clean increased his chances of survival. And among the many herbs and powders and ground substances with which I experimented, I found that some few worked, in a mysterious fashion, to drive back the shadow.

I travelled to Narbonne, and then to Toulouse. Here too I found the fear and the madness, and the shrieks and groans of the dying, and the endless processions to the churches, and the streets filled with corpses. Sometimes I could scarcely move through the alleyways, so clogged were they by the dead. There was no one to teach me but the sick.

I travelled to Bordeaux, where the pestilence had struck with particularly savage violence. The people of the city had responded in a time-honoured fashion: they hunted a scapegoat. I was astonished not that this had occurred, but that it had failed to occur in any of the other towns I had visited. The hunt fell at random: on the lepers, on the Lutherans, on the Jews, on the poor, on the outcasts. I saw people burned at the stake in streets already piled high with cadavers, and others thrown from the towers of the Château Trompette, to be dashed to death on the pavement below. Bodies piled upon bodies, fear piled upon fear. I worked desperately, far into each night, experimenting with the paste of sulphur and antimony and arsenic which I had found was the key which drove back the infection.

At length, in each of the cities through which I passed, the disease began to slake itself. As if it were a beast which had devoured all it could hold, it lingered, satiated, and finally crept away to some other waiting town. Like men limping crippled and wounded from some terrible battle, the townsfolk and the country folk of Provence commenced to pick up the shattered and mangled fragments of their lives. And as the plague withdrew its shadow from Toulouse, from Narbonne, from Bordeaux, I followed it. I had long ago decided that studying medicine at Montpellier meant nothing to me. The only thing that remained real was the battle with this enemy. I was no longer eaten with loneliness, nor haunted by frightening dreams. I was needed and useful. And if I could find a way to cure the disease, I could find a way to vindicate my solitary life.

VII

I followed the plague to Carcassonne, that ancient city on its lonely plain with the forty towers bristling on its buttressed walls. Here the ghosts of the hunted Cathari still walked. And here I found once again that world of nightmare where the dead lay everywhere in the streets amidst the offal, and the plague bell tolled brazenly from the cathedral in grim counterpoint to the groans and wails of the bereaved and dying. Everywhere it was the same.

My certainty deepened that the disease was connected with the surrounding filth. But the doctors of Carcassonne, like those of Montpellier and Narbonne and Toulouse and Bordeaux, would not believe me, and quoted Galen, and assured me that this outbreak resulted from the evil configuration of planets perpetrated by God to chastise the sins of His people.

I had been hearing this nonsense incessantly since the disease had struck, and I was heartily sick of it. I tried to tell them that among those I treated, I had met many good and decent folk. Yet men chose to believe that God, Who in their view was both omniscient and omnipotent enough to arrange the heavenly bodies in such a dire fashion, could mistakenly strike down the innocent with the guilty because His hand was a little clumsy. Besides, what, after all, was sin? But the doctors muttered and whispered of heresy and sorcery. I knew that I must in future keep these thoughts to myself, lest I find myself – like the scapegoats of Bordeaux – tied to a stake.

Eventually the pestilence abated in Carcassonne and moved away to seek fresh blood. I remained in the town for a year, long after the bereaved and shattered townsfolk had buried their dead. For it was in Carcassonne that I made a curious friendship which at first seemed a stroke of good fortune. Afterwards, however, it served to remind me that I could not hide from my fate in the imagined nobility of my physician's tasks any more than I could hide from it in my books.

I had begun to acquire a rather glamorous reputation. Rumours from the countryside had reached the town, and I was hailed as a gifted healer who could conquer death by a mere wave of my hand. I was still unsure enough of myself to feed on these praises, until I almost began to believe them. The local doctors were infuriated, as much by my increasing arrogance toward them as by my wooing away their wealthy patients. They spread the usual rumours of heresy and sorcery. And I realised how great a change had been wrought in me by my disillusionment; for I found myself growing daily more cunning, more calculating, more manipulative in the face of their opposition.

I decided it was time to befriend some powerful prelate to ensure my safety. And no sooner had I decided this than what I thought was luck played directly into my eager hands.

One day, as I emerged from the early mass at the church of St Étienne, the priest approached me. He told me that my reputation as a healer had reached the ears of the Bishop of Carcassonne, Monseigneur Ammanien de Foix. This cleric wished to make my acquaintance and consult me with regard to a slight malady which had been troubling him.

Thus occurred my first commission from one of high rank in the hierarchy of the Church. I determined to do my utmost to please this man; for the protection and good favour of a Bishop, particularly one of such a wealthy and ancient town as Carcassonne, would prove immensely useful to me. I envisioned a fat purse, and recommendations to other powerful prelates across the whole of Languedoc and Provence. I guessed that Mgr de Foix must have gout, or a troubled liver, or constipation. The commonest maladies among princes of the Church were those which stemmed from too much food and drink, or from ill-chosen companions in erotic pleasures.

These thoughts I naturally kept to myself, for they resembled too closely the Lutheran heresy which was spreading like plague from town to town. It was viewed with a horror not dissimilar to the horror reserved for the plague, and was thought, like the disease, to be an outbreak which, although destructive, would soon pass. I had some doubts about this. I had seen too clearly in the faces of the dying the shattering of the barriers that had held back the flood. But my sudden rise to status drove these dark speculations from the foreground of my mind.

I found that I had been mistaken in my conjecture. Mgr Ammanien de Foix did not have gout or a troubled liver or constipation. He was in fact a perfectly healthy man, portly and red-faced, with warm, humorous dark eyes. His only complaint was that at times a mysterious fatigue rendered him impotent and thus unable to please his mistress. She, it seemed, was only seventeen, the daughter of a farrier, and lusty enough to exhaust even the most virile of men.

I stifled my laughter, and promised him a love-philtre which I assured him would kindle sufficient vigour to satisfy a dozen mistresses. I had obtained this recipe at Montpellier – a pommade compounded of lapis lazuli, gold leaf, and powdered coral. It probably owed its efficacy solely to the belief of the recipient. Nevertheless it was laborious and expensive to make; and few purchasers would dare suspect that something so precious could prove useless.

The Bishop was happy to furnish money with which to obtain materials from the local apothecaries. Either the pommade, or more likely the very practical regimen I prescribed of more red meat and more sleep, served to produce the appropriate cure. For within a fortnight he was pleased to inform me that his fatigue had totally gone, and that his mistress had nothing further of which to complain. He recompensed me for my efforts with a large purse, which pleased me enormously. He also promised to secure me further patronage among the noble and wealthy of the town.

I concluded that luck, or the helpful configurations of the planets, was favouring me. I was fortunate, being fresh from university and not yet even qualified by a doctor's certificate, in having received such a highly desirable patron. And in the meanwhile I could seek some more genuine but less lucrative cures for the terrible disease which still lingered, albeit in decreasing virulence, throughout the south of France.

But I soon learned that the Bishop of Carcassonne was a far more complicated man than he had appeared. I began to wonder whether some other motive had prompted him to send for me. He invited me to sup with him, and I found to my surprise that this was intended as a private meeting. Once the food was laid out, he sent away all his attendants and servants, so that we were left alone in the comfortable dining hall of his luxurious town house.

We spoke first of the affairs of the country, and of the terrible sack of Rome perpetrated by the Emperor's troops under the Duc de Bourbon. To my surprise the Bishop did not express the mortification I should have expected from a prelate of the Church. Charles de Bourbon had died on the walls of the Eternal City, felled by a stray arquebus shot. But his men had gone berserk and had sacked the city, aided by the troops of Don Ferrante de Gonzaga, a prince of Mantua. The Pope fled in terror to Orvieto, begging the Emperor for peace. King François was ransomed and replaced in his gloomy Spanish prison by his two little sons. There was once again a king in France.

We spoke of the plague and current medical opinions concerning it. He inquired deeply into my own views and philosophy on the matter. I told him that I was inexperienced, having only had three years of training before venturing into the countryside to work with the disease. But he was respectful none the less of my words and ideas, and listened with an interest and a courtesy I had never found among my medical colleagues. I began to suspect midway through this conversation that Monseigneur de Foix was far less ignorant of medical principles than he had let me assume. I felt increasingly embarrassed about the pommade. He knew perfectly well, I now realised in shame, that it was merely a tangible and highly expensive means of reassurance, while the real cure lay in diet and sensible habits of living.

'Do not chastise yourself about your marvellous prescription, M. de Notredame, for I have found it useful in other ways,'

59

he said. 'I have been dabbling with it in some alchemical experiments, and have found that it suits a particular purpose admirably. Nothing else that I had tried seemed to succeed. I am grateful to you for offering it to me.'

This revelation, that the Bishop was an alchemist, left me sitting in astonished silence. It was not surprising in itself; there were certainly many prelates involved in various obscure and often illegal arts, under the protective cover of the ceremonies of the Church. But I could not understand why he should choose to tell me, whom he hardly knew, at a time when rumours of heresy were so rampant.

Once again he seemed to sense my thoughts. I was finding to my dismay that Mgr Ammanien de Foix was a most subtle man. Before, I had only looked at the flat and prosaic surface, finding him conventional, courteous, but not particularly imaginative. Now I realised how well-constructed a mask he wore.

He smiled in amused fashion, and said, 'You are wondering why I consulted you at all, when I could as easily have cured myself. In fact there was no malady in the first place. I beg you to forgive my little deception, but I wished to find out what manner of man you were. It is unusual to find one so young attracting so much attention in this town. I am relieved to find that you are as unscrupulous as you are gifted in your art. The Church has wealth enough to patronise you.'

I was torn between embarrassment and laughter. At the same time, I wondered whether this shrewd man had also sensed the subversion perpetrated by the plague against the apparently impregnable edifice of which he was a part. But I did not presume to ask, for fear that he was devout.

'I find your views on medicine refreshingly sound, M. de Notredame,' he said. 'I believe you will make a very fine physician. Please do not feel awkward. Although I have played a little game with you, you in turn played one with me. So consider that the score is even on both sides, and let us be friends. I have a mind to acquaint you with the principles of alchemy, if you find that it interests you.'

Of course it did. And so I remained in Carcassonne, and each day went to visit the Bishop at his Hôtel. We spent many long hours immured in intense conversation, and spoke of the Stone, the Lapis, of the great work of transformation and the release of the spirit from its prison of dense substance. We discoursed on the recent work of Paracelsus, who had passed through Montpellier only two years before me, and whom I longed passionately one day to meet. I began slowly to understand more of the philosophy of this great art, which has never truly been concerned with the creation of gold, but seeks to redeem the living god from within the soul of man himself. In the alembic of his own flesh, man is subjected to the consuming fires and transforming pressures of his own will to self-purification. And if the operation succeeds, that vision dawns which rends apart the veil masking the arcane nature of the world's substance, and exposes the design beneath – a design unfurled across the heavens and within the human body. And this wisdom I garnered carefully with the treasures which my grandfather had given me, for it too was part of the pattern.

I knew I would have to leave Carcassonne. It was increasingly evident that I must take my doctorate at the university if I expected fair treatment at the hands of my colleagues. Mgr de Foix accepted this in a manner which told me that he understood very well what ambition drove my spirit. He promised me I would not leave Carcassonne without a goodly sum of gold to speed me on my way. And then he made me a curious invitation.

'In a few days,' he said one evening as we sat in his study drinking wine, 'I am taking a journey south to Rennes-les-Bains, to visit a friend. It is only a day's journey by mule. Would you care to accompany me?'

And because I had learned that my companion was a man of rare subtlety, who did nothing without purpose, I accepted.

We lodged with his grooms and his servants in a little inn at Rennes-les-Bains, where the natural springs were said to possess miraculous healing powers. While the Bishop visited a gentleman of the village, I explored the countryside on my mule. I found it a disturbing place. There were mountains ringed all around, and on one of them brooded the ruined shell of an old preceptory of the Temple, lonely and eerie against the autumn sky. This land held in its bosom many strange memories of Templar and Cathar, whose blood had fertilised the earth; and the earth still suppurated like a great unhealed wound. One could divine the ghosts flicking one's back even in the cold sunlight of the afternoon. It made me uneasy, and I turned my mule once more toward the village.

The Bishop was interested in my reactions to the country-side.

'So,' he said with an amused glint in his handsome dark eyes, 'you can feel the spirits of the dead. Yes, this place is full of them. You should visit Montségur, where the Cathari were besieged before their massacre. It is said that one can smell their blood, and that the mountain itself cries out for vengeance. You have the peculiar sensitivity of your race, M. de Notredame. I hope you do not have distressing dreams here.'

I started at this. But of course, I thought to myself, he could not possibly know about my dreams. He is merely humouring my womanish fantasies.

Mgr de Foix was silent for a time, and then said, 'Tonight at midnight begins the thirteenth of October. Does this date mean anything to you?'

I shook my head. I could remember no saint whose feast-day claimed celebration on the morrow.

'It is the day on which Philippe le Bel invaded the precept-ories of the Temple, and took the Knights prisoner to be tort-ured and burned at the stake for the crimes of sodomy, blasphemy and secret worship of the Devil. And most strange is the fact that these Knights, five thousand of them, stronger than any army mustered by the King of France, went willingly to the sacrifice, as though they knew the fate awaiting them and accepted it. It was thus too with the Cathari, who came down from the heights of Montségur hand in hand, singing, into the flames.'

I had become increasingly uneasy as he spoke. Something lay hidden in this place which I could not comprehend. I felt a little shiver pass with a sinuous finger along my flesh. I began to wish I had not come to Rennes-les-Bains.

We stood now outside the inn to take some air after our sup-per. The setting sun streaked the sky with blood and smoke, and the mountain peaks loomed around me like ancient animals, curled in drowsing torpor, ready at any moment to awaken.

'Only one preceptory was spared,' said the Bishop. 'Look, over there, to the southwest, against the sky. You can see it from here. It is Bézu. The commander of that preceptory was a man called de Goth, of the Blanchefort family. He was cousin to Pope Clément. Did the blood link save these Knights from the King's men? Or did Bézu hold a secret which the Pope dared not violate? It remains a mystery.'

I looked, and saw again the battlements I had glimpsed earlier that day, broken and jagged, like rotting teeth grinning black against the deepening sky. The sunset had given way to purple shadows, and a chill was rising from the earth. A mist white as steam coiled gently over the bracken and the fields, and shrouded the foot of the mountain in a funereal pall. I longed for ordinary human company, the friendly warmth of the fire.

'I am going to climb Bézu tonight,' said Mgr Ammanien de Foix. 'I wish to be there among those walls by midnight.'

I said nothing, but only stared at his hearty, fleshy, florid face, holding my breath, feeling my uneasiness give way to gnawing fear.

'It is said that he who climbs Bézu on the anniversary of the fall of the Temple will be privileged to witness a miracle,' said the Bishop. 'The Knights of Bézu possessed a little silver bell, a holy bell. When they thought they too would be taken, they hurled this bell into the ravine beneath the walls. And the tale tells that at midnight, on the anniversary of the fall of their Order, the bell chimes, and its sweet note fills the wind washing the mountain. If one has courage and remains steadfast, one can see the ghostly shapes of the Knights, white and shimmering, with the great blood-red cross on their breasts. And a ghostly voice cries out, "Who will restore the Temple?" And a chorus of dead heads, speaking heads, answers thrice in unison from their coffers, "No one. No one. No one. The Temple has been destroyed."'

I waited while the perspiration streamed in chill runnels down my back. I knew what would follow now.

'And,' said Mgr Ammanien de Foix, the friendly Bishop of Carcassonne whom I thought luck had brought me as a patron, 'I would like you to accompany me.'

I shook my head vehemently. 'I cannot, Monseigneur. I am afraid. This place makes me uneasy. It reeks of strangeness and the whisperings of the dead. There is some secret concealed here. I am sorry if I seem to you childish, or full of women's vapours. But I do not wish to hear the silver bell or see the ghostly shapes of these long-vanished Knights. I have no doubt that they still walk here. I do not need to be convinced.'

'It is not for convincing that I ask you, M. de Notredame. You know much more of it than you realise. There may be some meaning in it for you.'

'These things mean nothing to me,' I said firmly. 'I am not concerned with what is past. I am only a medical student seeking to learn my trade. I beg you not to ask this of me, for I have a deadly fear.'

'I promise you that no harm will come to you.'

In the end he won. Perhaps it was because he was so gently persistent. Perhaps I did not wish to be thought a coward. In those days I was not a man who could be made to do what he did not will. But while I was still thinking of excuses to make, I found myself scrabbling up the rocky face of the mountain of Bézu on my hands and knees. Ahead of me the black shape of the Bishop moved nimble as a mountain goat, a shadow against the shadowy slope, climbing rapidly despite his heavy frame. At last, the ancient walls encircled us. Amid the lonely ruins of the roofless and gutted fortress, a navel, a chalice open to the sky, we sat down to share the wine he had brought in a skin. Above us, wisps of cloud sifted across the moon, as if the heavens had blinked their eye.

It grew colder. I wrapped my cloak about me, my teeth chattering. It was very late. I heard the church bell thinly toll eleven hours from the village below. The Bishop was silent. I could hardly see him in the close conclave of shadows between those walls. Only the wan starlight illumined his pale silvery face, his eyes which resembled opaque pools in the darkness. I knew he did not wish me to speak. As if it were a litany, I repeated to myself that it was only a night walk to an old ruin, that it meant nothing, that the Bishop was merely an eccentric with a taste for ghostly tales. Granted, the residues still clung here with frail fingers, vivid enough to my acute and vigilant senses. But silver bells, however sacred, would not ring of their own accord from the depths of the earth. The wind had risen, whipping with a sibilant hiss around the walls. Above, scudding clouds eclipsed the stars. Though I felt no pain at the time, I found next morning the wounds in my palms where my fingernails had dug into the flesh.

The breeze subsided. Once more, with quiet finality, the bell tolled from the village and was swallowed by the silence. Mgr de Foix put his fingers to his lips, placed his hand under my elbow and helped me to stand. And I will never know whether what I heard was real or engendered by my fear and the images he had so carefully planted in my mind. From somewhere, so faintly it might have been the wind, there issued a pale and barely audible tone, a fleshless tone, a note, sweet yet insubstantial as the colour of the wind.

I could bear no more. I flung myself down on the cold earth among the fallen masonry, and covered my ears with my hands to shut it out. I was shaking from the strain of my fear. Some time later, I felt the hands of the Bishop gently raising me, while his dark eyes looked into mine with sad compassion. The quiet had pooled itself around us in a thick cocoon. I could hear nothing. It was only an old ruin on a mountaintop. We did not speak, but silently began the long climb down.

He only addressed me once before he retired to his chamber, placing his hand on my shoulder and looking at me sadly.

'Perhaps I misjudged the moment,' he said. 'It was too soon.'

The experience cut deep, for I was awakened that night by a terrible dream. I stood in a great wood, where ancient oaks clustered like conspirators, blotting out the light. The earth was wet and rich and black and teeming with life. Instinctively, I knew this was a holy place, a sacred grove, for the spirits of the trees pressed about me as though I were an intruder. Overhead the dense branches met, like myriad clasped hands, forming the nave of some murk-green cathedral sculpted of membrane and bark. I knelt and bowed my forehead to the earth in obeisance. What place it was, I did not know. But I recognised the ancient power here, which was not of God the Father.

When I arose, the unnamed King had ridden into the wood, with trailing white damask robes and golden coronet on his brow. His hair streamed unshorn down his back, parted like a curtain from a thin, pale, sharply hollowed face, revealing eyes set like deep blue stones beneath a high chiselled brow. He was attended by five men-at-arms and a retainer who helped him from his horse and ushered him beneath the great trees to rest. He leaned back against a vast gnarled oak, so twisted and thick it must have been centuries old. He closed his eyes in weariness, while the retainer brought wine in a massive goblet carved of rock crystal, which glimmered with wan creamy luminescence in the greenish gloom. The men-at-arms were also weary, and settled themselves into sleep.

And then, while the King drowsed, I saw the retainer draw a lance from his equipment, and stealthily approach his master. And although I tried to cry out in admonition, I could not move or speak, and no sound passed my lips. With a great sweep the lance struck through the King's right eye. Red blood spurted like spilled wine across his white robe, gushed into the fallen goblet, bubbled into the black earth. A terrible wrath stirred the ancient trees, as though some tempestuous storm coiled among them, about to break. At last I cried out and awoke, shaking in the dark, not knowing where I was. Then I remembered the terror of the mountaintop, and the ghostly bell. I crawled out of bed, lit candles, and sat huddled in the dimness until the sun rose.

VIII

After four years among the dying and the dead, I returned to Montpellier. I found that the town had resumed its habitual life, though many walked about in mourning garb and a fearful, hunted look still clung to the faces of the townsfolk. But no matter how great the horror, how complete the disaster, the ordinary cycles of living and dying must ultimately reassert themselves. For it is not a trait of human nature to brood forever on tragedy.

I was welcomed back to the university with something less than enthusiasm. My reputation throughout the towns of Provence and Languedoc, fed by the superstitious awe of the grateful countryside, had swollen to mythic dimensions – so much so that the professors who had once praised my acumen and my diligent application now viewed me with suspicion. I had displayed the brazen arrogance to test remedies which they themselves had not taught me; and those remedies had succeeded where theirs had failed.

Nevertheless they could not fault me. I lived the same intense, lonely, indrawn life that I had pursued before the plague, plunging myself into my studies, denying myself all but the occasional furtive pleasures. Nothing had changed, except my own soul. Despite the almost tangible dislike of my professors, which settled about me like a miasma, I passed my examinations with outstanding honour and completed my doctorate in three years. I now had something at which I was competent, even superior. It constituted a bastion of protection against the irreconcilable alienness of the world. The praise I received was tainted with a heavy scent of resentment. I felt a thin pride, and a bitter satisfaction.

The time of hiding had come to an end. I stood poised like some animal sniffing the cross-currents of the wind, wondering which way to go. Ahead lay blank grey space, punctuated only by those vague intimations which my grandfather had vouchsafed me as a child.

You will rise higher than I ever could . . .

I could not see where the road led. It wound around the dim formless shapes of my fears and my fantasies, then vanished. I carried two burdens with me: the iron corset of my solitude and the unpredictable visitations of my dreams. I could speak of neither to any soul I met. The only man who might have understood had passed only briefly through my life, a flicker of flame that beckoned and mocked and hinted at some secret and disappeared, carrying his magical lute. I was haunted by portents of some strange thing that lapped insidiously at the borders of my

67

awareness but never quite surfaced – some sense that I had a destiny, that I must seek something, that something was seeking me. I sometimes endeavoured to peer directly at this shapeless shape hovering about me in that hollow and pregnant space between sleeping and waking, when the body is somnolent and the spirit flies free. Always, however, it eluded me.

I waited for a sign. I did not know that four times the signs had appeared, only to depart unrecognised. I examined my horoscope. Saturn, Lord of Boundaries and of Fate, was beginning his slow approach to that point where he lay at the moment of my birth. A cycle was ending, a new one beginning.

The students at Montpellier, those who were younger and just beginning their training, gathered together in a boisterous group and demanded of the faculty that I be appointed their professor. At first there was protest, and I heard the now familiar rumblings of heresy and sorcery whispered behind learned hands. But my career of healing was blameless, and they knew it. Even they, narrow and riddled with petty rivalries, could not justify jealousy alone as a reason to refuse me. They gave way. Thus I began my brief career of teaching at the venerable university of Montpellier, through which Paracelsus had once passed.

I became bored, then I became restless. I chafed against the restrictions of a Church-dominated programme of learning, which denied all freedom of thought and speech to both teachers and students. I was expected to lecture by rote from the manuscripts given me, and I could not interject my own views without incurring serious chastisement and the omnipresent but still veiled accusations. I did not care to be one of the first martyrs to the brood of black inquisitorial vultures hatched from Luther's egg.

I chafed, I fidgeted, fussed and fumed, and then one day I packed my bag and sold my few belongings, and bought a mule, and rode out through the gates of the town and left Montpellier behind me.

> Io son l'occello che non pò volare,
> Non me essendo rimasto piuma alcuna;
> Io son quel segno dove a saltare

Ve sforzano le stelle aduna aduna;
Io son stancho nochier in alto mare
Tempestato dal ciel e da fortuna;
Io son con lui che più de nulla cura,
Poi che dal ciel ogni uno ha sua ventura.

I was free. Or so I believed, as I fixed my eyes on the road dis-appearing into the shimmering gold heat of the summer sun, and the sky blue as lapis overhead, and the air full of possibilities and promise.

I travelled to Narbonne again, and to La Rochelle. I visited many of the villages through which I had passed while the plague ravaged them, and found that the country folk remembered me. I even visited Avignon, where in some other, darker incarnation I had once received into my bed, in the silent black womb of the night, a woman of my own flesh and blood. And where I had once seen in a procession a fair, strange, princely face with cornflower eyes of compelling familiarity – a face that sometimes, incubus-like, still haunted my dreams. I did not go back to St Rémy. My brother and I had long since ceased what tenuous and hypocritical communication once existed between us; and my parents and my grandfather Pierre were dead of the plague.

I thought of once more travelling to Carcassonne, to visit Mgr Ammanien de Foix. But I found myself making excuses to avoid the journey. I was always busy with something or wished to go somewhere else. I gradually came to see that it was fear which barred my return with an immovable black door. I tried to reason it out, attempted to convince myself that I had merely suffered an hysterical episode, brought on by my susceptibility to another man's eerie tales. Nevertheless, I did not take the road to the old city where the ghosts of the Cathari still haunted the shadows.

So I became at last that which I had always, in some secret place in my heart, known myself to be: the Wandering Jew with the burden of his knowledge and his secrets and his endless centuries of playing scapegoat to men's fears weighing on his back like a jongleur's sack of trinkets and tricks. And above him, the ambiguous light of his planetary lord illumining the road with its yellowish beacon, on a journey with no beginning and no end.

In time I returned to Toulouse, where I had made friends among the enclave of alchemists and kabbalists that flourished there. I took rooms and made it known that I would receive patients. Once again my reputation preceded me, and I had no difficulty in acquiring clientele, to the chagrin of the local physicians. As always, for the benefit of curious eyes, I displayed my piety by beginning each day on my knees in some church.

One day I received a letter from the town of Agen in the duchy of Guyenne, on the bank of the Garonne, across the border of Navarre. Jules-César de l'Escale, who called himself Scaliger, was a renowned and erudite scholar, hailed throughout the southern provinces as one of the greatest thinkers of the age. Having heard of me from the Bishop of Agen, he invited me to visit him.

It was the kind of offer calculated to excite my fantasies. I longed for the intellectual stimulation which a man like Scaliger could provide. I had never seen Guyenne, and I was beginning to think of finding some pleasant town where I might establish a permanent practice. I was thirty now, and had commenced to contemplate the idea of marriage.

In the past I had often asked myself why I felt no strong inclination to settle and establish a family. After my experience in Avignon I was careful to choose my nocturnal companions with care; I avoided those who stirred me too much, lest there be unleashed that black passion which I could not control. I had always formulated the same answer to the question: it was not the right time, there were more cities to visit, more places to see, more worlds to explore, more learning to acquire before I rooted myself like a tree in the earth.

Perhaps, I thought, I will marry in Agen.

But something about this letter from Jules-César de l'Escale irritated me like a gadfly. I had been recommended to him by the Bishop of Agen, which seemed at first consideration innocent enough. But when I inquired, I found that this Bishop was no mere local prelate. He was a wealthy and powerful prince of the Church, a *puissant* nobleman who sat on the King's council and owned many rich dioceses all over France. Agen was merely one of numerous towns whose revenues poured like a golden waterfall into his ever-expanding coffers. The Bishop of Agen was none other than Jean, Cardinal de Lorraine.

I felt torn by colliding desires. The prospect of meeting Scaliger was immensely attractive to me. It appealed to my intellect and caressed my ambitions, for a person of his connections could provide me with the noblest and most highly placed of patrons. I was also curious, despite my uneasiness, about Jean de Lorraine, and what manner of man he was. It was a puzzle to be solved.

Undecided, I tossed this way and that, like a boat on a tumultuous sea. I began to sleep badly, and woke up often with some half-remembered dream – in which the faces of the Cardinal de Lorraine and the minstrel of Montpellier coalesced and separated and laughed mockingly at me and coalesced again and vanished.

And then I had a clear dream, like the dreams of my childhood and youth. When I awoke, my indecision was gone.

I dreamed that I wandered down an endless dusty road, which stretched straight as an arrow into the vague light of the hazy distance. Like an old Roman road, it cut direct as a lance through hill and valley and field and wood, as though the will of man sought to prove its power despite the protestations of nature. The sun glared angrily overhead, and the dry scrub and coarse grass at the roadside were sere and parched, like the vegetation of the desert of Craux near my childhood home. I walked and walked, and it seemed as though I moved nowhere, for nothing changed, and the sultriness and the dust and the blinding light remained.

I began to feel weak with thirst, for I had no water, and the land was dry and cracked and bleached white in the heat. A few thin trees, bent under the incessant bludgeoning of the sunlight, straggled along the roadside like limping old men, dying. I tried to see into the distance, but there was only the endless horizon and the white sky.

I staggered and stumbled. Once I fell on my face in the dust, and tasted its acrid flavour in my mouth and nostrils. It filled my eyes and blinded me, but there were no tears, for every vestige of water had been baked out of my body by the

71

ruthless light.

I fell once more. When I managed to lift myself she stood before me, a small and slender woman with the large, deep-socketed and sensitive dark eyes of some exotic forest creature. Her pale colourless face looked fragile beneath the weight of heavy dark tresses coiled snakelike around her brow. Beautiful and frail and haunted, she nursed in her hands a cup carved of some veined dark red stone, brimming wine. For a moment our eyes met, and I became aware of infinite compassion and infinite despair, as though she were pregnant with some bitter sorrow that ate at her from within, that fluttered on the delicate blue-veined eyelids. At first I thought it was her own. Then I realised that the sorrow and the despair and the compassion were for me.

A twinge of fear pinched my heart. Something invisible beat the air about me with formless wings, something dogged me, some shade that masqueraded as sunbeam in the bright light. I turned quickly around, but there was only the endless road behind me. I turned again to the woman, and saw that she cast an enormous shadow in the brilliant sun – a shadow stretching from her feet like the gigantic silhouette of an immense dark goddess, faceless in the white dust of the road. This shadow seemed to be the reality, and the woman only the shadow. I drank the wine, and closed my eyes with weariness and relief. When I opened them again, she had gone, leaving me the red stone goblet full of dregs.

When I awoke I knew I must go to Agen, convinced that I would meet her there. In my blindness I thought her the woman I would marry, for I had an intense presentiment of her as a living creature. I believed I might at last perform those rites which would allow me to cease my endless wandering. But dreams do not lie. It is only the dreamer who fails to understand their meaning.

IX

As I rode my mule through the gate of Agen, I awaited some harbinger, some omen, some confirmation that my future lay here. Like a superstitious savage, I looked for a bird's feather drifting to the ground, a cloud across the face of the sun, the significant flight of a hawk – a portent, a sign, anything that would ease my forebodings. Agen perched coyly, like a nubile maid, on the bank of the Garonne, neat and white and almost antiseptic in the dry and vivifying air. Wealth was evident in the size and ornateness of its buildings, pride in the relative cleanliness of its streets, complacent well-being in the faces of its townsfolk.

No omen came. I settled myself in an inn, and proceeded to extract what gossip I could about my future host from the innkeeper.

Scaliger, the innkeeper told me, had left the town after the last outbreak of plague. He was now resident at his luxurious country property of l'Escale, beyond the walls of the town, overlooking the river. Apparently he was very wealthy, and held in such high esteem that the local populace had nominated him Consul. A wonderful man, said the innkeeper, a wise man, a great man. All the learned of Guyenne and Gascony, Languedoc and Navarre passed through his household on their way to Nérac, Pau, Bordeaux, Toulouse, Montpellier, Carcassonne. A noble man, fit to match any Prince of the Blood on the tilting ground, with a beautiful young wife and a charming three-year-old son.

I began to feel awed. Here, if the innkeeper spoke the truth, was one of the greatest intellects of our time. I told myself that I was unworthy of him. I wondered what service I could offer him, what gift that might persuade him to act as my mentor.

Thus, in the dry dusty air of Agen, I still sought vindication of myself.

The man who loomed over me and bowed with a theatrical flourish was a man of proud and magnificent bearing, strongly built, with a great leonine black beard and wild hair curled in deliberate disarray. Cold light grey eyes, reflecting the true dweller in the pure realms of thought, peered into mine.

'I am honoured by your visit, Maître de Notredame,' he said. Even the ringing, measured tones of his voice suggested careful cultivation. I found myself speaking to him as though he were some stern and adored father, and I a child.

His pride of bearing was not, it seemed, unfounded, for he claimed descent from the noble house of Verona. The lesser folk of the Guyenne countryside did not know what to make of this glorious and autocratic man with his gloomy Italianate tempers, his sudden passions and his bouts of icy coldness. He was much respected in Agen; but the townsfolk were afraid of him.

'They do not understand,' he announced to me, 'that the intellect in every man is God. You and I, we are brothers. We have climbed the mountain peaks and glimpsed the pure light of mind untarnished by petty emotion and banal desire. Naturally they fear me.' He peered at me again from under heavy brows. 'Men always fear what they cannot understand.'

The brittle glow of polemics was his lifeblood. Much of his scholarly reputation had been established upon his vicious exchange of letters with Erasmus of Rotterdam. These two learned men had quarrelled violently about their definitions of humanism, had published erudite Latin treatises, had torn each other to pieces in elegant Ciceronian prose. I was impressed. I thought I would find stimulation enough in this man to last me for a lifetime; for mine is the kind of mind that does not come alive without the inspiration of a greater one.

I could not imagine why he had been so intent upon courting my acquaintance, for he had an outstanding reputation of his own as a skilled physician. He had his pick of accomplished and renowned companions from all over France and Italy. I remembered with a certain anxiety that it had not been Scaliger, but Jean, Cardinal de Lorraine who had orchestrated our meeting.

As things transpired, I settled into his house – temporarily, it was understood, until I could establish my medical practice and purchase a home of my own. With a characteristic theatrical flourish he spread his arms and opened his massive hands.

'Treat everything in this house as though it were your own,' he said.

Scaliger's young wife, Andiette de la Roque-Loubéjac, was just twenty. When I arrived in Agen she was in Gascony at the home of her parents. I devoted little thought to her. I imagined some pleasant and inconspicuous woman, compliant and agreeable and colourless, living tranquilly in the shadow cast by her husband's overpowering dominance and magnetism.

But when I saw her at last at the dinner table, I could only stare in shocked astonishment, a goblet of wine poised halfway between the table and my lips. She was small, slender, fine-boned, beautiful and frail and haunted, pale-complexioned, almost bowed down by the weight of her heavy dark hair, her opaque eyes deep-socketed and full of sensitive comprehension and compassion. The dark eyes met mine and slid away like water over mossy rocks.

Urgently, I resolved that I must obtain my house in Agen as quickly as possible, must find some well-dowered girl of the town to marry me. Otherwise I should find myself in a dreadful entanglement. I cursed my stupidity and my blindness. How was I to know that the woman of dreams, the giver of life in a parched and dying landscape, would be Scaliger's? I had never met a man whom I admired as much as Jules-César de l'Escale. I was not prepared to toss away the gift of his acquaintance like a worthless bauble, because of some fantastical fascination for a woman. But I had never met a woman I desired as much as his twenty-year-old wife.

My fame had preceded me to Agen. The townsfolk were eager to entrust themselves to the famous healer of Provence who, it was said, had virtually conquered the plague singlehanded. In a very short time, I enjoyed a thriving practice, and soon had enough gold to buy myself a little house in the rue de St Georges, across the courtyard from the beautiful old church of

St Hilaire. And circumstance, or some secret design of my own soul, conspired to further enmesh me in the net of my fate. For the man who owned the property I purchased had a young daughter named Blanche, whom he was anxious, even urgent, that I meet.

I was invited to his home. There I felt an immediate compassion for the young woman who had been dressed up and bedecked like a wooden doll. She had obviously been terrified by tales of the famous doctor who might favour her with an offer of marriage. Her innocence, her docility, her desire to please had paralysed her with embarrassment. She sat at the table with a pathetic naked pride, her hands tightly clasped together, her grey-blue eyes wide and frightened, her back stiff, her head high. Her knuckles were white from the vicious frightened clenching of her fingers.

I tried gently to draw her into some conversation that might afford a glimpse of the woman beneath the rigorous schooling. But I saw that she was unformed, like a blank tablet before writing has been inscribed upon it. I felt an immense and irresistible pity.

Thinly, at the back of my mind, a small voice nagged me, insisting that pity was not a basis for marriage, that I was only using her to escape from desires I dared not confront. I silenced this voice by admiring the pale cloud of her hair, the smooth white skin of her neck and shoulders, the waiting innocence of her rounded body, the delicacy of her nose and lips. She was a silken cocoon, a cloak of fragile feathers to protect me from the chill of the night. She would do whatever I wished, and love me for it.

I accepted the arrangement, flushed by my power over her, preening myself before the obvious and ingenuous happiness that shone from her face when she realised she had pleased me. I curled myself within the silken cocoon, and promptly began to wipe all thoughts of Andiette de la Roque-Loubéjac from my mind. When I met her at Scaliger's house I avoided her eyes. I never knew whether she too had experienced that sharp and wrenching recognition that had gripped me like the vice of a hawk's beak. With the endless hubris that I misconstrued as cleverness, I believed I had tricked the portent of the dream.

76

The two years which followed my marriage were years of peaceful contentment, of silken tranquillity, of feathery mindless torpor. All that had haunted and tormented my youth seemed at last to have dropped away, releasing me into ordinary manhood to live an ordinary life. I was well pleased with my wife, for she was docile and gentle and loving. Her gratitude to me for marrying her made me feel strong, and I was never troubled by the dark currents of passion which had once subsumed me. She asked no questions, and left me to my studies and my moods. She did not complain when I spent evenings away from her at Scaliger's house, for she did not believe herself worthy of participation in his esteemed intellectual circle. At the end of our first year of marriage, she bore me a son.

My practice blossomed. My wealth increased. I spent what spare hours remained to me with Scaliger, watching his brilliant mind apply itself to every subject man has ever pondered – from Aristotle and Galen and Hippocrates to the laws of the Church and the corruption of the clergy and the heresies of Luther and Calvin, from the celestial sciences to philosophy and rhetoric and classical literature. I met men from everywhere in Europe who passed through Agen to visit the famous scholar. I tasted all that was new and coming to flower in medicine and theology, architecture and poetry. I consumed it all like a starving man. I devoured, and grew famished, and devoured again.

Endless evenings passed at the homes of the *noblesse*. Scaliger's circle was a hotbed of theological argument, for the sword-edge of his wit enjoyed dissecting subjects forbidden by orthodoxy. He received visitors from Calvin's enclave in Geneva, and from Germany, and from the court of Queen Marguerite de Navarre across the Garonne at Nérac, and from other centres of free thought throughout Europe. I recalled the stifling doctrines of my education at Avignon and Montpellier, and believed that I had found heaven.

So the second year passed. Blanche bore me a daughter, and my practice was so full that I was obliged to turn people away. I grew plump on good food, and grew convinced that the rest of my life lay here in Agen, somnolent, drowsy, placid, warmed by the sun, sheltered by my wife's solicitous care, cheered by the smiles of my children, stimulated by the lofty company which had allowed me into its midst.

I marvel even now at man's capacity to blind himself to the deepest commands of his own soul, if they do not suit his purposes. But hindsight is an easy gift.

X

Scaliger told me he had received an invitation to dinner at the château of the Bishop of Agen, who, during a rare tour of his far-flung dioceses and abbeys, was temporarily in residence. Jean de Lorraine now numbered among his benefices the Archbishoprics of Reims, Lyons, and Narbonne, the Bishoprics of Metz, Toul, Verdun, Theroenne, Luçon, Albi, Valence, Nantes, and Agen, and the Abbeys of Cluny, Marmoutiers, Saint-Ouen, Gorze and Fécamp. He was the wealthiest prelate in France.

To my alarm, Scaliger had been requested to bring me to the Cardinal's dinner. I accepted the invitation with not a little foreboding. Jean de Lorraine's wish for my presence was explicable enough. He had heard of my reputation as a healer long before. It was, after all, his suggestion that had prompted Scaliger to write to me in the first place. But the uneasiness crept through my cocoon of feathers and silk.

The Cardinal de Lorraine was at this time thirty-nine years of age, and had acquired an extraordinary reputation. He was said to be as prodigal a churchman as had ever graced the College of Cardinals, and squandered his immense ecclesiastical revenues in the most reckless manner – on extravagant fêtes, on rare *objets d'art*, in purchasing the favours of his innumerable mistresses. At court he not only sat on the King's council but served as the King's procurer; and so conscientious was he in this service that he always sampled the wares first. It was said that no woman, young or middle-aged, married or unmarried, beautiful or plain, was safe from his bright wandering eye. If nothing else, I concluded, this banquet should prove an illuminating experience. I had never attended any nobleman of such distinguished lineage as this profligate great-grandson of King René d'Anjou.

The château of Agen was small, but I had never seen accumulated in one place before such a collection of treasures. The banqueting hall glittered and shimmered with tapestries and paintings and sculptures, golden candelabra and alabaster vases and cloth of gold. Candlelight from a hundred scented tapers floated across the gilded and frescoed ceiling, across the silks and satins and jewels of the assembled company.

There were only some twelve people present besides Jean de Lorraine, a small gathering for such a display of pomp. Most of this conclave were unknown to me, members of the Cardinal's household or attendants at the court of Navarre, which he had recently visited. I knew only Scaliger and Philibert Sarazin, one of the schoolteachers of Agen and a notorious Calvinist. I observed with interest that the Cardinal was not as discriminating in his religious scruples as he was in his aesthetic tastes. He greeted Sarazin as an old friend, and placed him near his own chair at the great table.

I took my seat between Mme Jeanne Musset de Moncille, who attended the Queen of Navarre, and a Dominican monk who seemed aloof and remote from the wealth and gaiety of the surroundings. He sat quietly drinking wine with a look of amused interest on his face. My conversation with both my table companions was polite but cursory. Although Mme de Musset was both attractive and a charming conversationalist, my gaze and my interest returned repeatedly to the Cardinal de Lorraine. He sprawled in a great carved chair at the head of the table, laughing and telling ribald stories, feeding titbits of sweetmeats with his own hands into the mouth of the richly gowned lady to his right, who lolled towards him with passionate intensity.

After his initial greeting, when a flicker of interest crossed his face as we were introduced, he studiously ignored me. I could not understand this behaviour, for he had, after all, made certain I would be invited to this banquet. I looked uneasily at the great banners decked about the hall – the quartered lilies of Anjou and Sicily, the crimson bars of Hungary, the double cross of Jerusalem, and silver eaglets of Lorraine. I decided to be sanguine and enjoy the meal.

We had eaten our way through the pine-seed cakes and the cold asparagus and the goose livers and the roast deer, and the servants were bringing out trays of capons and pigeons. My head was beginning to swim. Whenever the wine level in my goblet dropped, it was magically replenished by one of the pages through some deft sleight-of-hand. Mme de Musset leaned over to whisper in my ear. I could smell the scent she wore, attar of roses, above the odours of venison and goose and capon and human sweat.

'Do you know,' she said softly, 'the Cardinal always carries about with him a large wallet, filled each day with three or four hundred écus. And whenever he meets a poor person, he puts his hand into his wallet and gives whatever he happens to draw out, without bothering to count it. He is said to be the most generous man in the world. Once, when he was walking in Rome, a poor blind man asked alms of him, and he gave, according to his custom, a great handful of gold. Whereupon the blind man cried out: "You must be Christ, or surely the Cardinal de Lorraine!" Is it not a charming story?'

Charming indeed, I thought, as the lady's adoring gaze rested on the golden-haired prelate. He now sprawled languidly, laughing, reciting snatches of obscene poetry, one arm about the neck of the lady on his right, the other hand halfway down the bosom of the lady on his left. Apparently he was already drunk, his bright cornflower eyes roving the table, watching the company make merry. Yet despite his apparent abandon, I saw that he did not miss anything at all that occurred in the room. In his gaze lurked a concealed alertness that monitored everything, everyone with carefully disguised intensity. I began reluctantly to re-evaluate my opinion of him. He was not so much the vain and jolly sybarite as he made himself out to be. I looked for Scaliger to question him about our curious host, but my friend was engrossed in vigorous discussion with a portly neighbour. My gaze locked briefly with the Cardinal's. He gave me a slight nod, and a charming smile, and turned again to his ladies.

As if by a sudden blow, I was struck by the same sense of

intense recognition I had experienced long ago in Avignon, when he was a mere lad of twenty and I a boy of fifteen. The man had some power, of a kind I could not fathom. I stared at his face, trying to pursue the nagging and elusive memory that haunted me. Now pouches of dissipation marked his eyes, and his face had taken on flesh. But he was still extremely handsome, and radiated immense charm.

His glance crossed that of the sombre Dominican beside me. For a moment some message passed between them. By this time the servants had brought out the roasted piglets and peacocks in white sauce. At the doorway of the hall, the musicians had arrived. One or two of the guests had already fallen into a drunken stupor. Others were becoming rowdier as the evening progressed. I was becoming increasingly aware of my black-gowned table companion, who had passed the evening observing, but saying little.

This amazing feast apparently amused him. Crystalline gleams of irony flickered across his dark face, and open admiration for the Cardinal. His name was Mathieu Bandello. His speech was thickened with a heavy Italianate accent, his face emaciated almost to the point of being skeletal, but not uncomely. Grimaces of droll, sardonic humour intermittently curled his long, thin lips. A white scar seamed his face from forehead to chin, along the fine line of cheekbone and jaw.

I was aware, from time to time, of his scrutiny, but his gaze held no enmity and I felt no discomfort. I asked him how he came to be in Agen. He was staying, it transpired, at the house of an Italian noblewoman, Costanza Fregosi, whom he had accompanied from Venice after the battle of Pavia. According to rumour, he was a French agent at the time. He had connections with every noble house in Italy and made the difficult journey over the Alps with some regularity, bearing missives and information for whomever he served. He also had some reputation as a poet. Scaliger had met him once at Mantua.

The lute player, accompanied by a viol, a flute and a tympanum, had ensconced himself in the gallery above us, and was tuning the strings of his instrument in the shadows. I found myself thinking sadly of that other lutist long ago in Montpellier, with the melancholy, veiled eyes. A hush descended over the banqueting table. The lutist bowed low, first to the Cardinal and then to the rest of the company, and began to play.

My thoughts had wandered again to the Cardinal, who managed in such effortless fashion to offer service to both God and his senses without any apparent conflict in his conscience. I was jerked violently out of my reverie by the clear sexless voice of the lutist rising above the murmuring voices around me.

'Fruit de la nature
De très noble naissance,
Ida règnera
Dans la justice et la sainteté.

'À la légitime comtesse de Bologne,
Avec un encens brûlant,
Chantons de pur chants,
Et aussi au Duc de Lorraine,
Le fondateur de la dynastie,
La Fleur de l'esprit chevaleresque,
Godefroi, l'honneur du coeur.'

Intensely disturbed, I overturned my goblet of wine, which, in a red pool, sloshed over the table's edge and into my lap. A page materialised behind me and began to clean up the mess, while I sat with a myriad bizarre reflections careering through my bewildered mind. The Cardinal was watching the lutist intently, while he chatted to his ladies. The ladies watched the Cardinal. And Mathieu Bandello watched me, with a faint smile hovering at the corners of his mouth.

The lutist finished his motet, and the musicians began a *chanson*. It is chance, I told myself, mere chance. There is no reason why he should not play that piece, old as it is, for the honour of the house of Lorraine. It is mere coincidence. There is no meaning in it. None at all.

Mathieu Bandello turned and conferred on me a gentle smile.

'If you ever travel over the Alps,' he said conversationally, 'you must visit the court of my master.'

I waited politely.

'It is the sanest court in Italy,' he continued. 'The Gonzaga have been able to show their dead with honour for centuries. My lord Don Ferrante de Gonzaga, the Count of Guastalla, is a great soldier. But he is also a patron of the arts, and has many astrologers and kabbalists around him. You would find many of your own kind there.'

He gave me his gentle smile again. For no accountable reason, something ominous prickled at the back of my neck. It was an absurd surge of indirected fear, brought on, no doubt, by the music and the memories it evoked. I tried to escape into banter.

'I understand that the Count of Guastalla is a loyal subject of the Emperor. I would probably be hanged as a French spy before I had a chance to take out my astrolabe.'

I had, of course, neither desire nor intention of travelling to Mantua. I was content in the serene and somnolent haze of Agen.

'For you, there would be a welcome,' Mathieu Bandello replied. He watched my face. I became aware that I was expected to make some connection; but none occurred to me. I looked back at him blankly.

'There are many holy relics in Mantua,' the monk said. 'There is an ampulla which is said to contain the sacred blood of Our Lord, gathered by St Longinus from His body while it hung on the cross. And my lord of Gonzaga has in his possession a remarkable red porphyry cup, of great beauty and age, which was given to him by Antoine, the Duc de Lorraine, who inherited it from King René.'

He waited again, but I said nothing.

'Did your grandfather never tell you,' said Mathieu Bandello, 'about King René's sacred cup?'

'I have heard nothing about any red porphyry cup,' I said sullenly. Across the length of the table, the Cardinal de Lorraine was contemplating me musingly. He tossed me his charming smile again, as a young girl might throw a posy. This time I did not return it.

Bandello retreated a little. He was a skilful chess player, this sombre Dominican with the scarred face. 'It is said to be the cup in which Our Lord transformed water into wine at the

Wedding of Cana.'

'France abounds with holy relics,' I replied sourly. 'I do not need to travel to Mantua to see another. How do you come to know of my grandfather, Fra Bandello, and what do you wish of me?'

He spread his hands in an innocent gesture, and gave me his gentle smile again. 'I only know that your grandfather served King René,' he said, shrugging.

I stared into his dark eyes, but could divine no secrets in them. He looked back at me with a calm, sympathetic gaze. The long white scar suddenly resembled a seam, stitching the dark, ascetic face like a mask to some unknown thing beneath.

'Fra Bandello,' I said, 'have you ever met a wandering minstrel who calls himself Plantard?'

The dark gentle eyes gazed back at me innocently, without a flicker. 'Plantard? What an odd name. No, I do not believe that I have ever met such a man. Has he much skill?'

'I do not know if he is still alive. I met him long ago. I have never heard such a brilliant lutist, with a voice of liquid gold.'

'Then I shall be sorry if I never meet the man. The Cardinal is a lutist of some skill himself. And I am told that his nephew, young Charles de Guise, who is only fourteen, possesses a rare gift on the instrument. But,' Mathieu Bandello said, smiling into my eyes, 'the most skilled player of all was said to be Charles, Duc de Bourbon, the Constable who fled and trounced the King at Pavia. Those who heard him play declared he had the hands of an angel.'

You know. You know, Michel, where the minstrel Plantard has gone. Can the notes of the lute be heard wafting where his pale ghost flits along the walls of the Eternal City?

One minute passed, and then another. The music and the chatter hummed and bubbled and buzzed around me. No, I thought. It is impossible. No.

'Fra Bandello,' I said carefully, more than a little drunk, 'I know that you wish something of me, but I do not understand you. Do you wish me to become involved with the politics of Mantua, or perhaps the politics of Lorraine? I am happy here at Agen. I am a loyal servant of the Church and of His Most Christian Majesty. I do not wish to know anything about dukes or princes other than the common gossip that every man knows. Evidently I have been brought to this banquet for some reason. Well, I am telling you that I have no interest in it. I have a lovely young wife and two children, and a thriving practice, and a comfortable house. Please let us discuss astrology, or medicine, or, if you insist, even theology. But not what you are hinting at. I do not wish to know.'

Mathieu Bandello replied with a gently derisive ripple of laughter.

'Jésu, but you are a touchy man,' he said. 'You do not even know what I am going to say, yet you tell me no. I mentioned nothing of politics.' He laughed again. 'You speak proudly, but without understanding. You have been involved with us from the beginning. But there is much that an old man cannot tell a child.'

'For some reason which I cannot fathom, Fra Bandello, you are baiting me. Go and bait Scaliger, who has been in Mantua and has undoubtedly drunk from your lord of Gonzaga's sacred cup. Whatever my grandfather was to you, I make no allegiances except those which I choose.'

Bandello seemed to capitulate and retire into himself. Perhaps I was not as he had expected; perhaps I had disappointed him. But he had shown no malice during our exchange. Rather, there had been an expression of concern in his face, as though he were trying gently to make me aware of something I should know, yet was too blind to see. He took a deep breath and exhaled it in a long sigh, then swallowed another mouthful of wine.

The anger drained away, and I felt suddenly blundering and sorry, as though it were I who had offended him.

'I will remember your recommendation to the Count of Guastalla,' I said more gently. 'But I do not see that I shall travel to Italy in any predictable future. My children are too young, and I do not wish to leave my wife.'

'No. Of course not.' He looked full at me, and the compassion and solicitude were obvious in his dark face. He reached into some pocket in the voluminous black folds of his robe, and drew forth something which glinted in the candlelight. It was a ring of gold, carved with the device of a bear. He proffered it gently to me.

85

'Take this. If you prefer, it is a recompense. You once un-knowingly performed a service for a friend of mine, in Mont-pellier, when he was in need. And if you ever travel to Mantua, take the route through Chambéry into Savoie, and over the pass of St Bernard into the Milanese. When you arrive, present that ring to my lord Don Ferrante de Gonzaga. He will know then that our paths have crossed.'

I looked at it shining in his palm in the candlelight. I did not wish to take it, and glanced away. At the head of the table the Cardinal de Lorraine's bright cornflower gaze was fastened intently upon me. I looked back at the ring. Something of terr-ible importance was occurring, but I did not know what it was. Amidst the din of voices and the noise of lute and viol and flute, some profound and endless silence stretched on a tight thread between the Cardinal's eyes and mine.

How do I know you? I have known your face for a thousand years . . .

Despite every inner prompting to refuse the gift, I reached out my hand. After all, I reasoned, I will probably never see either of these men again. The Cardinal rarely comes to Agen, and Bandello will most likely return to Italy.

'I thank you, and I will remember. But will you not tell me why you are so anxious that I go to Mantua?'

Bandello smiled at me. 'Why, on a pilgrimage, Maître de Notredame. To see the red porphyry cup of King René d'Anjou.'

XI

I can remember perusing my horoscope, and noting a malign influence impending: Saturn was approaching the opposition to Venus. I recall telling myself that it undoubtedly referred to some disappointment over a new house I had wanted to obtain outside Agen.

For long periods I did not even look at my own horoscope, being, as I told myself, more concerned with those of my patients. Nor did I perform my customary examination of the charts of my wife and children. I existed in a blind haze and, like a mole, buried my head in the earth. But perhaps we are deliberately blinded, so that we can experience and choose with a semblance of free will, and not disclaim responsibility.

My peace was first shattered by a letter, a month after the banquet at which I met Mathieu Bandello. It was delivered by a messenger in a plain tunic and cloak. He would not identify himself, but handed me the parchment, mounted his horse and rode off with a clatter down the street. The letter was brief and to the point.

'To Maître Michel de Notredame at Agen.
From Jean, Cardinal de Lorraine at St-Germain-en-Laye.
Greetings.

'By order of His Most Christian Majesty King François, Louis de Rochette, Inquisitor of the Faith for the Province of Languedoc and the Duchy of Guyenne, is *en route* from Toulouse to root out the heretics who are said to have infested His Majesty's town of Agen. If you are wise, you will undertake a little journey.'

I stared at this letter in bewilderment. My first question was not what I would do, nor where I would go, but why this eminent nobleman and prince of the Church should concern himself with me.

That the Inquisitor of the Faith should smell heresy at Agen was not surprising, for the town had indeed been infested. Virtually every leading citizen, including Scaliger, was implicated; Calvin's doctrines had been assiduously circulated throughout the town. Sooner or later, someone was bound to incur a guilty conscience and notify the authorities.

Accepting the Cardinal's advice, I travelled to Bordeaux to visit my friend Nicolas de Vicheray, the alchemist. I took Blanche and the children with me, leaving only the servants in the house. My own conscience was clear as crystal. At Agen, as elsewhere, I had been exceedingly careful to display an irreproachable piety toward all ceremonies and dignitaries of the Church.

We returned to Agen a month later. By then the tumult had died down. The story turned out to be more of a farce than a tragedy, no doubt due to the Cardinal's unseen intervention.

Early in March, Louis de Rochette had arrived and preached a long sermon of fire and smoke at the church of St Fiary. He urged the townsfolk to denounce all heretics in their midst. Those who fulfilled this sacred injunction would be recompensed in gold écus.

People being what they are, more than seventy depositions were received. This number astonished me, for I was, at that time in my life, still surprised to find that ordinary folk, with whom I shared my daily life, were somewhat less reasonable than I assumed. The depositions accused, among others, Philibert Sarazin, the school regent, and Jules-César de l'Escale.

Several people, including M. Sarazin, were thrown into prison. But the Inquisitor of the Faith himself apparently harboured secret sympathies for the heretics, allowing M. Sarazin to escape the city without obstruction. A week later Louis de Rochette was arrested as a sodomite – a charge concocted, no doubt, to cover the embarrassment of a tainted Inquisitor – and taken under arms back to the stake at Toulouse.

Another Inquisitor appeared, named Antoine Richard. To the mortification of the Tribunal in Toulouse, this second Inquisitor too was influenced by the Calvinist doctrines. A few days later he in turn was arrested and burned in the town square. A third Inquisitor arrived, to continue the trials.

Scaliger was lucky. He was gifted enough to muster for himself a brilliant and eloquent defence. More importantly, he was able to answer his charges before a group of men who were predisposed, by their learning and his reputation, to be sympathetic. Behind this moved the Cardinal de Lorraine's powerful hand. Although he could not interfere directly with an Inquisition sent at the King's request, he could, as Bishop of Agen, appoint the ecclesiastical judges he wished to try the accused.

Thus, when I returned from Bordeaux, the uproar had subsided. It had been terrifying for many, and costly as well. In the end, however, no deaths were claimed save those of the two

Inquisitors themselves.

There had been one inquiry concerning me, for I had been seen often enough at Scaliger's house, bandying theological theories with his suspect circle. But no one in Agen cared to place a deposition against me. The idea that I might be a heretic was considered so preposterous by everyone who knew me that the questioning proceeded no further. My grandfather would have been pleased with me.

Again the days flowed by like a peaceful river, sunrise to sunset, melded into a golden current of tranquillity. I believed that life would return definitively to its normal placid course. In consequence, the second blow, when it descended, was far worse than the first – not only in its nature, but in its utter unexpectedness. Yet like other turning points in my life, it was heralded by the recurrence of the dream.

There had, of course, been other dreams, equally strange and equally incomprehensible; and the dark pool and the shadowy abbey had gradually dimmed in my consciousness. I thought of it only rarely. And only during those moods of melancholy to which I have always been prone did I discern a meaning beyond the augury of death and change. On such occasions I would sit for hours staring at the fire, trying to cultivate a sense of the place, the landscape I had never seen in waking life. But when I surfaced from such moods, my mind was quickly diverted by other things. My life with Blanche, my wealth and comfort, my increasing reputation and honour, the warm glow of the prestigious little circle blooming under Scaliger's delicate tutelage – all conspired to efface the dream from my memory. Men are such vulnerable beings, even the wisest, when flesh is sleek and pride satisfied.

I had passed a contented day. I had treated M. Castelan, the notary, for a bad attack of the rheum. I had helped deliver a child to Mme Duperron. I had spent the evening before the fire playing with Jacques and showing him my astrolabe, in which he displayed great interest. I had made love to my wife. I had fallen asleep with her arm curled across my chest and her warm breath on my cheek, my stomach surfeited with wine and suckling pig.

I stood by the stream, gazing down upon the pool, and all

was familiar and as it had been before. I was again suffocated by the dense closeness of the atmosphere, as though devoid of air, and again endured the fear coiling up my spine, nestling in my belly. The lightless abbey squatted on the crest of the hill, humped and silent. And the bell began to toll, measuring out its slow, lugubrious notes like a gigantic heartbeat. It was the plague bell, tolling as it had done at Narbonne, Bordeaux, Toulouse, Montpellier, Carcassonne.

From the shadows of the abbey rolled the death cart, its small silvery bell ringing counterpoint to the great one. The figure which followed the cart and steered the oxen was robed and cowled in black, a shadow against the shadows. As he passed he lifted his head to me and smiled. His face was half eaten away by worms and corruption – a pair of holes in place of a nose, eyes sunk into dark pits, half the jaw eroded to disclose the sockets of his teeth. In greeting, he raised his hand, on which winked a huge golden ring, set with an immense ruby that glowed molten with its own inner light. The cart was piled with decaying bodies, some still twitching, such as I had seen a thousand times before. A terrible stench rose to meet my nostrils. And then, buried beneath the mound of dead on the cart, I discerned one body which seemed eerily familiar. Protruding arm and shoulder clothed in the black serge of a doctor's fur-trimmed gown, head face down with the flat doctor's cap on chestnut hair . . . The cart passed into the shadows, while I stood rooted and blind. It had been my own corpse in that macabre pile. I looked up to where the solitary monk now stood at the crest of the hill. As before, I knew that he watched me, though I could not see his face. I awoke with a cry in the arms of my wife.

I realised then that the plague would come to Agen. Although I could see no indication of death portended in my horoscope, I was nevertheless prepared to accept the omen. It was in the lap of the gods. I resolved to quietly register my will with a notary. I knew that dreams do not lie. But I forgot that there are many kinds of death.

Early the next morning, I warned the town magistrates. My astrological reputation led them to believe I had foreseen it in the stars. That would be within the bounds of orthodoxy. I was not about to declare to all the world, a week after the Inquisition had left Agen, that I suffered from prophetic dreams. I was faintly surprised that I felt no fear. Perhaps, I thought, it is as it should be: one accepts one's fate and makes one's peace with the gods.

As I returned from my day's rounds, M. Duperron rushed to meet me in the street. He had been searching frantically for me everywhere. I stared into his distraught face and knew in one blinding shocking instant what kind of death that dream had prophesied.

I found her stretched on the bed, coughing and gasping and retching, her forehead burning with fever, her body already beginning to twitch with the terrible convulsions; her pillow was spattered with the blood she had coughed up. It was the pulmonary plague, the rare one which I had never been able to conquer. I found Jacques in his little cupboard bed, delirious, lying in a putrescent pool of his own vomit. Renée, shrouded in her tiny crib, was already dead.

By nightfall all three had gone. The disease had bitten too deep when I found them. Had I come sooner, there might have been a chance. But it had all been forewritten, and my famous remedies, my wonderful cures which had earned me fame and gold throughout Provence and Languedoc, were useless. While my wife gasped out her last rattling breath, I heard the great church bell beginning to toll. My family were the first to die.

I do not remember much of the time that followed, for I was not sane. I remember the coffins – I refused to allow those precious and pitiful corpses to go with the death cart – and the quiet, hurried burial. I remember cursing God, and screaming and shouting and smashing the crockery, and beating my fists against the stone walls of the house. I remember weeping, and lying prone on the floor. I remember rising in a stupor, and drinking myself to oblivion, and awakening to the same terrible pain. I remember sobbing in the arms of Scaliger, who had come from his house to tend me. I remember the compassionate look in Andiette's dark eyes as she wiped a cool damp cloth across my forehead and forced me to eat. At some point I managed to stand and totter out with Scaliger to minister to the sick. But I moved in a trance, and spoke to no one.

I knew that I must either attempt to resume my life or renounce it. I chose the former, but the choice was a tenuous one. For I had indeed died. Much more had been consumed by the flames than my comfortable bourgeois life. I could smell the currents of the future, harbingers of that which awaited me patiently despite my evasions and my blindness, like the far-off smell of salt clinging to the wind, long before one glimpses the sea.

My apparent faith in Holy Church, so carefully nurtured for the benefit of interested eyes, now mocked me. There were too many gods, and not all of them beneficent. The townsfolk of Agen showed their pity, and while a few acquired some doubts in my competence, most of them retained their faith in me. Did I not have a long history of wonderful cures? It was a tragedy, they said; but life went on.

It was my faith in myself that had shattered. If I could not heal my own family, what kind of physician was I? If I could not foresee this disaster, of what use were my celestial studies? I clung to Scaliger as though I were drowning, and felt an absurd gratitude to him for giving so generously of his time.

Among those few who turned against me were Blanche's parents. I could understand their bitterness, but had underestimated their pettiness. Within a fortnight of her death they instituted a lawsuit to recover the dowry she had brought into our marriage. This included the house in which I still lived. Thus, to my loneliness and bereavement and the presentiment of some terrifying future was added the additional curse of a bevy of notaries and solicitors banging on the door. Each time I sent one away with subtle arguments or imprecations, another would appear.

The legal proceedings, brutal farce that they were, continued over many months. I knew that my property could not be wrested from me. Had there been any real danger of it, I would have appealed to the Cardinal de Lorraine to bribe the town magistrates. But it soured me toward Blanche's parents and toward the town, though this was unreasonable. Increasingly I sensed the fate that was dogging me, and stubbornly turned away, determined to refuse it. Thus the Goat beats his head against the wall until his forehead is bloody and his skull cracked, believing to the end that the persistence of his will can bring him victory.

Before the year was out and the suitable period of mourning over, the ranks of fathers with marriageable maidens began to form again. I was, after all, one of the most eligible men in town, being wealthy and of an honourable reputation, having produced a healthy son and daughter to demonstrate my virility. I made the polite responses and refused.

They thought it was because I still grieved over Blanche. In part, this was true. But nothing dies that has not been lived out, and with Blanche's death that seed I had so ruthlessly stifled proceeded to sprout with alarming rapidity, as though to take vengeance on my former suppression of it. I began to dream at night of Andiette de la Roque-Loubéjac; and now there was no sweet and willing buffer to protect me from my own desires.

I tried to counter them with self-denigration. I could not imagine that this refined and delicate and sensitive woman would favour me. I thought of Scaliger: handsome in his saturnine way, tall, gaunt, with his thinking eyes and noble brow, his wonderful intellect and biting wit – dark locks curled and perfumed, long ascetic fingers glittering with rings. I thought of myself: plump, overfed, barely of middle height, my cheeks comically rosy, my blunt earthy fingers hardly shaped for a courtier's gestures and caresses.

I thought with irony of the declaration I had once made to my grandfather: *I would like to be a court gentleman*. No one was less suited for the role.

Time passed and I succeeded, with enormous effort of will, to blot Andiette from my thoughts. I was lonely, but I had long ago grown used to that. There was still the pleasure of Scaliger's company and that of his friends, and the obvious affection of the people of Agen. I asked myself why I did not take some friendly local girl as mistress, and answered that I was simply not interested. I prided myself on not being so driven by my desires that I must rut with any trollop for relief. So it went on, for a year after the plague.

But I did not anticipate that Andiette had far fewer scruples, and far less hypocrisy, than I. For there came a day when I sat at my calculations in my solitary house, watching the waning light of the late afternoon sun insinuating itself through the shuttered windows, and heard a knock at the door. Outside stood Andiette, with a basket on her arm, paying, to my astonishment, a social call.

I was thoroughly confused. I had never seen her alone in the town, for Scaliger possessed her like a precious object, and she was always with him or surrounded by serving women. I had barely exchanged a dozen words with her since my arrival in Agen. It was beyond my comprehension that she should seek my company. I offered her a chair, and some wine, and some supper which she refused. She spread her skirts about her – they were of some deep blue stuff that made her skin seem very white – and I noticed that beneath her self-possession she was frightened, for her hands trembled.

For a moment, as I studied her, I saw the road white with dust, the ruthless searing sun, the vast shadow that extended behind her, the stone cup, the red porphyry cup, the cup . . .

I jerked myself back to find her sensitive eyes upon me with a quizzical expression.

'You do not look well, Michel. Perhaps you should go away for a while.'

'I am well enough. It will take time, that is all, to find my balance again. You must not be concerned if I seem morose or solitary. It will pass.'

It was a bizarre dream-conversation, a juxtaposition of converging dreams . . . I heard myself speaking the ordinary words as though we had been friends all our lives. And at the same time, somewhere above it, I watched, peering down owl-like from a cold height, astonished.

'I know. That is not what I mean. It is the way you are with Scaliger, the way you worship him. I have watched the look on your face when he speaks and the way you follow his words. He insults you in his veiled fashion, and you accept it and smile and nod, as though you were some idiot at the feet of a saint. Since your loss it has got worse. You follow him about the house like a dog. You need time away from him, to heal. He has taken you over, while you were unable to defend yourself.'

I was bemused by this speech, not least because I had never heard her utter so many words before. I felt a mounting

94

indignation that she should speak so disloyally of him to me, an anger that she should thus bare her private complaints, as though to turn me against him. Certainly he was arrogant, theatrical, bombastic, sometimes supercilious. But I could not see, in return for the admiration and devotion I offered him, any sign of contempt.

'Why do you speak like this of him?' I demanded. 'If you harbour a grievance against your husband, it is none of my concern, and I do not want to be involved in it. Go home, Andiette. I do not know why you have come here. Your place is by his side, and your duty to be a loyal wife.'

'Oh, do not pontificate so, Michel. You are like a pompous little cock, strutting on a dung-heap. You are too blind to see what Scaliger is. You find his posturing endearing, yet every idea of yours he seizes as his own. There is no thought that comes out of you that he has not borrowed. He is jealous of you, and has always been so. He picks the brains of his friends like a jackal, and you, little fool, think it an honour.'

I shook my head as though to clear it, for I was increasingly bewildered. But despite myself, awareness filtered through my determined blindness, rousing the mole from his somnolent sleep. So many dinners, so many discussions, during which some statement of mine would be dexterously, brilliantly refuted, dissected, laughed at, only to reappear on his lips the following evening. And his guests would nod, impressed.

'Why do you tell me this? I thought yours a happy marriage,' I said unwisely.

She gasped hoarsely, disdainful laugh and cough commingled. 'What do you know?' she snapped. 'You know nothing of me. You are so obtuse the roof could fall on your head, and you would sit there puffed up like a partridge, blinking and pondering the source of the loud noise.' She was almost spitting with rage, her face flushed, her eyes glittering.

'Why are you so angry with me? I have done nothing to offend you. Let us say that you are right. It makes no difference to me. He is my friend. He is the architect of all the good I have accrued in Agen. Before I met him I was unsettled, footloose, lost. He has given me a home here, and when my grief was unbearable he stayed by me and helped me through it. If he is jealous, then he is a fool and does not see his own worth. And I shall tell him as much.'

'Ah, Michel,' she said, and I realised that she was weeping. Blind, blind, so utterly blind . . .

But she had not the refuge of blindness. Being a woman, she would not cheat her own heart with evasion, though it had made her suffer. How long? I wondered, and then I remembered her look sliding away from mine like water.

I felt her body trembling like some captured forest creature beneath my hands. For a few seconds she clung to me, then broke violently away.

'This will not help us. It can only bring shame and misfortune to us all. I came today to ask you to leave Agen.'

'Leave Agen? Are you mad? That is unthinkable. I cannot leave now, now that . . . I have been blind, as you say, but that is because . . . because . . .'

'Because you know nothing of women, and nothing of yourself. I have lain awake in the night so often, cursing the fate that married me to the wrong man. I knew it very soon, long before you came to Agen. It does not matter. You must go. I have a terrible premonition. I do not wish to be the cause of further pain.' She paused and breathed deeply and straightened herself. 'I know what kind of love it was between you and Blanche. It was good and gentle and sufficient. You were happy. All of us would have grown old and grey together and never had to confront it. But since she died, I think of you here alone, and watch you trailing in Scaliger's shadow, and I cannot bear it.'

'I cannot leave.'

'I am certain that Scaliger knows. I can tell by the way he watches us both. He is like a great dark spider, spinning webs. You think him a shining knight. Oh, you do not realise . . . You can begin again, somewhere else. You have money, you have fame. Any town in Provence would be honoured to receive you. You can meet someone else and marry again and be happy.'

My instinct for survival, which has taken me through a long life with knee bent to the service of Church and kings, with a smile on my face and a heart full of secrets, told me she was right. I might avoid discomfort if I left Agen while it was still possible. I have never been made of the stuff of martyrs.

'I will think about it,' I said. But the next moment I was on my feet and kissing her, feeling her lips open under mine in response. And then somehow she lay white and beautiful and fine-boned across my bed, her eyes staring into mine. And from the shuddering in my own body, I knew it would be the same dark journey I had made before, into those murky depths from which I emerged without remembrance, weeping and shaking. But this woman was not Marguerite; and she had kindness.

Afterwards she looked for a long time into my eyes, and said, 'I understand now why you have been afraid. Is it always like this?'

'No. Only once, long ago. I have never comprehended it. But with you I can bear it.'

'Where do you go, Michel?' She stroked my hair, and traced the outline of my face with her finger.

'I do not know. I only feel as though my soul has been torn out of me, and that in some way I have died and come back, and that for a moment something else has possessed me. It terrified me, the first time, for the woman was not someone I would have trusted with it.'

'Who was she?'

'My father's sister.'

She looked at me again for a long moment. 'You have many secrets, Michel. I sometimes think you are surrounded by some mystery, and that a strange fate indeed awaits you.'

A cool shiver ran along my spine. I tried to flee the nagging ghostly shapes and voices by burying my face in her heavy hair.

The following morning, my reality in Agen collapsed completely, shattered like a smashed eggshell. A letter arrived from Scaliger. In his best Ciceronian prose, he stigmatised me with every villainous epithet in his extensive vocabulary, and warned me never to show my face at l'Escale again.

I was torn between shame and anger and anxiety for Andiette. I knew that Scaliger must have beaten her savagely, for his tempers, even over small and unimportant things, were violent and frightening. Over the loss of his friendship, I discovered that I felt nothing.

I did not know what to do. I decided to wait until I received some word from her. I waited for three weeks.

The town gossiped of our quarrel. He put it about that we had fallen out over religious differences. We had always argued about the new heresies, and his explanation was therefore plausible. It caused a stir for a while, and much shaking of heads. A pity, the townsfolk said, that two such brilliant doctors should fight like schoolboys. But it could not remain a matter of real interest for long. There were still the sick and the dying. Once I passed him in the street, and he turned his head away.

There came at last a foul night of rain and chill wind, and, as midnight reverberated in the belfry, I heard a tapping at my window. She huddled in the courtyard, bundled and cloaked so that her face was indistinguishable in the gloom. But I would have known her anywhere, from the way she stood, and the fragile line of her shoulders under the heavy cloak.

'Michel, you must leave Agen immediately. What I have feared has happened. He has made a deposition to the Inquisitor at Toulouse. You have been accused of heresy. Pack your things and go. You must go quickly. The messenger will arrive in the morning, summoning you to the Tribunal.'

I was stunned. 'Heresy? What nonsense is this? There is no one in Agen less likely to be charged with heresy. I was thoroughly exonerated when Louis de Rochette came.'

'He has named you a Calvinist agent, responsible for the spread of the doctrine in the town. The Cardinal de Lorraine cannot help you, for the court at Toulouse is beyond his jurisdiction. You must go.'

'Jésu, I cannot believe that he would stoop to this.'

'That is how he is. He uses such things when the opportunity comes. You are not the first. I told you you were blind to what he is.'

'How have you managed to come to me?'

'I crept out through the kitchens. I will be beaten when I return. He will know. He has known all along. It does not matter. Please, you must go. You are in danger. I pray that God will protect you, and keep you from harm.' She began to weep, but held herself straight. 'It was too late when you came to Agen. I cannot fight against fate.'

'What did he do to you?' I said, taking her by the shoulders. She flinched away from me, but said nothing. As I slipped her gown from her body I gasped, for her back was covered with a savage pattern of weals, half-healed, stitched across the smooth white skin. Tears of pity and anger filled my eyes.

'Oh, my dear, I am sorry, so sorry . . .' But deeper than the anger lay the guilt.

Although it pained her at first, we coupled with desperate hunger, like animals, for we knew we would never see each other again. We were both weeping by the end of it. Here was the evil fate that dogged me, dogged me persistently, ruthlessly, tortuously. There was nothing to be done.

In the morning the messenger from the Inquisition arrived on an exhausted horse, his white and silver uniform splattered with mud. He informed me that I had two weeks to present myself at the Tribunal in Toulouse.

'But this is madness,' I snapped at him. 'Of what heresy have I been charged?'

He removed a parchment from his pouch. 'It is known that you are an agent of Calvin, receiving documents and blasphemous literature from Geneva, which you have been disseminating to the innocent townsfolk of Agen.'

'That is ridiculous. Anyone here can tell you that there is no one in this town more devout than I. When the Inquisitor of the Faith passed through Agen I was completely cleared of even the faintest suspicion.'

'New information has come to light,' the man said in a bored voice. He had heard such protests many times before. No doubt he had also seen the protesters tortured and burned many times before. 'I have here the order demanding that you present yourself before the Inquisitor in two weeks' time. I would advise you not to consider avoiding it, lest the charge of heresy be compounded with others. However, the Inquisitor at Toulouse is a compassionate man. He can often be persuaded to leniency by a donation attesting to one's contrition.' He gave a curt bow and withdrew. I listened to his horse clopping through the mud down the street.

I stood at the window in a stupor. All would depend on the Inquisitor. If he were a tolerant man, and if I possessed sufficient gold, I would merely suffer inconvenience and a depletion of my coffers. If he were intolerant, or if I were not sufficiently rich, or if he had headache that day, I might be tortured and burned. I did not fancy any of the alternatives. I shook myself out of my stupor and began to pack.

It took me three hours to prepare. I charged M. Duperron, whom I trusted, to sell my house discreetly in a few months' time, and to retain possession of my grandfather's library. I would contact him from some safe place to collect the proceeds. Clothes and furniture and household items would have to be sold as well. I packed the most precious of my books, and my instruments, and my gold, and donned a plain grey travelling robe. I waited until nightfall, mounted my mule and passed quietly through the gate without a glance back. I left only death, bitterness and frustration behind me. By dawn the following morning I was far from Agen, taking the side roads through the countryside of Guyenne, moving east.

Not until the next evening did I feel safe enough to stop at an inn for some supper and a bed. I dug into my pouch for coins and my fingers closed on the golden ring Mathieu Bandello had given me over a year before at the Cardinal de Lorraine's banquet. Amid the gloom of my cramped little room at the inn, the ring glinted and glittered in my hand, while the wind beat at the window and the shadows crept stealthily about me. I knew then that he had foreseen it all long ago.

He, or some careful masters for whom he worked, had kept track not only of my movements, but of the movements of my horoscope as well. They had read there the impending crisis, which I in my stupidity had so sublimely ignored. Bandello had been sent at the appropriate time, to point out the next stage of the journey.

I began to shiver as the net fell softly around me. I had been avoiding it for too long. Now I felt something harden and crystallise inside me. Very well, I thought. I shall play your little game. We shall see who wins in the end.

Mathieu Bandello's quiet voice resonated in my mind: *I mentioned nothing of politics*. What, then, was it? If they toyed with alchemy and magic and the old rituals of the Temple, surely there was no need for this game of cat-and-mouse secrecy. It was obvious enough that I was steeped already in the occult arts. I remembered the monk's gentle smile, the compassionate look in his eyes. Of course he had been compassionate. That sensitive man had known, or guessed, a little of what lay ahead of me, and had, in his fashion, pitied me.

I stared at the ring. It became increasingly obvious that I had no other choice than to travel to Chambéry, and proceed through Savoie over the Alps toward Mantua.

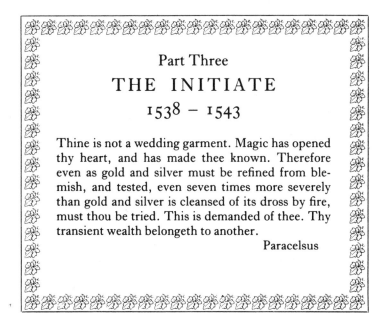

Part Three

THE INITIATE
1538 – 1543

Thine is not a wedding garment. Magic has opened thy heart, and has made thee known. Therefore even as gold and silver must be refined from blemish, and tested, even seven times more severely than gold and silver is cleansed of its dross by fire, must thou be tried. This is demanded of thee. Thy transient wealth belongeth to another.

Paracelsus

XII

From the height of the severe mountain masses I turned and looked back at the imposing vista through which I had passed. The tortuous road wound like a gigantic serpent round one peak and disappeared behind another, fading into the darkened jumble of jagged rocky crevasses as though it plunged into the very bowels of the earth. Above me glittered the eternal snows where some distant aloof gods of ice and stone cavorted and laughed in the endless reaches of space.

Ahead of me, perched like a frail bird on the topmost mass at the roof of the world, was the little monastery of St Bernard, which marked the pass to the Val d'Aosta and the Milanese. The very air seemed filled with the jewel-like fluttering of sylphs and devas and godlets of wind and cloud.

I needed food and rest. It had taken me a full month to reach Chambéry, another three weeks to reach the pass. I turned my mule to the unimposing squat shape of stone with its simple bell tower topped by a cross, stark black against the vivid blue of the sky. The monastery shone ancient and warm in the golden light. I envisioned friendly, simple faces, ordinary good fare, a cup of wine, a straw pallet for a bed. But even here – in this bizarre and antiseptic domain of crystal and ice and white sunlight and emptiness, where the squabbles and bickerings of kings and the bloody clash of arms and the black reek of plague seemed nothing more than a frightening and half-remembered nightmare – even here, the daemon dogged my steps.

At first it seemed pleasant enough. I was exhilarated by the brilliant light and the invigorating air, and felt my sorrows drop away from me under the gentle ministrations of the white-robed monks. The Prior told me there had been many travellers all through the summer, most of them on urgent business.

Since the new truce signed between King François and the Emperor in June, a vast exodus had passed through this little eyrie – Italians fleeing into France and French fleeing into Italy – each anxious to affirm his allegiance before the next débâcle occurred and plunged the two crowned squabblers into another Peninsular war.

I wondered to whom this homely monastery, nestled so cosily in the heights of the vast mountains, owed allegiance, and to whom it transmitted information about travellers passing through its doors. Probably, I thought, to both. The wine was excellent, far from the simple vintage I had drunk throughout my journey, and the fare was rich. The donkeys and horses stabled in the courtyard were fat and sleek, and the cross in the Prior's study was of solid gold.

I held out to him the safe-conduct passes I had obtained in Chambéry, marked with the seal of the Duc de Savoie. With the gentlest of gestures, he refused them.

'There is no need, Maître de Notredame,' he said. 'We have been expecting you these two weeks or more.'

'Word travels quickly across the mountains,' I said sourly.

The Prior smiled at me. 'The air is thinner,' he replied.

I removed Mathieu Bandello's golden ring from my pouch. 'Do you know this?' I asked him.

'Of course. But it was not necessary to show it to me. I know already of your business with the Count of Guastalla. You should keep that ring hidden, until you are face to face with him to whom it belongs.'

'Perhaps you can tell my business to me, since I do not know it myself.'

'It is not my place,' said the Prior, smiling at me again, 'to meddle in the secrets of others.'

I could get no further information from him. He was courteous, pleasant and aloof. After showing me the little cell in which I was to sleep, he asked me if I would join him in prayer in his private chapel. It was meant as an honour, and I could not refuse, although I felt some discomfort at playing the hypocrite before this gentle old man.

But when I entered the tiny shrine, preparing to kneel, I stopped, catching my breath in astonishment. Amidst the perfumed smoke from the censer and the frail light of a single taper, the figure of the Virgin glimmered before a small altar. She was black, black as pitch, carved of some ancient wood, and so old, so terribly old, that the very stones of the chapel, already worn from five centuries of devoted hands, seemed fresh and new and hardly born. The wood was cracked and seamed, and her form stood stiff and archaic in the rigidly pleated carved robe, lips curled in a serene and enigmatic smile, eyes blank and mysterious and full of secrets, hair coiling like a swarm of serpents across narrow rigid shoulders and outstretched arms.

There was no Child.

I stood in the shadows and watched the Prior kneel and make the sign of the cross and begin to murmur in his thin old man's voice, while the smoke brought tears to my eyes and the candlelight flickered and winked through the gloom.

He rose from his knees and turned to me. 'You do not pray, Maître de Notredame.'

'What is she?' I whispered. 'What is it you worship here? That is not the Virgin. That is an ancient thing, from some remote dark past.'

'That is Notre Dame,' the Prior said quietly. 'Do you not recognise her for whom you were named?'

I could only stare at him, while he met my eyes with unperturbed serenity. Far away, I heard the thin note of a bell, summoning the monks to vespers. The rich bitter aroma of frankincense filled my nostrils and made me cough.

The Prior moved close to me and took between his gnarled old fingers the little silver crucifix which hung around my neck. He smiled up at me, a gentle little old man with dark eyes full of kindness and hidden things.

'Do not put too much faith in this,' he whispered, 'for it is too young.'

And before I could answer, or even catch together the reeling and tangled threads of thought which spun through my bewildered mind, he had knelt again before the altar and resumed his prayers.

I backed out of the little chapel, and walked slowly to my cell, and threw myself down on the straw pallet, fresh and sweet, which they had laid for me on the floor. As I sank into sleep, the stiff form of the ancient figure seemed to hover and waver in the darkness, lips curved in an enigmatic smile.

Do you not know me? Surely you must remember. I existed before the mountains and the seas came into being, or any living thing . . . Do not forget that you are mine.

XIII

When I reached Turin I followed the winding coil of the Po, avoiding Milan and restricting my lodging places to little village inns and farmhouses. All around me I saw the ravages of war, the burned farms, the stripped fields, the tumbled towers and ruined villas. But the life of the earth itself was too strong here even for centuries of foreign invasions to extinguish the ancient beauty of the gentle hills crowned with poplars and cypresses, the cloudless sky, the crystalline light, the silvered olive groves and vineyards, the rich ochre and sienna and cream of the stuccoed buildings.

I passed the field of Pavia, where King François had met his humiliating defeat at the hands of the Duc de Bourbon. Now it was the domain of grazing goats, and the olive trees drifted and flicked their silver leaves in the wind.

Once I had asked Scaliger whether he thought Italy would ever accept the Lutheran and Calvinist heresies.

'Italy? Never!' he had thundered. 'Italy can never be made Protestant. She has been made nominally Christian. But she will never embrace those grim preachers, for her soul is pagan, and belongs to the old gods.'

Along the banks of the ancient river, among the thickly wooded slopes and the pure golden sunlight, I was convinced that he was right. The old gods still dwelled here in the cypresses and the currents of the water and the stones and the earth, invisible to the sight of man.

I have also been in Arcadia.

Sometimes the peace and beauty of the countryside eased my pain as I travelled, and I was released from the grief I had carried since Agen. At such moments I did not think of Blanche and my children, or of Scaliger, or of Andiette de la Roque-Loubéjac, or of the collapse of everything I had held precious. I did not even think of the wild journey I made, at the request of an unknown man, to an unknown destination, for an unknown purpose. I gave myself over to birdsong and olive groves and sunlight; and sometimes I lay prone on the earth, face buried in the fragrant grass, hands outstretched, feeling the power that coiled in the bowels of this land over which so many nations had futilely tramped, seeking conquest and power and treasure and gold.

But at other times the melancholy would rise and overwhelm me, and I would sit enmeshed in a black web of bitter thoughts, brooding over my failure and my blindness. Beside me, the endlessly flowing brown river seemed to me as fruitless in its journey as I myself.

So I wandered, shifting like the currents of the river between sad serenity and black despair, nourished by my tenacious determination to unravel this welter of snarled skeins. And at length I reached the great conjoining of the Po with the Mincio, which flows from the Lago di Garda, that jewel embedded in the high mountains. I turned my mule and followed the trail of the lesser river north, and at last, surrounded by her lakes, the towers and turrets of Mantua soared upwards to impale the horizon. Sunlight shimmered on the cream and sienna and ochre of the houses, and the great golden dome of the Basilica Sant'Andrea, and the ancient and sombre fortress-palace of the Gonzaga, crouching like a great lion and overshadowing the town.

I had expected to be ushered into the presence of the Count of Guastalla, or of his brother, the duke Federigo. Instead, to my surprise, I was led to the *sala dello zodiaco*, which served as audience chamber for Donna Isabella d'Este, dowager-marquesa of Mantua. It was lined with frescoes of the tutelary deities of the planets, and beneath the presiding figure of Saturn, the marquesa sat in a gilded chair, fondling a pomander filled with cloves. Her seamed and wrinkled face still retained vestigial shreds of a great and noble beauty. Beneath her snowy hair surmounted by a black jewelled widow's cap, beneath her wise old black eyes, her thin lips parted in a gracious smile.

I understood at once why Mantua, womb of culture and wisdom for the whole of northern Italy, was said to owe its stature to this diminutive old woman. Hers was indeed a great light.

'My sons are in Milan,' she said, her voice like a whispering of wind among dry leaves. Her skin was pale and stretched taut as parchment, while her eyes shone with a brilliant and strenuous vitality in a face already set for death. 'The Count will return this evening, or tomorrow. Until then you are my most welcome guest.'

I handed her the golden ring Mathieu Bandello had given me.

'That is for my son,' she said. 'You may give it to him when he returns.'

She made a little sign, and a servant ushered into the room a man who at first seemed old, until I scrutinised him more closely. His countenance was twisted and engraved with lines, a calligraphy of great pain and sorrow. Although hardly more than forty, he was crippled, and hobbled on two beautifully carved malacca canes topped with silver heads.

'Maître de Notredame,' she said in her perfect French with only the faintest trace of an accent, 'I wish to introduce you to my astrologer, who is called Luc Gauricus. You and he will have much to say to each other. Into his hands I commend you, for I am old and ill, and cannot spend the time with you that I would like.'

Luc Gauricus and I bowed courteously to each other. His name was well known in France, for he was reputed to be the most brilliant astrologer of the time. He received commissions from every great ruling house in Italy, and had prophesied also for King François. It was rumoured that he had predicted the débâcle at Pavia, but for some reason, known only to himself, had neglected to warn the King. He had also prophesied the death of the Connêtable de Bourbon. But that rash and noble man, ignoring all admonitions and laughing gaily at his fate, had heedlessly sortied to his doom, storming the walls of Rome.

Luc Gauricus had paid dearly for his great gift. He was a blunt man, and had never bothered to school himself in the arts of court diplomacy. Unwisely, he had prognosticated the fall and demise of the tyrant of Bologna. With faulty logic, Bentivoglio had him recompensed by subjecting him to torture on the *strappado*. True to the prophecy, the tyrant had been exiled and murdered. Luc Gauricus had never recovered.

I did not think that this renowned man would know of a simple Provençal doctor who was famed only in his native province for healing plague. But he surprised me.

'I am pleased to make your acquaintance, Maître de Notredame,' he said in an unexpectedly rich and vibrant voice. 'I have eagerly awaited your coming. The Goat has not yet begun his long climb to the mountaintop. I see you now after your tragedy, when your fortunes are at their lowest. But soon all things will be made clear to you.'

I stared into the intense dark eyes with their heavy pain-laboured lids. They knew everything, while I knew nothing.

I turned to the marquesa. 'Madame, is there some service I can offer you during my stay in Mantua?'

She replied with a little cackle of a laugh, brittle with amusement. 'No service, Maître de Notredame. The only one who could serve me now I await eagerly, for I am weary of this sick and useless body. I merely wish you to take your pleasure in Mantua. Think of this visit as a means to heal your grief.'

The audience was ended. I retired with Luc Gauricus to his chambers. I learned more from him in a day than I had learned from the entire conclave of astrologers and occultists that I had met during my travels in France. I languished in the sunlit courtyards of the Reggia dei Gonzaga, and drank the clear and potent wine, and ate grapes and olives and pomegranates, and watched peacocks spread their brilliant plumage beside spraying fountains, and wandered through heavily scented hanging gardens with bright birds in golden cages. Luc Gauricus and I spoke of the stars, and of alchemy, and of philosophy, and of magic, and of fate. We did not speak of why I had come to Mantua.

*　　*　　*

That evening, the Count of Guastalla's black and impenetrable eyes perused me carefully from a gaunt and striking face.

'You are welcome in Mantua,' he said with the curtness of the soldier, taking the golden ring without a word and placing it in a little carved box.

'My lord of Guastalla,' I began, foolishly thinking I would at last receive the key which might reveal all the dark secrets of my journey. 'What is it you wish of me? You know that Mathieu Bandello sent me here. But the reason for my summons has not been made clear.'

'Reason? Summons?' He laughed at me. Intrepid soldier of fortune, tireless lover of women and young boys, artist, sybarite, occultist himself, he was a formidable and daunting man. 'Reason?' he said again. His teeth were very white against the dark olive of his skin. 'I thought you had your own reason. I know of no reason I might have to summon you to Mantua.'

As I stared at him, a heavy anger began to stir within me, the anger of so many weeks' futile journeying, of expectancy, of troubled dreams and timorous hopes. Three months on the back of a mule across France, over the high mountains, through Savoie and into Italy, had been for naught. I could not believe it.

While I struggled to disguise my rage, he reached gracefully for a cup, into which he poured a stream of wine. It was a large cup and very old, carved of deep red porphyry veined leaflike with white and olive and gold.

'To Our Lady,' he said smiling, watching me over the rim of the red porphyry cup as he sipped his wine. His dark pupils never moved, never blinked. Black as ink, as onyx, I felt them boring into the veins and arteries beneath my skin, twisting and ferreting among my thoughts, sucking at my soul, dragging it struggling and squirming out through my eyes. It was a scrutiny the like of which I had never experienced before. I could only stare defiantly back at him. But my anger seemed stupid and futile.

'Maître de Notredame,' said the Count of Guastalla abruptly, 'I believe we should play a game of cards.'

'Cards?' I said faintly.

From a carved mahogany box, inlaid with ivory and ebony, he gently lifted a deck of painted cards wrapped in vermilion silk. Shuffling them expertly, he sifted through them until he found one he wanted, and placed it face upward on the table.

'This is your essence,' he said. *'El Gobbo.'*

The Old Man, the Wandering Jew, peered up at me, exquisitely wrought, with his sack of secrets on his twisted back. The frail translucent old hand shielded the lantern, which radiated the caged glow of the six-pointed star. It was myself staring up at myself, a painted man and a real one. Or both painted by the same skilled hand, for I no longer knew.

Ferrante de Gonzaga held the deck out to me. 'Choose ten cards,' he said.

I selected them blindly. I had thought it a joke. Now the inky gaze began to frighten me.

'This covers you. *La Rotta.'*

You are a seaswept mariner, buffeted by the gods and by fortune . . . You thought, Michel, that you could fix time and space with a woman's fecund body, with a pile of sticks and stones to make a house – as a sculptor fixes for ever a face wrought of stone. But Fate is the dappled darling of all the gods, and She cannot be wooed as a lover or coerced as a servant. She is as full of caprice as a frolicking fish in a bottomless pool . . .

'This crosses you. *La Morte.'*

It is the death of those you love that dogs you . . . You thought, Michel, that you understood death in the reeking cadavers and the filth and the charred bones. But life nurses at her breast the seed of death like the stone in a fruit, and death lurks in everything that lives; and that which immures life creates death, more surely than the frozen sea incarcerates in polished ice the foolish swimmer . . .

'This is beneath you. *La Fortez.'*

You thought, Michel, that strength meant survival, the naked wit and animal cunning of the scapegoat, the dexterity of the mountain goat. But the strength that closes the lion's gaping jaws is not the strength of hoofs and horns and brittle rock. It is the strength of the waves that flow fluid and sweet around the forms of life, and embrace death willingly. For strength is the strength to die, to die and thereby beget new life . . .

'This is behind you. *La Sagitta.*'

You thought, Michel, that the death of the form meant death, but the death of the form only releases life into life. As la maison de Dieu *shatters under the lusty thunderbolt, so life is freed to build another form, for only that which can destroy itself is truly alive* . . .

'This is above you. *Il Bagatella.*'

You thought, Michel, that you mastered the jongleur's tricks because you could name the names of the saints and make a pommade of gold and lapis and powdered coral. But the true jongleur is he who can dance between the form and the abyss, between the mask and that which hides beneath it. For every- thing is paradox and parable, and in the filth of the gutter may be found the alchemical gold . . .

'This is before you. *Lo Impichato.*'

You thought, Michel, that your solitude earned you the key to the gilded door, that your pain balanced the scales like the fea- ther of Tahuti and left you free to devour the bread of the mysteries. But you must be hanged upside down on the cross of that which you call reality, that the blood may drain from your eyes and mouth as once did St Peter's. Thus it may nourish the seed which grows beneath your head, the seed which becomes the vine whose fruit contains the seed of God . . .

'Your greatest fear. *L'Amore.*'

You thought, Michel, that you could hide from the shuddering plunging, the clawing blackness, the subsuming beast that nes- tles in your belly and your loins. But you have not understood that death yields life, and that the arms on the far shore of black sand wait and wait because you have not dared to part the veil that hides Her face. You thought She would eat your manhood, but in truth you are no man at all without Her . . .

'Your greatest desire. *Imperator.*'

You wanted to be a court gentleman . . . You thought, Michel, that you could quiet the whispering ghosts that haunt you by trailing in the shadow of Rex Mundi, *the Lord of the World. But he is a capricious friend who only guards the door to death. As there are myriad flowers in a garden, there are myriad forms of death; and there are myriad forms of power, and the power you seek is not the form which Fate has chosen. You have not learned what is your true master . . .*

'Your image in the world. *El Mato.*'

You thought, Michel, that you possessed wisdom because you knew the names of flowering plants and wandering stars. But it is the profane fool who walks to the edge of the precipice and believes his learning will build a bridge. The Holy Fool dances to the edge, seeks no bridge, leaps into the abyss of blue. For he knows that in his own soul the precipice and the drop and the grinding impact of flesh against rock and sea are but a dream . . .

'Your future. *La Papessa.*'

Do you not know me even now? Surely you must remember, for you are mine . . . mine . . . mine . . . mine . . . mine . . .

'I cannot endure any more,' I whispered at last, and buried my face in my hands. Several minutes passed in complete silence. When I raised my head he still sat quietly sipping his wine from the red porphyry cup, watching me.

'Who are you?' I murmured.

'I am the Count of Guastalla,' he replied with a white smile. 'Who are you?'

I could think of nothing to say. I moved my eyes blankly around the little study, dimly glimpsing as through an opaque mist the tapestries, the frescoes, the statuary, the richly carved furniture, the reliquary studded with rubies which echoed mockingly the huge ruby winking from the index finger of his right hand.

In an ornate frame of gold hung a painting. My eyes returned to it, for here the mist thinned. The fragile figures of Madonna and Child beckoned me, surrounded by brilliantly costumed and jewelled courtiers, like a cloud of summer butterflies. The woman's lips were painted red and voluptuous, her eyelids heavy and somnolent and sensuous over vivid blue eyes the colour of cornflowers – eyes that befitted the Magdalen better than the Mother of God. My scalp began to prickle, for no explicable reason. Behind her loomed a monumental backdrop of crumbling archways and porticoes, pillars and columns, all rotting to ruin. Far in the distance washed a cold blue stretch of shimmering mountain peaks. I looked away. And then I looked again at that mountainous landscape. At the rising hill to the right, which reared behind the gaudy shape of an alchemical peacock perched insolently on a broken pillar. At the decaying walls of the roofless fortress which formed a gigantic navel, a chalice open to the sky.

I knew that I was not mistaken. Thrice I had seen it before. Once from the back of my mule. Again while I stood with the Bishop of Carcassonne outside a little inn, while the sun set and shadows slithered into a pool around us. And a third time while I huddled within the black walls and listened and did not wish to hear.

'Do you find the painting attractive?' said Don Ferrante de Gonzaga, gently breaking into the frantic chattering of my thoughts. 'It is the work of Sandro Filipepi, he who is known as Botticelli.'

'Beautiful,' I murmured sullenly, avoiding what I knew to be mockery in the inky eyes.

'The landscape is most evocative,' he said lightly.

'If I were not a peaceable man, and a coward,' I said between my teeth, 'I would kill you.'

He laughed at me again, white teeth glittering in his dark insolent face, and proffered the red porphyry cup.

'Drink,' he said. 'The wine will cheer you and cool your anger. The cup is very old. It is said to have magical properties.'

'Perhaps the wine will turn to water as it touches my lips,' I said bitterly, 'since I am *El Mato*. I do not wish to drink your wine. I wish to have answers. What do you want of me? What does the house of Lorraine want of me? Why did Mathieu Bandello send me here? What do you all know of my grandfather, that I do not know myself?'

'So many questions!' laughed the Count of Guastalla. 'You waste your anger on me. I am not aware that you were compelled in any way to make this journey to Mantua. Perhaps the answers to your questions lie within yourself.'

'That is clever, my lord of Guastalla, but not to the point. I did not ask for the golden ring.'

'Peace, Maître de Notredame. I wish nothing from you save but to meet you, which I have done. I must admit that I like you, despite your evident wish to slit my throat. I wish you to enjoy Mantua.'

I sighed heavily. He only tormented me, and reached inside my soul and twisted it to show me my wounds. A great fatigue, a paralysing languor descended on me.

'When you have had your fill of Mantua,' Don Ferrante de Gonzaga continued, 'I have a commission for you. There is in my possession a parcel of letters and documents. They must be carried to the Duc de Lorraine at Nancy. I would like you to bear these for me across the Alps into Lorraine.'

'I have had my fill of both Mantua and Lorraine,' I said wearily. 'But I have nowhere else to go. I will therefore do as you ask.'

XIV

I followed the Meuse from Toul, because it was the route suggested to me, and because all my life, when I could not foresee the end of my journey, I had followed the rivers. It was the season of rains, and I grew accustomed to being drenched by downpours, spattered with the yellow mud of the riverbank. I drove my shivering mule fetlock-deep through potholes and bogs and drowned grasses, trusting that my resilient constitution would preserve my health.

Frequently I travelled for days without meeting another human being, avoiding the main roads, clinging closely to the curve of the swollen river. I limited my resting places to abandoned cottages and the smallest and least prepossessing of village inns, often knocking at the door of some solitary farmhouse perched in isolation amid the waterlogged fields. No one displayed any curiosity about my past or my destination. They provided me with food and a bed, and took my florins, and asked no questions. They were a cautious and reticent folk, these half-German, half-French peasants straddling two countries whose rulers were perpetually at war.

Only briefly did I allow myself to ponder the history of the land through which I passed. The enigmatic Duc de Lorraine, fair like his brother the Cardinal, had granted me a brief audience at Nancy – only long enough to entrust to me certain missives and to direct me to Stenay and Orval. By his curtness and aloofness he had rendered me even more reluctant to become involved in his duchy's politics.

I hugged the French bank of the river, and mused on the Grail romances which had once issued from this province of Champagne, born of the romantic court at Troyes. I wondered how such perfect jewels of vision and beauty could be shaped in such a bleak and unfriendly climate. But then, I had never seen it in summer, when the fields bloomed with poppies and buttercups and mustard, and the vines were heavy with fruit.

I avoided Verdun, and returned to the river two days' journey north. And at last I arrived at the great forest which lay south of Stenay. I reached it at mid-afternoon, but it was so dense that the trees shut out the light and a brooding darkness pressed upon me. I rode as though into a tunnel where no living sight or sound from the outside world could penetrate.

I did not welcome the thought of spending the night in this forest, for it was a place redolent of legends known even in Provence. But I had to pass through it, as it surrounded the town to the south, the east and the west for many miles; and I was annoyed at my own superstitious fear. It was called the Forêt de Woëvres, the Wood of the Serpent. Strange tales were woven about it from the most ancient of pasts. It was said to be a sacred wood where once the Goddess Rosemertha had been worshipped beneath the great oaks.

I reminded myself that it was only a forest, that I had two days' worth of bread and cheese and dried meat and wine in my bag. I was not afraid of residues. And because it was so ancient and so close, the foliage shielded me from the rain, promising a more comfortable journey. So I told myself, as I drove my mule into the first clumps of oak and birch and poplar, into the sour odour of damp mould and rotting leaves. Some of the great tree· were still bare from their winter's sleep, or showed fat buds ripening. Some were already in young leaf, or dappled with the brown and gold garments of the previous autumn. Their boughs entwined above me like a myriad tightly clasped hands so thick that the greenish-brown murk exiled the sun. I was imprisoned within an irridescent shadowy world, as though within a leaf or a bole, compelled to wait for the time of flowering in order to be released.

As dusk drew its cowl about me and the thin track faded in darkness ahead, I seemed to pass into the great hall of some sacred and ancient temple. I knew that the anger I still carried sullenly within me was an affront to the powers presiding over this place. There was no wind to disturb the interlacing of dense branches. Sometimes I heard the gentle plop of a branch or a twig falling, or some animal scuttling for shelter, fleeing the slippery suck of my mule's hoofs on the damp black earth.

A curious tightening gripped my stomach. My mule felt it too. He slowed, then stopped and listened, ears twitching, nostrils quivering, eyes rolling in fear.

A full moon would rise tonight, very late. The darkness spread in a black pool around me. I decided to break my journey and sleep, for I did not fancy trying to follow the narrow track through the darkness, with the trees huddling so close about me and the sense of some ancient thing breathing softly at my back. I knew it was not inimical to me, but it unnerved me. In sleep I might find a refuge. In the morning, with the rising sun, there would only be forest again.

I tied my mule to a tree, and spread my cloak on the wet earth, and managed with considerable effort to light a small fire, using my tinder on the sodden and odorous fallen branches. I drank half a skin of wine and crouched close to the flames. Dizzy and drowsy, I silently cursed Mathieu Bandello and the Count of Guastalla and the Duc de Lorraine. And I slept.

No disturbing dreams plagued me. Nevertheless I awoke unaccountably two hours before dawn. The opaque silver face of the moon shimmered through the latticework of black branches. I could discern the dim shapes of the trees circling the little cold heap which was all that remained of my poor fire. Something disturbed me about the formation of those trees, the branches locked overhead like clasped hands. Before me stood a great oak, so gnarled and thick and twisted it must have been many centuries old. I stared at it, heavy with fear and foreboding, for I had arrived at the place of the dream I had dreamed the night I climbed the mountain of Bézu with the Bishop of Carcassonne, and heard the resonance of a ghostly bell chiming for white-mantled Knights who died two centuries before.

I peered around me into the darkness where the old oaks stood sentinel. I had slept in that sacred grove where some ancient and unnamable power, older than God the Father, had made its home. No spectral white-clad King rode into my vision with unshorn hair streaming behind him. The grim and lonely oak was terrifying enough. Here, where I lay, his blood had gushed forth in a bright and violent stream, a scarlet offering, to inseminate the black earth.

With immense relief, I entered the little walled town of Stenay and approached the old church of St Dagobert, with its pitted and roughly carved portals. My relief, however, was short-lived. The church had fallen into disuse, and smelled of the must and damp and mould of many years of abandonment. I surveyed the squat columns, the stained vault that bore the marks of fire, the broken shards of windows scattered like a fragmented rainbow across the floor, the ruined altar with its ancient statue of the saint, carved in the stiff and unyielding pose of centuries past. The face was so eroded by the ravages of time that it seemed the face of a leper. There was a desolate feeling about the empty and ruined place, and I turned towards the door.

I heard a rustling behind me. The Curé of the church of St Dagobert of Stenay stood waiting for me in the shadows by the broken altar. He had appeared as silently and abruptly as though he had materialised out of the stones.

He was a wizened little man, with snowy hair, and a face wrinkled and brown as a raisin, and impenetrable black eyes which reminded me of the caged monkeys in Avignon. There was an aura about him that disturbed me profoundly. I could not fathom the feeling of him. It was as though he danced away each time I sought to intuit his nature. He had a thin, droning voice like the scrape of a fiddle through some ancient and tuneless song. His lips quirked in a perpetual twitch which threatened to break into a smile but never quite did. Nevertheless, it conveyed the impression that he was mocking me.

'I understand that you are travelling north, to the abbey of Notre Dame d'Orval,' the Curé said, and gave me that peculiar smirk.

I kept my face carefully blank and nodded. I was heartily sick of being baited.

'It is only half a day's ride,' said the Curé. 'You will find it easier than your journey through the forest.'

I said nothing.

'Before you set out for Orval, I would like you to explore our church. It has an interesting history. The Duc de Lorraine of course told you of it.'

'The Duc de Lorraine only told me to come to the church of St Dagobert. He said nothing of the place.'

'One should know something of the place,' said the Curé in his curious sing-song, as though intoning to himself. 'A place has a soul, as a man does. One should know the soul of a place, so that one can make one's peace with it. Long ago this town was called Satanicum.' He began to drone a chant, black monkey's eyes peering at me.

> 'Corpus terra sublevatur,
> Sathanacum deportatur,
> Ac devote veneratur,
> Per ejus confinia.

> 'Martyr Christi praelecte,
> Deo placens et perfecte,
> Martyrio coelo vecte,
> Duc nos ad celestia.

> 'Ipsum votis collaudemus,
> Voce, corde exultemus,
> Ad beati suspiremus,
> Dagoberti gaudia.'

I fell silent again. Here were more hints, inferences, nuances. I felt the anger stirring within me again, the futile, fruitless anger. But I determined to hold my tongue. Had I unleashed it as I had to the Count of Guastalla, I would only have received the same ambiguous evasion.

'Beneath this church lie the ruins of an ancient temple to Saturn, *Rex Mundi*,' said the Curé of Stenay. 'It is a sacred site.'

'No doubt every place is sacred to something,' I said.

He ignored my sarcasm. 'The soul of this place is not one which any good Christian soul would care to meet. That is why the church of St Dagobert is abandoned. No one will set foot in it. They fear the spirits of the dead Kings of the line of Merovée, the Long-Haired Kings, the Sorcerer-Kings, who are said to walk here still. They are quite right to fear the dead,' the Curé said with a little titter which reminded me again of the monkeys at Avignon. 'But the living are much more dangerous.'

I suppressed a shudder. What sacrifice had I witnessed beneath the great oak?

'Come,' he said, putting his clawlike hand at my elbow. 'We will go down to the crypt beneath the church.'

'I am sure it is very interesting, Monseigneur, but I fear I must depart for Orval. I wish to reach the abbey by nightfall.'

'You will be there by nightfall, Maître de Notredame, never fear. What is the matter? Are you frightened of an old church? Or is it the old Curé who frightens you?' And he tittered again.

With great effort I curbed my temper and refrained from slapping him. 'What is so interesting about the crypt beneath the church?'

'It is an old chapel of the Knights of the Temple,' the Curé replied.

The words pitched me headlong into an urgent desire for flight. 'No,' I said firmly, backing away from him. 'I have been through this before. I wish nothing to do with the ruins of the Temple. The Temple has been destroyed.'

'Has it indeed?' tittered the little old man, malignant with the petty vituperativeness of the very old who have outlived any real usefulness.

'By Christ,' I exclaimed with violence, 'why must you all torment me so? Can you not simply tell me like honest men what it is you wish of me, without playing upon my fear?'

My only reply was another burst of that awful laughter. I

walked to the door, then turned to face him.

'Who are you?' I demanded.

'I am the gatekeeper, Maître de Notredame,' he said, smirking.

I stalked from the church and scrabbled on to my mule and rode north from Stenay. And for many miles, echoing in the wind and the rain at my back, I thought I heard the Curé's tittering, monkeylike laughter.

I rode at a furious pace until I had exhausted my anger, then slowed my mule as we entered another patch of forest that lay across the road to Orval. My stomach had knotted itself so tightly that I was almost doubled over with the pain. This materialisation of nightmare after nightmare terrified me – as though the borderline between my dreams and my waking life, like a sandbank before a river in flood, had suddenly dissolved, flinging me into a chaotic world where there were no longer any boundaries or landmarks of sanity.

By the time I emerged from the wood I was very tired; I was also shivering, although the late afternoon sun streamed thinly on my back. The rain had temporarily ceased, and the fields were steaming with mist. The track straggled through clumps of ivy oak and birch, then meandered across a broad meadow to which the fractured light imparted a heavy and preternatural cast. A few very ordinary sheep dotted the grass like mushrooms. The dying sun glimmered on the moving surface of a small stream, which followed the muddy road to the left. A ragged hill, dark and humped and thickly wooded, crossed the horizon before me. The road wound around it, out of sight.

I continued twenty more paces before I knew, with the sudden shattering impact of a violation. And there it lay, burbling and chuckling gently over the mossy rocks, waiting for me, laughing at me, a long silvery laugh, a laugh of thirty years, exhausting itself from its own laughter into the dark pool. To the east, beyond the tangled silhouettes of the clumped trees, lay the village of Orval. To the west, at the crest of the hill, stood an abbey.

An insane chant began in my head: *I have walked out of the real world, I have stepped through the veil that hides dreams from the light of day, I have fallen by the roadside, am lying on the sodden ground, writhing in the grip of some fever or pestilence, dreaming that I am dreaming that I am dreaming . . .*

But it was not the same abbey. That other had been a dark, squat, ominous structure, some monstrous beetle, black with age, torn from an ancient tapestry. This was a gothic jewel, mellow in the dying afternoon light, its spires pointing gilded fingers upwards.

If I enter this place, this final place of dreams, I will vanish from the face of the earth, trapped in some fragment of vision spinning through the dark abyss of space, imprisoned in a dream-death like a fly in a fragment of amber . . .

The road forked. To the left it narrowed, dwindled to a donkey-track, passed between the two ancient and pitted stone pillars through an iron gate which hung open in mocking welcome; then it continued up the hillside, through an orchard, to the abbey. I wondered whether, at junctures such as these, there was any vestige left of human choice. I could no more turn about and head back toward Stenay than I could metamorphose into a unicorn and gallop into the wood. And indeed, I was no longer certain whether Stenay had existed at all, or whether the old church of St Dagobert had itself been a dream.

But it is you yourself who have chosen to come here, Michel. No one has coerced you. Only your own dreams.

I passed through the open gate and up the hill among the bare apple trees, which would soon be bursting into blossom. A man approached me from the shadow of the abbey. At first he was only a silhouette, a wraith, a shadow against the shadows of the edifice behind him. I pulled up my mule and dismounted, waiting for him, suspended in a species of trance, watching the slight sway of the black robes, listening to the faint slap of sandalled feet on the wet earth. As he reached me, the dying light caressed the dark emaciated cheeks, the sombre eyes, the long delicate lips, the jagged scar of Mathieu Bandello.

'*Deo gratias*, my friend,' he said, giving me his gentle smile as though it had been four days rather than four years since we had met. 'You are undoubtedly tired and chilled. You must come in and share some wine with me.'

As the lean black back moved ahead of me, I abandoned

myself to the confused compound of exhaustion, fear, anger and relief yeasting within. A fire burned brightly in his study. The walls were hung with an array of wonderful tapestries, and I glimpsed hues like those of butterfly wings, or the petals of flowers. Firelight shimmered on the coloured panes of the narrow window, cast fantastic volatile patterns over the bare stone floor. I smelled cedar and sandalwood burning. He pulled the door shut and bolted it, and slid a richly carved chair toward me, its legs softly scraping across the tiles.

'Well, Fra Bandello, I am at last at the centre of the spider's web. You may do with me what you will. I have very agreeably played the puppet in this merry dance. I am too weary to fight you, and too cold to be heated by the anger which by all right I should bear you. You would, perhaps, like a recipe for quince jelly, or a cosmetic cream to soften your white hands?'

'I wish to do nothing with you, Maître de Notredame, that you yourself do not will. How did you like my lord of Gonzaga?'

'I was too angry with him to like him, Fra Bandello. I fear my patience with you all has long ago been exhausted.'

'That is a pity. Don Ferrante de Gonzaga is a noble and learned man.'

'He has a most peculiar deck of playing cards.'

Bandello smiled. 'And a most peculiar collection of paintings as well.'

'He sent me to the Duc de Lorraine, who sent me to Stenay, about which you naturally know. The Curé showed me the church of St Dagobert, and offered to lead me to the crypt of the Temple underneath. I fear I rejected his offer, for I lost my temper with him as well.'

'That too is a pity, Maître de Notredame. There is something in that chapel which would have explained a good deal to you. I fear you must learn to curb that temper of yours.'

'Perhaps it would help my temper if you ceased baiting me, Fra Bandello. No doubt the Temple is bound up with your little mystery as well?'

'No doubt,' Mathieu Bandello said pleasantly, ignoring my hostility. 'Will you have some of our excellent wine? It is from the Duc de Guise's private stock at Joinville.'

He offered me a cup, an exquisite goblet carved from a solid mass of rock crystal, through whose yellowish translucence the firelight fragmented and winked. I examined it in fascination, and then saw the inscription carved into the crystal.

Qui bien beurra
Dieu voira.
Qui beurra tout d'une baleine
Voira Dieu et la Madeleine.

'I did not know you trafficked in magic goblets,' I said with irritation. 'Is it the cup, or the Duc de Guise's wine, which promises me a vision of God and the Magdalen?'

Bandello smiled delicately. 'That depends, my friend, on the hand that holds it. It is one of King René's treasures, a legacy to Orval.'

I sighed in exasperation. 'Am I to be plagued for the rest of my life by King René and his accursed cups?' I put it down sharply, secretly hoping it would splinter in two. 'I am a poor chess player, Fra Bandello. You say I must do nothing except what I will. Explain to me clearly, please, without guile or inference, what you wish of me. I have had enough of omens, hints, signs, legends and symbols.'

Mathieu Bandello placed his fingertips together. His hands were very long and thin, a scholar's hands. The golden ring, I noticed with a start, was back on his finger.

'Are you not too tired for a tale?' he said. 'It can surely wait until tomorrow.'

'I am well enough. I would like to hear your story now. Where is the abbot of this house?'

'Dealing with abbots' business. He is called Mathias Delvaux. He is a very great scholar, and a friend of mine. We will not be disturbed.'

'Despite my strenuous efforts to decipher the meaning of your elaborate game,' I said carefully, 'I can make no sense of it. I can only surmise that it concerns the claims of the house of Lorraine to those lands which once belonged to King René, and which were wrested from him by King Louis.'

I waited for confirmation, but none came. Bandello only

watched me quietly, the gentle smile hovering on his lips.

'If this is the case,' I continued, 'then it is the oldest story in the world, the eternal cry of the dispossessed, mingled with the eternal cry for power. That my grandfather might have been involved I am willing to believe.'

'Your grandfather,' said Mathieu Bandello, 'was more than "involved", Maître de Notredame.'

'As I told you in Agen, I have no interest in politics. France has changed, Fra Bandello. The great feudal states of my grandfather's time are gone. There are new problems now. Luther and Calvin do not know what they have unleashed. I have had presentiments of bloody religious war in this land. I cannot believe your masters still think they can wrest their lost duchies from the King now. If they do, then they are fools, however noble ones, and doomed to self-destruction. The tides within this nation flow now to the centre. One cannot reverse time.'

But Mathieu Bandello only laughed at me, and poured more wine into the strange crystal goblet. I realised only then how quickly I had gulped it down.

'You are as I remember, Maître de Notredame: ever ready to jump to a conclusion, without knowing of what you speak. This is no political vendetta, nor an attempt to gain a vanished state. Political power is only the garment which hides the form. We are not Sforza or Borgia, though we may use the means of both.'

He stood up and paced back and forth across the narrow chamber. Entranced, I watched the thin black-draped frame, still struggling to evolve a sense of what was happening to me. Far away, I heard the faint silvery tones of a bell ringing compline. The aromatic wood hissed and sputtered as it burned, filling the room with its pungent scent.

'You must believe that I too would not waste my time,' said Bandello. 'I am fonder of poetry and philosophy, and of my life, than I am of heroic commitment to a lost cause. My lords do not want King René's lands, my friend. They want nothing less than the throne of France on the one hand, and the throne of Rome on the other. Why do you think Claude de Guise and his brother, the Cardinal, work so assiduously at King François' court? It may take years, even generations. But if a Lorraine prince mounts the throne of France, he can, being of a German house, take the throne of the Empire as well. The whole of Europe would be united. And with a Lorraine prince on the papal throne to crown him . . . Why, who wants Anjou and Provence, Maître de Notredame, when we can have the whole of Christendom?'

I shrugged, swallowing my trepidation at the enormity of this assertion. I could see nothing in it for me save disaster.

'That, too, is an old story,' I said. 'But the claim of Lorraine to the French throne is a very tenuous one. In between stands Prince Henri, with a newly pregnant wife. And after him the house of Bourbon, the Princes of the Blood.'

'You know nothing about the claim of Lorraine,' Mathieu Bandello said softly.

'I have not heard anything that might change my mind, Fra Bandello. And I am made exceedingly uncomfortable that you tell me these secrets when I have shown no sympathy for your schemes. It makes me fear you have no intention of permitting me to leave this place alive, should I persist in my refusal.'

He stopped his pacing and resumed his seat. Perhaps it was something in his expression, or the lingering memories of my journey. But I could not remove my gaze from his sombre eyes.

'Believe me, Maître de Notredame, I wish you neither harm nor suffering nor danger. I find it difficult to speak of all this. Your grandfather's hand lies in it. You were meant for us from the beginning. But it was necessary to leave you alone for a time, to see what you would become. And we thought, at first, that you knew more than it seemed, and were being coy with us . . . I did not know what would happen to you in Agen. I am but a novice in the celestial art. I only realised that some crisis lay over you, some great change. I am truly sorry for your wife and children.'

'Sorry?' I snapped at him. I had been holding my pain at bay for many weary months. Now it began to flow afresh, like a wound from which the scab has been torn. 'It does not sound as though my feelings, or my wishes, are of the least account. You and my grandfather and those for whom you work have evidently mapped out my life for me. A death or two makes no difference, so long as I arrive at the appointed time and perform the appointed tricks, like a baited bear in a ring.'

Mathieu Bandello shook his head and rose, placing his scholar's fine-boned hand on my shoulder. 'You misunderstand, my friend. Nothing has mapped out your life except your own soul. We have tried on certain occasions to make you aware of us. But it was not the time. It may be that others see where your journey leads before you see it yourself.'

He looked down at me for a moment with amusement and detached compassion.

'I understand that the Inquisition has been interested in you, at the instigation of our dear Scaliger. You should have been more discreet, my friend. But then, you do not take affairs of the heart lightly, like the Cardinal de Lorraine.'

I only clamped my lips shut and stared at him in miserable anger. It seemed that every secret was being picked over like a sack of bones thrown to the dogs.

But Mathieu Bandello ignored my smothered rage. 'I would like to show you something,' he said.

He removed from his bureau an illumination executed on parchment in a delicate and controlled hand. Tints of sapphire and slate and indigo portrayed the mocking stream, and the pool shading to purple and obsidian shadows. A full moon like a white eye rode high in the black firmament. The hill crouched in one corner, an ancient animal; but no abbey crowned it. At the water's edge, a splash of blood picked out in gold, glowed the russet gown of the ringed woman. And from the frothing ripples of the surface rose a fish, a fish such as I had never seen, a magical rainbow-hued fish with emerald eyes bearing in its mouth a golden ring set with a great ruby . . .

I looked up, stunned, to meet Mathieu Bandello's curious eyes.

'You have seen this before?'

'Only in my dreams,' I said bitterly. 'Since I was a child. Who is she?'

'Mathilde de Bologna, Marquise of Tuscany, wife to Godefroi le Bossu, Sieur of Bouillon and Stenay, Comte de Champagne and Duc de Lorraine. Four and a half centuries ago she wandered from her castle at Stenay into the Forêt de

Merlanvaux, seeking consolation for the loss of her husband to the assassin's knife. She found the pool. When she dropped her husband's ring, she prayed to Our Lady for a miracle. She was answered by the fish which leaped forth, bearing the jewel in its mouth. Does it not remind you of another tale?'

'It is the legend of King Solomon,' I said slowly. 'He retrieved the golden ring from the belly of the fish, thus proving himself the true King of Israel.'

'Precisely,' said Mathieu Bandello. 'A circle of hermits had come from Calabria, a strange circle said to be monk-magicians, seers, prophets, Pythagorean initiates. They made their home in the forest. Mathilde de Bologna gave them this tract of land in gratitude for the miracle, that they might build an abbey. She called the place Val d'Or. And she gave to them her foster-son, young Godefroi de Bouillon, to be taught the mysteries.'

He rose and took the miniature gently from my hand and replaced it in the bureau, in a locked drawer.

'There was another monk who lived in the forest,' he continued, 'called Peter the Hermit. It was he who inflamed young Godefroi, heir to the duchy of Lorraine, with a great secret. Between them they instigated a Crusade, and took Jerusalem from the Saracen, and Godefroi was crowned King. The vine branches from Godefroi to King René.'

'What secret is this that you speak of?'

'The descent of King René from the house of Bouillon is generally known,' said Mathieu Bandello. 'What is more interesting is the origin of the line itself.'

Unaccountably, a slow creeping fear seized my hands, my forehead, the back of my neck – the deadly fear of my childhood dream, the premonition of some terrible revelation, some unknown creature that would rise from the depths of the obsidian pool. It was only a fish, I told myself inanely. But I drifted into a strange dissociated state of mind, while Mathieu Bandello's voice receded to a disincarnate echo, and the room grew dark, and the fire guttered, and the tapestries vanished in the gloom.

And suddenly, the spirits of the dead clustered around me, probing me with frail cool incorporeal fingers. With them, the presences of the forest entered the room. I could smell the wet black earth and the odour of rotting leaves, while the sombre shadows of the great trees closed overhead, denying the light. Through my vision passed the other dream, the dream of the white King seated beneath the great oak, and the sudden piercing blow of the lance, and the blood surging in great gouts over the earth. I reached for King René's crystal goblet and steadied myself with the Duc de Guise's wine.

'The house of Bouillon descends from King Dagobert II, slaughtered eight centuries ago, the last of the sacred blood of the line of Merovée,' Fra Bandello's quiet voice continued. 'The first Kings of France, the Elect, the Long-Haired Ones, the Sorcerer-Kings, the Children of the Sun . . .'

I passed my hands over my weary eyes. *You know nothing about the claim of Lorraine . . .*

'Rome had sworn allegiance to the line, to the sacred blood it bore. But the Bishop of Rome sent an assassin to crown King Dagobert anew, with a lance through the eye. Perhaps, like Judas, the assassin did not know how great, how sacrilegious was his crime. He had murdered the *sangraal*. But the King's son escaped in secret, and fled to Languedoc, to the mountains south of Carcassonne, and there perpetuated his lineage . . . What is it, my friend?'

He reached out his hand to me, for my own had begun to shake, and the wine sloshed over the rim of the goblet, and spread in a red pool across the floor.

'Has this too come in your dreams?'

'The white King with the lance through his eye . . . How is it possible that I have always known these things?' But I could hardly speak, for like a mosaic the coloured shards had begun to form the outlines of a fantastic picture. *Sangraal*, royal blood, vessel of Christ's blood sung by Chrêtian de Troyes and Wolfram von Eschenbach to the whole of Christendom. A cup that was not a cup . . .

This is my body, this is my blood . . .

I saw it all now, but my shock was too great. Feebly I tried to find some other meaning. I gripped the crystal goblet as though I were drowning.

'This *sangraal*, this royal blood.' I listened to my own voice, and it cracked and wavered like that of a pubescent boy. The

131

presences of the wood crowded around me now, pressing against my eyeballs and my forehead and my throat. 'What blood line was this, this line of sacred kings?'

'But you know already, Maître de Notredame,' said Mathieu Bandello gently. 'You saw Sandro Filipepi's painting. She is beautiful, is she not? It is said that the long sea journey from Jerusalem to Marseilles brought her to bloom like a goddess. What mother, and what child, did you think those were? Look at the goblet you hold in your hand. *Qui beurra tout d'une baleine, Voira Dieu et la Madeleine.*'

'You are mad!' I snapped, leaping from my seat and grasping his arm in my deepening confusion. 'You must be mad. I do not believe you, I cannot believe you. What proof do you have of this monstrous story?'

'Incontrovertible proof, Maître de Notredame. Did you think we could make such a claim without proof? That is why those Nine Poor Knights who later became the Temple embarked for Jerusalem. It was a little matter of reclaiming certain things pertinent to the lineage and ancestry of their feudal lord, the Duc de Lorraine. These things were offered for your perusal in Stenay. But you refused to see them.'

'Fra Bandello, this is a mad tale. I am no Christian, as well you know. But this . . . Do you know what you are telling me?' I was very near to weeping. 'If I had not dreamed these things, if they had not haunted me all my life, I would laugh at you for a gullible fool. Why have I been brought here? Am I to die?'

'Not in any sense that you mean, Maître de Notredame. But is it not a death and a true rebirth that you know the truth? Now do you understand why we wait and wait for the right time? Here lies the reality of which all else is but distorted shadow. These formalised rituals of Holy Church are richly carved cups from which the precious fluid has escaped. Their meaning has been distorted and forgotten, and their husks reduce man to less than a beast. He has come to believe he was conceived in the sin of carnal love, that the very body he inhabits is tainted, that he must seek intervention for God's aloof mercy through celibate priests . . . Perhaps you will have more tolerance now of King René's heirlooms. Truly, it is a joke on the grandest scale ever known to man. I am overwhelmed, at times, by the irony of it. Does it not make you weep?'

But I was weeping, though not from irony. Here was the heresy of all heresies, yet it had an irresistible logic. No matter how I applied my critical reason, I could not disbelieve it. All paths had brought me to it. I bowed my head in acceptance.

Images careered before my eyes, a multitude of shimmering fragments, as though the world, the past, spun by me with astonishing speed. My wife and children convulsed in their terrible deaths, my serene grandfather with his books and his snowy beard and his gnarled hands, the silver *ailerons* fluttering like living creatures in the wind above the crimson and cloth-of-gold of the Cardinal's litter, the filmed gaze of a minstrel scrutinising me above a throbbing lute, the silvery chime of a spectral bell taunting me from the heart of a great sacred oak . . . A whirlwind of images flitting like bats, like birds, like smoke, and the voluptuous face of the blue-eyed Madonna smiling and smiling and smiling . . . There was a terrible spinning, a vertigo, and a voice alternately sobbing and giggling, which I recognised as my own.

'Madame de Musset told me in Agen, at the Cardinal's banquet,' I managed to sputter in the midst of this fit, 'that he had been passing through Rome and gave a blind man alms, and the blind man said . . . Ah, Fra Bandello, I think I will go mad.'

The tears poured unceasingly down my cheeks, and I laughed like a lunatic as the implications radiated through my mind, like ripples spreading from a stone dropped in a pool. How could I refuse him now?

'It is enough for the moment,' said Mathieu Bandello. 'You should sleep. There will be time enough tomorrow, and in the months to come, for you to learn the whole of this tale. It is only the beginning. Perhaps you will find it in your heart to forgive me for what must seem a childish game. But I felt sure you had some knowledge, some prescience of it. I gambled on finding some small thing that would kindle your recognition. And when it seemed you understood, you recoiled again like a frightened horse. You drew near so many times and pulled away. We did not mean to torment you.'

He gave me his gentle, compassionate smile. 'I know some of what is in your heart. I went through it too, once. And I, you must remember, am a Christian. I thought the world had ended. But truly, Maître de Notredame, has it not only just begun?'

He led me to a small chamber, an austere room with a narrow bed and the thick wall pierced by a single small window, in which stood a jug of budding Judas tree blossom. There was a crock of water, and a simple cross hanging over the bed, a rose carved at its centre.

'Fra Bandello,' I said, 'tell me one final thing. Why should it be me? I am a good physician, but so are many others. Surely it cannot be only that my grandfather served you.'

He laughed. 'Why, Maître de Notredame, have you not read your own horoscope? With very little effort, we can make of you the most puissant astrologer-prophet in the whole of France. There are things we cannot see, and we need your eyes.'

'Why have you not gone to Luc Gauricus?' I asked, and then realised the absurdity of that question.

'Tomorrow at dawn we will ride toward Joinville, to see my lord of Guise and his two eldest sons. The first thing you can do for us is to see what may be discerned in the futures of these two precious seedlings. François, the Comte d'Aumale who will one day be duke, is twenty-three. Charles, Archbishop of Reims, is but eighteen. It is upon these that our hopes now lie. Two generations of planning have brought them within a step of the throne.'

I would like to be a court gentleman . . . No wonder that my grandfather laughed.

'As for what may follow,' Bandello continued, 'we shall see. But remember that you can go where no courtier can. Astrologers are privy to the secret souls of kings. To the world you are only a Provençal physician, whose political slate is spotless, who is a loyal subject of the King and a devout adherent of Holy Church. And you are a showman, my friend. You know how to sell your wares. If my instincts tell me true, you are a master of dissembling as well. Who knows where we can place you? I told you we had been waiting these hundreds of years for the right time. Who but an astrologer-prophet can tell us when the right time has arrived?'

XV

As we rode through the gates of the town, the ancient château of the old Sieurs of Joinville loomed grim-faced above us on its high wooded hill. Larger even than King René's vast pile of stone at Tarascon, its stern and ominous keep, its bastions, its towers and turrets and crenellated battlements clawed the reddening sky.

In the cavernous and gloomy hall, Claude de Lorraine, Duc de Guise, stood motionless before the fire, waiting to receive us. That layer of superstitious fear which infests even the most civilised men had gripped my bowels. I avoided his eyes at first, staring instead at the vivid pattern of the Byzantine carpet. But when I looked up, I saw only a man, albeit a comely one. He was forty-six years of age then, fair, with wheat-coloured hair and beard, magnificently but soberly dressed in black velvet doublet and mantle trimmed with ermine. The scars of old sword-wounds marked his stern face, and I saw the look of careful calculation about the hard disciplined mouth and the narrow, pale, heavy-lidded greenish eyes.

His close friendship with King François was an object of rumour and admiration throughout the country. What the gossips did not know was the meticulous and ingenious fashion whereby this friendship had been architected, like a chess game in which each piece was moved with diabolical cunning upon the great board – no opening ever missed, no mistake ever made. Claude de Guise had proven his bravery and his warrior's skill again and again, in Italy, in Spain, in the constant border wars intruding upon his domains and those of his brother the Duc de Lorraine. *Heureux et genereux*, he was called – lucky and gallant. With polished diplomacy he had contracted an unromantic but advantageous marriage to a daughter of the house of Bourbon, which stood next in line to the throne. And with disarming charm, he had contrived to extract from the King the honour of being raised from Comte to Duc de Guise, a status equal in rank to any nobleman of French blood save the monarch's own son. In addition to the vast French fiefs he had inherited from his father, he had wooed from his bemused sovereign governorship of the rich province of Champagne, cradle of legends and chronicles of the Holy Grail.

Heureux et genereux. He was not as attractive a man as his sybaritic and dissolute brother Jean, Cardinal de Lorraine. But a greater power resided within him – something formidable and unbreakable and adamantine.

The duke dismissed his servants, leaving the three of us alone in the vast shadowy hall. He held court here like a king, so sumptuously had his refined Italianate taste furnished the immense and oppressive fortress. Yet he himself practised the bleak austerity of the man of war. He was in fact about to plunge into another. For the King was preparing yet again to challenge the Emperor Charles. By midsummer an army, under the Duc de Guise's command, would invade Luxembourg. We had seen, as we rode south from Orval, the sluggish serpentine line of ordnance and provisions moving slowly along the roads to the border.

'It is a depressing place, is it not, this old château?' he said conversationally. A single huge ruby winked at his throat, blood-coloured in the firelight, while his pale catlike eyes appraised me through the gloom. 'I am having a small house built among the woods, in the valley below, which will be more to my taste. I have commissioned Primaticcio to draw up the plans for me. He is calling it the Château du Grand Jardin. I do not care for these feudal mausoleums.'

I must have betrayed my discomfort, for he was obviously making an effort to charm it away.

'It is fitting that we should meet at last, Maître de Notre-dame,' said the duke, 'for your reputation is not unknown to us here in Champagne. Besides, your grandfather was the good servant of my great-grandfather. A noble house should not forget those who do it service. Our Dominican here has told you a strange tale, has he not?' He seemed perfectly relaxed as he spoke, as though passing on to me some choice morsel of court gossip. 'What do you think of it?'

'Think? I do not know what to think, my lord. It is only the day before yesterday that the world collapsed around me in ruins. Rest assured that I am pledged to your service. When I am able to think again, I will perhaps have some answer. In any case, I hope I will prove worthy of your confidence.'

Claude de Guise laughed, and I saw in the sudden lighting of his austere warrior's face, and the flash of good white teeth, the dash and charisma which so endeared him to the romantic King. I saw too, in the charming smile, a resemblance to his remarkable brother.

'It is hardly a matter of a confidence, is it?' he said. 'After all, to whom could you tell it? They would think you mad.'

'I myself think I am mad, my lord, or will be very soon. But do not let this concern you. They say that we astrologers see further when our sanity is in question. How may I be of assistance to you?'

'I wish you to inspect the horoscopes of my two eldest sons. I myself am somewhat versed in the art. But I understand that you have some insight greater than the study itself, as did your grandfather. I would therefore be pleased if you would tell me what lies ahead for these two youths, whom I love, but upon whose shoulders a great burden now lies.'

I knew that François de Guise, at twenty-three, had already proven himself a formidable and courageous fighter, promising to outshine even his brilliant father in the arts of war. About the young Charles I knew nothing, save that he played the lute, and would one day inherit the wealth and benefices and title of his uncle Jean, Cardinal de Lorraine. Upon the shoulders of Claude and his son François the military destiny of the country slowly and quietly accumulated. Upon the shoulders of the Cardinal and his nephew gathered its financial and ecclesiastical affairs.

Move the knight to check the king, but protect him with a bishop . . . By the time these skilled players had performed all their convoluted moves, there would be nothing left to parcel out to the nobility of France. The house of Lorraine would hold it all.

'I will introduce you to them now,' said Claude de Guise, 'and we will sup. Then you will retire to the chambers I have had laid out for you. In the morning we will peruse the horoscopes. It is late for such work after a tiring journey.'

Mathieu Bandello sat quietly at the duke's left. A great love for this austere nobleman was written in his ascetic face. Well enough, I reflected; no doubt he is the sort that inspires it, aloof though he is. I myself felt nothing. I was in a state of curious detachment, suspended from all emotion, as though I were watching a masque in which I were one of the players.

But this state of serene tranquillity was abruptly curtailed. Charles de Guise, Archbishop of Reims, entered the hall, followed by his elder brother, the Comte d'Aumale. I was suddenly staring into eyes that flickered and danced with the wisdom and cunning and ancient sorcery of a serpent. The sense of shocking recognition was so profound, so intense, that my winecup dropped from my hand and rolled with a clatter across the stone floor.

It was a fresh fair face, worthy of Sandro Filipepi's angels, but with a precociously corrupted innocence. And the bizarre eyes gazed back at me – large, limpid, long-lashed, blue as lapis, enigmatic, cynical and wise. He had inherited his father's elegant tall frame, and carried it with grace and dignity. Here was a veritable Adonis. His forehead and nose were chiselled with the delicacy of a Greek marble, his skin pale and almost waxen. Yet there was something frightening about him. His mouth was small and perfectly formed, imprinted with a profound but controlled sensuality that spoke of love and secrets, not litanies. More than a hint of vanity and cruelty lurked in the curl of his lips. The first faint beard, nut-brown and elegantly curled, already shadowed his upper lip and chin.

I had the uncanny sensation that he was reading my thoughts. He offered me a terribly knowing and intimate smile, and seated himself like an insolent peacock at the great table, admiring his own long white hands as he poured himself a cup of wine. *Seduisant*, they would call him later: the irresistable, the dazzling, the fascinating, the seductive one. This ancient house of kings, I thought, has bred a serpent.

I turned away, my mouth dry, feeling the sweat film on my

forehead. The sense of inexplicable familiarity had been disturbing enough when I first saw Jean de Lorraine in Avignon, when I met the veiled eyes of the minstrel Plantard in Montpellier. Now that familiarity was overwhelming. I seemed to have slipped into some ancient never-ending dream world, where I had danced an eerie dance with this deadly and dazzling creature for thousands of years.

How, I asked myself desperately, had I come to be among these men? There was a patina over all of them, father and sons – a sheen, a glaze, which might have been their pride of bearing or might have been something else. In the gloom of the great fortress, power beat about me with invisible wings. It was not power of the kind men make with money and arms, but rather an inner power, an intrinsic *virtû*, which is forged in the soul and manipulates from the world's substance what forms it pleases.

The resemblance of François de Guise to his brother was pronounced, but François was more olive of complexion while his hair and beard shone dull pale gold. The same clear patrician features ennobled his face, the same finely shaped, insolently sensual mouth. Eyes that glowed greenish with his father's catlike insensity stared arrogantly, almost irritably, at me, challenging my curiosity. But while the young Archbishop's face exuded charm and mobile intelligence and cunning, this young lord radiated courage and valour, impetuousness, even brutality. Beneath the surface control, like a vein showing bluish beneath translucent skin, the thread of explosive violence ran, ready to be triggered by a trifle. I could see it in the line of the jaw and the stubborn set of the mouth. Here was the unmistakable stamp of Mars, the warlord, which I knew I would find dominant in his horoscope.

I stared at them, a serpent and a lion, and they smiled indolently back. I looked at the jewels, the velvet, the fine pleated linen, the gold and silver tracings of their doublets, the delicately worked boots of Spanish leather, the rich furs. I looked at the black triangular *biretta* and the massive gold crucifix studded with rubies and amber and jasper that hung about Charles de Guise's graceful neck. Irony began to clutch at my entrails, an immense, hilarious, utterly shattering irony.

Despite my efforts, I felt the corners of my mouth drooping into a twisted smirk. To my horror, I began to laugh uncontrollably, until the tears welled in my eyes. I glimpsed a sympathetic grin on Mathieu Bandello's face, and the affronted dignity, shifting to amusement, in the features of Claude de Guise. Then they were all laughing, and the terrible spell was broken. It was, after all, a very great joke. As Fra Bandello had said, the greatest joke in the whole world.

Mathieu Bandello rose and clapped me on the back. 'He has had a little shock,' the monk said apologetically to the duke, pouring me more wine. 'But he will recover.' He smiled gently. 'After all, he is a Jew by birth and a pagan in spirit. Beyond the irony, it means little to him either way.'

Claude de Guise waited in his study with the numerous horoscopes we were to examine. I was hesitant at first, and shy of him. But he encouraged me gently, until I realised it was absurd to be coy with this man. Had I pronounced his imminent death he would have sat with the same impeccable dignity, discussing the appropriate measures to follow. He was true to his birth sign of the Scorpion. There seemed to be no fear in him at all.

The burden these men carried had bred strange effects in them, varying according to their temperaments. To live with their secret, I thought, must be near unbearable. One had to cling to sanity somehow in a world which to them must seem insane. It had driven the Duc de Guise into himself, so that he lived within a deep solitude, behind a vast bastion of grim self-restraint. It had spawned the reckless idealism and brutality I had glimpsed in the handsome features of François de Guise. And it lurked in the shadows of depravity that haunted young Charles' ancient eyes.

The duke unrolled before me Charles de Guise's horoscope. For some minutes I merely stared at it, finding nothing to say. I recalled the prophecies of eighteen years before, when the plague first struck Montpellier. Six heavenly bodies conjoined in the sign of the Fishes, and appeared at dusk in the wake of the setting sun as a great star. This had ignited a rash of terrified prognostications – the coming of the Antichrist, the end of the world.

Despite the plague and the debâcle of Pavia and the imprisonment of King François, the world had continued to exist. And here was this *seduisant* young man, born under that strange massing of sun and planets, observing the world through his haunted nacreous eyes, daily parading a suffocating ritual of dogma to the world. He escaped from it into lovemaking and luxury and cruelty, while the terrible irony of his own blood ate at him from within.

The sign of Virgo – the craftsman, the scholar, the politician – was rising in the east at his birth. Mercurial, versatile, blessed with a brilliant wit, an astonishing and tortuous mind and memory, almost supernormal perceptions. What moral code could guide him? He saw too much and knew too many answers, so that everything was relative and therefore permissible.

'Why do you recoil?' Claude de Guise said. I jerked around with a start from my preoccupation.

'I have not seen a horoscope such as this before,' I murmured, 'with all the planets conjoined in a great star.'

'Have you not?' he replied, watching me with his cool cat-eyes. I looked away.

'The power of the Fishes,' I managed to declare at last, 'lies in a genius to embody what the secret currents of the time require. Your son is a medium, a mouthpiece. For what, I cannot even imagine.'

He merely nodded and rolled up the horoscope and put it aside. There was nothing further to be said.

We turned next to the horoscope of François. Here was something more concrete with which I could work. It did not flicker and shimmer and slide away from my grasp as did the other. He was another of the Fishes, but earthier and stronger. Leo, the lion, the *chevalier sans peur et sans reproche*, the King, the lightgiver – Leo lay in the east, ascending at his birth. I told the duke of the marks of power and honour and wealth, the almost ferocious courage, the loyalty, the chivalry. I remained silent about the patterns of danger through treachery, and the deadly grip of blind idealism, and the slow rot of disillusionment, and the violent death. Before he reached his goal, an assassin would cut him down. I felt deeply saddened, for this young man was a true knight, worthy of King René's tales of chivalry and courtly love.

Claude de Guise could read my face, however blank I strove to maintain it. He pried the truth from me.

'How long will he live?'

I could not meet his eyes, for it was a terrible thing to tell a father about his son. But something in this grim feudal lord compelled it from me.

'He is in great danger in three years. But I do not believe it will be death. Saturn moves in quadrature to Mercury and in opposition to Mars. Most likely it will be a wound in battle. But he will survive. It is in his forty-fourth year that the malefic influences are strongest.'

'That is twenty-one years in the future,' said the Duc de Guise. 'We have ample time.'

I gave him a surprised look, disturbed by this callousness. He met my eyes levelly, calmly. It was not callousness at all, I realised, in that cool, dispassionate stare, but the harsh and painful realism of the stoic. He loved this eldest son deeply, above all else. But it did not matter.

We examined the other horoscopes piled atop his bureau. Here was the entire garden of the French nobility's most vivid flowers, all those who might be in any way bound to the fortunes of the house of Lorraine: Anne, Connêtable de Montmorency; the Emperor Charles; Henri d'Albret, King of Navarre, and his young daughter Jeanne; Diane de Poitiers, the Dauphin's mistress; Madame d'Estampes, the King's mistress; Antoine de Bourbon, Duc de Vendôme, First Prince of the Blood; the Dauphin Prince Henri and his ambiguous Italian wife.

The horoscope of the last, though I only glanced at it, produced an ominous foreboding. I could not say why.

'You feel it too,' Claude de Guise said. 'The design seems innocuous enough, until you study it. The cross of Mars and Saturn and the moon is a subtle and ugly configuration. It is said that she poisoned the King's eldest son to make way for herself as future Queen. No one yet knows what Catherine de' Medici is. They think her self-effacing and humble and unimportant, because she gives way to her husband's mistress with apparent good grace. And now,' he said with disgust in his voice, 'after ten long years, she has managed to become pregnant, and is useful because she may bear a future King of France. But I have had many dealings with her at court. And I know what lies behind those blank and colourless eyes.'

I saw for the first time a blaze of anger flare in his pale gaze and distort his austere face.

'I have told my sons to court Diane de Poitiers. The Dauphin will be faithful to her. She is their only hope of safety when the Italian woman becomes Queen. When it was thought that she was barren, my son Charles, whom Prince Henri loves, sought to influence the King to divorce her from his son, so that Henri might marry a more fruitful woman. He had selected my daughter Marie. But the seed has at last quickened. We must wait to see what foul creature is produced.'

It occurred to me for the first time how useful a tool to this prolific house was the dynastic marriage. How could one play chess without willing pawns? Graft a branch on to the royal vine here, another branch there, suffuse the corrupted house of Valois with fresh, vital Lorraine blood, until the upstarts, the foreigners, had surrounded with a silken net the chosen prize – a net woven from the fruitful bodies of noble ladies who, entering the first gentle flush of womanhood, were auctioned like cattle to the most estimable bidder.

For a moment it made me angry. Thus was Andiette de la Roque-Loubéjac traded to Scaliger when she might have been mine. But that was long buried, and I did not wish to learn if any life still stirred behind the closed door. Moreover, such barter might, to some, be acceptable, even welcome.

And so it went on, throughout that long day – who were the enemies, who were the friends, who could be trusted, who could bring harm wittingly or unwittingly. Marriages and divorces, conflicts and deaths. Whether there would be children for François to carry on the line.

The duke prepared us a sumptuous meal that night. In addition to his eldest sons the younger were present as well: Louis, who was also destined for the Church, Claude, René, another François. And I met too Antoinette de Bourbon, Duchesse de Guise. It was at once apparent that this rather tragic woman –

plain, lonely, capable, with the pale and faintly fanatical face of the blindly religious – knew nothing of the secrets of the German house into which she had married. She had spent most of her life immured in the ancient fortress, bearing children for her duke. She had not been touched by the bright burgeoning of art and learning which had flowered at the court. She was a feudal châtelaine of centuries past – stern, devout, managing the great estates of her husband with rigid yet efficient hand. Only her deep blue eyes, blank now after years of ruthless self-abnegation and endless good works, had passed on to her beguiling second son. I felt pity for her, a pawn like myself.

A lute and a viol tipped their plaintive chords down from the gallery, for Claude de Guise was fond of music. I listened to the melancholy rise and fall of the liquid notes and reflected that this meeting was only the beginning. I would be needed at each crisis, each moment of decision, each childbirth, each marriage, each turning point. The long endless road stretched ahead through the years, to what unknown end? I was once so independent of spirit, had repudiated my comfortable teaching post at Montpellier because I cherished my freedom. How had I stumbled here and so willingly surrendered myself to these men?

But whenever I glanced at François de Guise and his brother, the noble lion and the enchanting serpent, I was forced to acknowledge that these youths had bewitched me. I was ensnared by their power, and bound by my recognition of them, and trapped by my own dreams.

Once the Archbishop leaned across to me and said quietly, in his melodious voice, under the ripple of the lute, 'You do not look happy, Maître de Notredame. Is there anything amiss that I can remedy?'

He looked so sincere at that moment, so young, so gentle, so concerned, that my heart opened to him.

'I thank you, my lord, but it is no concrete thing which disturbs me. I am bewildered rather than unhappy. Perhaps your noble father, the duke, and I have spoken too much of life and death today.'

'Perhaps you look upon life and death with too much intensity, Maître de Notredame,' said Charles de Guise, offering

144

me a sweet smile and passing me a plate of sugared marchpane. 'One should live each moment as though it were the first and the last – passionately, but laughing. You will learn.'

It was fair enough advice, though specious coming from one so young. But when I pursued the thread of it, I shuddered with alarm. It was like the offering of the apple: the beguiling voice, the sweet smile, the limpid blue eyes, the bottomless abyss beneath. Turning away, I began to chatter inanely to the duchess on my left, while a cold chill ran up my back like a gentle finger.

When it had grown very late, and the scented tapers had burned low in their silver sconces, and the duchess and the younger boys had retired to their beds, Claude de Guise turned to me.

'Do you believe, Maître de Notredame, that we can escape our fates?'

I shrugged. I was already very drunk. 'I have seen too many things to believe we can avoid what must be. Yet I believe we have freedom, of a kind. There are always choices. Perhaps certain events are destined. But the road one takes to those crossings, that is one's own. Perhaps one has a destiny to live in the world. But one also has the freedom to be great or petty, noble or malicious, as one chooses.'

'Then you do not feel a man's soul is bound by fate, as are his circumstances?'

'I do not know whether these two are not secretly the same. There is a terrible paradox in it that I cannot comprehend, although I have tried.'

I passed my hand over my flushed forehead, and looked away to gather the wandering skeins of my thoughts. My eyes met the shimmering blue stare of Charles, Archbishop of Reims. The duke followed my gaze, and read my face.

'You are disturbed by my son,' he said very softly under the cloak of the music. It was a flat statement, rather than a question. 'Virtually all who meet him are enthralled, enchanted. He is hailed as a gifted spirit, a *santorello*, with a brilliant future before him.'

'I too am enchanted, my lord.'

'But you see the dark shadows that move beneath the surface, deep in his soul. Does he have a choice?'

A long moment passed while the Duc de Guise and I studied each other. At last he smiled and put his hand on my shoulder.

'I am being unjust in posing such questions to you,' he said. 'Forgive me. I know our world is strange to you. But I trust your wisdom.'

'I do not know the answer, my lord. I am well versed in the occult arts. I know much of the inner structure and correspondence of things, the plan upon which the universe is said to be built, the secret powers of nature. I have studied astrology and alchemy and the kabbalah. I can often sense the inner heart of men, and my dreams sometimes foretell what is to be. I have always believed, like Paracelsus, that there is some consciousness, some life inherent in all things, even in the very stones, a life which strives to develop itself through all the kingdoms of nature and seeks its real awakening in man. So we struggle through the ages, reaching for light, because what we call God itself longs for light. This is of course the great heresy of the alchemists: that God seeks His redemption in man. Perhaps whatever the substance we are given, that is fated, but what we shape of it is not. Yet what I do not understand is the nature of this dual God, who shows me one face in men like Socrates or Pythagoras or Jesus of Nazareth, and another in war and torture and pestilence and human cruelty and death.'

'You see both faces in my son.'

'I see both faces in you all. Perhaps there is a great mystery here that I am only beginning to understand.'

'We are only men. We feel anguish and lust and loneliness and hate and greed. We bleed and die. My son François was wounded in a skirmish in Spain. An arquebus ball shattered his ankle. He suffered as any man does, and cried out in his pain. I told him that men of our blood ought to take pleasure in building a reputation upon the ruin of the body. He bit his lips until they were torn and bloody, trying to prove his courage.'

'Yet there is magic in you, my lord, and even greater magic in your sons. They hold a sheen of destiny upon them. I will pray, in my fashion, for you all.'

And as Mathieu Bandello and I rode north from Joinville through the yellow mud and the grey rain along the flooded banks of the Meuse, I did indeed pray, after my fashion, for these men. For I had discovered, during the last two days, that I had begun to love them as my black-gowned companion did – irrationally, compellingly, unwillingly. And most of all the young Comte d'Aumale, the lion with the stamp of the warlord upon his noble face, whom I knew in my heart would barely miss his goal and fall to a bloody death.

XVI

For eighteen months the sheltering walls of the abbey of Notre Dame d'Orval embraced me. After a few weeks, Mathieu Bandello departed for Italy on business. He left me in the care of the Abbé, Mathias Delvaux, but assured me he would return before it was time to release me into the world again.

Although still confused and disoriented, I was no longer unnerved by what had happened. The symmetry of the pattern had locked into place. Now that I could see it, I accepted it. I became an embryo in some strange stone womb, immured behind the sanctified walls, gradually forming limbs and eyes, developing sight and hearing and touch and taste and smell. In time the gestation would be complete and I would emerge into a world I would no longer recognise, because I myself had so changed.

Mathias Delvaux, like Jules-César de l'Escale, had dabbled in everything. A linguist and a theologian, he was versed in both medicine and astrology besides. He possessed the same acute intellect as the polemicist of Agen, the same love of scholarship, the same delicate and effortless manoeuvrability in the realms of systems of thought. But Mathias Delvaux was a gentler man, and did not use the keen edge of his mind to hack at the lesser defences of others. He had acquired a serenity which one should expect but rarely finds among men of God. The hair around his tonsure still retained some of its youthful dark colour, and he had an exquisite fondness for good wine.

He maintained his imperturbable serenity while the war

raged around us along the border. For King François, as he had planned, invaded Luxembourg, with an army led by the Duc de Guise, and the countryside was torn and looted and pillaged in its wake. Although we could hear the boom of the cannon even through the dense forest and the high stone walls, the abbey did not suffer. Claude de Guise carved a careful berth around it. Its lands, untouched by the conflicts of kings, were rich and fecund. The orchards yielded their succulent fruit, and herds of sleek cattle provided milk and cheese and butter. The cellars were stocked with fine wine from Champagne and Lorraine. While Luxembourg was ravaged I dwelled in cocoon-like comfort, enveloped by that strange and beautiful womb sequestered in the Forêt de Merlanvaux, dreaming amidst its legends.

Each night I retired to my little cell with the high narrow window and the rose-embellished crucifix. Each morning I attended matins and lauds with the monks, kneeling on the cold stone floors, breathing the scent of frankincense, listening to the sad watery cadences of the *Salve Regina*, hiding my ironic laughter.

Each day, Mathias Delvaux led me into the crypt where the old manuscripts were kept rolled in silk and nestled in their ancient carved chests. By the guttering light of the tapers, I read parchments and scrolls of immense antiquity, exquisitely illuminated, in Greek and Latin and Hebrew and Arabic. I devoured and grew famished and devoured again.

The Abbé wished me to learn more of the Merovingian tree, that I might better appreciate the fruit now ripening on its branches. He showed me genealogical tables of great age, tracing the descent of the house of Lorraine from Clovis, first Christian King of the Franks. In even older parchments, in Latin and Hebrew and Aramaic, the great trunk descended back through Merovée to its roots beneath the earth – the ancient tribe of Benjamin, the First Chosen who had abandoned Israel when Judah rose in its place. The Benjamites, vilified because they placed the Mother above the Father, who migrated to Arcadia and thence to Gaul, settling at last in the virgin forests and fields of Languedoc and Provence. The irony intensified, by this revelation that the house of Lorraine, pillars of Holy Church, secretly claimed descent from the ancient blood of Israel. Here indeed were wandering Jews.

The abbey's greatest treasure was at last offered to my hungry eyes: a book which had been recopied many times over the centuries, from Aramaic into Hebrew, from Hebrew into Greek, from Greek into Latin, bearing on the ancient rotting binding the seal of the Order of the Temple, the blood-red cross *pattée*. It spoke of the great design of the world, beginning with the first embryonic life that emerged from the timeless depths of the womb of the sea, weaving its path in increasing complexity through the tangled and bloody threads of the aeons of human history. It spoke of the evolutionary plan, and of the soul of the earth itself seeking development through all its kingdoms, so that each line – mineral or plant or animal or human or devic – might unfold itself according to its own destiny. It spoke of the races of men; and of the secret currents of history – like silent underground rivers spewing forth on the visible shore those individuals whom the times call great and whom men believe shape the times, when in truth it is the time-spirits of the aeons, the dancing gods, which call such genius into being as eternal present, as myth. It spoke of the geometric patterns of matter and space and time, and of the slow wheel of the precession of the equinoxes, and of the great round of the millennia, ceaselessly spiralling toward some distant goal when man as God in flesh, and God as man incorporeal, would meet and recognise each other as one substance.

And it spoke too of that which Mathieu Bandello had hinted to me and which in my first astonishment I would not countenance: of the desperate and secret flight from Jerusalem after the sacrifice, and the landing of the exiles at Marseilles, and the hidden treasure that was borne among them – blood of Judah and Benjamin conjoined, the Chosen of the Chosen, the Heir to the Kingdom, the *sangraal*, the blood royal. And a thousand years later, Godefroi de Bouillon had merely returned home, to reclaim his rightful heritage.

I reflected upon my own name and erupted in mordant laughter at the thought of my grandfather. Old Pierre de Notredame had been compelled, like Jean de St Rémy, to repudiate his heritage, to choose a Christian name; yet he, who had been close to my grandfather Jean and had no doubt been privy to his secrets, had had the last laugh after all. And here too were the tendrils of churches and abbeys which had sprouted like summer vines beneath the guiding spirit of the Temple, snaking in a great serpentine spinal column northward from Marseilles, through Paris, to Notre Dame d'Orval. A myriad edifices brooding in silent stone mockery, laughing down the ages, dedicated to Our Lady who was not after all the Virgin, but that other, her heavy indolent cornflower eyes peering languorously from Sandro Filipepi's eerie mountainous landscape.

The house of Lorraine had inherited an awesome and terrible burden as her fate. The crowned heads of Europe, the papal throne itself, would rock and shudder and topple. The very fabric of Christendom would rend apart, were this secret exposed to the light too soon. For the Rock of the Church was built upon the doctrine of Original Sin, the sin of the serpent, the sin of carnal love which through Adam's fall denies man access to God's grace save through His chosen mouthpiece. Lorraine had been wise in her caution. For the masses – blind as nodding sheep in their centuries-old adherence to the dogmas of Holy Church – would surely go insane.

So I have spoken in the language of number and anagram and symbol and dream, and told the story of what has been and what will be and also what must be done by those who hold the key, for these were my instructions from my masters. But none save those for whom I write will understand. Others will interpret these things as the rantings of a fool or a charlatan, or the obscure visions of a solitary lunatic. They will not discern the gigantic design of which the lunatic is the oracle.

And I have named my eldest daughter Madeleine, as Claude de Guise named his Marie. And we have both laughed, as my grandfather Pierre must once have done, over this ironic little conceit.

XVII

Slowly, with unutterable patience, Mathias Delvaux taught me to contemplate the fire. At first my eyes watered and my head ached, and I saw nothing save the flames and the crumbling ashes and the pulsing red blood of my own eyelids.

'In your dreams you have sight, Maître de Notredame,' he would say to me. 'The waking world of your earthbound eyes is not the real world at all. You must pierce the veil that masks the real world, the world of dreams, from the one which your eyes perceive. There is only a veil of finest gauze draped across your dreams. You have only to walk through it. It is as thin and insubstantial as mist. It is Michel de Notredame who is the dream and not the dreamer.'

I laboured for many weary hours, many weary weeks. With my intellect, I could grasp what he told me, and it formed a clear and diamond-bright picture in my consciousness. But it remained beyond my reach.

I drank myself blind with wine, and weakened my stubborn body by fasting until I was dizzy and my eyesight spattered with shifting shapes of light. I drank tinctures of poppy and belladonna, and stared in drugged stupor at a pinpoint of flame for hours in the heavy darkness, while the pulse thudded dully in my temples. Still my eyes could not see.

'You are of the earth,' Mathias Delvaux told me. 'You are the Goat, sure-footed on the rocky mountain crags. Yet there is fire deep within you, fire like the volcano's heat within its bones of ash and stone. That clear hand and eye that make you a skilled physician cloud what is truly yourself from the mask of sinew and flesh in which you walk. Part the veil, Maître de Notredame. Do not fear. You will still be here alive when it is over.'

I fell into despair. I was a creature of earth, I cried out to him, not a salamander. Paracelsus and Agrippa could speak of fire with impunity, could themselves perceive the *lumen naturae*. But fire was not my element. Fire only evoked for me the horror of consumed flesh at the Inquisitor's stake, and the stench of burning corpses in the wake of the plague.

I had common sense and rationality and insight. Could I not serve him with these? My knowledge of the stars was no trifling matter. Would that not suffice? My visions visited me only in sleep, when my earthbound body was numb. I felt in my stomach and my heart the souls of other men. I could not see visions in the fire. I pleaded with Mathias Delvaux to use what abilities I possessed, not try to extract from me, like blood from a lifeless stone, those I did not own. Then I pleaded with him to let me go. I declared myself a failure, as I had failed before.

But he had the patience of a wise parent with a child. Gently he coaxed the gift out of me, seeing it clearly long before I had glimpsed its existence. It was a long and hard labour, a bloody birth, and it cost me great pain. Every wound I had suffered in my life, known or unknown, rose like foul gaseous bubbles to the surface of a stagnant pool. I was overwhelmed with loneliness and self-pity and melancholy. With ruthless compassion, he wrung from me every motive, every hope, every dark and secret desire, every dream. Often, instead of the visions I hoped to see, I imagined over and over again the face of Death in sickness and at the stake. He seemed to call my entire soul out of me as the snake-charmer calls the serpent with his magic flute, exposing it, blind and quivering, to the light – so that each hidden abcess, each obscure scar, each buried and festering sore might be cleansed and understood and made whole flesh again.

And then one day, as I stared at the flames for the thousandth time, exhausted and tense beneath the grinding hammer of a clawing and relentless headache, something within me released its lifelong grip. I felt it heave and shudder and roll over and die, as though some heavy earthy beast had exhaled its last breath and abandoned itself to a dignified but inevitable death. I did not realise until then how much of my father there had been in me.

The room wavered and darkened around me, a negation of

light. I was abandoned and alone, the last man on a dying earth or the first on an earth being born. I stared at the flames and saw a great sarcophagus carved of black wood fastened with facings of brass and studs of gold. It was carried by faceless men, robed and cowled in black, into the maw of an enormous dark vault beneath the earth. Seven children, their faces silvery white and glistening in the gloom, surrounded it where it lay. I heard a howling and a crying, as though some massive incorporeal creature were in pain, and I saw the shapeless misty dead of the ages rising and coiling about the coffin as the door of the vault swung shut with a muffled clang . . . I gasped and choked, and the sound of my own breath rasping in my throat awakened me. Shaking and perspiring, I faced Mathias Delvaux, who sat calmly in his usual chair, watching me with interest.

'What did you see?' he inquired gently.

I tried to describe the vision, but my tongue was heavy and sodden in my mouth. 'Whose death have I foreseen?'

He shook his head. 'I do not know, Maître de Notredame. Come, let us set up the horoscope for this moment and determine, if the heavens reflect in the ethers the birth of this unborn event. I have never been able to read the fire. But I have some inkling, some faint feeling that you have spied upon the end of the Valois, conceived in the womb of the future. We shall see. It is the beginning.'

It was indeed the beginning. I did not always remember what the fire revealed to me. Sometimes I fainted afterward; sometimes the fragments were so cloudy, so obscure, that I could not retain them. Sometimes too they belonged to the past rather than to the future. Time was undifferentiated, as though some gigantic tapestry were weaving itself in the dream of the sleeping heaven-god Ouranos, and past and present and future melded together in an endless shifting dance of disparate threads, waiting to be born in matter and space and time.

We would always map the moment afterward and scrutinise the movements of the heavens for whatever influences were at work. These would sometimes tell an obvious story. At other times they were obscure, and the heavens and the visions remained mute.

I asked him if these were truly prophetic visions, bound by fate. He smiled benignly at me.

'What is fate, Maître de Notredame? We do not understand time, we poor earthbound creatures. We think there is a present and a future and a past. In truth it is all now, all happening at this moment, like the pictures of a dream which span centuries in a second and a moment in a millennium. For each link in the chain, each intersection point, there are many possible branches, many possible futures. Thus the great vine of the *sangraal* has many branches, many possible futures: Lorraine, Guise, Blanchefort, Gisors, Joinville, Chaumont, Courtenay, Montpezat, Gonzaga, Charnay, Brienne, St Clair. Break any link in the chain and the future shifts and changes its shape.'

'Then I do not understand the purpose of this work.'

He laughed. 'You thought it was to predict the future. No, my friend. Our business is to choose one clean thread among many, and bend the future to our will in accord with our own designs.'

We spoke at length of the principles of magic, which I understood well enough as theoretical philosophy. But I had never attempted to invoke, within the protective pentagram, those forces which stand midway between the portals of spirit and matter. Now I was told I must learn the rituals to focus power and summon the aid of that which guards the threshold, to help me call the visions into being at will.

I refused. I told him I did not wish to dabble in black sorcery. All I had learned of magic could be safely couched in terms of philosophy and the natural sciences. It was permissible to allow my clairvoyance to perceive images in the fire, for I was then but a passive recipient and assumed no responsibility. I did not wish to invoke the elemental powers and risk a battle of my will with theirs. I made erudite excuses. The truth of it was that I was afraid.

'You do not understand, Maître de Notredame,' said Mathias Delvaux. 'Ah, I know you protest in the most persuasive manner on theoretical grounds. But I can see the fear in your eyes. You must remember that in this shadow-world in which you are learning to swim like a young dolphin, all is raised to the dignity of symbol and parable. The only demons you will meet, my friend, are those which make their abode in your own soul.'

Thus we began the next phase of the training. I found, after many months, that I could put myself into trance at will, without the violent shock to body and soul that had previously accompanied my visions. It was like setting a lute in tune, so that the notes would play true. The images became clearer, more focused. I learned to see them in a pool of still water, and sometimes in the air itself against a whitewashed wall.

The rituals of magic are abhorred by all Christendom. But I, who have never been a Christian, learned that magic, like the rituals of the Church which are honoured as holy, stills the buzzing and ceaseless nattering of the mind. It gently immerses the little will of man in a watery half-sleep, so that the Other can speak and be heard.

Thus, having been a physician and an astrologer, I became a magician under the kindly and patient tutelage of Mathias Delvaux, the gentle and saintly Abbé of Notre Dame d'Orval.

XVIII

At the end of eighteen months, the Abbé told me my training was nearly at an end. All he had hoped to see accomplished had come to pass. Delight shone in his serene hazel eyes. He was as pleased with me as though I were a responsive child in school.

I had indeed learned my lessons. Very little remained of that Michel de Notredame who had once ridden his mule into the town of Agen, seeking a comfortable marriage and highly placed patrons and easy fame and ready gold.

I wondered what Order I had unknowingly entered, what Order I was now bound to serve. For the network was too scattered and apparently disconnected to be bound only by blood, and too impeccably organised to be without structure, hierarchy and leadership. It was enough, Mathias Delvaux told me, that I knew of the Order's existence, sufficient that I had gleaned its essence and shared its secret. I asked if it was the remaining life-thread, arcane and hidden, of what had once been the Temple. He smiled and replied that the Temple, that powerful soldier-state of monks of war, had itself been created by the Order. I did not dare question him further, for his usually benign and smiling face had become sober and austere. I bowed my head in acquiescence, and we spoke of the future, when I would emerge from the womb of Notre Dame d'Orval.

He wished me to return to Provence. The role in which I was cast required an aura of the quaint and naïve back-country provincial doctor – *El Mato*, the Fool, ignorant of the court's sophisticated patina. I laughed. Sophisticated the court might be in matters of poetry and love and domestic politics. But compared to this labyrinthine spider's web, it was scarcely more than children at play.

Mathias Delvaux told me I must choose as my place of residence a town called Salon, in the little desert of Craux, south of Avignon. I inquired how such a town of such small consequence could further his plans.

'Because of Mgr de Santacroce, the Archbishop of Arles,' the Abbé said. 'His château overlooks the town. He is one of us.'

'How many of you are there, then, in the ranks of the Church?'

'More than you would think,' replied Mathias Delvaux. 'All that St Bernard created belongs to us.'

Even now I could still be astonished. Orval, of course, was a Cistercian house. Now I recalled the tiny Cistercian monastery nestled in its eagle's eyrie among the distant folds of the Alps, haunted by the ancient and enigmatic shape of a Notre Dame older than time, black in the flickering light of the tapers.

Do not put too much faith in this, for it is too young . . . Pope and Antipope, Christ and Antichrist, Virgin and Antivirgin, white and black, the Beauséant, the banner of the Temple. A pristine and snowy cross reflected mirrorlike in an onyx pool . . .

'And what am I to do in Salon?'

'You must marry. You must become a family man, respectable and devout, a loyal friend to the town magistrates, a generous donor to convents, monasteries, hospitals and the poor. A pillar, in effect, of nation, town and Church.'

My lips tightened. I did not wish to marry again. There had been a surfeit of agony in Agen. My dreams were still sometimes stained and shadowed by the inert corpse of my wife, unrolled over and over again in an endless chain of mirrors. And by the slender small-boned body of Andiette de la Roque-Loubéjac, laced by a latticework of scars.

Mathias Delvaux watched me with compassion. 'I know what you must feel, my friend. But you will not suffer again. Believe me, it is behind you. You will make a *mariage de convenance* with some attractive widow, who is pleasant and agreeable and brings with her a large and useful dowry. She will bear your children and minister to your needs without prying into your secrets. We will find a woman for you of whom you need not be afraid.'

Once I would have found this complete manipulation of my most intimate life outrageous. But a shroud of curious and opaque apathy enclosed me like an inverted goblet. I nodded my head in docile acceptance.

'When you have settled in Salon,' said Mathias Delvaux, 'you will begin to prepare your yearly almanacs. You will prophesy the events of the months of worldly change and turmoil. By this means your reputation as an astrologer will increase, earning you fame and gold and a devoted following that extends far beyond Provence. There is no one who will compete with you. You will hold the secret of reading the future in the fire. You will also hold the secret of the unfolding plans of your masters at court, as they manipulate the hands of King and government. And if all goes according to our design, your real work will then begin. For you will incarnate, in words which can be read by all men, the past and the future of our strange story. You will do so in language no man can understand, but which every man imagines he comprehends. A glimmer, a flicker, a flash may leap forth like a fish from a pool, but nothing will truly be grasped, save by those who know and need to understand the pattern. You will write for those who are dead, to enshrine them; for those who are living, to bemuse them; and for those yet unborn, to instruct the few among them who hold the key. A few things will stand clear as a monolith in the glaring light of day, to set ignorant men's minds racing. Much more will be shrouded in shadow. In the end no one will know whether you are fuddled in your cups, or a madman, or inspired by God.'

'You have chosen a charming role for me, M. Delvaux.'

'It should appeal to your sense of irony, Maître de Notredame. Have you not always wished for wealth and a name that resounds across France?'

Once, I thought, once . . . But the court gentleman now lay a charred heap of ashes, consumed by its own absurdity in the purgatorial and purifying fire. This new Michel was a husk, the flesh and bones drawn from the bodily cavities and steeped in bitumen, an Egyptian mummy whose heart and brains and entrails lay stored neatly in sealed canopic jars. I knew the dull apathy would cease once I left Orval. But I could not yet measure how much in me had truly, irrevocably changed.

'And when I have acquired this name that resounds across France, what then?'

'You ask too many questions, my friend. We must see what the future unfolds. Many years will pass before that time. By my calculations and yours, King François has left to him only four pox-ridden years of life. New powers will rise at his death. And at the centre will be our own, François de Guise and his brother Charles, Archbishop of Reims, who will rapidly obtain the Cardinal's hat. The second generation of the house of Guise shall build a new Temple of Solomon on the foundations laid by the first. Thus we begin.'

'Why do you trust me with this great responsibility? How do you know I will not fail, or turn against you?'

He only smiled at me. 'You forget, Maître de Notredame, that I have seen your soul, which you have held before me bleeding while tears ran down your face and you clung to me as to a father. I have also seen your power, and know that the depths from which it springs are not those of fantasy and delusion. You will not fail. As for treachery, though I do not doubt you are an accomplished liar, you will be bound by three things. You will be bound first by your own oath, which you will give to us on the night of the thirteenth October.'

'I cannot believe you are sentimental about dates,' I said.

'That too. But the sun then will be entering the sign of the

Scorpion and the moon will be full, a lunar eclipse that crosses your horoscope in the house of death. It is a fitting time for a death and a rebirth into life.'

'And the second thing?'

'Your own fate will bind you. For you realise as well as I that you have been driven to us along your thorny and lonely path from the earliest years of your life. And you have been driven so by your own soul. I know you now believe yourself apathetic, drained, devoid of will. The process to which you have been subjected absorbs the life-force for a time. That will pass. But the pattern which has enmeshed you will continue to guide you, for it is the substance of your innermost self.'

'And the third?'

'The final thing that will bind you is your loyalty to the house of Guise. The ties of human love are more powerful than almost any other, Maître de Notredame. This cord encircles you more tightly than any you have experienced in your life, save perhaps your love for your grandfather, Jean de St Rémy. You will not fail it, nor it you. You do not even know yet to what depths it has taken root. You think it bemused fascination. Yet you have recognised each one of them. Do you think such love as this springs full-grown from a few brief encounters in one short lifetime? It is a tie of the soul.'

Part Four
THE PROPHET
1547 – 1566

Blessed is he that is born during sleep; he shall know no evil. For thou hast purified with great care, and hast endured much in thy days. Thee no one hath overcome, and no one shall there be that will again awaken thee, even as long as there is counted as much as thine enemies have counted from their eyrie.

Paracelsus

XIX

For two years I wandered aimlessly through Provence, tending the sick and decocting confitures and jellies, prescribing love-philtres and casting horoscopes. In each town, great or small, I was careful to remain just long enough to make an impression on the townsfolk, then moved on. I left an increasingly swollen reputation behind me. And everywhere I travelled, I sought out the *noblesse*, and scrupulously befriended the rich and the powerful, and listened, and learned, and stored horoscopes and information, and preserved an enigmatic silence.

The slow and inexorable collapse of King François was whispered behind hands wherever I went. Riddled with the pox and the gnawing disillusion of a glamorous but ineffectual reign, robbed of his best-beloved heir and confronted with a younger son whom he detested, it was apparent that he had not long to live. The nation waited breathlessly for the new reign to begin, the new galaxy of stars to rise in heaven. Once again, peace was wearily declared between King and Emperor, this time at Crépy. I heard one name above all others, praised over and over as saviour and hero and defender of the country: Claude de Lorraine, Duc de Guise.

The stealthy spread of the Lutheran and Calvinist heresies was no longer a minor irritation, no longer a mere seasonal rash. It could no longer be extirpated by a few well-placed immolations or preached into nullity by persistent clergy. Like water, it had permeated into the secret vacuum left by the plague's passage and the blatancy of Roman corruption, sinking to the very roots of the nation. It had acquired the solemn dignity of a holy movement. The consequences were as yet unreadable. I sought answers in the fire; but I saw only a torrent of blood.

I was summoned by the terrified town consuls to Aix, then to Marseilles, where the pestilence had broken out again with renewed rapacity. Through my efforts there I acquired a considerable degree of fame and a considerable quantity of gold. At times, sparingly and in the appropriate place, as a skilled cook uses a rare spice, I displayed that gift I had learned at Orval. Using my occult powers, I would astonish some bemused nobleman by prognosticating one or another petty household drama. The word spread. When I entered a new town, people spoke of me not only as a skilled healer, but as a prophet.

I travelled to Chambéry to see the Holy Shroud of Our Lord, brought from Constantinople by the Knights of the Temple three and a half centuries before. I stared for a long time at the stiff and ancient piece of linen, yellow with age, stained by fire, marked with the unknown imprint of twisted limbs and injured hands and a man's face in the calm repose of apparent death. I had no visions or presentiments. It was only a piece of cloth. But the face haunted my dreams for many weeks after.

I was told I must be established in my new role by the time King François died. That was, by my reckoning, still two years in the future. Nevertheless, I found myself delaying the journey to Salon. I travelled restlessly back and forth, from the borders of Savoie to the borders of Navarre, as though I were in flight from something. I received no messages or instructions. I wondered sometimes, in the obscure lonely hours of the night, if I had dreamed it all. But if I chose to drive from my mind what could not be unlearned, others unwittingly reminded me of it.

I visited my friend, Nicolas de Vicheray, in Bordeaux. I had not seen him since my flight from Agen with Blanche and my children, when the Inquisition descended on the town. He stared at me lengthily, a deep frown creasing his brow.

'Something has happened to you, Michel,' he said. 'Oh, no, I do not mean your tragedy, which we heard about with great sorrow. That too has left its mark. But there is something about your eyes. There is a distant look, as though you peered through things, and a strange bitterness. If I did not know you so well, I would be frightened of you. Perhaps you need to settle down again. You have been a long time without a wife.'

I nodded, and murmured agreement, and said my strangeness must undoubtedly derive from many years of rootless and solitary wandering.

I visited Monseigneur Ammanien de Foix in Carcassonne. Nearly twenty years had passed, and he was an old man now, grown grey and fat. But his handsome dark eyes still shone with the same shrewd and amused look. He offered to take me again to Bézu, suggesting I might view it differently now. I declined. It was enough that I was one of them. I had no need to meet the dead ghosts of the Temple when my life had become inextricably entangled with the living ones.

I travelled to Tarascon, and presented myself to Claude de Savoie, Comte de Tende, Governor and Grand Seneschal of Provence. He too was a thread in the network – a round, red, jovial man fond of his cups, whose ready laughter and conviviality belied the stern competence with which he held the reins of his fief. Like any ordinary patron, he invited me to stay at his residence to discuss his horoscope with him. So I followed my grandfather's footsteps at last into the great feudal château of King René d'Anjou, which brooded over the swift-flowing Rhône. In the shadows of the winding staircases, amidst the turrets and towers, flitted the spectres of the Order of the Crescent, King René's equivalent of the Garter and the Golden Fleece. And it was here, while I visited with the Comte de Tende, that I received the first communication from Claude de Guise.

Within a twelvemonth of its signing, the Treaty of Crépy had been rendered waste parchment. King François had never overcome the humiliation of Pavia. He longed for some glorious victory, even now, at the shadowy demise of his reign, which would vindicate his ghost in the eyes of a dreaded posterity. In consequence, the French army besieged Boulogne, captured by the English a year before.

It was at the siege of Boulogne, Claude de Guise wrote me, that his son François, Comte d'Aumale, had been brutally wounded and lay at death's threshold. According to the doctors, he could not possibly live. And if by some miracle, some divine intervention, he did indeed survive, it was feared he would be blinded. A sacrifice like that shadowy and spectral ancestor of my dreams, that white-robed Sorcerer-King whom Rome betrayed, François de Guise had taken a lance thrust over the left eye, just above the eyebrow. The head had passed down through his nose and right cheek, and out through the neck below the ear.

I was summoned to the ancient château-fortress of Gisors, the old capital of Vexin, northwest of Paris. The journey would require three weeks on horseback. If the Comte d'Aumale lived, he would be carried by litter to meet me. If he died, we must quickly make new plans.

Claude de Savoie loaned me a horse. With my rational mind, I knew the young count would live, for I had read this crisis in his horoscope. Yet as I galloped madly through the plains of Guyenne, hardly stopping to snatch a brief hour's sleep or a scrap of bread and cheese, I recognised the truth of Mathias Delvaux's words. I had not perceived how deeply the roots of the bond had dug and ferreted their way into me, like a silent mole burrowing underground. But at the thought of François de Guise's death, I felt as though it were my own heart that had been lanced.

Through the labyrinthine honeycomb of underground tunnels and passageways, dank and foetid with the odour of sour soil and mould, I was led into the heart of the fortress. Past the empty prisoners' cells marked with the desperate graffiti of long-dead Knights entombed in their own preceptory, my guide moved silently ahead of me through the half-gloom.

O Mater Dei, memento mei.

I heard only the sound of water dripping, and muffled footfalls on the hard earth.

François de Guise was a piteous sight. He had stubbornly clung to life, thanks to a grim determination to survive born of the impassioned conviction of his mission, and to the near-miraculous recuperative powers of his young body. I wondered, with a certain vague awe, whether there might not indeed be something unnatural, or supernatural, about this blood. The King had sent his own physician, Ambroise Paré, who – with a pair of enormous farrier's pincers – had endeavoured to extract the embedded lance head. He had put his foot on the young prince's face, had wrenched out the broken stump through bone and muscle and nerves and veins and arteries. Now the Comte d'Aumale lay mending in the shrouded bed in his dimly lit chamber, weak from fever and loss of blood. His face was still a torn and twisted nightmare, despite the weeks that had passed since his ordeal. One eye was completely closed with a great puckered lesion over it, the other was half-shut with a blossom of purple bruise. His nose was broken, his cheek swollen to twice its size. Like a black flower clotted with dried blood, a gaping wound disfigured the white skin of his neck.

Only the whisper of the fire and the sputtering of the tapers troubled the silence in the chamber. Almost overnight, Claude de Guise had metamorphosed into an old man. He stared at me with his austere cat-eyes, ringed by the dark shadows of his anxiety.

'You warned me he would be wounded in battle,' the father said softly. 'You said he would live. It was the only reason I consented to let Paré draw out the lance. I wish to thank you.'

'There is no need, my lord. It was his fate that he should recover. I did not know how terrible the wound would be.'

The duke paced back and forth for a few moments, his eyes bleak. No sound emerged from the curtained bed.

'Each physician who has examined him has offered a different opinion. From you, I know I will have the truth. Will he be blind in one eye?'

I probed the wound. François de Guise did not cry out. He gritted his teeth and muttered to me, in a hoarse voice, to get on with it. When I had finished, I inspected his horoscope again.

'He will regain his sight. There will be a scar. But that is all.'

A little hiss of relief, gentle as the hissing of the fire, escaped the Comte d'Aumale's lips. He shifted laboriously on to his side, his back turned toward me, and the fur coverlet slipped from his bare shoulders to reveal, between the shoulder-blades, a curious blemish against the white-olive skin. A birthmark shaped like a small cross, blood-red.

I stared unashamedly at the mark, for I had never seen its like before. I looked up into the duke's cool cat-eyes.

'We are born with it,' said Claude de Guise quietly. 'It is the sign.'

For three days I remained among the ghosts of the Temple at Gisors. Although he was already mending and did not need my care, I eagerly tended the young count. I mixed the poultices as my grandfather had taught me, poultices that would knit torn flesh, and prevent mortification, and ensure a clean scar. François de Guise was restless and irritable, resenting intensely this bondage to bedclothes and possets and cosseting. Only the music of a blind lutist, whom his father had brought from Joinville, seemed to soothe him. But he never complained nor uttered any sound that might betray the pain he still suffered. He could scarcely open his mouth to sip the broth we served him, for it wrenched the unhealed torn flesh beneath the skin, where the lance had passed through his nose and the inside of his cheek. Along with the curious birthmark, he had obviously inherited his father's iron control.

I told him that men of our blood ought to take pleasure in building a reputation upon the ruin of the body.

Sometimes, to comfort himself, he would whisper to me of his dreams. The vision of kingship never left him, even in the midst of his pain.

'I will resurrect the Temple,' he murmured between swollen lips. 'I will restore the Order. Can you envision a King of France surrounded by his bodyguard of white-robed Knights, each bearing the cross *pattée*, a King to whom Rome will once more swear allegiance?'

And it seemed, when he spoke thus, that the ghosts who haunted the château-fortress of Gisors pressed close to listen, to drink in his promise, to whisper amongst themselves through the sputtering of the tapers and the hissing of the fire.

On the day that I prepared to leave Gisors, Charles de Guise, Archbishop of Reims, swept in with his train from the court at Fontainebleau. As fresh and cool and sanguine as a flower on a spring day, he exhibited no anxiety. He merely gave a little moue at the dreadful mask which peered at him from the shrouded bed.

'They say the ladies find a battle wound irresistible,' he said sweetly in his smooth musical voice. 'There is no telling what some men will do to earn the approval of women.'

The trace of a pained smile cracked his brother's face. The Archbishop turned to me gracefully and bowed.

'It is a pleasure to see you again, Maître de Notredame. You said he would live, and lo! he has returned from the threshold of Pluto's realm. He has been more fortunate than King Dagobert. But you did not warn us of the form of my brother's new incarnation. I hope it does not completely spoil his beauty.'

He seated himself on the bed, spreading his robes about him, and gently touched the terrible wound with his long white fingers.

'A scar won in battle is a useful thing,' he said. 'It reminds people that you have spilled your blood in their defence. We will call you le Balafré. It will be a good name to be known by, when we place you on the throne.'

For another year I roamed the towns of Provence. And at last, on a chill and crystalline day in January, while a cold sun shone, I rode into Salon-en-Craux, south of Avignon.

I took residence under the aegis of Monseigneur de Santacroce, in the great sandstone château of the Archbishops of Arles which towered, ruddy and ornately imposing, on its steep rock above the town. From there, I cultivated the local citizens in leisurely fashion, like a gardener. I was in no hurry to leave the sheltering walls of the palace. I knew what was required of me here, and I did not relish it. I dispensed my cures and ointments from the lavish apartments which Mgr de Santacroce had appointed for me. I made frequent trips into the barren countryside, to gather winter herbs and savour the remaining days of my solitude.

And one day when the sun blazed like a brilliant white eye in the cloudless heavens, while the burgeoning spring brought crocuses and cherry blossoms to flower in lavish carpets and bursting canopies of vivid saffron and purple and dusty pink, we heard that King François, the *roi chevalier*, the Sunflower, the *vieux galant*, had died in his château of Rambouillet.

Mgr de Santacroce told me of the forlorn scene at the royal deathbed. The King and his son had hated each other with a stony and inflexible hatred. At the end, however, nudged by the omnipresent reminder of the waiting gates of heaven and hell, they had embraced amidst the prayers and sobbing of the attendants. Both had wept. The dying King had begged the Dauphin to retain his old ministers, as well as to banish from power Anne de Montmorency, Constable of France, disgraced and retired several years before. He had pleaded that kindness and understanding be accorded his mistress, Madame d'Estampes. And finally, as the shadows descended to claim him, he whispered that above all things, Prince Henri must beware of the house of Guise – whose aim, he gasped, was to strip him and his children to their doublets, and his people to their shirts.

Whatever the old King's revelation, it eluded his son. Which stars would shine in the heaven of the new court quickly became evident. King Henri II now ruled France. But Diane de Poitiers, Duchesse de Valentinois, twenty years his elder, ruled King Henri. And the Connêtable de Montmorency, the dogged and loyal and humourless old warrior whose ambitions had been pruned so ruthlessly during the old King's reign, was promptly recalled and offered the reins of government.

It was said among the gossips of Salon that an old wetnurse and a decrepit watchdog now controlled the King. But it was soon apparent that the true sovereigns of the new reign would in fact be a trinity. Like the Star of Bethlehem, a new double luminary had risen in the east, over Lorraine. At the third point of the triangle, the pivot upon which all balanced and turned, stood François de Guise, *le Balafré*, twenty-eight years of age, now Duc d'Aumale and Governor of Dauphiny and Savoie. Hand in hand with him, united with him in all things, was his sleek and elegant brother Charles, duke and Archbishop of Reims, Duc de Chevreuse. Although only twenty-three, he was already head of the King's household, Chancellor of the Order of St Michel, Master of the Chapelle Royale. And now he had been dispatched to Rome, to receive his Cardinal's hat.

As they had promised, they found me a wife.

She was called Anne Ponsart Gemelle, a well-connected and wealthy widow. She was sensible and clever, well-educated and widely read, with that dry wit and peaceably realistic attitude toward life and people which reflects a deep and imperturbable serenity. She was intelligent but not inquisitive, capable but not managerial. I appraised the smooth dark hair coiled beneath the modest widow's cap, the finely chiselled bones of her face as clean and pure as a young boy's, the lucid brown eyes, the firm lips. And knew I need not fear her.

We married in November, taking up our residence in the small but elegant house I purchased in an impasse off the Place de la Poissonnerie, overshadowed by the crenellated towers of the Archbishop's palace. On our wedding night, no ghosts whispered, flittered or brooded about me to remind me of other lips, other eyes. No frenzied dark yearnings erupted from the recesses of my soul to churn my blood and lodge in my throat. I was safe.

In the nocturnal solitude of the little observatory I built at the top of the house, I began my work at last. I could not control my *daemon*, though I could summon it at will. It issued out of my trance and gripped me with vicious talons, leaving me numb and bloodless afterward. The visions which emerged were often chaotic. Sometimes they terrified me, and I remained shut in my study for days, unable to continue. Sometimes I plummeted into profound melancholy over the pathos of what I had seen. Sometimes I laughed like a mindless lunatic. And the work grew, like some strange luminescent fungus in the darkness, burgeoning with its own autonomous and unknowable life.

And the machinery which those I served had set in motion began to reveal its first harvest, its first early green fruit. The new King had spent the opening year of his reign in festivities, hunting parties and the white arms of his middle-aged mistress. Now, prompted by the exquisitely gentle pressure of Charles de Guise, his Master of the Chapelle Royale and spiritual advisor, he proceeded to exhibit the same fatal predilection for Italy as did his father.

I received a series of letters from Charles, now Cardinal de Guise, who was happily embroiled in the convoluted and festering web of Italian politics at Rome. Imperiously but charmingly, he demanded from me prognostications, advice, insights into the horoscopes of those with whom he treated, from Pope to lackeys. And all the while, with his superb seductive diplomacy, he fished in the Papal pool for the crown of Naples – once an heirloom of the dukes of Lorraine, now to be reinstated upon his brother's golden head. Charles de Guise's mission to Italy, nominally undertaken to receive from the trembling arthritic hands of His Holiness the honour of the Red Hat, was in fact carefully calculated to enmesh France in another Italian war.

Nurtured by his skilful machinations, revolt against Habsburg rule erupted in Parma and Piacenza. The Emperor's troops – led by Ferrante de Gonzaga of Mantua, Count of Guastalla and Lieutenant-General in Italy for the Imperial crown – flooded the Milanese. Fearing another sack of the Eternal City, the Pope appealed in desperation to the Cardinal de Guise for French aid. Charles de Guise was treating with Rome and, in secret, with the Count of Guastalla simultaneously. He smiled sweetly and promised His Holiness the mighty assistance of the armies of the King of France – for the modest price of Naples.

He almost succeeded. But at the last moment King Henri panicked and withdrew his offer of support. Ferrante de Gonzaga gobbled up Parma and Piacenza. There was no war, and the Cardinal de Guise, drooping like a wilted poppy in a summer shower, returned to France with an empty hat.

Unquenched, he brought another prize with him from Italy – a marriage for his brother François to Anna Atestina d'Este, daughter of the duke of Ferrara, granddaughter of King Louis XII of France. War in Italy would have enabled François de Guise to prove his soldier's skill and steal a crown. As an alternative, this marriage brought him a powerful Italian ally, an enormous dowry, and a princess descended from the royal blood of the Valois. Move the knight one step closer to the king, graft a branch here, another branch there, suffuse the dying house of Valois with fresh Lorraine blood . . .

Three years after I had settled in Salon, I prepared my first almanac. Most of the prognostications, arranged month by month, were strictly astrological. Some came from my visions. Some were based on the practical knowledge I possessed of the plans and machinations of my masters at the court. Despite

Mathias Delvaux's predictions of the work's success, I was astonished by the extent and immediacy of its popularity. A new prophet was greedily accepted into the ranks of the *illuminati*. No astrologer before me, it was said, had possessed such an uncannily accurate faculty of judgement. My reputation among the gentry of Salon and the surrounding countryside blossomed like a spring garden. For this gloss and glitter I paid a price. The poorer townspeople grew increasingly suspicious of me.

I saw it first in the way they recoiled from me in the street, making the sign of the cross and muttering uneasily behind their hands. Familiar whispers of heresy and sorcery began to wisp about like pale elusive shreds of smoke. The populace was in an incendiary mood, for Huguenot congregations were proliferating and included many of the aristocracy. Availing themselves of this excuse, the peasants would rally under the banner of religious fervour and satisfy their ancient grudge against their social superiors. Banding together in *cabans*, they would periodically riot and, with insane glee, pillage the houses of the rich.

As I was becoming increasingly wealthy, I became increasingly alarmed. I withdrew from all contact with the ordinary townsfolk. I tried to assuage my fears with the familiar view from my study window – the massive Archbishop's palace on its steep rock. I would also recall, with reassurance, the château at Tarascon, where lived my friend Claude de Savoie, Governor of Provence. And I continued my work.

Another event of immeasurable significance occurred at court. Charles de Guise, in addition to his other dazzling talents, displayed a positive genius for matchmaking. Little Marie Stuart, his niece and six-year-old Queen of Scotland, was shipped from her stormy and war-torn realm to the court of France. Here, to the horror of the Connêtable de Montmorency – who had increasingly assumed the role of implacable enemy to my masters – she was betrothed to the King's firstborn son, the Dauphin François. By this match, her handsome and cunning uncles, *heureux et galants*, were abruptly transformed from the status of foreign princes to members of the royal family.

The unborn children of my visions stirred in the dark silence of the womb. The pieces were set on the board for the first game.

In the spring of the Year of Our Lord 1550, I was visited by a dream, brief but clear as a piece of crystal. It reminded me with gentle and inexorable insistence that those who served the Order, and manipulated the secret threads of government, were not gods, but only men.

Passing slowly before me as through a dark mist, a great sluggish funeral procession wended solemnly along a dusty and empty road to a vast vault of marble and porphyry and jasper, the lintel of the gaping black doorway crowned by the double-armed cross of Lorraine. An unending line of mourners, draped and hooded in black like creeping beetles, bore on their shoulders two biers, two lonely and eloquent biers, shrouded in jet velvet and cloth-of-gold. The sound of wailing women threaded itself like an eerie shuttle between the leaden tolling of bells and the dull heartbeat of tympanums and the unearthly chanting of monks, while white tapers flickered and danced madly and at last were snuffed into darkness.

In the morning I sent an urgent messenger to Claude, Duc de Guise. But it was only a futile gesture, an empty mummery. I had inspected his horoscope carefully, and seen what we both had recognised eight years before. That grim warrior had known from the beginning the length of time he had left.

My messenger crossed *en route* with one from François, telling me of his father's death at Joinville on the thirtieth of April. In his last moments, it seemed Claude de Guise believed he had been poisoned. Only his dignity forbade him making a specific accusation. It was known he had been pressuring the King to take arms against the quarrelling Genoese and invade Italy. Someone had seen fit to forestall this plan before it bore fruit, just as the young Cardinal had been thwarted in a similar enterprise. And one black-draped bier had vanished into the maw of the vault.

A second letter followed a month later, announcing a second tragedy. The old Pope had died and the sacred throne of St Peter lay vacant and sweetly beckoning. Charles de Guise had once more travelled to the Holy City, this time with his uncle Jean, Cardinal de Lorraine, King Henri's candidate for the papal tiara. Vast sums of money were squandered on fruitless bribes in the College of Cardinals – which obligingly swallowed the gold and elected an Italian pontiff instead. The disappointed pair returned, seething, to France. At Lyons they received the news of Claude's death. Jean, Cardinal de Lorraine, the golden sybarite with the cornflower eyes, was dining at the home of a friend when the courier arrived. And although he had known, although he had been warned long ago, something human and vulnerable to grief within him displaced the Order's steely mouthpiece. He was seized by an apoplectic stroke and fell dead amidst the roast venison, and the stuffed partridges, and the wine.

Amid the critical opening moves of the great game, the first generation of the house of Guise thus passed into the darkness, making way for the second. And even their deaths were characterised by the impeccable and unerring timing which those two extraordinary brothers had possessed throughout their charismatic careers. The poisoner had defeated his own ends. François was now Duc de Guise in his father's stead. And the title of Cardinal de Lorraine, as well as the staggering accumulation of wealth and benefices which Jean had gathered into his coffers, spilled *en bloc* into the dexterous white hands of his enigmatic nephew.

For the first time I began to appreciate how little the individual personalities mattered in this many-armed and many-eyed scheme. As a man, Claude de Guise was now insignificant, merely a dead nobleman whose embalmed body awaited ritual interment in the family vault. As a repository for the sacred blood, Claude de Guise possessed meaning only as long as his lifethread extended and his work was accomplished. And Jean de Lorraine, whose eyes had tracked me through so many years, so many journeys . . . When the mission was completed, what then happened to the man?

Their faces – the ascetic, austere, scar-seamed face that could brighten so suddenly into a handsome smile; the fair, charming, blue-eyed face exuding dissipation like a potent scent – seemed to materialise like shadows in the shadows of my candlelit study, seemed to flicker in the embrace of the fire. Somewhere deep within me, despite the impersonality and the irrevocability of these passings, there gnawed a great grief.

In the following year I published another almanac, which proved even more successful than the first. I also began work on my *Traicte des Fardemens*, a little book on cosmetic preparations and recipes for confitures. And a year later, when the treatise was finished and the third almanac begun, Charles de Guise – now Cardinal de Lorraine – at last succeeded in pulling the royal roof down upon the King's obtuse head. War between Valois and Habsburg burst once again into brilliant blossom.

King Henri seized from the duchy of Lorraine the three bishoprics of Metz, Toul and Verdun. At the instigation of their duke, the inhabitants of the towns opened their gates like willing women. The Emperor, his pride stung, irritated as by a gadfly, led an enormous force to besiege Metz, the ancient capital of the Merovingian kings.

It was generally believed that the city, ringed by crumbling walls, poorly fortified and ill-prepared for a siege, would fall in a matter of days. The King sent the young Duc de Guise – whose bravery as a soldier was undisputed, but whose prowess as a strategist was as yet unknown and unpredictable – to defend his newly acquired possession. The Emperor was delighted to find that a mere mincing courtier had been placed on the board as his opponent. It would be almost too easy.

'I will bring the walls of Metz down,' he told the French ambassador, 'upon M. de Guise's head.'

But that ambitious golden head was not destined to be bowed beneath the rubble of a fallen city. We had planned it with the greatest care, the most meticulous efforts, making use of propitious configurations that favoured his horoscope to ensure the foregone conclusion. A popular soldiers' ditty began to make the rounds of the inns and taverns.

> My lord of Guise is here at home
> With many a noble at his side,
> With the two children of Vendôme,
> With bold Nemours in all his pride,
> And Strozzi too, a warrior tried;

Who ceases not, by night or day,
Around the city walls to stride,
And strengthen Metz in every way.

At last, so stout was her defence
From Metz they moved their guns away;
And, with the laugh at their expense,
A-tramping went their whole array.
And at their tail the noble lord
Of Guise sent forth a goodly throng
Of cavalry, with lance and sword,
To teach them how to tramp along.

Le Balafré had entered the stage in a great starburst of magnificent panoply. From Metz, the unknown and untried young commander returned as a national hero, the darling of Paris. The Emperor burned down Theroenne in peevish retaliation, and limped away from his lost cities into a slow decline.

The stars and *La Rotta*, it seemed, conspired in amorous delight to nourish the designs of my masters. Yet I sensed, even without the aid of my visions, the slow coiling and compression of fire and smoke, like a tight spring within the heart of the sleeping volcano. Forces were at work in the soul of the nation which were ungovernable by the nimble mind of Charles de Guise and the military prowess of his brother.

Persecution of heretics had attained a new level of atrocity. Violence sanctioned by the assiduous Huguenot-hunting of both King and Church erupted everywhere among the poorer classes like monstrous boils. The peasant *cabans* proliferated with the rapidity of rabbits. Half the court, people said, was infected with heresy. Even the Queen had been seen reading Calvinist literature. The hypocrisy of a court which encouraged persecution yet steeped itself in the very object of its hunt fostered further enraged conflagrations. I stared into the fire and saw ominous visions, like a great running river of blood emptying into a corpse-ridden sea.

One morning a young man knocked at the door of my house: a slight, graceful, dapper man with pale grey eyes that mirrored the winter skies of Lorraine, and a winning smile that revealed slightly prominent teeth. His name was Jean-Aimé de Chavigny, and he had travelled from Beaune, where he had functioned as the town's mayor. He possessed degrees in both law and theology, was a linguist and a classical scholar besides. He had resigned his office, he said, that he might come to Salon. Here he wished to study judicial astrology under the celebrated Michel Nostradamus, whose prophetic almanacs had created such a stir throughout the country.

I surveyed his beautifully cut and understated clothes, his cool clever eyes, his sleek smile, his carefully manicured hands, his long, narrow, mercurial face full of craft. It was obvious that he reeked of the court.

'Who has sent you to me?' I asked, although I knew the answer.

'I have a friend at court,' he said, 'named Jean Dorat. He is a poet, a friend of *La Pléiade*, and an ardent admirer of your almanacs.'

'Has the Cardinal de Lorraine then decided that I am in need of a watchdog?'

He burst into delighted laughter. 'I am not your watchdog, Maître de Notredame. I am your servant. Truly, I have not been sent to pry into your business. I am here to help you, for the task you have undertaken will be more taxing than you realise.'

'I was not aware that I needed help.'

'Often we are not aware of our own needs,' replied the young ex-mayor of Beaune with a sunny and tooth-filled smile. 'But the *Centuries* will need careful editing and copying. According to my understanding, seven of them must be ready for publication by the end of this year. I write a fair hand, and will make you an excellent scribe and secretary. I am also said to possess an unusual gift for cryptography.'

I began to laugh. Amidst war and religious persecution, while the nation rocked perilously as a fragile boat on a hostile and tempestuous sea, Charles de Guise concerned himself with the perfection of my bizarre work, born of fire and darkness. I reminded myself carefully that it was not being written for him, but for those who would follow.

'We must be attentive to the future,' said M. de Chavigny, as

178

though he had divined my thoughts. 'When you are dead, someone must be able to portray your innocent face to the world. Your name will bear too much notoriety not to provoke question. Who better than I, your humble and devoted student, who has lived with you over the years and tended faithfully to all your affairs?'

I stared into those distant grey eyes and again saw the two noble bodies carried on their black-draped biers, into the depths of the massive vault. The pathos of their passage pinched my heart with insistent fingers. So vast, so cold, so unconcerned was this infinite silken web that I felt a bleak desolation. We were all – myself, the old duke, the bright Cardinal, the nameless minions and agents and scions and pawns – only very small grains of brown dust blown about in a little breeze, motes that would vanish without trace, invisible insects weaving the sounds of a passing summer's day. Even my death was already arranged, already accounted for, already screened with the appropriate camouflage for the years to come when, as Mathias Delvaux had prophesied, my name resounded across France and down the labyrinthine corridors of time.

But I was bound. Mysterious and elusive ties bound me, as well as the explicit ones. M. de Chavigny and I studied each other for a few moments, each taking the other's measure.

'Do not be distressed by my apparent callousness, Maître de Notredame. You know we must plan for all contingencies.' He smiled. 'And if nothing else, you will find me a faithful servant. I will keep the dogs of Salon away, so that you are free to perform your work in peace.'

Another sort of marriage had been arranged for me. In the end I accepted it. I liked Jean-Aimé de Chavigny, and discovered that it was indeed easier to share the burden. He was born under the sign of the Twins, and acquired gossip and information as though he breathed it into his lungs from the air itself. Anne was fascinated by him, and found his talk of court affairs intriguing. She was happy to offer him a room in the house. By this time she was pregnant once again, and willingly entrusted to him much of the management of the household. His presence was not questioned. It was usual for an astrologer to train an apprentice, as my grandfather had once trained me.

And so my famulus, my *döppelganger*, who would justify my name to posterity, took his abode with me in Salon.

In the spring of the following year, Jean-Aimé de Chavigny rode on horseback to the publisher Macé Bonhomme at Lyons, bearing in his pouch the first seven sections of the *Centuries*. I had at last given birth, after a gestation spanning thirteen years. The child had been torn from me and given to the currents of the river, like Moses in his basket of reeds. Now it must float to its august destiny. I dedicated the unfinished book to my newborn son César. Two children had issued from my seed, one born of the womb of my gentle and sensible wife, the other born of fire and smoke and the terrifying embrace of my *daemon*. I felt a sour gratitude that my masters had laid claim to only one of them.

I returned to my confitures and my beauty creams and my love-philtres and my horoscopes and my almanacs. And waited. The manuscript was published in May. I received a brief note from Charles, Cardinal de Lorraine, informing me that he had seen several copies of the *Centuries* at court, and that one had reached the hands of the Queen. The opinion of *La Pléiade*, his little cultivated garden of poets, was that the style was appalling. The courtiers sat shaking their heads in confusion, trying in vain to decipher the flickering images that leaped forth like flailing fishes from a dark pool, only to vanish in ambiguity.

A madman, a drunkard fuddled in his cups, a prophet inspired by God: Mathias Delvaux had foretold what reception would await me. In Salon I was known as all three. To the local populace, the book was incomprehensible, this enigmatic new progeny which had flowed from the pen of the strange Jew in their midst, who performed mysterious and nameless nocturnal deeds in his secret study, who lived bastioned behind the powerful protection of the Archbishop of Arles and the Governor of Provence. I began to hear, among the whisperings of heretic and sorcerer, that of devil-worshipper.

It was closer to the truth than was comfortable – as it had once been for the Temple. I withdrew further into sullen silence, and forbade Anne to walk in the streets without the protection of M. de Chavigny or the household servants.

And I waited.

My masters waited too. The King rode and hunted and supped with his ageing mistress and played endless games of tennis with his dear friend François, Duc de Guise. The Emperor Charles, weary and sick and disillusioned after the siege of Metz, began to abdicate his bouquet of thrones, flower by flower, to his son, Philip of Spain. The Peace of Augsburg was signed in Germany, granting freedom of worship to the Lutherans. The French peasantry rebelled against King Henri's salt tax. They were brutally suppressed by the Connêtable de Montmorency in Guyenne, and quieted by the Duc de Guise with gallantry and mercy in Dauphiny. The Italian Queen produced another Valois spawn. The royal-blooded Duchesse de Guise produced a golden-haired son, christened Henri after the King. I was immediately requested, of course, to inspect the child's horoscope. As I did so, the rumbling of great underground currents in the maw of the earth grew louder. I thought of the earth-shaking god Poseidon, lord of the subterranean waterways, rising from his bed in the womb of the Mother to tear the land to pieces. And I waited and waited.

And then one day my waiting was over.

XX

In the beginning of July in the Year of Our Lord 1556, I received a messenger from the household of Claude de Savoie, Comte de Tende, Governor and Grand Seneschal of Provence. I was to attend him immediately at the château at Tarascon, upon the King's business.

It seemed that Queen Catherine de' Medici had been given a copy of the *Centuries* by some unnamed courtier. A curious quatrain had been marked which disturbed her profoundly.

> Le lyon jeune le vieux surmontera
> En champ bellique par singulier duelle;

Dans cage d'or les yeux luy crevera,
Deux classes une, puis mourir, mort cruelle.

This quatrain, Claude de Savoie told me, smiling behind his plump hand, bore a strange and terrible similarity to a prophecy made years before by an Italian astrologer called Luc Gauricus. It foretold the King's death in his forty-first year, from a head wound incurred in single combat, in an enclosed space.

'Tell me,' said Claude de Savoie. 'Did you truly see that in the fire? Or was it contrived to fit the other?'

'I saw it in the fire. But I knew well enough whose death was portended. That is one of the reasons why the first seven *Centuries* had to be published so soon, unfinished.'

'It seems that Gauricus has sent the Queen a letter. It arrived from Mantua almost simultaneously with the mysterious appearance of the marked *Centuries* among her papers.'

'I hope I do not meet Luc Gauricus' fate. I do not think I would survive the *strappado*. My incipient gout is punishment enough.'

'You are safe enough, so far. The King cannot decide whether to believe the prophecies or not,' said the Comte de Tende. 'The Cardinal de Lorraine has written to me of the royal response. It is a sad and amusing story. M. le Connêtable de Montmorency was present in the chamber when Gauricus' letter was read. The King said:

'"See, my *compère*, what death they predict for me."

'"Ah, Sire," replied M. le Connêtable, "would you believe these rascals? They are nothing but liars and babblers. Throw it in the fire."

'"My *compère*," said the King, "why should I? They sometimes tell the truth. I do not care if my death is in that manner rather than in any other. I would even prefer it – to die by the hand of whomever he might be, so long as he was brave and valiant, and so long as I kept my honour."

'That,' finished Claude de Savoie, 'is a brave man, and a man of honour. It is a pathetic affair that he cannot govern his own realm, but must keep Montmorency beside him like a clumsy and faithful old dog. Who knows what might have been achieved already without the obstinate enmity of that old man?'

It was fortunate that King Henri possessed no great love of history, and would not think of that other King's death beneath the sacred oak nine centuries before, a death that still awaited vengeance. In the eyes of the Queen and the court, my role was to warn him of his impending danger in order to preserve his life. So far as my masters were concerned, I must help render him suggestible and vulnerable to certain advisors. These advisers, mindful of the malefic influences impending three years hence, would ensure the King kept his appointment with fate.

On the fourteenth of July, I embarked on the long road to Paris. After two weeks of hard travelling, I reached Lyons, where at the house of M. Macé Bonhomme, a letter from the Cardinal de Lorraine awaited me. It was brief, sardonic, and – typical of Charles de Guise – not at all to the point.

> 'Agrippina is filled with anxiety over the fate of her Nero, though two sons have preceded him out of the putrid womb. If the stars were in favour, what would she not do to make him a King?'

I read it over and over, struggling to divine what was required of me. *Il Bagatella* stood on a precarious tightrope, with an ominous sack of balls to juggle. This was no small quiet passing of messages from hand to hand, nor remote celestial advice transmitted from the secluded shelter of my study. I must play my little move, my small pawn's step, with unerring skill, or I would probably lose my life. I thought of Luc Gauricus with his twisted and crippled legs, his heavy pain-ridden eyes. As a subject and a Jew, I risked something much worse than the *strappado* if I could not maintain the mask of a blameless and innocent visionary. On one side of the tightrope the pit of heresy gaped open; on the other, the abyss of treason.

I almost turned my mule back to Salon. If I understood the Cardinal aright, I must plant in the Queen's mind – so subtly that she would never recognise whence the inspiration issued – seeds which would flourish as the murder of her two eldest sons.

Exhausted and filthy, I reached Paris on the fifteenth of August. The untrammelled sun beat down upon my head with the impact of a brass hammer, while the stench of rotting garbage and offal rose to clog my nostrils and swarms of flies trailed after my mule like a dancing black banner. But the great royal city of Paris was bustling with celebration of Our Lady's feast-day. The omen was favourable.

I threaded my way wearily through the teeming streets. At length, I discerned the river, thronged with busy barges, and the island set gemlike at its centre. From a nest of luxuriant green foliage, the spires of the cathedral of Notre Dame reared their dazzling tracery over the agitated water. One façade shone pure and cool and formal, austere and virginal as a nun. The other beckoned salaciously, lewd and lush and profane as a harlot's leer. A mocking, centuries-old laughter hung chiselled in silent stone about the buttresses and gargoyles and porticoes – the eternal laughter of Notre Dame, who, Janus-faced, existed before the mountains and the seas came into being, or any living thing . . .

I found a pleasing inn across the river from the southern harlot-face of the cathedral. Here too, the benign omens proffered themselves to me. For it was called the Inn of St Michel.

I had spent all the money I brought from Salon. The proprietor of the Inn of St Michel refused to believe my business in the great city was at the Queen's request. How, he asked me, did he know I was whom I purported to be? Certainly everybody had heard of Nostradamus the astrologer. But why was I so dirty and penniless and unaccompanied? He demanded payment in advance for the night's lodging. I was furious, livid with my own impotence and my lack of foresight in bringing so little gold. But the portents – the feast-day and the inn's name – had promised truly. A young gentleman named Jean Morel was lodging at the inn. He courteously loaned me two écus because, he said, I had an honest face.

I slept for a time, and awakened to find the sun had set and the streets were drenched in torchlight. In the crowded dining hall of the inn, I seated myself beside my benefactor, M. Jean Morel. He was kind enough to furnish me with the latest city gossip. I had of course already heard it from my own sources.

But I did not wish to deprive him of the obvious satisfaction he derived from acting as my informant. Like Jean-Aimé de Chavigny, he was born under the sign of the Twins, and told a good tale.

Paris hummed and buzzed with the impending prospect of another Italian war. Thus far, King Henri had clung with sullen stubbornness to the pact signed with Philip of Spain at Vaucelles. The Connêtable de Montmorency, discerning what opportunities another Peninsular squabble would furnish for the house of Guise, also pressed for peace. But the Cardinal de Lorraine gnawed ceaselessly at the King's secret ambitions, tempting him to break his word and dispatch an army to Italy. Charles de Guise had already contracted a secret treaty with His Holiness, to expel the Spaniards from Naples and the Milanese.

Italy, the golden chimera, beckoned anew. The Cardinal de Lorraine urged the King to assert his ancient ancestral claims. Italy, as Charles de Guise's honeyed tongue cajoled, hung like ripe purple fruit, ready to be plucked by a bold hand. If France won the duchy of Milan and the kingdom of Naples, she would hold the papacy between upper and lower millstones. She could then compel the new Pope to serve the whims of His Most Christian Majesty with the obedience of a docile courtesan. Would this not, the Cardinal prompted, raise France high above the Empire, and make her the Queen of Christendom? Charles VIII had conquered Italy in the last century as easily as one might catch a fly. To be sure, he had lost it equally quickly, as if, when he opened his fist, the fly had escaped. With wise heads in the cabinet, however – heads like those of Charles, Cardinal de Lorraine and François, Duc de Guise – such carelessness would not occur again.

I listened to this recital by M. Morel and kept my face carefully noncommital. I had heard it all before. It was the same mad plan that Anne de Montmorency's stubborn interference had thwarted nine years previous. I knew too well the shining pattern that Charles de Guise had woven from elusive wisps of fantasy. He imagined Naples, like a succulent plum, would fall into his brother's waiting hands. If the duke wore on his fair head the Neapolitan crown of his Angevin ancestors, and if one of the King's own sons ruled Milan, no one enjoyed greater likelihood of obtaining the papal tiara than the Cardinal de Lorraine himself – already recognised as being even more *papabile* than his eminent and wealthy uncle, still mourned, it was said, by the ladies of the court.

During our long correspondence I had warned him that this Italian enterprise could not succeed. The auspices of the heavens were unfavourable. Simple common sense also warned that Philip of Spain, angered by a rupture of the truce, would undoubtedly invade France from the Netherlands, from the Germanies, and – supported by the arms and men of his royal and barren English wife – from Calais.

The Duc de Guise, always reasonable, was prepared to listen to me and bide his time. The Cardinal de Lorraine was not. And now Paris seethed with the rumour of the imminent Italian adventure. At first, the Constable had bitterly opposed the Cardinal. In the end, however, he turned face. With his entire council snapping like hungry dogs at his heels, the King had no choice save war. He was an honourable man, but weak and vacillating. And my advice meant nothing in the face of Charles de Guise's glorious and gilt-dusted dreams.

M. Morel tactfully refrained from questioning me about my business at court, for it was obvious enough. I would be asked to prognosticate on the future of the nation, and on the possibilities of the Italian war, and on the meaning of that mysterious quatrain prophesying the King's death. Since the letter from Luc Gauricus at Mantua six months after the publication of the *Centuries*, it had been on the lips of every courtier in Paris.

I did not sleep well that night at the Inn of St Michel. A host of spectral apparitions reeled in a faery ring before my sleepless eyes – the tall bulky form of the King and his heavy slow-moving Italian Queen, the proud armour-clad figure of François de Guise and the sly and seductive Cardinal in scarlet robes, the Valois children moving hand in hand, seven glistening white faces in the gloom of a dark sepulchre . . .

My visions pursued me relentlessly into restless slumber, until the great bell of Notre Dame awakened me. It did so moments before the hammering commenced at the door to my chamber. The innkeeper – who had yesterday scorned the poor traveller claiming to be the King's Prophet – now bowed obsequiously to me, an oily grin smeared across his fat face, his forehead shining with sweat. He stammered a thousand apologies, for his ill-considered conduct of the day before. But how could he, a poor innkeeper barely able to keep his family fed, know whether I was the man I claimed to be, or simply some sly thief trying to obtain board and lodging for nothing?

I wondered what had happened to transform the manner of this offensive little man so dramatically. I learned soon enough. Awaiting me below was no less a personage than Anne de Montmorency, Grand Constable of France, come to conduct me to the court at St-Germain-en-Laye.

I was prepared to despise the Constable at once. Were it not for his deadly enmity toward my masters, the power of the house of Guise over the King would be complete. But Anne de Montmorency had bound himself fondly and intimately to King Henri; and the King, so taciturn and solemn and slow to trust, would not, once a friendship had been cemented, break it. King and Constable were cut of the same cloth: simple, plodding, turtle-like. François de Guise and his brother, radiating arrogant glitter and polished breeding and supple subtlety, wove brilliant circles about the two somnolent and stately buffoons. Like a bear baited by sleek greyhounds, the Constable was profoundly uneasy in their presence, seeing himself contemptuously reflected in their eyes.

I perceived a humourless face pocked by narrow, intense eyes, slashed by a thin and brutal mouth, reeking with the bigotry and dogged determination and boorish belligerence which had earned the man a reputation for loyalty. He was a fossil, a bone, a limestone monolith, calcified and ossified in the past. I entertained an irrepressible suspicion that here was the hand that had poisoned Claude de Guise.

Concealing my revulsion, I made my most courtly bow, telling him what great honour he bestowed upon a humble provincial physician by coming in person to conduct me to court.

'I come under the Queen's orders,' he growled. I was obviously as distasteful to him as he was to me. I knew well enough his opinion of astrologers: we were nothing but a crowd of babblers, liars and rascals. The celestial art was frowned upon by

Holy Church. If not actually heresy, it should be left to foolish and frivolous old women.

Like drunken butterflies, the flowers of the court lounged in the vast and glittering vestibule to the palace of St-Germain-en-Laye, dripping in silks and satins and velvets and damasks and cloth-of-gold, winking and sparkling with pearls and rubies and diamonds and emeralds in constellations of earthbound stars. They twittered, chattered, clustered about me, eager to see what manner of curious creature it was who consulted the heavens and spouted disturbing prophecies. They were patently disappointed to find a rather dumpy and elderly doctor in fur-trimmed gown and sadly travel-stained black hat, hobbling from an attack of gout, who peered owlishly around him at the shimmering splendour of *la noblesse*.

One of the courtiers, pushed and nudged by a group of chattering friends, minced forwards, bowed flamboyantly, and demanded that I tell his fortune in love. I courteously apologised and declared I had been summoned to see the Queen. But his frivolous query unleashed a flood. I was surrounded by a buzzing swarm of men and women who flung both mocking and serious questions at me, anxious to hear what the strange old prophet would say. Starved for novelty, they were prepared for any outrageous response. Had I rolled my eyes and spat yellow foam and crawled away babbling on my hands and knees, they would have been delighted. To all of them, I muttered the same reply: I could answer no questions until I had seen the Queen.

Out of their midst, François de Guise abruptly materialised before me. I had not seen him since he lay torn and mangled at Gisors, after the siege of Boulogne. The appalling wound had healed cleanly and miraculously, leaving virtually no trace save for the knotted flesh over the left eye and a slight crookedness where the broken nosebone had mended imperfectly. One eyelid hung down, curiously sardonic, as though perpetually about to wink. Janus-like, he stared down at me from his graceful height, two faces melded together, two eyes that belonged to two polarised souls.

He was clad in full court dress for the feast-day, in a *pourpoint* of grey satin embroidered with silver and a cape of gold cloth, in boots of gold tooled leather with facings of figured scarlet satin. From his shoulders hung the great ducal cloak of *cramoisie violet*, trimmed with ermine, studded with silver eaglets and crosses of Jerusalem worked of stiff gold fabric. A cap of scarlet velvet perched in precise insolent tilt on his pale gilded head, and a huge diamond winked coldly at his left ear.

This regal apparition, more sumptuous than the King himself, grinned mockingly at me. The courtiers around him subsided into unwonted silence. Even among these jaded flowers, the hero of Metz was viewed with awe. The scions of Lorraine, I reflected, made the noble blood of France resemble hamfisted peasants. Pricklings of vague awe crept up my neck. Who, in truth, were they?

'And will you tell my fortune in love and war?' he asked with his cat-eyes opened wide and innocent. I heard titters tinkling like crystal chandeliers among the cluster of ladies surrounding him.

'I beg pardon, my lord. But I can answer no questions until I have seen Madame the Queen.'

'But it is only a little request,' he persisted, and the titters bubbled again in a delicate froth. Someone beside him murmured softly, 'You must tell him Italy will fall into his hands like a ripe cherry.' Someone else whispered, 'Madame de Clermont is a riper one.' There was a suppressed gasp and another snicker while he fixed his peculiar double gaze upon me, waiting.

I looked back into the right eye, which I recognised.'I humbly beg apology, my lord. But I must await Madame the Queen's pleasure.'

A little moan of disappointment wafted like a faint breeze from the ladies. Only one among them – willowy and dark, with a sardonic smile curling her full mouth and olive-black eyes that watched me with amused sympathy – did not partake of the frivolity. She stood apart, her skin silvery pale as a crushed lily, serene, aloof, clothed in a white damask gown, her black hair roped with pearls: a Selene, a white moon riding a black sky. Her enigmatic gaze met that of the Duc de Guise. Some signal passed between them. He stared down at me for a moment longer, then turned elegantly on his heel and stalked away, the great velvet cloak swinging about him like a bell. The crowd of courtiers followed him, whispering and giggling.

I had squandered my anxiety and apprehension during the waiting. When I stood before Queen Catherine de' Medici, therefore, an utter and unreasonable calm had descended upon me. She motioned me to a chair, and the pages and ladies-in-waiting removed themselves in a rustle of silks and satins, like a flock of pigeons erupting into flight. I knelt, and kissed the pale be-ringed hand, and looked up into the blank, inscrutable eyes – expressionless mirrors, as Claude de Guise once warned me, which concealed a myriad deadly secrets. They were almost colourless, grey as wet slate or granite or a stormy opaque sea. On the table lay a copy of the *Centuries*. With a supple and fluid feline movement, the Queen reached out and opened the book.

'Tell me what this means, Maître Nostradamus,' she said. Her voice was furry and low and heavily accented. Watching the stillness of her heavy body, balanced as though poised to pounce, I thought of the big cats in the King's menagerie. This woman was a hunting leopard, masked to bemuse the prey.

'Which, Madame?'

'You know. Must I read it out to you?

> Le lyon jeune le vieux surmontera
> En champ bellique par singulier duelle;
> Dans cage d'or les yeux luy crevera,
> Deux classes une, puis mourir, mort cruelle.

What does it mean?' she demanded again, never removing her bleak, opaque gaze from my eyes.

I offered her the most polished gaze of innocent sincerity I could muster.

'Madame, I do not know. Like my other visions, it came in trance, before the fire. Although the image was clear, I do not know to what event, past or future, it refers.'

'Do you mean to tell me that you have written a book whose meaning you do not understand?'

'Precisely that, Madame. These visions come upon me through the grace of God. I only heed them and record them for posterity. It is only when some specific place or person appears, or when I hear a name spoken, that I have some inkling of its meaning.'

She was silent, obviously impressed.

'You must know that the prophecy of Luc Gauricus about the King is in everyone's mouth,' she said quietly.

'I know that, Madame. I have taken the liberty of inspecting the King's horoscope myself. It is certainly true, there are malefic influences occurring three years hence, in the month of July. If I were in Madame's place, I would ask that the King refrain from open combat during that time. But I truly do not know to what death this terrible vision refers.'

'If it is the King, do you think it possible to avoid?'

'Madame, you ask me a question every astrologer and philosopher and theologian would dearly love to answer, if such an answer could be found. I suspect there are many possible futures. It is conceivable that several deaths await each of us at different intersection points, like forks in the road leading to different villages. Different choices may conjure one or another of these deaths into being.' I bowed my head. 'I would strongly advise the King to beware of open combat during the month of July in his forty-first year.'

My advice would, I hoped desperately, produce precisely the opposite result. The King's reactions to his wife were well known and predictable. A firm suggestion from the Queen would probably prompt him to do the contrary, for the uncomfortable mixture of guilt and distaste which he held toward her compelled him to treat her with contempt. I did not allow myself to dwell on the Cardinal de Lorraine's wrath, should my surmise prove incorrect.

She closed the book with a slap and replaced it quickly on the table, as though it had bitten her. I scrutinised the peculiar masked eyes, the heavy pendulous lips, the sloping chin, the dazzling waxy complexion, the crinkled and unbecoming coarse hair dyed startlingly yellow. At thirty-seven, she had begun to coarsen and thicken. Even in her youth, however, she had never been beautiful. In his mocking and lascivious way, the Cardinal de Lorraine had written me of her constant torment over the Duchesse de Valentinois, and the hole in the floor through which she peered at the lovers in the chamber below, her heart consumed by twisted excitement and jealousy and rage. A thin strand of irrepressible pity was intertwined with my revulsion, but I dared not acknowledge it. At this woman's instigation, the Florentine cupbearer had offered the fatal drink to the young Dauphin, the present King's brother and rightful heir to the throne. Poison was part of the heritage of the Medici court. She would not hesitate to utilise its quiet diplomacy again.

Yet so superstitious was this woman, so fascinated by occult power of any kind, that I could see the concealed fear lurking beneath the opacity of her eyes, and the faint beads of perspiration on her upper lip.

I removed from my robe a copy of the *Traicte des Fardemens*, and handed it to her with a bow and a flourish.

'Knowing Madame's interest and great skill in the arts of beautification, I am honoured to present you with my latest humble work. I hope it will afford you pleasure.'

The sombre stare brightened a little, and a pale smile hovered at the corners of the heavy, sullen mouth.

'I did not know that the Prophet of Salon dabbled in cosmetic recipes,' she said.

'It is my business to study the secrets of the stars, Madame. Among these are the arcane properties of herbs and flowers and metals. There are recipes in this book which are guaranteed to preserve the bloom of youth on any woman, if exercised faithfully each morning and night. And although Madame's complexion is flawless and perfect as a magnolia petal, I am nevertheless confident that the book will be of interest to you.'

The threatening atmosphere subsided. She leafed through the book, and questioned me about creams and potions and perfumes and ointments. We spoke for nearly an hour of the wiles and concoctions by which a woman might retain her beauty, the sheen of her hair, the whiteness of her skin, the suppleness of her hands, the brightness of her eyes. All of it, I knew, was a sounding. This subtle and devious woman wished to determine precisely what I was. Only then would she disclose the real purpose of my summons to Paris.

For a time we debated cosily about fate, and whether it could be altered or was indeed the inexorable will of God. She was well versed in Greek and Latin literature and philosophy and works of magic. Her nimble mind quoted passages I never expected to hear on lips other than those of scholars like myself. But she had not played her delicate game for so many years through lack of wit and subtlety. Conventional behaviour having proved futile, she had cultivated the only alternative: recede like mist into the background, draw a veil over the eyes and the manners, smile, be civil, be courteous, maintain dignity, keep silence, and wait – wait until the moment arrives, the moment to seize power.

I knew that moment would be the King's death. She knew it too. Although she loved him, although it lacerated her soul to see him so completely the possession of another, there was something in her which would not be sorry to see him dead. Buried and mourned, he could no longer be unfaithful. He would then be wholly hers.

Delicately and gently, like careful physicians, we probed each other's minds and natures. While we did so, I thought of François de Guise and the Cardinal de Lorraine. Of all their enemies, this woman was the most resourceful, the most cunning, the most lethal. Anne de Montmorency was stubborn and immovable as a granite pillar; but he could be outwitted. Queen Catherine de' Medici could not. She, like the house of Guise, wanted absolute power, and would not hesitate to sacrifice any life – even her own issue – to see it placed in her hands. I wondered whether she might not ultimately prove too formidable an adversary. For the duke and the Cardinal were, despite their united strength and brilliance, driven by their dreams, and thus vulnerable. The Queen of France, on the other hand, had no dreams left her. She therefore had nothing further to lose.

By the end of our interview we were chatting amiably, joking and laughing. Despite myself I appreciated the versatile wit, the sinuous cunning, the flexible intelligence of this astonishing and repellant woman. It was a pity she was not beautiful. Had King Henri loved her, she might have helped him to rule like a true King, rather than weaving black plots in the secret darkness of her tortured heart.

I recognised in her a creature like myself, a survivor – *La Fortez*. Had we been other than what we were – a Queen who sought to rule through the house of Valois and a servant of that line's eternal enemies – we might have become spiritual siblings. As it was, I knew that in my understanding of her lay my power to influence her as I willed.

Two hours had passed. She rose, to let me know that the audience was at an end.

'Maître Nostradamus,' she said, 'I find that I have not enjoyed myself so much for a long time. I believe we will be friends. I shall send you now to the palace of the Cardinal de Bourbon, Archbishop of Sens. There you will be given apartments until I summon you again. The royal children are at the nursery at Blois. It is to Blois that I wish you to go, to inspect their horoscopes and that of the young Marie Stuart, my son's bride-to-be. In the meantime I enjoin you to take your pleasure in our great city of Paris.'

The first phase was achieved: I had won her confidence. I held my breath until I had passed through the antechamber and out into the great hall, then exhaled a vast sigh of relief. Before me stood the chattering, twittering clusters of courtiers, whispering and speculating on what had passed between the Italian woman and myself. I imagined them leaning against the doors, trying to overhear some fragment of conversation. A grotesque image coalesced in my mind – of velvet and satin and silk and damask-clad bodies piled atop one another, peering through a keyhole to listen to pronouncements of great import, and hearing instead that white lead mixed with rosewater and lemon juice was an excellent remedy for unsightly pigmentations of the skin.

XXI

I received from the Queen an embroidered velvet purse containing one hundred and thirty gold écus – barely enough to cover the expenditures my journey to Paris had incurred. I fumed and fussed and furiously cursed her parsimony as I paced my sumptuous apartments at the Hôtel de Sens. But in time I began to realise that royal patronage brought another kind of recompense.

Before nightfall, the entire court knew of the Queen's approval. My apartments were besieged by all kinds of clients: old lords who wanted prescriptions for gout or stone or debilitated virility, young ladies who sought secret remedies for the decay of their complexions, anxious mothers who demanded horoscopes for their children, clandestine lovers who wondered when an ageing husband might die, young courtiers who hoped some advancement in their fortunes was imminent.

The stream of visitors continued in full spate, like a rain-swollen river, from early morning in to the late evening; and sometimes an impertinent noble, forgetting that lesser souls, too, need their sleep, would pound on the door far in to the night. Despite my fatigue and the pain in my feet, I turned no one away. The records of these horoscopes would be useful later, as would the bits and snippets of relevant gossip I gradually accumulated about the flowers of France.

And they showered me with gifts: clothes, plate, jewels, and money. One elderly and heavily rouged woman, seeking advice on her desperate but unrequited passion for the young Duc de Nemours, presented me with a brilliantly coloured parrot from the Indies, which had cost her a thousand écus and which whistled at me and shrieked raucously, 'Vive le roi!' At first I thought the bird amusing. After a few hours, I gave it to the Cardinal de Bourbon as a gift.

That poor sum of a hundred and thirty golden écus was but a grain of sand compared to the fortune I amassed in five short days. Behind it stood the Queen, mentioning a word here, passing a suggestion there. I silently lauded the subtlety with which she rewarded me. Had she offered too much outright, she would have appeared a gullible servant of superstition.

Amidst this insane round of noble visitors, the enigmatic dark woman in white damask knocked at my door. Graceful as a birch-tree, she stood in the little sitting-room with its lavish tapestries and carved furniture and paintings and gilt. She looked about her with a faintly amused smile on her lips, as though she knew the irony of my encasement in these luxurious surroundings. She did not seek a consultation about her horoscope, nor a recipe for beauty cream. Instead, she brought me an invitation – to sup the following evening at the Hôtel de Cluny, Parisian residence of the Cardinal de Lorraine.

'Monseigneur wishes your presence to grace his humble table,' she said, that sardonic smile on a mouth like a blown carnation, 'since you are now the sensation of Paris.' She seated herself languorously on a delicate bench inlaid with ivory which stood by the fireplace. 'How do you like the court, Maître de Notredame?'

Her manner of address interested me at once. To the court I was Nostradamus, the Prophet of Salon.

'It is a court, Madame. Wealth and splendour and power are always impressive.'

'It depends in which hands they lie, does it not? And what do you think of Madame the Queen?'

'I will answer your question, Madame. But first I would like to know your name.'

She laughed, revealing a row of small and slightly pointed white teeth between the full red lips.

'I am Marie de St Clair. I am Scots by descent, of the Earls of Caithness, but my family have lived in France for many generations. I attend Madame the Queen. I have a brother called Jacques de St Clair, who is an archer in the King's Scots Guard. My husband . . . my husband is interested in viticulture.'

I waited, but she offered nothing further, enigmatic and pregnant with silence as the moon in a quiet sky. Clearly she was part of the network. Her face was too full of hidden things and sly amusement for it to be otherwise. And she was, of course, implicated by virtue of her connections with the Cardinal and the duke. She stared at me boldly, watching the questions flicker across my face. I knew I could conceal nothing from her. From the look exchanged between them, I guessed she must be François de Guise's mistress.

'Do not look so perplexed, Maître de Notredame,' she said, smiling broadly at me. 'With all that you know, are you so surprised that women too can bear secrets?'

She wafted a cloud of some exotic scent behind her –

sandalwood and spice. Marie de St Clair. The name tormented me with nagging familiarity. I brooded on it, trying
first this association, then that. Suddenly the pieces snapped
together, and I heard the voice of Mathias Delvaux weaving the
tapestry of the great vine with its myriad branches: Gisors,
Joinville, Chaumont, Courtenay, Gonzaga, Brienne, Montpezat, Charnay, Blanchefort, Guise, Lorraine, St Clair.

This woman too was *sangraal*.

XXII

The Hôtel de Cluny, Parisian residence of the Abbots of that
powerful monastery, stood on the south bank of the river overlooking the Sorbonne, amidst an elaborate garden profuse with
lime trees and white roses and shaded cobbled walks. Its delicate turrets were graced with intricate lacework of stone,
fraught with angels and gargoyles copulating in bizarre
embrace. Once it had been a cloister. Now it housed the subt-
lest political machinator in the whole of France.

The Hôtel had been built on the site of the archaic Roman
baths of Lutetia, and the Cardinal de Lorraine had ordered
tons of earth carted away to expose the ancient structure's
crumbling stonework. He had planted it with vines and flowering shrubs and sweet-scented herbs. Now it formed a humped
shadow beside the gothic marvel of the Hôtel itself, an ominous reminder that what is holy must be forever conjoined with
the dark. In the little courtyard beyond the ornate gate, horse
chestnuts had showered their fruits prolifically on the cob-
blestones.

The profusion of treasures at first swept away all thought of
the evening to come: gold and alabaster statues from Egypt and
Greece and Rome, jewelled crosses and reliquaries and clois-
onné enamel plaques, painted jars and gilded urns and silver
plate and faïence, a great blossoming of tapestries and embroidered hangings. I had known the Cardinal was a collector,

whose avidity in purchasing rare works of art perpetually dismayed his competitors. What I saw now confirmed his exquisite taste. Each piece was itself a jewel, a perfect example of its kind.

François de Guise lounged by the massive marble fireplace, still clothed in his elegant costume, a winecup of gold studded with jewels in his right hand, his left on the shoulder of Anna d'Este, his plump and pregnant duchess. Marie de St Clair stood erect as a tall white taper beneath a tapestry like a rainbow, which illumined the shimmering white silk of her gown sewn with seed pearls. Beside her stood a comely young officer in the gilded cuirass of the King's Scots Guard, his features so closely resembling hers that they appeared to be twin heads stamped on a coin. A young, emaciated, fine-strung Cistercian monk whom I recognised at once as an occasional visitor to the library of the abbey of Notre Dame d'Orval, a fanatical genealogical scholar, sat on a velvet-coloured bench conversing heatedly over the origins of the Joinville line with one of the court poets of *La Pléiade*, Pierre de Ronsard. With them sat another officer of the Scots Guard – Gabriel de Montgoméry, Sieur de Lorges, a young tawny-haired giant, ruddy, freckled, flushed, who held a fragile crystal goblet in one great red fist as though it were a halberd. Already drunk, Louis, Cardinal de Guise, artist and poet and dreamer, third son of Claude, sprawled with undignified grace across a pile of embroidered cushions. The Cardinal de Lorraine glided up to me, all smiles and charm and soft appeal. His vivid eyes aglow with warm welcome and affability, he proffered me a goblet of wine.

I bowed before Marie de St Clair. 'Madame, forgive me for not at once understanding when you told me your name. I must offer as excuse the trying time I have had these three days in Paris.'

'Your trying time has not yet begun, Maître de Notredame,' she said, offering me her sardonic smile. The scent of sandalwood and spice and juniper gently caressed me. 'I fear Blois will be a saddening experience for you. You know well enough the future of those pitiful children.'

'I do not doubt it will sadden me. I am already saddened by the Queen herself. But perhaps pity is out of place here.'

She bowed her dark head in assent as Charles de Guise approached us. Once again I felt the inchoate creeping uneasiness and fascination which he invariably evoked within me. Eleven years had passed since I last saw him face to face at the château of Gisors. He was thirty-two years of age now, and the beguiling, seductive young *santorello* had matured into an equally seductive yet deadly courtier and machinator. Anne de Montmorency had once referred to him as a great calf. But the calf was full-grown now, tough and wiry and cunning beneath the sleek mask. He was both adored and hated at court. I had heard more than a little gossip and speculation about him from the stream of visitors circulating through my apartments at the Hôtel de Sens.

Numerous ladies were desperately in love with him, although his favours were conferred with fastidious discrimination and no scandal ever marred the finely polished veneer of his sanctified private life. Not a few of the young men courted him too, and here he was even more discreet. And a great many distrusted him profoundly, finding him too perfect, too charming, too exquisite – a *tentatore* full of guile and shifting volatile moods, like the moving surface of a stream reflecting a changing sky. They were ensnared and disturbed – as I had been – by the ingenuous and fascinating eyes, the melodious voice that poured forth such eloquent cascades of oratory and could shift so nimbly and gracefully from sermons to Greek classics to the most revolting of obscene jokes.

'The Cardinal is both King and Pope in this country,' the Venetian ambassador had told me at the Hôtel de Sens while I predicted his future fortunes in France. I had stilled my face into blankness, for the Prophet of Salon was uninterested in court gossip. But it seemed that Charles de Guise had everyone, even the King himself, dancing like puppets on invisible strings.

'So, my friend,' he said, casting over me the golden net of his notorious charm. 'The Queen is said to be vastly impressed by her new astrologer. I trust that you left her suitably frightened by your strange quatrain of the two lions.'

'I told her,' I replied nervously, 'that I did not know what it meant.'

He stared at me for a moment, then answered with a silvery ripple of laughter.

'Even better,' he said. 'All Christendom knows the Fool is holy.' He clasped my arm, exuding sinuous serpentine grace like a fragrance. 'Come. I would like you to meet my very dear friend Captain Montgoméry, Sieur de Lorges.'

I met the young giant's greenish flecked eyes, and could not but warm to his open, honest face beneath the cap of tawny curls, majestic as a lion's mane.

'You see?' said the Cardinal with a graceful white hand on the Captain's shoulder and a gentle smile on his lips. 'He is like a young lion, is he not? It is fitting, for I have taken the trouble to cast his horoscope, and he is born at sunrise under the sign of Leo.' The bright eyes fixed me as though I were an insect on a pin. 'Are you not pleased with our young lion, Maître de Notredame?'

A long moment passed before I understood. I stared at the Sieur de Lorges, then turned helplessly to Charles de Guise. He merely laughed.

'There is fate and fate,' he said, raising his goblet high in histrionic toast. 'Behold the creation of man-made fate, in perfect coupling with the web of the Grey Ones. Which is destiny, and which contrived? There is a riddle for you.' He turned with a graceful swirl of the red satin robes, and led the way into the dining hall. I felt a strong hand on my shoulder, and turned to face François de Guise.

'Why are you afraid?' he asked, giving me the stern but sympathetic look he probably bestowed on his soldiers when they baulked before a battle. 'It must not be said that the house of Guise slaughtered its way to the throne of France. You know we must work in this way. You have helped to create it yourself. Why do you tremble now?'

'I was comfortable enough seeing visions in the fire. But there is something unholy in all this. It reeks of sorcery.'

He laughed easily. 'Come, my friend, do not play the hypocrite with me. You are not one to fear sorcery. Besides, we are only doing what any man does when he conceives a vision or a possibility and adjusts his circumstances to actualise it. Therein lies the essence of any creative act. We are all magicians. Do not brood on it.'

We spoke at length of the Italian venture, and ate roasted peacock and lamb stewed with herbs, and drank an enormous
quantity of very fine wine. The young Cistercian monk had
begun to argue again with Pierre de Ronsard over the Joinville
family, pounding his fist on the table to punctuate his pronouncements and inadvertently overturning his goblet of wine.
François de Guise cut coolly across this dialogue and asked the
poet to give us a song.

The poet bowed, pleased to comply with the request. He
never tired of singing his own sonnets, or of hearing them set to
Janequin's delicate music. He was a strange little gnome,
wizened and hunched like an old man, though he was the same
age as myself; and he was nearly deaf, so that one had to shout
to be heard. From the cold spaces of his silent world he spun
fantastic frostings of silver and gilt, finely honed and sculpted,
exuding a faint cool fragrance of lemon blossoms. His poetry
did not move my spirit, for it was too chill, too precise. But it
suited the Cardinal's exquisite taste. He lavished M. de Ronsard and his friends with largess and tender patronage, so that
their little circle blossomed like an orchard of crystallised fruit
beneath his delicate hand.

These poets and musicians that the Cardinal gathered lovingly around him were slowly but inexorably transforming the
very language of France. And they would leave behind them a
silver and gilt monument exuding the fragrance of lemon blossoms, which eternalised him and his house for all posterity.
That monument would glisten and shimmer unextinguished
down the dead years, would one day strike sparks in the souls of
the yet unborn.

M. de Ronsard gazed at his patron with adoring myopic
eyes, took up his lute and began a lengthy piece which he called
his *Hymn to Justice*. It was florid with exultant and hyperbolic
admiration for his master.

> 'Prince si jeune d'ans et de moeurs si chenu,
> Celui sera nomme le Prelat de Lorraine,
> Charles, dedans lequel ta fille souveraine

Miraculeusement tu feras transformer
Pour les faicts vicieux des humains reformer;
Elle prendra son corps;
Mon Charles, mon Prelat, mon Laurier de Lorraine!'

I listened with faint embarrassment to this flood of senti-
ment. But the Cardinal did not seem in the least disturbed by
it. As though it were merely his due, he sat with an amused
smile curled on his finely shaped lips. I suppressed a bitter
laugh. The Huguenots, who hated him, would not have put it
that way.

Charles de Guise had been appointed Papal Legate and
Grand Inquisitor by His Holiness in Rome. Now the rumour
was abroad that he intended to bring the Inquisition to full
flower in France. I knew this rumour to be untrue, for he
lacked the blind fanaticism to be a persecutor. In fact he was
more sympathetic to the heretics than they could ever have
comprehended. Yet the trace of cruelty I glimpsed so many
years ago had blossomed and was already bearing fruit. The
fragile and finely cultivated sensibility which had chosen these
perfect works of art, and which shone with such utter sincerity
from his elegant face, could so easily metamorphose into violence and mockery and spite. Not for the first time I remembered his father's question: *Does he have a choice?*

Throughout the meal Marie de St Clair had said little. She
sat listening and observing like an enigmatic Egyptian statu-
ette, her red lips lightly pursed with good-humoured irony, her
pale skin luminescent in the candlelight. Insistently, I reminded myself that I was now in middle age and growing old, that I
had a good and respectable and loving wife. It made no difference.

Charles de Guise absently extended a white hand and fon-
dled her arm as it lay gracefully across the table. With the gentlest and most unobtrusive of gestures, almost an afterthought,
his slender ringed fingers moved in languorous rhythm up
and down the vulnerable pale skin. I rose impatiently, sour
with stifled jealousy, and stalked out into the great hall to
brood.

There was wine to quench the burning, and then more wine.

Louis de Guise lay asleep, young and vulnerable, cocooned in some gilded dream on the pile of cushions where they had abandoned him. The company drifted lazily into the hall, and M. de Ronsard played his lute again. A somnolent, faintly corrupt atmosphere suffused the room, like the steamy odorous sweetness of some tropical garden, heavy with exotic blooms but also redolent with decay. Nothing was said of the role the Sieur de Lorges must play. But it preyed upon my mind like a succubus, as did Marie de St Clair's olive-black eyes.

The long evening unfolded like settling mist, bittersweet, insubstantial, as though I swam through heavy belladonna dreams. Recognising that some melancholy lay upon me, they left me alone, and the murmur of voices and gentle plucking of lutes hardly disturbed my dark reverie. The Cardinal and his guests wandered in and out of the hall, vanishing and reappearing like actors on a stage. I sat beside Louis de Guise's supine and oblivious red-draped body, staring at the embroidered blazon on the tapestry, *la dame et la licorne*.

Mon seul desir.

At last I rose, stumbling slightly, and made my way outside to the silent gardens. My senses were askew from the wine and the dreamlike strangeness of the atmosphere. I recalled the words of Mathias Delvaux, spoken from the darkness before the fire in which I watched the dim and wraithlike shapes of my visions.

We do not understand time, we poor earthbound creatures. We think there is a present and a future and a past. In truth it is all now, all happening at this moment, like the pictures of a dream . . .

Here, coalescing before me, was one of those intersection points at which the realm of possibilities met the controlled will of man. One of the multiple futures in the fan-shaped web of time was that King Henri would die in three years. This nascent embryo, quietly nurtured in the womb of the future by Luc Gauricus and myself, would soon be midwifed to concrete birth. The midwife, it seemed, had already been chosen.

I thought too of M. Ammanien de Foix, Bishop of Carcassonne, speaking quietly of alchemy and the act of voluntary liberation required to precipitate the tincture. No irrevocable hand of nature would ever bring it into being. God and fate were both prisoned in dumb oblivion until the act of sin, the act of consciousness, the hubris of deliberate choice, brought God to birth, and in doing so, damned man.

Moonlight lay cold and white as drifted snow over the gardens of the Hôtel de Cluny. The still, heavy leaves of the chestnuts and limes were silvered to a semblance of translucent marble, some mad sculptor's fantasy of a bleached white world patterned lacelike against jet. I walked toward the black humped shape of the ruined Roman baths, frosted with silver, festooned with twisted garlands of vines and young ice-flowered trees. Everything was moon-bleached to a pale bone whiteness, fine shapes eaten colourless by the moonlight's acid, like the delicate lines of an etching. I could still hear the faint thin melody of M. de Ronsard's lute wafting across the blackness between the ghostly trees.

How did they dare? I could not quibble that the King must soon die. Like his father before him, he was already suspicious of this fascinating and *puissant* house of Guise, with its vaulting ambition and its irresistible strength. When the young and pliable François II mounted the throne, they would rule through his little Scottish Queen. The Duchesse de Valentinois would be dismissed from court. The Connêtable de Montmorency, their most bitter rival, ageing and snappish and incompetent as an old dog, would be ousted from power. Absolute governorship would be theirs. And I knew well enough that the Order's work must at times be bloodstained.

But I would have felt more peaceful conspiring in some grisly plan – a poisoning, a dagger thrust, an apparent accident. There was something terrible about this eerie magic of peering through the smoky lens of vision and the reeling patterns of the stars. And choosing, with human wit and human boldness, the crossed threads of dream and incipient reality. Choosing them in the form of a solid man, of flesh and blood, who must become the living vessel through which the forces of fate would work. He would undoubtedly die for his act. It seemed he was willing. Here was black sorcery indeed, with its own sacrificial beast. My skin crawled at the deadly arrogance of it. Who were they, and how did they dare? Yet I was as guilty as they; and, as

François de Guise had pointed out with his blunt soldier's tongue, I was far more of a hypocrite. Through my visions in the fire, had I not outlined the design?

I seated myself within the shadowy enclosure of the ruin, beside the still pool. Reflected on the water's obsidian surface, the moon's staring eye transfixed me. I recalled that other pool, the pool of dreams, which concealed some dreadful revelation. At first I thought the sound issued from my fantasy, or that I myself in my weariness had exhaled the faint sigh. Then I heard it again more clearly, a woman's tense moan wafted from the ruin across the pool. I could see only darkness, the black shape of the crumbling masonry, shadows against shadows, a faint silvering of moonlight as a breeze ruffled the water and sent gentle ripples toward the reflected moon and shattered it into fragments.

I held my breath and moved my head cautiously around the buttress of stone that obscured my sight. I told myself it might be someone in pain, someone in need of help. Despite this excuse, I knew in my heart I must not look upon what was being enacted here. I knew it was forbidden me, knew it belonged to the dreamlike fabric of that ghostly garden. Nevertheless, I could not control the blind impulse that drove me to peer over the sheltering and concealing stone wall, to watch them stretched white and moon-bleached among the flowering plants.

Her head was thrown back, her profile cut sharp and pure and cameo-like against the darkness; her hair trailed loose and black and snake-like in the water at the pool's edge. The ghostly and beautiful bodies locked and unlocked in rhythmically undulating motion, a dream-slow convulsive dance – pale limbs like living lace, hands rippling and sliding over white shoulders and plunging thighs. In willing complicity the frail light bleached to pale silver even the satin of the crumpled and discarded red robes. And I saw, black against the white skin, the birthmark in the shape of a small cross.

Sol et luna, sulphur and salt, the Red King and his White Wife . . . *And Tiresias looked upon the serpents coupling in the shrine of the sacred grove, and knew that the gods had sent him a holy mystery; and he stamped his staff upon the earth three times, and demanded of the Goddess which of them, male or female, knew the greater ecstasy . . .*

Another sigh, a deeper and wilder sigh, wafted toward me across the water. It was followed, in eerie counterpoint, by his sharp and almost painful cry, something like a sob – as though he could not bear the exquisite intensity as he twisted and plunged and abandoned himself to the climax of his pleasure. I turned away and huddled behind the stone and buried my face in my hands.

Some time later, I heard the whisper of their voices and the gentle rustle of the grass, and then I knew they had gone. Yet I remained crouching in the ruin, digging my fingernails into the palms of my hands, seeing over and over again those white bodies locked in their embrace, while the moon's unwinking eye impaled me with coy laughter from the now motionless obsidian pool.

I am an ageing man now, I told myself, smitten with an old man's disease. I have never been able to take my pleasure freely of women. If I am consumed by a foolish fancy for this young sibyl, it is the blind and common curse of old men. I tried to shrug it off by making bitter mockery of it. Yet the wound seared into my soul, as though a lance had pierced me with some strange poison. I hated them both.

Much later, when I had recovered my composure, I returned to the Hôtel de Cluny and joined what remained of the company in the great hall. M. de Ronsard had retired to some upstairs chamber to sleep. The Cistercian monk had vanished. Anna d'Este, delicately pregnant and easily fatigued, had returned to the Hôtel de Guise. Louis de Guise still sprawled, clumsy and poignantly childlike in his drunken stupor, across the embroidered cushions. The two soldiers of the King's Scots Guard lurked in the shadows, deep in hushed exchange. The candles had burned low in their sconces, and the room was redolent of strange underwater currents and the sweet scent of burning sandalwood and spice and juniper.

Marie de St Clair stood sinuous as a pale birch tree in her white silk gown, her hair neatly coiled, glistening with damp and roped with pearls. Her white teeth gleamed from her laugh as she jested with François de Guise. The Cardinal sat at their feet on a carved ebony stool, his dark head bowed, M. de Ronsard's lute across his rumpled scarlet lap. Lazily, he toyed with the instrument's strings, his long white fingers plucking a melancholy melody.

As I passed him to fill my cup – I had no solace but to drink myself to oblivion – he raised his head and gazed brazenly at me, his brilliant lapis eyes dancing and mocking, his delicate lips curled in a terribly knowing and intimate smile. With shame and anger, I realised he had known all along of my presence in the garden. No doubt he found it amusing, my undignified old man's passion for his beautiful and enigmatic mistress. I turned away, choking on my bitterness. But I felt his hand on my arm as he rose and leaned toward me.

His eyes were full of gentle compassion. Expecting some kindness, I flushed with embarrassment and bowed my head.

But he said quietly in my ear, 'Next time we will perform for you by torchlight, to the music of a viol and a tympanum. Afterward you can join us for the second round. It is much more interesting that way.'

And as I whirled on him in pain and fury, he glided away like the serpent he was, still smiling, and returned to his lute.

XXIII

For a week, I rode, accompanied by the Queen and her armed guard and her train of attendants, through the valley of the Loire, to the château at Blois. All during the journey, a black melancholy roosted in me like a foul bird. Their tragic fates were all too well known to me – those pathetic Valois children so newly come into a world changing too quickly and too violently to tolerate their frail and burdensome presence. The royal nursery was infested by reeking sulphurous fumes, a stinking miasma. What could I tell the mother?

There was François, the Dauphin, aged twelve, destined for childhood marriage to the dazzling Marie Stuart – a sickly and sallow boy who would be a sickly and abject King, doomed to a one-year reign.

Premier fils veuve malheureux mariage
Sans nuls enfans deux Isles en discord
Avant dix-huict incompetent age,
De l'autre près plus bas sera l'accord.

No one had questioned that quatrain yet. People would do so afterwards, when he lay in his grave.

And the Princesse Elizabeth, just ten years old, marked for a cold and loveless marriage with Philip of Spain, consigned to a land of barren rocks and women robed in black, of sterile vines and red dust, where she would die in childbirth with her child. And the Princesse Claude, who would one day marry a young scion of Lorraine, but whose life thread would be severed in her twentieth year . . .

And the melancholy little Charles de Valois, with haunted eyes and the seams of madness already stitched across his pale face. He would be King at the age of nine, would die at twenty-five, with the monstrous burden of massacre laid like an ox's yoke across his frail shoulders . . .

And the prancing five-year-old, best-beloved of his deadly mother, Nero courting Agrippina – Henri de Valois, Duc d'Anjou, who would also be a King, painted and bedecked like an alleyway whore, until the assassin's dagger pierced his belly and ruptured his bowels . . .

And the baby François-Hercule, Duc d'Alençon, only two years old, who would die of the plague . . . And little Marguerite, prettiest Valois princess to grace the nurseries at Blois . . . She would be thwarted in love, compelled into barren marriage, doomed to a futile quest for passion and a bitter old age, childless, throneless, disgraced by adulteries that failed to appease her yearning . . .

From this poor pale brood there would be but one issue – the Princesse Claude's child, who would one day be Duc de Lorraine.

And finally, last but first in the hearts of my masters, the Dauphine-to-be, Marie Stuart, thirteen years old, her slender body already budding into womanhood, her bright sienna hair like rich red earth under an Italian sun . . . A Queen of Cups become a cracked and useless chalice, cherished niece and precious pawn of her gilded uncles, useful for a time and then tossed like an unwanted bauble to her own lonely fate, agonised in love and ignominious in death . . .

What a grim nursery of fates to prognosticate, I reflected morbidly. Tied to a stake before the cathedral of Notre Dame, smelling the stench of his own burning flesh and hair, feeling the noxious smoke eat at his eyes and throat, the last Grand Master of the Temple had pronounced his curse on this line. I could only marvel at the utterness with which his imprecation would be fulfilled.

> De maison sept par mort mortelle suite,
> Gresle, tempeste, pestilent mal, fureurs . . .

Haunting the shadows of every one of my visions over the years I had seen only war and massacre and death, not only for this pitiful lineage, but for those whom I served as well. For I knew in my heart that the house of Guise would fail in its design. The currents of the times were too strong. With the splintering of the rock of the Church would come, ultimately, the collapse of the royal throne, and Pope and King would dance their dance to merry hell together. A brief golden age of glory, and then the decay and dissolution that would not cease until France was kingless and in ruins, her cities – like her rivers – running with blood.

I had spoken of these visions once to Mathias Delvaux during my sojourn at Orval. He believed it still possible to avert disaster. The house of Lorraine was the sole bulwark between France and chaos, for only Lorraine could claim right to the throne. If she failed, there would be no hope for half a millennium.

I had spoken too to François de Guise, hoping his superb soldier's courage might allay my fears.

'I cannot judge such things,' he replied, with his sanguine acceptance of brutal reality. 'But we are the servants of our mission. Perhaps you are right. Perhaps we cannot realise it. Nevertheless our honour compels us to try.'

And I had spoken to the Cardinal de Lorraine, begging him

to take care as he laid his webs and wove his convoluted plots. I had hinted of the shadows I sensed hovering beyond the bright circle of his ambitions and his dreams.

But he had only smiled his sweet and mocking smile. 'What does it matter if we fail, Maître de Notredame? The throne of France is but one objective. There are other thrones to be had. And even should it take a thousand years, the cycle will turn again to its beginning. The *roi perdu* does not die, my friend. He is not a man. He is a myth.'

'I do not understand,' I had said, troubled.

'An eternal present,' he replied. 'The times themselves will choose him, so long as he be of the sacred blood. In the end he cannot fail, because the secret soul of every man seeks its salvation in him.'

'But the sacrifice,' I began. 'The sacrifice is too great . . .'

'There is no birth without blood,' the Cardinal had replied, smiling.

I rode with blank face and tormented spirit along the dusty road to Blois. Ahead of me pranced the men-at-arms, the arquebusiers and the halberdiers carrying the great banners. Behind me followed the palanquins of the Queen and her *Escadron Volant* of court ladies, streaming like vivid silk pennons unfurled in the summer sun. My oppression intensified as the royal château loomed into view on its high hill overlooking the river. I felt I was about to choke, so acute was my discomfort. With narrowed eyes I peered into the sun, trying to discern the outlines of the castle shimmering through the blazing light. But a black shadow obscured my vision, an ominous shape veiling my destination from me.

I remained at Blois for three days. Much of my time there was my own. I was intensely grateful for this, as I had to struggle constantly against being sick. On the evening of our arrival, I inspected the children in the royal nursery and spent several hours on their horoscopes – which I had already cast long ago for the Cardinal de Lorraine. Later that night, a dream revealed to me why I feared Blois, and why I smelled there the reek of blood.

I dreamed I stood in the King's apartments. The rooms were

empty, with the kind of breathing and pregnant vacancy that masks some terrible but yet unseen presence. Around me the tapestries hung silent, the curtained and canopied bed stood motionless, the carved and gilded writing bureau waited, the chairs hunched like dumb animals in the gloom. The paintings and marbles, the reliquary, the floor polished to a diamond-hard glitter, the rich carpets, the golden candelabra – all frozen, all mute.

A man strode through the curtained doorway – not stealthily, but proudly, as though to prove he was not afraid of this empty room with its silent presences. He was tall and fair and well-made, and at first I thought I recognised François de Guise, for the resemblance was strong. But this man was younger, and the left half of his face was disfigured by a dreadful scar. Half the cheek had been blown away, and a piece of the ear, and the skin had puckered and twisted over the ragged wound. His pale hair curled in thick ringlets above a broad white brow, and his eyes were dark blue and astute and bright with intelligence. After a moment, he moved to the centre of the room and stood motionless, waiting. I felt the presences draw near, and tried to give voice to some warning. But like the furniture and the tapestries, I was mute.

It was over very quickly. As though from the air itself, six men materialised from behind the hangings and the tapestried nooks, masked, brandishing naked daggers. And when they had finished their work, the young man's body lay stretched across the shining floor, with dark blood pooling over his velvet *pourpoint* and ruffled silk, over his white scarred face, his hands, his legs, his belly. Half a dozen hilts jutted from his carcass as though he were a broken doll pricked full of pins and discarded by a bored child. In the enveloping silence, his life seeped away over the polished parquet.

I awoke quietly with terrible clarity, feeling as though a great fist were crushing my heart within my ribs. For though this dream pointed far into the future, beyond my own death, I recognised its import. I had never met the son whom François de Guise loved so dearly, first fruit of his marriage. In portraits, I had seen the thick golden curls, the intense dark blue eyes, the broad white brow. I had heard praise from every quarter heaped upon this noble and perfect scion of the house of Guise. Many hopes rested upon him, for where the father might fail, the son would surely succeed. At his birth I had cast his horoscope. But blinded by my loyalty and my illusions, I did not recognise the destiny.

And I, who did not wish to bear this burden, had now foreseen his bloody end, here at Blois.

For three terrible days I shared the château of Blois with the ghosts of the unformed future. At last I was granted one hour of audience with the Queen. She asked me the question I expected.

'What will be the fate of my four sons?' she said, her cold grey eyes, reservoirs of a cheerless ocean, boring into mine.

I bowed my head. 'I see four crowns, Madame,' I replied.

'They will all be kings?' she said, unable to keep the shock from her voice.

'I see four crowns, Madame. I do not know more than this.'

'If they are all to be kings, then there can be no issue from any of them.'

'There will be no issue, Madame,' I said, almost in a whisper. 'You know their fate yourself. It is as you wish it to be.'

One minute passed, then another. She stared at me in the attenuated silence.

'As I wish?' she echoed at last, in a grating voice.

'Yours will be the power, Madame, unto the end.'

'And the Duc d'Anjou? What of my third son?'

'He will be King, Madame. You will not live to see the day when he is not.'

She continued to stare at me and I felt her enigmatic gaze probing mine, seeking treachery or deceit.

'How is it that you read my soul so well, Maître Nostradamus?' she said, and I heard the catch of fear in her voice.

I looked up to meet her eyes. My own were full of tears. She believed them to be tears of sympathy, of understanding, of sorrow, for her and for her children. They were not false tears, but they were not shed for what she imagined. I had vowed never to tell François de Guise of what I had seen at Blois, for he would not be alive to know of it. None the less, before this woman bent on the destruction of their house, my grief breached its barriers, and I wept.

As her eyes cleared, the anger and fear and suspicion slowly drained out of them. Almost gently, she asked, 'For whom are the tears, Maître Nostradamus?'

'Forgive me, Madame. I must seem foolish and impertinent. I weep for you, and for the King, and for the house of Valois. Perhaps God in his mercy knows why the future must unfold thus, despite the will of men. Perhaps Heaven will be a kinder place for us all than this sad earth.'

'I do not believe in Heaven, Maître Nostradamus, nor even in God. I believe in power. You know this of me, you whom I cannot deceive. I know that you will help me, for we are friends. And I am content with what you have prophesied for me. It seems that I will have power through my sons, for the length of my life. It is all I ask. When I am dead, I will be a rotting body in the earth, devoured by worms. Then I will not care. Do not be afraid. I am content.'

And so will be the Cardinal de Lorraine, I mused bitterly as I left the Queen's chamber. I had accomplished what was required of me. Knowing what I had told her, Catherine de' Medici, Queen of France, would not stay her hand. She would not shrink from removing those who stood between her best-beloved son, Henri de Valois, and the throne. Those who stood so were her own children. So be it, I thought. The seed has been planted. It will be many years bearing fruit. Now there will be the long waiting, while one by one they take their places, white-faced, in the shadowy sepulchre of my dreams.

When I returned to my apartments at the Hôtel de Sens, I found a message awaiting me. Marie de St Clair wrote that she must see me in secret, and that I must speak to no one of her visit.

She arrived close to midnight, after most of the household had retired. She was dressed in luminescent white, as was her wont. At first I had ascribed to affectation this perpetual lunar paleness, which flattered her exotic dark beauty and moon-white skin. Now, however, I began to discern a subtle irony in the pretty conceit.

'Maître de Notredame, you must leave Paris at once.'

I could not help smiling an unpleasant smile, while distant echoes fluttered about me like a flock of taunting birds.

'The gentlemen of the Palais de Justice are inquiring after you,' she said. 'It is Anne de Montmorency who has instigated this. They wish to know the methods of your work, to determine whether you are in accord with Holy Church.'

'This is a familiar scene,' I said wearily.

'I do not doubt it. The Queen will of course protect you. But it would be wiser and safer for us all if you return to Salon at once. Too much probing may reveal what should not be revealed.'

'Madame, I wish for nothing more than to leave Paris. I will be on my mule by sunrise. Do not fear. I have had enough of the court of the Valois to last me for a lifetime.'

'I warned you that Blois would sadden you.'

'Blois has saddened me beyond all bearing. I do not even wish to remember it. I will never return there as long as I live.'

She watched my face with detached solicitude. There was no mockery in it now. 'Monseigneur the Cardinal has asked me to tell you he is well pleased with your work at court.'

I had not wished to burden her with my own burning, futile dreams. But my lips spoke before my will could prevent it.

'Why did he send you to tell me this?' I said. 'Why did he not send me a letter, or come himself?'

She saw the bitter hunger in my eyes, and said softly, 'You must not hate him. He is a complex man, unfathomable even to one so astute as you. But he is not evil.'

'What, then, is he?'

'A paradox, Maître de Notredame. Men are frightened of paradox. They wish each other to be consistent, so they can say, "This is a good man," and "That is a bad man." That which is paradoxical inspires fear and sometimes hate. But he wishes you no harm.'

'Yet he wounds me through you, knowing it is the one thing against which I cannot defend myself.'

'I told you that you do not understand him, Maître de Notredame,' she said gently, eyes black as olives, skin white as a lily, her lips a blown carnation, smiling. The candlelight blazed luminescent against the whiteness of her gown as she moved gracefully toward me. The touch of her hand burned terribly. 'Perhaps he does not intend to wound. Perhaps it is meant as a gift.'

XXIV

In the last days of December, the Duc de Guise crossed the Alps with thirteen thousand men, and was joined in the plain of the Po by the Army of Piedmont. They marched on Valenza and carried it by assault. On the thirty-first of January, war between His Most Christian Majesty Henri II of France and His Catholic Majesty Philip II of Spain was formally declared.

Following the eruption of this long-desired conflict, I received a brief note from the Cardinal de Lorraine, written in his own elegant hand.

'Watch carefully, and you will see a dance of step and counterstep. Sometimes one tool may be put to more than one use.'

I knew the venture would fail. As I anticipated, the Pope, previously so eager to aid his French allies, had made a secret treaty with King Philip. He provided neither troops nor money to the French army in Italy. Sick, exhausted, starving, unused to the burning Neapolitan sun, François de Guise's troops were harried and besieged. The duke was finally compelled to retreat, falling back on Rome. At the beginning of August he received orders from King Henri to return home.

The Italian escapade was over.

I tried to fathom the Cardinal's letter. All I could see was a foolish and disastrous expenditure of men, money and ammunition. It was a debâcle. What was the counterstep?

Philip of Spain hastened to take advantage of France's vulnerability while her greatest general lay sick with fever, exhausted with failure somewhere in Italy. He gathered in the Netherlands a force of sixty thousand men, commanded by the Duc de Savoie and the Count of Guastalla. At the beginning of

August, this army invaded Picardy and besieged St Quentin. The timing was curious, for it coincided precisely with the Duc de Guise's recall to France.

I began to see dimly at last. The governor of Picardy was Gaspard de Coligny, Anne de Montmorency's nephew. Upon his shoulders lay the defence of the province. Desperate, he called to his uncle, the Constable, for aid. The dogged old soldier frantically scraped together an army to relieve St Quentin, which was otherwise doomed. And as my masters had no doubt anticipated, the Connêtable de Montmorency proved, in dramatic and unmistakable fashion, his absolute unfitness for military command. The Duc de Savoie and the Count of Guastalla thoroughly trounced the fragmented French forces, taking the Constable and his nephew prisoner. It was a second Pavia.

Counterstep.

Although I deplored the slaughter of so many men, I could not but admire the brilliance of the stratagem. Ingeniously, the ancient and inevitable conflict between Valois and Habsburg had been twisted to other ends, been reduced to a mere move in a much greater game. Never had the players seemed to me so omnipotent – the duke, the Cardinal, the Count of Guastalla. Even Emmanuel Philibert, Duc de Savoie, was part of the network, although nominally, like Ferrante de Gonzaga, the servant of Philip of Spain.

Despite the tragedy of the war, I laughed. Who fought for whom? I laughed helplessly until tears rolled down my face. This extraordinary group of men, whose tentacles extended to every noble house in Europe, cared not a jot for either religious or political ideologies. They used whatever material came to hand.

The Spanish army inexplicably refrained from marching on Paris, continuing to batter down the walls of St Quentin. And France waited, breathless, for the advent of the one man who could save her from being overrun.

He arrived at St-Germain-en-Laye in October, and encountered no opposition at court. The Connêtable de Montmorency was in captivity, thoroughly disgraced. There were no more snide whispers in the King's ear, no plots, no intrigues. François de Guise was quickly forgiven the Neapolitan fiasco, which was, after all, hardly his fault or his brother's, but that of the vacillating and treacherous Pope. As the duke rode through the countryside, he was hailed as a saviour. The rural *noblesse* armed themselves and joined his entourage. At the Cardinal's reasonable and modest suggestion, the King promptly appointed him Lieutenant-General of the Kingdom. Royal orders were dispatched to the governors of every province and city in the realm, enjoining them to obey the Duc de Guise as they would the King himself.

Nothing else could have so quickly catapulted François de Guise to such power. And then, in the new year, as the malefic planetary configurations which had dogged him in Italy receded, he seized Calais from the English. The siege lasted a mere six days, restoring to France a town lost for two centuries. Philip of Spain was mortified, for Calais had been the precious dowry of his unwanted English bride. The Duc de Guise was the golden darling of France. More than once I heard whispered:

'It is a pity he cannot rule in place of the King.'

My masters did not hesitate to turn their magnificent success to political account. The marriage between the sickly young Dauphin and the little Queen of Scots was precipitated with almost obscene haste. The Duchesse de Valentinois, who now feared the house of Guise, tried to dissuade the King from the match. The Constable wrote frantically from his prison, violently protesting. The Queen pleaded that the Dauphin was too young, and that the wedding should be postponed. But my masters had won. The ceremony took place in April, with a splendour that surpassed anything seen before.

'The duke discharged all the functions that M. de Montmorency exercised as Grand Master of the King's Household,' Claude de Savoie told me, laughing. 'And he did it so admirably that people are saying it is a pity the Constable must be ransomed.'

'The house of Guise has a taste for extravagance,' I said. 'I can imagine what sort of majesty this wedding entailed.'

'It was more than extravagance or majesty, my friend. All the Lorraine princes took precedence over every noble of French blood. The Bourbons are in an uproar.'

'Well, it is wise to propagate the idea that they are the real pillars of the throne. It is a smaller step to the throne itself.'

'There is more,' said Claude de Savoie. 'They have persuaded their little niece to sign a secret treaty. In the event of her death without issue, it guarantees to the King of France the Kingdom of Scotland, and all rights to the English crown as well.'

I was silent. They knew very well there would be no issue. I had told them the young Dauphin had only a year in which to reign. And I saw now what the next step would be. They had fashioned their *coup* with superb and impeccable statesmanship. Now King Henri must die.

XXV

'I have had a most interesting visit to Peronne,' said the Cardinal de Lorraine, toying restlessly with a dirty folded piece of parchment. 'I wish to have your opinion on it.'

He had summoned me to Reims in June, fairly bursting with a strange brittle excitement which warned me his head was full of new machinations. He was like a child who has discovered a treasure-trove of sweets, is virtually exploding with his secret, yet prolongs the delicious torture as long as possible. No mention was made of my visit to Paris and its dreamlike termination. I wondered with some bitterness whether he still maintained his liaison with Marie de St Clair. But I did not dare ask him, for fear of his mockery.

'At Peronne I was introduced to an extraordinary man,' said the Cardinal. 'He is called Antoine Perronet de Granvelle, Bishop of Arras.'

He watched me with his enigmatic eyes, waiting, while I searched for the name among the cluttered cabinets of my memory.

'The Bishop of Arras,' I finally said, 'is King Philip's most trusted agent.'

'Of course. Did you think I would deal with a man he did not trust?' He gave me one of his smiles of rare sweetness, the kind so notorious for melting the hearts of court ladies. 'King Henri sent me to him to treat for Anne de Montmorency's release. As you may imagine, I did not devote much time to the matter.'

'Sooner or later peace must be made.'

'Later, perhaps. The Bishop of Arras has given me two gifts. The first is a letter.'

He handed me the crumpled parchment. It was a communication from the Sieur d'Andelot, one of Montmorency's three nephews, to his brother Gaspard de Coligny, incarcerated in a Flemish prison. In it, he confided his conversion to the Huguenot faith.

'That is not all,' said the Cardinal de Lorraine. 'M. de Coligny has become a heretic as well.'

'The implications of this are explosive. Despite their rank, they could both be burned at the stake.'

'Naturally. But there is no point in that. It will be sufficient to throw M. d'Andelot in prison. That, I daresay, will create sufficient scandal and further disgrace M. le Connêtable in the King's eyes.'

'Why did the Bishop of Arras give you this?'

'That should be obvious to you.' Charles de Guise assumed his most pontifical air. I was forcibly reminded that in his slender ringed hands lay the religious future of France. 'We are, the Bishop and I, deeply concerned about the inroads made by the Huguenot heresy among this country's nobility. The letter affords most compromising evidence, does it not?'

He suddenly discarded the severe countenance, and leaned toward me. I thought for a moment he was about to take my hand, so intimate was his gaze.

'I am, lest you forget,' he said in the lightest, most charming of voices, with the gentlest of smiles, 'Grand Inquisitor in France for the Faith. And King Philip is as deeply anxious as King Henri for the preservation of the Faith. They both long to lay down their arms and join together to oppose this enemy which gnaws like a mole at the foundations of Holy Church.'

'Since when, Monseigneur, have you become so passionately

concerned about the preservation of the Faith?' I said caustically.

'Since the Bishop of Arras reminded me that I and my brother, the duke, hold in our hands the destiny not only of France, but of Europe as well. According to the Bishop, our zeal for the Church is known and lauded throughout Christendom. He also declares it is our imperative duty to conclude peace at the earliest possible moment. Only so may France and Spain unite in a joint endeavour to extirpate heresy in their dominions.'

'The Bishop really means that Philip of Spain has exhausted his treasury and can no longer afford a war.'

He laughed. 'You are cynical, my friend. Of course that is true. King Henri has exhausted his treasury as well. And I have assiduously helped him, since he must then borrow money from me and incur the ensuing obligation. But can you not understand what this implies?'

I took a deep breath and passed my hand over my eyes. 'I begin to see,' I said, speaking my thoughts aloud as they coalesced in my mind. 'You would no longer be *parvenu* foreigners. You would be spared the petty intrigues of the court, the slander of the Bourbons and the Montmorencies. You would no longer be obliged to seek protection from a powerful favourite such as the Duchesse de Valentinois. Your cause would be that of the Faith, your sacred duty the protection of all Catholics, your role the custodians of orthodoxy in Europe. Any attack upon you would constitute an attack upon God.'

'Very good,' said the Cardinal, smiling winningly at me and stroking my arm. 'A new image for the supple house of Guise, far greater than the old. Do you not think it has endless possibilities?'

'Yes, possibilities indeed. But I fear they are bloody ones. Can you not work to counteract the spread of heresy by persuasion, by gentleness? You have a golden tongue. Even Théodore de Bèze, a fanatical Calvinist, has said that if he had your graces, the whole of France would be Huguenot.'

'I thank you for the compliment. But the truth is that Calvin and Luther are scarcely inferior alternatives than Rome, and the populace know it. It is too late for gentle persuasion. The

Huguenot heresy encourages men to think for themselves. In principle, I applaud this. But the time is not yet come for us to grant that kind of freedom. Besides, you know that our work is futile without a Catholic Apostolic base on which to build. Without a Pope to guide it, Europe will fragment into petty states, each with its own definition of God's will. It is through myth and ritual that we must rule, not through the favour of some parliament of querulous burghers.'

He leaned close to me, so that his face was only a hand's-breadth from mine. The heavy blue eyes shimmered coldly, and I smelled the faint scent of lavender with which he perfumed his linen.

'I will tell you a secret,' he said. 'Before the siege of Metz, when King Henri was quarrelling with the Pope, he asked me a daring question. He asked me if we should found a Gallic Church, and break free, like Henry of England, from bondage to Rome. If I endorsed such a step, the King promised to make me Spiritual Patriarch, Pope of France. Do you know what I did?'

I stared at him blankly.

'I wept,' said the Cardinal de Lorraine, smiling. 'I wept large, copious tears. I replied that His Majesty must ask this question of his conscience, knowing full well his conscience was riddled with visions of hellfire and the stench of sulphur. But I did not weep for the tender spiritual agonies of my King. I wept because of what I had to relinquish. I am not prepared to see that sacrifice wasted.'

'Monseigneur, you will create civil war.'

'I will create a united Christendom with my brother as its ruler.'

I shook my head sadly. 'Your mind is full of fantasies, Monseigneur. If I imagined you to be religious, I would warn you that you are damning yourself.'

'If I am to take the word of my detractors,' said Charles de Guise with a gentle smile, 'I was long ago damned. *Flectere si nequeo superos, Acheronta movebo.*'

'I cannot countenance tearing France to pieces in the name of a God in whom you do not even believe.'

'Maître de Notredame, you are always admonishing against

wars. How do you expect anything to be accomplished? We are not selling flowers. You should understand now that individual lives are not important.'

'That is easy for you to say,' I snapped, 'who have never fought a battle.'

The charming smile faded from his lips, and the brilliant eyes grew chill and wintry as they fixed on me. 'I do not believe,' he said quietly, 'that you were asked to assume the role of nurse to my conscience.'

'I could not if I tried,' I said bitterly. 'I do not believe you possess one.'

He replied with a melodious ripple of laughter. 'You are a jewel beyond price,' he said, and the charm returned to his finely moulded face, and the delicate lips smiled again, and the vivid eyes shone at me. 'I do not know what I would do without you. If ever I seek a confessor, I will come to you.'

He took the letter back from me and tucked it away in his robes.

'I have something else to tell you,' he said. 'When we have negotiated peace between King Henri and King Philip, it must be ratified by the customary dynastic marriages.'

'The Queen of England is dying,' I said flatly. 'You will give the Princesse Elizabeth to Philip of Spain.'

'That was my thought. Do you agree?'

'It does not matter. She will die in childbirth, leaving no heirs.'

'Poor King Philip has no luck with his brides,' laughed Charles de Guise. 'Perhaps there is something deadly in his lovemaking.' He gave me that knowing smile again, and I saw where his thoughts had wandered. I squirmed uncomfortably in my seat, feeling the hot colour seeping up my neck. She would, of course, have told him everything.

'The second marriage I have already arranged with the bridegroom,' the Cardinal continued. 'I trust you will approve it. Emmanuel Philibert, Duc de Savoie, will marry the King's sister Marguerite.'

'Excellent. I commend you on your genius at nuptial arrangements,' I said, then clamped my lips shut in embarrassment.

'I have taken the liberty of instructing the Duc de Savoie to prepare for a wedding next summer. When I return to Paris I will suggest this date to the King.'

He smiled into my eyes, waiting. At first I did not understand.

'When next summer?' I said slowly.

'Why, the very date, by some peculiar coincidence, that you have mentioned to me in connection with another matter. The beginning of July. And I wish you to be in Paris to attend the wedding, though your presence there must be in secret. It will provide many unusual sights for you.'

> Le lyon jeune le vieux surmontera
> En champ bellique par singulier duelle . . .

As the gilded figures of my vision materialised once more before my eyes, the Cardinal's velvet voice purled on.

'There are so many delightful pleasures at a royal wedding. The feasting, and the drinking, and the women, and the masques. The pageants, and the jousts . . .'

'You have sealed his fate.'

'I?' said the Cardinal de Lorraine, blue eyes opened wide and innocent as daisies. 'I? I have only arranged a royal marriage.'

But King Henri was doomed now. For he could hardly cower in his bedroom while festivities were celebrated around him. He could hardly shun the tournaments in abject terror because a pair of astrologers had warned him against open combat. He could not risk the ridicule of the entire court – particularly if peers like the Duc de Guise mocked him by entering the lists themselves. The King's honour would not permit it. And although slow and ponderous, he was, as Claude de Savoie had said, an honourable man.

'I do not wish to go to Paris for the royal wedding,' I said. 'It is enough that I have helped you create this monstrous thing. I do not wish to see it.'

'I fear,' said Charles de Guise blandly, putting his delicate white hand softly on my arm, 'that you have no choice, Maître de Notredame. I need your presence there.'

'What if I am recognised?'

'You will not be recognised. You will merely be one of the

crowd. No one outside the court knows your face. And there are details of timing which only you can provide.'

'Monseigneur, you are placing me in grave danger. If this thing comes to pass, I will be implicated. No astrologer who has successfully prophesied evil or death escapes without suspicion. I am reminded of what happened to Luc Gauricus. It is natural, in grief and anger, to blame the prophet.'

'I tell you that you will not be recognised. Enough of this quibbling. You will write a letter of warning to the Queen at the beginning of June. M. de Chavigny will send it by courier for you, as you will be bedridden with a particularly painful attack of gout. In the meantime you will actually be on the road to Paris. The Queen must be reminded in time, so that she is sure to badger her royal spouse.'

I gave a great weary sigh and bowed my head. I could not disobey him.

'There will be but a year of reign, Monseigneur, when King Henri is dead. Are you sure you wish this? The Dauphin is tubercular. If his lungs do not kill him, his mother will.'

'Much may be accomplished in a year,' said the Cardinal de Lorraine. 'We will be rulers of France in all but name.'

'Then you must aim for a stable government, careful management of finances . . .' I began.

He laughed at me. 'Stable government? Careful management of finances? I would think, rather, the extermination of the Huguenots would be far more pleasurable.'

I lost my temper at last and slammed my goblet down upon the tabletop. My hands shook with the strain of the conflict between my anger and my fear of him, my remembrance of who he was.

'You are a fool,' I snapped at him. 'All you can speak of is persecution and extermination, this holy new role for the house of Guise. Is that what your brother, your father, your grandfather fought for? You will destroy all our plans and kill us all. François de Guise is loved by the people of France because he is gallant. He has a reputation for justice and mercy. You will blacken him along with yourself. Do you think the people of this nation wish to see a tyrant on the throne?'

But he only laughed harder, showing his small white teeth.

At last he subsided, and gently took my hand between his cool ringed fingers.

'My dear friend,' he said, and despite everything I gave way before the extraordinary power of his charm. 'You must not believe everything I tell you. I fear you do not understand me at all.'

'I do not and never will, Monseigneur. Why do you bait me?'

'Because it amuses me to see you hurling enraged moral diatribes. It helps to restore my faith in human nature, which seventeen years at the Valois court have tended to erode. Do you think I am such a fool, or that my soul is indeed so black as you paint it?'

I stared into those unfathomable eyes and could not answer. Fluttering at the threshold of my memory were the many testimonials to his kindness and generosity, his refinement and taste, his nourishment of learning and the arts. The King loved him. His family adored him. And yet . . .

He rose. 'You must return to Salon, and I must go to court, to show M. d'Andelot's letter to the King. We will expect you in Paris next summer.' He smiled sweetly into my eyes. 'I am certain you will enjoy meeting Madame de St Clair again.'

XXVI

In mid-October, the treaty of Câteau-Cambrésis patched together a tenuous peace between Philip of Spain and King Henri. The duchies of Savoie and Piedmont, long clutched tightly by French hands, were returned to Emmanuel Philibert, Duc de Savoie, who also accepted an offer of marriage with Princesse Marguerite, sister to the King. King Henri renounced all claim to the Milanese and Naples, for ever extinguishing Lorraine's cherished dream of the ancient and chimerical Angevin crown. The Connêtable de Montmorency and his nephew, Gaspard de Coligny, were released from imprisonment. Ageing King Philip, a widower at last, accepted the hand of the prepubescent Princesse Elizabeth de Valois. Young Charles, Duc de Lorraine, was betrothed to Princesse Claude de Valois, receiving Stenay and 300,000 écus in dowry. France retained the three bishoprics of Metz, Toul and Verdun. And Calais, the Duc de Guise's great prize, wrenched so boldly from English hands, remained in French possession.

François de Guise was livid at the terms of the treaty. Much that might have been retained by hard bargaining was irresponsibly signed away, for the King was anxious to retrieve the Constable from his Flemish prison. France emerged from the negotiations with little to show for so many years of bitter fighting. And the Constable, in the gloom of the dungeon, had assiduously nursed his virulent hatred for the house of Guise. Now he undertook to destroy their credibility in the King's eyes. For the moment, the two golden and infallible princes of Lorraine seemed to have fallen from royal favour.

But other patterns evolved that were more to my masters' satisfaction. The wedding of the Duc de Savoie to the Princesse Marguerite de Valois was firmly set for the twenty-seventh day of June in the Year of Our Lord 1559. The King would then be forty-one years of age, and the malefic configurations in his horoscope would be at their most fatal.

The old lion and the young would at last meet on the *champ bellique*.

On the fifteenth of June, I arrived in Paris, where I was discreetly lodged by Jean Dorat, poet to the court, in his elegant little town house. I dared not venture out, and passed a week cosily ensconced in M. Dorat's library, carefully examining the daily movements of moon and planets across the King's horoscope. When my voluntary imprisonment and my onerous task became unbearable, I at last risked strolling the nocturnal streets muffled in a grey cloak. Ridiculous enough, of course, for the Cardinal had been right. I would hardly have been recognised. Who in Paris besides the *noblesse* would know my face? I had left my doctor's robes and cap behind, and trimmed my beard to the fashionable length, and wore a simple doublet and subdued black cape. I resembled any prosperous merchant, a grey stone among innumerable others. Nevertheless, a profound uneasiness haunted me, stemming from my sense of guilt.

On the twenty-first day of June, Emmanuel Philibert, Duc de Savoie, made his formal entry into Paris. He was mounted on a black charger and attended by a splendid and formidable train of men-at-arms – tactful reminder that he had smashed St Quentin and now ruled an independent duchy. Behind this display of Savoie's martial might rode a hundred and fifty gentlemen of the household, in doublets of fiery red satin, crimson shoes and cloaks of black velvet embroidered with gold lace which shimmered in the ruthless sunlight. As the procession passed, crowds poured from their houses, filling the flower-strewn streets with a seething flood. I stood at the window of M. Dorat's snug library and looked down with interest at the middle-aged warrior of severe countenance, his great hooked beak of a nose and clever deep-set black eyes suggesting a bird of prey. He rode with immense dignity toward the court, lodged for the occasion at the Hôtel des Tournelles. For many centuries the house of Savoie had been inextricably bound, by marriage and blood, with the vines of the Order. I wondered whether Emmanuel Philibert would participate in the lists.

The city was in perpetual uproar. Having barely recovered from the celebrations of one royal wedding – that of King Philip and the Princesse Elizabeth – it plunged with insane glee into another. Fête succeeded fête, and largess from an exhausted treasury was prodigally distributed among the crowds. The streets churned and streamed with merrymakers, vandals, drunken fights and brawls. Everyone succumbed to the pervasive and irresistible spirit of hysterical gaiety, which sanctioned every possible crime as well as every possible pleasure. I buried myself in my books, as I had once done at Avignon and Montpellier, and awaited word from the Cardinal de Lorraine.

He arrived very late on a steamy and oppressive night, accompanied by the young lion, Gabriel de Montgoméry, Sieur de Lorges. I was seated at a bureau in the library, head bent over my horoscopes by the light of a single guttering candle. I turned to see those two tall figures standing shadowy and inexorable as fate in the doorway. The short hairs stiffened at the back of my neck.

The Cardinal glided into the room cluttered with books and parchments, and lolled languorously into a chair.

'Well, Maître de Notredame, when shall the appropriate moment be?'

I licked my lips, which were very dry, and swallowed convulsively. 'On the third day of the tournaments. The thirtieth of June, at four o'clock in the afternoon. The moon moves into Capricorn, ignites the opposition of Saturn to its natal place, and accentuates its natal quadrature to the sun.'

'Excellent. It cannot be too soon, for I fear our good graces at King Henri's court have been worn threadbare. He begins to suspect the truth of his father's dying words. I shall ask Madame de St Clair to collect you here in the early afternoon. You may watch from among the crowds beneath the galleries.'

I stared at the Sieur de Lorges, but he stood stolidly in the doorway, mute. I felt a sudden urge to seize him by the shoulders and shake him, to cry out, How can you perform this deed? How can you offer yourself in sacrifice? Refuse, leave Paris, flee to England, flee anywhere, anywhere but here . . . Desperately, I sought words which might persuade the Cardinal to let me return home. But he answered my pleading gaze with his usual cool amusement, and smiled, and took the Sieur de Lorges by the arm, and left me alone with my horoscopes and my black visions.

Marie de St Clair was as exotic and enigmatic and beautiful as my tormented memories had recalled, her olive-black eyes shining with unholy anticipation. She was clad in a simple white gown, like any bourgeois wife. A demure heart-shaped white satin cap studded with small pearls was perched on her dark head, while a sardonic smile nestled in the corners of her red lips. By the time I saw her, I was beyond all sanity. My head was seething with terrible visions of lance-wounds and dust and shadowy kings locked in mortal struggle on endless tilting-grounds of bloody sand. I could no longer distinguish between reality and dream. She looked at me intently. Gently, she insisted I drink a goblet of wine before we emerged from the shelter of Jean Dorat's town house into the thronged and noisy streets.

228

The crowds swarmed thick as ants wherever I looked, on the rooftops, in the streets, perched atop the turrets and towers of the palaces, balanced like storks on the stonework statues of the churches. I had never seen so many people in one place. The din was deafening, the cloying stench of sweat suffocating. The sun pounded blindingly on the chased silver and gold armour of the contestants, the swaying plumes of the helmets, the brilliant liveries of pages and squires and grooms, the embroidered blazons and banners, the gleaming and sweating backs of the great chargers. I peered up at the galleries, to where the Queen, in cloth-of-silver, sat surrounded by her retinue, a nacreous pearl set among vivid jewels. To her left sat the Cardinal de Lorraine, graceful and bright as a poppy in the sun. To her right sat Marie Stuart, the Dauphine, in cloth-of-gold, her bright hair a sienna cloud around her pale face. Behind her hunched the young Dauphin, with Madame de Valentinois in her widow's black and white, stark against the exotic plumage of ladies and courtiers. I fixed my eyes on the grey dust and garbage at my feet. Marie de St Clair's gentle but firm fingers pressed my arm.

'You must watch, Maître de Notredame,' she whispered into my ear above the din. 'Nothing has been planned but the moment. It is in the lap of fate. We shall see if fate is willing to be seduced.'

Tall and imposing as an ancient sun-god in his dazzlingly polished golden armour, the King rode a magnificent black horse belonging to the Duc de Savoie. Emmanuel Philibert himself sat in the galleries beside the Cardinal. I stared again at Charles de Guise, most brilliant and most deadly of all the handsome princes of Lorraine, elegant and fair, with sunlight beaming brightly on his gold crucifix and scarlet robes. Even at this distance, I could discern the vivid blue of his eyes.

The cornets blared an imperious prelude. King Henri rode out first against Jacques de Savoie, Duc de Nemours. The young duke sat his horse badly – from lesser ability, or from some instinctive wisdom, or perhaps from a knowledge of what this day meant to us all. In the first course, the King's lance splintered against his cuirass and he tumbled into the dust with a resonant crash. Unhurt, he staggered from the field. The crowds cheered the King wildly. Looking away, I again felt the intense pressure of Marie de St Clair's fingers on my arm.

'Watch,' she murmured with her red lips.

King Henri rode out next against Alphonse d'Este, Prince of Ferrara, brother-in-law to François de Guise. He too was unhorsed in the first course. The crowds cheered even more tumultuously. This display of skill on the King's part proved him as brave a knight as his charismatic father. It compensated for the sombre melancholy of his ponderous personality.

The third opponent in the lists was the Duc de Guise. He rode astride a snowy charger, bearing the silver and crimson and gold *ailerons* and the double-armed cross of his house, crimson plumes streaming against the shimmering silver of his exquisitely chased helmet. Behind the silver eaglets and the cross of Jerusalem floated another banner: the black and white Beauséant of the Temple, unfurling mockingly in the sun. The cornets dinned again. As though in a dream I watched the two figures shining gold and silver in the merciless light, their black and white steeds like chess pieces on a board. They approached each other at a thunderous gallop. Then, there was a great clang as lances struck and splintered against breast-plates. Both riders swayed and struggled to retain their mounts. Neither man was unhorsed.

They prepared to tilt again, with fresh lances. 'He is more skilled than the King,' Marie de St Clair whispered in my ear. 'But he will give the victory away.'

And as she spoke, the ominous clang of steel upon gilded steel resounded again, and François de Guise toppled, reeling, into the dust.

As he was helped from the field by his squires, the King sent a gentleman to the Duc de Savoie in the galleries. His Majesty thanked the duke for the loan of the magnificent black, to which, he said, he owed the honour of his victories. Moments later, the gentleman returned with Emmanuel Philibert's reply. He was delighted his horse had been of service. At the same time, he begged the King – as did the Queen and her ladies – to refrain from further exertion. Three triumphs were enough, the hour was late, the weather extremely hot, the tour-nament concluded.

Amidst my clouded confusion I thought of Catherine de' Medici, seated silvery and pale and impotent in the galleries above. She had no doubt received my letter warning her against the King's participation in open combat. In conformity with his nature and with our plans, King Henri had defied the admonition.

He now insisted he was ready to run another course. He demanded a fresh lance. He raised the golden visor of his helmet, which resembled a gilded cage, and I could see the sheen of sweat pouring down his brow and into his eyes. His eyes . . .

Alphonse d'Este and the Duc de Guise, armourless and streaming with sweat, strode out into the lists. Both begged the King not to joust further that day. He had suffered a swooning fit the week previous, after a particularly strenuous game of tennis. They were concerned about his health. The more they entreated him, the more obstinate he became.

'Send me the Sieur de Lorges,' the King demanded angrily. 'He will run a course with me.'

I drew a long slow breath. Wanly, hollowly, from some remote distance, the great bell of Notre Dame tolled over the babble of the crowd, marking the hour of four o'clock.

'How can this be?' I hissed to Marie de St Clair. 'He has requested the man himself. How can this be?'

She shook her dark head. 'Be silent and watch.'

Gabriel de Montgoméry, Sieur de Lorges, Captain of the Scots Guard, excused himself and implored the King not to command him. The King grew more irritated and repeated the order. The Sieur de Lorges bowed his tawny head – the immemorial gesture of the sacrificial beast going willingly to the knife. He was helped astride his horse and given a lance, then trotted to his position at the end of the lists.

Marie de St Clair gripped my arm with sudden impulsive violence.

'The King,' she whispered. 'He has forgotten to fasten his visor.'

It was as though I watched the underwater dance of two monstrous sea-creatures, as though a waking nightmare crawled sluggishly across my vision. Something had happened to my eyesight. The sky was greenish, like a great brass bowl

231

overturned, and the heat clawed at my throat. I stared at the engraved lion on the King's golden helmet, expecting it to come alive and roar over the heads of the crowd. My breath issued in ragged rasping gasps. The presences of the wood, the ancient wood, pressed upon me, and I saw the great oak rooted in the dust of the lists, for the galleries had receded into blackness, and the spectral king rode clad in white, but it was the king who held the lance now, two kings, two lances, *deux classes une, puis mourir, mort cruelle* . . .

Embroidered banners unfurled like smoke, soundless, ethereal, and the two ghostly gilded and glittering shapes seemed to meet in mid-air, to collide with a burst of white flame. There was a violent crash and a terrible abyss of silence, a bottomless hole in the fabric of reality. The King reeled and desperately clutched the pommel of his saddle, striving with stricken clumsiness to recover his seat. A dreadful shriek from the Queen pierced the hollow stillness, echoing like a pennon streaming raggedly through emptiness. Suddenly, the lists were filled with servitors, rushing to help the wounded man from his horse. They relieved him of his armour and I saw his face, his dreadful face swamped in blood and the splintered lance head driven through the eye. He had fainted. The Queen sat rigid as a lump of stone now, her hands pressed to her mouth, her face a ghastly white. Beside her the Cardinal de Lorraine had risen from his seat and held his gold crucifix in both hands, his lips moving in prayer. People were rushing madly everywhere while attendants carried the unconscious King from the field, into the Hôtel des Tournelles.

I covered my face with my hands, shuddering. Marie de St Clair, cool and composed as steel despite the carnage she had witnessed, gripped me firmly by the arm and led me away.

I did not regain my senses for many hours. When I at last opened my eyes, I discerned the carved beams of the ceiling in my room at Jean Dorat's town house. I was in my bed, and Marie de St Clair was seated beside me, her face still and white as crushed lilies.

'You will be well enough now, Maître de Notredame,' she said quietly, offering me a cup of wine. 'I should have guessed that it would take you in this way. What did you see?'

I shook my head wearily. 'Nothing. I do not know. It was the same state in which I see my visions. When I stare into the fire. But it was much worse. I saw . . . something other than what was there.'

'Tell me.'

'The King, the white King with the unshorn hair . . . I could not see the Sieur de Lorges. I saw something else.'

I looked up into her still, exquisitely carved face.

'Please,' I said. 'I do not wish to speak of it.'

'I understand.' She placed a cool white hand across my brow. A hot shudder coursed through my body at her touch. 'When I brought you back, you were in high fever. It has passed now. But you must wait until the Cardinal is able to see you. There will be chaos for a time. I fear the King will linger long in his agony before he dies.'

The guilt began to gnaw me mercilessly. 'He was not an unfit King,' I whispered. 'It is a hideous death. It seems unjust. He was an honourable man. A little slow, but honourable . . .'

'Hush. It was his time. You know that as well as I. You heard him yourself, refusing the pleas to quit the joust, demanding that the Sieur de Lorges fight.'

'That is easy to say. But we all bear the guilt.'

'Guilt?' she said, and her dark eyes mocked me. 'There is no guilt, Maître de Notredame. We are all only vessels for fate – midwives, if you like. Does the midwife bear the blame if the child is monstrous?'

I stared into her eyes, her marvellous black eyes in which I had once drowned. Charles de Guise had taught her well. Or perhaps she was made like this from the beginning, a serpent to match him.

My desperate desire for her was subsumed by an intense, overwhelming need to sleep. She had put something in my wine.

'Marie, ah, Marie,' I managed to murmur before my eyes closed, 'I thank the gods that the prelates of the Church cannot marry. For I dare not imagine what line of unholy princes you and he would breed.'

As I drifted gently downward into velvety darkness, I remember only her gently sardonic laughter, and the butterfly touch of her lips on mine, and the mocking echoes of my own words resonating in my ears.

When I awoke the Cardinal de Lorraine stood over me, elegant and composed, his excitement betrayed only by a high spot of delicate colour on each pale cheek.

'I fear,' he said with a little moue of his lips, 'that we must get you out of Paris quickly, Maître de Notredame.'

'Why? Have I been recognised?'

'No. But the good citizens of the town are burning your effigy in the street. And calling on the Church to do the same to you. They are clamouring for vengeance against you. They believe you to be a sorcerer and a Huguenot.'

'A Huguenot?' I said weakly, beginning to laugh.

'I must return to the King's bedside. He is failing quickly. The surgeons are working on him with all their desperate skill, but the lance splinters penetrated the brain. He is completely blind.'

I turned my face into the pillow.

'I have contacted my agents in England,' he continued. 'The Sieur de Lorges will be quietly spirited away by nightfall. The King forgave him, declaring he had only fulfilled his obligations as a noble knight. But the Queen seeks vengeance against him.'

'And does the Queen seek vengeance against me too?'

He smiled gently. 'No, my friend. She vows you did your best to warn her, and intends to protect you. But you must leave Paris tonight. I will send two men to accompany you back to Salon.'

'Gladly. I do not wish to see Paris again as long as I live. I do not know why you forced me here to witness this terrible tragedy.'

The vivid eyes smiled down on me with compassion. 'Perhaps you will one day understand. The artist's creation, or the gods', cannot be actualised unless one infuses it with his own soul. Only then is it an authentic creation. Had we not been present to witness this event, it would not have come to pass. Your very anguish was its lifeblood.' He stood for a moment silent, toying with his rings. 'I must go, for there is much to be done. We must appropriate the young Dauphin quickly, before his mother rises from her prostrate grief. There must be no doubt who are the real rulers in this new reign.'

'Monseigneur,' I said softly, 'you served him for seventeen years. Do you feel no remorse for the manner in which this has been done?'

The pale beautiful face broke into a charming smile, and the brilliant eyes mocked me. 'Done? I do not know what you mean, Maître de Notredame. The King has met with a tragic and unfortunate accident. His astrologers attempted to warn him of it. He did not heed the warning. It was his fate.'

XXVII

King Henri spent ten days dying. As Marie de St Clair had warned me, chaos ensued. The Queen remained incarcerated, blind with grief, in her black-draped chamber of mourning. Quietly, the Cardinal de Lorraine and the Duc de Guise mustered into Paris several hundred men-at-arms, who were installed as sentinels about the silent palace and in the Dauphin's apartments. These troops ensured that no Bourbon Prince of the Blood dared challenge the house of Lorraine. And when the royal party at last emerged from the Hôtel des Tournelles, they were shepherded by the princes of Lorraine – in whose capable and ambitious hands the whole of France's ecclesiastical, financial, political and military affairs now reposed.

As is customary with a change of monarch, a general reshuffling commenced, a repositioning of pawns about the board. My masters gathered around them the friends who had abetted their ascent, and quietly dismissed their opponents. There was no sensational disgrace, no petty revenge. Madame de Valentinois was politely requested to retire from court. The two Bourbon brothers, Louis and Antoine, were gently ushered from the *conseil des affaires*. The Connêtable de Montmorency was courteously dismissed from service.

But though the Cardinal and the duke were now the darlings of fate, I knew they struggled with an almost impossible burden. The treasury was gutted, the country's resources having been voluptuously squandered by the sybaritic extravagance of François I and the vain wars of Henri II. For this last, Charles de Guise was himself largely responsible. Now the entire burden of restoring stability weighed like an enormous cross upon those graceful shoulders. That he was capable of performing this task, I had no doubt. It was the opportunity he had long awaited. But the implacable hatred of his enemies was a beast not easily caged. He could not undertake his Herculean labour, could not sweep the nation's Augean stables clean without cost to his popularity.

It was no secret who these enemies were, nor what the reasons for their enmity. The new reign lurched to a promising dawn, a slow sun clambering up the sky. But as the young King was consecrated by the Cardinal de Lorraine at Reims, my fears were confirmed. Charles de Guise and his brother performed like gifted *jongleurs* of almost superhuman courage and skill, applying themselves to the débâcle of affairs heaped before them. Yet something undermined everything they sought to accomplish, subtle and persistent as woodworms gnawing silently in the darkness.

Behind much of this quiet disruption stood Catherine de' Medici, now Queen-mother. As she had made known to me, she intended to have power, had expected it upon her husband's death. Now the princes of Lorraine ruled as regents, and she was impotent. I could imagine what thwarted anger and hatred seethed within her. Only the slightest opportunity, the merest gentle bending of fate need present itself, and she would not hesitate to destroy her son, so helpless a pawn of the usurpers. In dispatching the young sovereign, his mother would rid herself of his mentors. Already, like maggots in rotten meat, her agents were at work in every province, fomenting rebellion, treating with Huguenots and malcontents, fanning anti-Guise propaganda through vicious and obscene pamphlets and tracts. To the unknowing populace, these two men, with greater claim to the crown than the King himself, began to appear as tyrants, usurpers – parvenu foreigners who had seized the rightful honours of the Bourbon Princes of the Blood. It did not signify that they championed the Catholic cause. This too was cunningly twisted. They were depicted as savage and implacable persecutors, eager to crush Huguenot and Catholic alike beneath their ruthless yoke.

There was another who was equally tenacious in his hatred, equally dangerous. I had met him in Paris, when he visited my apartments at the Hôtel de Sens to request advice in love: Louis de Bourbon, Prince de Condé, the dandy little man with the crooked shoulder, the penniless younger Prince of the Blood whose waspish catty wit was a byword for malice.

From the very beginning of the new King's reign, Louis de Bourbon resolved to topple the upstart house which had stolen the regency he coveted. Jealousy ate at him like acid. At the same time, he was shrewd enough to know he could not remove the duke and the Cardinal by public action. Despite their unpopularity with the Huguenots, their management of affairs was faultless. And Louis de Bourbon could not voice his real grievance as justification: that they were too charismatic, too brilliant, too wealthy, too strong. So he plunged underground like a mole, yeasting public hatred in his underground tunnels by the most outrageous lies.

At the moment of the brothers' triumph, fate – angered perhaps by their manipulation – seemed to be repudiating them. I wrote futile letters, warning them that the Saturnian influence in their horoscopes, though malign, was not irrevocable. But the Lord of the World requires payment for the journey in his own coin: patience, forbearance, tact, reflection, steadfastness. These qualities François de Guise possessed in abundance on the battlefield. He could not maintain them, however, in the face of more petty human enmity. Such enmity wounded him brutally, turned him savage. And the Cardinal de Lorraine – brilliant, mercurial, volatile, fluid as water – could not restrain his own bitter vindictiveness.

Salon did not escape the shadows' slithering encroachment. A prominent Huguenot leader of Provence was assassinated at Draguignan. The common folk of Salon, fanatically Catholic, celebrated this atrocity with wild rejoicing. But many wealthier citizens, some of them kinsmen of the victim, were sympathetic to his cause. Bitter fighting ravaged the streets, and riots, pillages and rapes violently shattered the town's quiet placidity. Claude de Savoie, Governor and Grand Seneschal of Provence, dispatched two hundred men-at-arms to quell the uprisings.

My situation was now even more delicate than during my interview with the Queen. As a partisan of the house of Valois, and an apparently devout Catholic, I was hated by Huguenots. As a Jew and an astrologer, I was hated by Catholics. As a man of wealth – for my reputation had increased vastly since my return from court – I was hated by the tumultuous peasantry. Threats and insults began to proliferate, as though behind a dam liable to break at any moment. Claude de Savoie sent me an armed guard, who made his bed in the parlour every night. Caught by the ferocious currents now mounting to violent crescendo, I spent each day smelling the faggot. Jean-Aimé de Chavigny purchased a pistol. My wife and children dared not show their faces in the streets.

And amidst this grinding and splintering which rent the whole of France and tortured my visions and dreams, there erupted the Tumult of Amboise. It began as political machination, and ushered in civil war.

Here was the overripe cankerous fruit of Louis de Bourbon's labours. Nursing and cherishing it like a child from his own loins, he fashioned for himself a conspiracy. Although truly devout Huguenots refused to be implicated, the prince attracted to himself like a lodestone disparate fragments of wasted and despoiled humanity, bits of flotsam drifting on the sea of social failure, vicious malcontents who strayed within reach of his indiscriminate net. He procured funds from Elizabeth of England, who welcomed the opportunity to strike back at the victor of Calais. Louis de Bourbon called himself the *capitaine muet*, remaining an obscure wraithlike figure pulling strings behind the scenes, but never showing his face. He chose as his figurehead a Périgordin gentleman named Godefroi de Berri, Sieur de la Renaudie, who also harboured a festering hatred of the Duc de Guise. Together they spun a web that stretched throughout the country, into Lutheran Germany, across the stormy channel to Protestant England. La Renaudie travelled back and forth like a shuttlecock, placing the agitators in contact with each other. He informed them of the great work soon to be performed, the salvation of France. For they meant, with all possible speed, to murder the Cardinal de Lorraine and the Duc de Guise.

Like a proud and doting father, Louis de Bourbon watched his conspiracy grow. But there were too many accomplices to be kept secret, too many loquacious mouths. Rumours of the plot filtered back through the Cardinal's agents in Germany. Warnings filtered from Paris through one of his creatures in the Huguenot camp. And the danger was crowned with farcical irony. Godefroi de Berri, Sieur de la Renaudie, decided to consult an astrologer for the auspices of the time. Reliable authorities had assured him that the Prophet of Salon was secretly sympathetic to the Huguenot cause. He arrived in the town to consult me.

The auspices in his horoscope could not be better, I assured him, although in truth they could not have been worse. I remained noncommital during his vicious denunciations of the duke and the Cardinal. I agreed it was deplorable when a noble nation was overrun by those who sought to feed only their own craven dreams of wealth and power. By the time we were finished, he was sweatily embracing me as a fellow conspirator, and I had solemnly proposed a date on which he would be wise to strike. It was the tenth of March. If I understood the patterns of the heavens correctly, this would be the date of his death.

I wrote immediately to Charles de Guise. I received a reply from François, who declared the royal family were in a panic, convinced they would all be slaughtered. Even the cool and sanguine Cardinal had loosened his steely control and wished to rouse the army. But François de Guise, with the calm resourcefulness bred of years of war, would not cause a public disturbance, preferring to confine his knowledge to his own immediate circle. He moved the royal entourage to the impregnable château-fortress of Amboise, filled the town secretly with his troops, and prepared for la Renaudie to fall into his hands.

239

'I am as always grateful to you for your timely service, as is Monseigneur my brother. Do not fear for us. We all know who stands behind this plot. I promise you that before this year is out the *capitaine muet* will be truly so.'

I was not reassured. It was not his life for which I feared. He, I knew, was safe – for a time. But I could not rid myself of the vision of his face, as I had seen it on my first visit to court – the left eye clouded by some savage spirit, something that had entered it as though with the lance long ago, and now waited to burst its bonds.

Regaining his composure, the Cardinal de Lorraine issued an edict relaxing measures against heretics. Only crimes of conspiracy against King and government were now punishable by torture and death. He thus made a mockery of the religious idealism behind la Renaudie's insurrection, dispelling the rebels' chief grievance. Then he invited the Huguenot leaders – Gaspard de Coligny, Louis de Bourbon – to Amboise, to discuss amicably the means by which freedom of worship might be granted without undermining Church authority. He thereby supplied himself with potential hostages, should there be an attack.

The conspirators were plunged into confusion. Panicked traitors revealed their movements. A clumsy band of them were captured in a fortified house. A disorganised attack on the château was easily and efficiently repulsed by the duke's soldiers. And on the tenth day of March, Godefroi de Berri was killed. The duke's cavalry scattered the assembling forces like grains of dust blown before a wind, and the peasants – loyal Catholics all – fell upon the stragglers with wolflike ferocity.

Louis de Bourbon's conspiracy collapsed like an inept chef's soufflé. But though François de Guise escaped, unwounded by sword or arquebus or pistol, another wound, more lethal than any inflicted by tangible weapons, had been incurred. The untrammelled savagery lurking in the duke's dark spirit, dwelling quiescent in his left eye, at last burst free from its confinement. As the captured rebels revealed the scope of their network, he realised Louis de Bourbon's débâcle was no mindless peasant uprising. It was a conspiracy of gentlemen – his own aristocratic class, his own peers who had grown to manhood with him at court, who had fought beside him at Metz and Calais and Thionville, who had toasted him with speeches and songs at sumptuous banquets in his honour when he returned victorious from battle. These men had been his friends. Their betrayal shattered his idealism, poisoned his heart; and the beast was unleashed.

The punishments inflicted upon the prisoners were atrocious. Many were immediately killed by a swordthrust. Many others were drowned in hessian sacks, like unwanted litters of puppies. After brutal torture, the remainder were hanged by hands or feet from the windows and battlements of the château, left to the carrion birds which swarmed in noxious black clouds overhead. It was said afterward that the Duc de Guise, the gallant and chivalrous hero of Metz and Calais, personally supervised the executions with the vicious ferocity of a pain-maddened beast. It was said that his elegant and sanctified brother, the Cardinal de Lorraine, forced the child-King François to stand at the windows of the castle, watching the carnage as though it were a masque.

Popular response to Amboise was immediate and inevitable. The Cardinal de Lorraine's properties at Meudon and Cluny were fired, his effigy hanged and burned in the streets of Paris. Charles de Guise bore the full brunt of the Tumult. A pamphlet began to circulate mysteriously through the countryside.

'Ravening tiger! Venomous viper! Sepulchre of abomination! How long will you continue to abuse the youth of our young King! Will you never put an end to your robberies? Detestable monster! Everyone knows you, everyone sees you, and yet you are still alive. Begone, then! Have done with your tyranny! Escape the hand of the executioner!'

The Cardinal, now that the conspiracy was suppressed and his equilibrium restored, found this tract immensely amusing.

He sent me a copy.

'The style is a little florid, is it not? But perhaps it will ensure my immortality.'

I did not find it amusing. This festering hatred which swelled like a rancorous boil was terrifying and incomprehensible. They had not earned it prior to Amboise; they had merely pursued their ambitions like other men, but with greater skill. Not for the first time, I wondered whether there was something about this blood, this mysterious line, that attracted such martyrdom. It was as though the populace sensed some strange glimmering, some alien aura that clung like a pale mist about the house of Guise. The cry of foreigner was meaningless, for the blood of St Louis flowed through the veins of Lorraine's princes as much as it did through those of Bourbon or Valois. Men could not name the true thing, and manufactured reasons to attack it. Here again, under the dark lordship of the seventh planet, was the Scapegoat.

In the letters I received from François de Guise, I detected a subtle transformation. Some bright cord had snapped after Amboise. The golden and untarnished dreams of his youth, now in his forty-first year had shattered. He had fantasised a magnificent shining restoration of the sacred blood, but the country whose crown he sought for this purpose was sick and rotten and putrefying at the core.

Louis de Bourbon fled to Navarre, to the court of his brother Antoine. Irrepressible, they proceeded to fashion another conspiracy against the King's ministers. This time they did so with greater clumsiness than before. Letters were found by the Cardinal's agents, implicating both of them, as well as the Queen-mother. Shortly thereafter a formal invitation bearing the King's signature – so polite, so gentle, so delicate that Charles de Guise's charming hand was unmistakable – summoned the brothers Bourbon to court.

If they obeyed this summons, they would be walking helplessly into the wolf's jaws. Yet there was no alternative. To refuse the royal request would constitute a declaration of war against the King. And the Duc de Guise had assembled an enormous force on the borders of Navarre which, like a massive hammer, would crush whatever armed rebellion the princes might foment. In the meantime, Catherine de' Medici was made a virtual prisoner in her own palace, impotent to help. And the young King was but mouldable wax in the hands of the house of Guise.

Louis de Bourbon, Prince de Condé, displayed unexpected courage. With his tamer elder brother trailing diffidently behind him, he arrived unarmed at court. Antoine de Bourbon, King of Navarre, was placed under household surveillance. The Prince de Condé was arrested, thrown into solitary confinement, and condemned to death.

With horrible clarity, I foresaw what the next move would be, and sent a desperate letter to the Cardinal. But it was too late. The Queen-mother, seeing an opportunity to at last exorcise her incubi, acted with the speed of a leopard. In November, while out hunting, His Most Christian Majesty François II of France, *premier fils veuve malheureux mariage sans nuls enfans*, died – of a chill, it was said. The Connêtable de Montmorency swaggered back to court from his retirement. François de Guise and the Cardinal de Lorraine were unceremoniously dismissed from office. And at the Queen-mother's instigation, Louis de Bourbon, Prince de Condé, was exonerated of all charges and freed.

Nine-year-old Charles de Valois, the mad one, the haunted one, was King of France.

Calm and apparently unworried, the Cardinal de Lorraine retired quietly to his archiepiscopal see at Reims, where he devoted his vast and versatile energies to inspiring his flock and conspiring with the German princes. The Duc de Guise retired quietly to Joinville, bitter and morbid and disillusioned, and amused himself with his field sports and his children and his unfaithful wife. The court whispered fearfully of the quatrain by the Prophet of Salon – about the unhappy son of the widow who would die young and childless. Once again, we waited.

Catherine de' Medici, Queen-mother of France, at last possessed the unlimited power she had so long coveted. Now she did not know what to do with it. She sided first with the Huguenot party, then with the Catholic. Powerless to prevent the bloodshed and the violence and the increasing distrust in which she and the new King were held, she sought appeasement through vacillation.

I knew it heralded the end of the Valois line. There would be only one more after this mad boy. But the sacrifices which must be made in the process were too appalling to countenance. Black dreams visited me at night. As though my ageing body conspired with the *daemons* of my dreams, attacks of gout tormented me with increasing frequency and severity. I stared at the heavens and drank more wine. Sodden oblivion was preferable to witnessing the avalanche crush the patient labours of so many long years. With intense grief, I watched the inexorable disintegration of François de Guise, who had abandoned his soul to brooding despair.

What does it matter if we fail? The roi perdu *does not die. He is a myth, not a man.*

But what of the man?

The Cardinal de Lorraine began to treat secretly with Philip of Spain, the only prospective ally left against the Queen-mother. Still gifted at nuptial arrangements, he offered the widowed Marie Stuart to Don Carlos, heir to His Catholic Majesty's throne. But King Philip was too crafty and too fearful to countenance this deadly uncle, working like yeast against his own country from the safety of Spanish domains. The match was refused. And Marie Stuart, no longer useful because no longer marketable, was shipped back to Scotland to embrace her own tragic fate.

Thus dawned the Year of Our Lord 1562. Bitter fighting continued. Across the length and breadth of France, priceless and precious holy relics of centuries of human devotion were defiled and smashed to pieces. François de Guise at last stirred himself from his black depression. As leader of the Catholic Triumvirate, he entered into military alliance with the Connêtable de Montmorency and the Maréchal de St André. Antoine de Bourbon turned traitor against his brother and his Huguenot wife, returned to the fold of the Church, and joined them. The Queen-mother retaliated by allying herself with Gaspard de Coligny, the Prince de Condé and the Huguenots. The pieces were laid on the board for the next game, neatly aligned, black and white. But which was black, and which white?

Often I wondered where I would be, had I turned my mule away from the abbey at Notre Dame d'Orval. But one can also peer backwards to the beginning of time, and wonder what might have happened had there been no Serpent in the Garden.

XXVIII

At the beginning of the new year, a vicious and terrible dream invaded my wine-fogged sleep. I dreamed I stood amidst a welter of dead and mutilated dying, surrounded by bloody bodies hacked and torn by arquebus and sword, some with heads lolling or severed arms and legs, some still alive and trying vainly to crawl to sanctuary. Corpses lay everywhere, piled so high I could not see beyond the grisly mountainous mass of putrefying flesh. Fear constricted my throat, for I knew that somewhere at the centre of this carnage was François de Guise, in mortal danger. Dark clouds swooned like massive fungi over the hellish spectacle, blotting out the light. I struggled frantically through the mounds of carcasses, spattering myself with gore. Sometimes hands reached out to snag my ankle as I passed, and the groans and cries dinned as an infernal chorus in my ears. I opened my mouth to shout, but no sound emerged. And over it all, like a monstrous metallic heartbeat, a lugubrious church bell clanged, tolling the dead.

As I floundered onwards, the dark clouds thinned and the light cast twisted shadows across the funereal arena. And when I at last broke through the ring into the centre, smeared with the marks of my passage, I saw François de Guise, illumined by the pallid glow of some yellowish heavenly body. His sword was glinting and streaked with gouts of blood, his pearl-strewn white doublet stained with red blossoms, his mouth distorted in a savage grin across his teeth. His right eye burned at me in silent desperation, wide and bleak and staring. The left was half-shut and aflame with malice. It fixed me malevolently, as though enraged that I should witness its triumph.

He opened his lips and whispered, 'Help me. For the love of God, help me.'

The news meandered for several days before reaching me at Salon. Journeying back to Joinville from Germany, where he and the Cardinal had visited the Prince of Würtemburg, the duke and his entourage passed through the town of Vassy, in Champagne. A large Huguenot congregation was gathered for a service in a mouldering barn. Curious, the duke's soldiers elbowed their way into the building, and a scuffle ensued with the irritated congregation. As such things do among a mindless mob, it quickly spread. François de Guise, merely a disapproving bystander, ·was attacked and injured by stones. His troops, shocked by this act of outrage against their noble master, retaliated. The entire Huguenot population of Vassy was mercilessly massacred. The bloodbath had begun.

I listened with rage and impotent bitterness. Once he would have held back those soldiers, would have acted with calmness and mercy. He was changed now.

I bring not peace, but a sword.

But how much choice had he had? I knew his intense pride. Here was the curse of Leo, rising in the east at his birth. If he were truly attacked without provocation, the results would indeed be inevitable. And the beast uncaged at Amboise was as much the creation of unbearable circumstance as a quality of his own soul. Soul and circumstance, circumstance and soul: which was choice, and which was fate? Who was the martyr, who the persecutor?

Long ago I had trusted the wisdom of Mathias Delvaux. I had sought to help my masters choose, from the myriad patterned threads of the future, the single strand which would fulfil the dream. Now it was tangled and knotted and broken, and the dark flood of a poisoned nation gushed through the dykes.

Help me. For the love of God, help me.

I knew I must try. But he would no longer reply to my letters. Only the Cardinal de Lorraine wrote from his retreat at

Reims, cool, enigmatic, full of malicious gossip, revealing nothing of his current plans.

I dispatched a letter to the duke in the crudest, most violent language I could muster. He was a fool, I informed him. He had wantonly destroyed everything with his mindless and primitive savagery. I no longer considered myself his servant. I gambled, of course, on my knowledge of him. Perhaps he would have me murdered for my betrayal. But I knew the pride of the Lion. More likely, his injury would compel him to confront me face to face, before he removed me.

For weeks, I could not rid myself of the smell of blood. In the wake of Vassy, uprisings and assassinations proliferated. François de Guise had set a fine example. I tried to focus myself on the most mundane of my labours. I attempted to resume my work on the unfinished quatrains of the *Centuries*. I stared at the fire and pondered the movement of the equinoctial point into the constellation of the second Fish. The reversal was at hand.

I thought of Rome's long corrupt rulership over her naïve and ignorant flock. I thought of the plague that had so shaken men's faith. I thought of England's rebellion, of King Henry whom God had not struck down in rage. I thought of Luther and Calvin, also spared divine wrath and even withstanding human vindictiveness. As I surrendered to the violent onslaught of my visions, I sensed the great heaving and groaning of the vast time spirit, dying amidst its labour of giving birth, spewing forth war and confusion and a turbulent quest for some panacea to ease the agony of its pangs. The world rocked and careered around me as though it had fallen from its orbit and was hurtling directionless through the void. Like huge abcesses on the soul of humanity, the poisons, long festering in the entrails and bones, were rising to the surface to be cleansed.

Having waited for so long, the propitious moment might indeed have arrived for the house of Lorraine. At such junctures, the call for the Redeemer invariably rose above the smoke and fire and ash of what lay dying. But the path that Redeemer must tread along the precipice was so narrow, so impassable, so flanked with unforeseen dangers. Only a god might traverse it. François de Guise was no god. He had committed the unpardonable error of displaying his too-fallible humanity. Whatever his lineage, he was in every sense unbearably, heartbreakingly human. And if I read his horoscope aright, his life would soon be forfeit.

'So the great prophet has proved a coward after all,' snapped the Duc de Guise contemptuously. 'I had thought better of you these many years, Maître de Notredame. But perhaps the Jews are indeed a lily-livered race.'

I said nothing.

'Of course,' he continued, his Janus-gaze hard as stone, 'you cannot expect to live this night out. One does not resign from my service as one resigns from the post of notary, or sells a sausage-shop.' He began to chew furiously at his beard, as was his wont in extreme anger. I knew, meeting his vehement glare, that I had gambled wisely.

I shrugged. 'I have only a few years left in any case, my lord, so it does not much signify. Had you a brain even the size of a pea, you would have foreseen the consequences of Vassy and stayed your hand.'

'You dare, *you* dare, to pass judgement on *me*?' he rasped. His face was very flushed, and the scar above the heavy-lidded alien eye was knotted and white and ugly. 'Did you fancy this work of ours would be like making beauty creams? I tell you I could happily slaughter every accursed Huguenot in this realm. Or any other man, woman or child who presumes to stand in my way. And I would sleep sweeter at night.'

He whirled and paced the chamber like a cat. His fingers, laden with jewels, rested on his sword-hilt. His raw power seared me afresh, the inexplicable and overwhelming power of this line – as did the pathos of its inexorable corrosion. Here might have been a King indeed.

'Do you know they tried to stone me?' he snarled, and I heard the mortal wound hidden beneath the anger. 'I was struck on the head and cheek,' he said bitterly, 'I felt my own blood running into my eyes. To bleed, not from a noble blow received in battle, but from a rock hurled by a pubescent Huguenot peasant brat!'

He ceased pacing and stood still as a stone pillar in the centre

248

of the room. His hands were trembling. The right eye stared at me, anguished, bleak, hopeless.

'Why do they hate me so?' he whispered. 'After Metz, after Calais, after Thionville, why do they hate me? Before Amboise, we did everything in our power to set the kingdom's affairs aright. No one else could have shouldered that task. We worked so hard, so long. We poured our own money into the treasury. We sacrificed everything. What did I do? What mistake did I make? Tell me, Maître de Notredame. You always tell me the truth. Why has it come to this?'

I shook my head. His pain had buried itself in my own belly like the hooked talons of a malignant bird. I remembered the whispered voice from the shrouded bed at the château of Gisors, telling me of his dream to restore the Temple.

'My lord, I beg you to listen. France is a powder-keg. Try to remember what is happening around you. The Queen-mother plays you against Condé and Coligny, Catholic against Huguenot. Because if civil war erupts, she alone will be the conciliator, the peacemaker, the saviour. It is such an old strategy. Have you forgotten? For any hatred the people bear you, she has sown the seed. But there are many all across France who love you. You are the king of Paris. Have you forgotten how they cheer you? My lord, your enemy is not the Huguenot. It is the Italian woman. She is destroying your soul. She is intent on your death. You are a bigger fool than ever I believed possible, to fall into her snare so readily. Can you not see that only moderation and tolerance will deflect her? If you ally with Condé and Coligny, she cannot stand against you. She knows you court the throne. But she dare not use her own hand against you, lest the Catholics rise in turn and depose her. It is easier to give you rope, that you may hang yourself – as you are so obligingly doing at this moment.'

He had begun to pace again. I did not know if he even listened. I plunged on.

'I do not judge you. You should know by this time that I serve you without blame. I would do anything within my power to help you. What man in these times can have clean hands? Only try to keep your sanity. I know the wound you bear from Amboise. You must not let it corrode you, for you

249

are toppling all you have so painstakingly built.'

But it was no use. He was trapped. He needed a banner under which to fight, yet in fighting he defeated his own ends. And his blind sense of mission, his desperate urgency to attain his goal, deceived him again and again. As the glittering vision of kingship receded like the memory of a dream, he clawed the harder to retrieve it. And perhaps he sensed – as I did in my great grief – that it was already too late.

He ceased his pacing again and stared at me. The firelight shone balefully on his jewels, on the dull gold of his hair and beard. 'You are right, of course. I see you have done this to get my ear. You have a woman's wiles, my friend. But Jésu, what can I do?' He laughed harshly. 'It is only as paladin of the Catholic cause that I can seize the throne. Only so can I keep the Bourbons out. I have no choice. I must shed blood. If I grant the heretics peaceful worship, they will put Antoine de Bourbon over me. Then all will be truly lost, for he has a strong son. I cannot slaughter my way to the throne of France through both Valois and Bourbon. Yet I am only engendering hatred around me. What can I do?'

'If you must kill,' I said quietly, 'kill Catherine de' Medici.'

'We have thought of that, of course. In fact, my brother and I deemed you the most likely candidate to proffer the poisoned cup.' I paled. 'But,' he went on, 'you must see that here too I am trapped. It is too soon. The King is mad and only his mother can control him. Destroy her and suspicion would fall at once on our heads. Louis de Bourbon would not forego that opportunity. The King would have us all executed, my children as well.'

No matter which way he turned he could not escape. He was like a caged lion, maddened by his impotence, unwilling to believe the dream was lost, flinging himself uselessly against the immovable bars.

The mood shifted abruptly, the despair and anguish drained slowly from his flushed and contorted face. The bizarre duplicity of the double gaze vanished. He was only a handsome man with an injured eye.

'I often ask myself,' he said slowly, 'what kind of God it is that truly guides us. These religious quarrels are all mummery, as well you know. I care not a jot whether I sing psalms or the *Salve Regina*, for it is all a means to an end. As you and I both know, there is no right side on which to fight. God is both present and absent in all of it, for God is in man. Yet when the black despair comes upon me, I still pray my Catholic prayers.'

He motioned at last for me to sit. As he poured wine, I stifled a groan of relief.

'You must think it laughable,' he said, 'that I am so devout.'

'Ironic, perhaps, my lord, but not laughable. All incense wafts to heaven, whatever the scent. The pity is that there must be this persecution in the name of God.'

'You know that is not why I have perpetrated these things.'

'I believe you. But that is what the world sees. Religion and politics are interchangeable in this war. You carry a burden and a secret that would drive most men mad. No, I do not think your beliefs laughable. A man must cling to something, if he is to remain sane.'

'You know so little about us. Yet you remain loyal. Why?'

I shrugged. 'I assure you it is not for religious reasons. My grandfather used to say that one name for God was as good as another. To me Apollo or Dionysus or Aphrodite are no less aspects of God than Our Lord. If you claimed to be the son of Poseidon, as Theseus of Athens once did, I would remain as loyal to you.'

He smiled broadly at me. 'My brother, the Cardinal de Lorraine, is the wealthiest and most powerful prince of the Church in our Catholic realm. He has a wondrously unquenchable and divinely inspired faith in the instrument between his holy legs. If I am to believe his own words, he wields it with incomparable versatility and dexterity. He worships Priapus, the Horned One, and Dionysus, bringer of drunken ecstasy. There is no sensual excess he has not sampled, with either sex. He has an obscene tongue. In private banter, he viciously mocks those very tenets on which he discourses with such magnificent eloquence to his entranced flock. He is the last man on earth one could call devout.'

'Then he is a true Cathar,' I said.

'Yes,' said François de Guise, laughing, 'an Adamite. He is committed to satiation of the flesh as gateway to the spirit. But

I am perplexed by it all. After my grandfather's death, my grandmother, Philippa de Guelders, became devout in the extreme. I remember with great clarity how, when I was a child, she witnessed a miraculous vision while praying in the chapel at Joinville. She came to us as though in a trance, her face distorted with a terrible ecstasy. It seemed her soul would burst forth from her eyes. She swore she had seen the Holy Ghost. Yet I have glimpsed the same expression of searing ecstasy on my brother's face when, at some drunken banquet, he has lifted his red robes and taken a woman on the floor. At the height of his pleasure, he has stared into my eyes. The look is the same.'

I was silent. Unwittingly, I had drifted back to the moon-bleached gardens of the Hôtel de Cluny, transfixed by those white bodies writhing in the shadows, serpents locked in serpentine embrace.

'How different these gods are, Maître de Notredame! What the one demands, the other abhors. Yet though our poor minds cannot comprehend it, I often suspect these gods are the same.'

'I have seen the face of neither god,' I said quietly, 'so I cannot say. I have met many demons. In the fire, in the arms of women, in my own soul. I have never encountered God. Or perhaps I have not recognised him.'

'Well,' said the Duc de Guise, 'I have envied both my grandmother and my brother, for I have never glimpsed such heights either. Yet I think too much of any god can drive one mad. I have killed for power and wounded pride, not for God. At least I am not a hypocrite about it.'

We are all of us poor puppets, I thought bitterly – this scion of such mysterious lineage no less than myself. Whose hand guided the strings? I looked at my own hands, clean of blood. And knew that I could judge none of it.

'In his fashion,' I said with a perfectly sober face, 'perhaps Monseigneur the Cardinal too seeks salvation.'

He let out a burst of delighted laughter, and clapped me on the back. 'Do not let him hear you say it, my friend, or he will find a way to make you suffer. He could not receive a greater insult.'

'I would not dream of insulting him. He is far too deadly.'

252

'Deadly, yes. But he is the cleverest man in the world. Do you know that he has hatched a new scheme at this moment of precarious balance? He has conceived the idea of a Holy League. An aristocratic brotherhood of all Catholic princes, prelates, governors, magistrates, officers and noblemen throughout the realm, united by treaty under the banner of the Church. Their formal commitment will first be to wipe out the Huguenot heresy. And second, should the Valois line cease, to place the Duc de Guise on the throne of France. A united League, bound by sacred oath, ratified by signature, backed by arms and sanctified by the Pope. And with the pledged support of Philip of Spain . . .'

'No,' I said abruptly. 'You cannot bring Spanish troops into France.'

'No Spanish troops, my friend. Spanish gold, and Swiss and German mercenaries purchased by a Spanish treasury. King Philip distrusts the Italian woman. She has been too lenient with the Huguenots. He would like the Inquisition fully installed in France, not thwarted, as now, by the Parlement. In return he will support us. He deems a Catholic prince of Lorraine preferable to a French Huguenot.'

'I do not like it. If you owe Philip your throne, you will make France a vassal of Spain. You will enrage the entire kingdom if you give untrammelled power to the Inquisition. The country will rise against you. Catholic or Huguenot, the people are united in their hatred of Spain. I cannot believe you would risk such a thing. Your brother has been using his golden tongue to fuddle your wits.'

'Do you think, if I were King, that I could not make Philip dance to my tune?'

'Your arrogance blinds you. I am afraid, my lord. When you speak of this thing, I see only a vision of blood and carnage.'

He looked at me intently. 'Tell me the truth, my friend, by the love I know you bear me. Is it my death of which you have come to warn me?'

I breathed deeply and managed to meet his eyes. 'No. But you are in great danger in February of next year. I do not like the transits across your horoscope. I beg you to discard this plan of joining with Spain, my lord. If word of it leaks out, you will be prey to the assassin's dagger. You must befriend Condé and Coligny; you must grant their people right to worship. There must be a middle path through all this. A few deaths, perhaps, but not disgraceful slaughter. I fear a ravenous beast has been set loose which will not rest until it is bloated with blood.'

'Then I will allow you to do my worrying for me, my gloomy prophet. And I will keep your counsel in mind.' He clapped me on the back again, a friendly soldier's tap which almost unseated me.

'My lord, I am an old man. I pray you remember your strength.'

He laughed, his eyes clear and merry. He had understood nothing. But he had assuaged his conscience, and now could think of other things. For a moment he resembled the twenty-three-year-old youth I had met eighteen years ago at Joinville – *un chevalier sans peur et sans reproche*, bright and golden and shining with the patina of destiny.

'Go home to bed, then, old man. And remember, if your gouty feet ache from climbing palace stairs, you have only yourself to blame.'

We parted with great affection. Yet I could hardly stumble down the stairs, so blind were my eyes with tears, so great was the grief in my heart. For I knew now that I would never in this life meet François de Guise again.

XXIX

He entered Paris in triumph a few weeks later. The Parisians, always his from the beginning, went wild, for in Paris he was already King. There was not a soul amongst that fervently Catholic multitude who would not have gladly died for him had he commanded it.

To assuage his wounded vanity he had bedecked himself in typical and most magnificent fashion – the great and noble champion of Holy Church, the bastion of the Rock. He wore a crimson satin doublet and hose, with a black velvet cloak unfurling behind him, a black cap adorned with rubies and diamonds and an enormous scarlet plume. He rode a black stallion caparisoned in black and silver. Behind him marched a troop of four hundred men-at-arms, bearing the cross of Jerusalem and the colours of Lorraine and the piebald banner of the Temple. And as he paraded through the streets, bowing and smiling, the crowds pressed about him, cheering and throwing flowers and making the sign of the cross, while shouts of *Vive Guise!* reverberated to heaven.

News of the approaching pageant had thrown the Queen-mother into dismay. If apparent to her before, it was now obvious to everyone that here was a man worthy of the sceptre and crown – far more so than the sickly and half-mad eleven-year-old child with the shadowed, terrified eyes. Goaded by her own guilt and duplicity, Catherine de' Medici thought the duke had come to seize the government. Undoubtedly he might have done so, had he been a different man. But despite the corrosion begun at Amboise, there still remained some vestige of the idealist – the *chevalier* who had suppressed the *gabelle* revolt with decency and mercy. If he gained a throne, he wished to do so with honour in the people's eyes.

The Queen-mother fled with her son to Fontainebleau. The duke and his men followed them, demanding the royal presence to vindicate his own triumph and stamp Vassy with kingly approval. He burned to ashes and rubble the two unpretentious Huguenot halls of worship, granted the heretics by the King two years before. He entered the city as a conqueror, prepared to inaugurate civil war.

As he had said to me, there was no other way. If he could not rule as the King's minister, he would rule as the King's tyrant, until his own moment was conferred by capricious fate. Had I not seen this insane religious war in the shadows of the fire long ago? Yet on the pregnant eve of its advent, I still pondered whether it might have been avoided. Where had the crossroads been? Where might another turning point have midwifed to birth another possible future? Where was the serene wisdom of Mathias Delvaux, which sought to shape the best of possible futures in accord with the cosmic plan? Perhaps, I thought darkly, this impending destruction was itself the plan.

If Henri II had divorced Catherine de' Medici and married Marie de Guise . . . If poor sickly King François II had lived to give Marie Stuart a son . . . If Anne de Montmorency had not assumed the reins of power when my masters began their ascent . . . If, and if, and if . . . So many turnings, so many vanished choices, so many neglected paths. My head reeled when I pondered it. And behind all these questions loomed another, which dogged me like my own shadow. If Charles de Guise, Cardinal de Lorraine, had been any man other than himself – other than the sleek and elegant shape behind the puppets, like a great scarlet spider at the centre of an impenetrable web . . . The further I distanced myself from it, the more inexorable it seemed. Had Luther and Calvin not begun their erosion of the Rock, had they not given voice to the tormented souls of the lost flock, there would have been someone else.

In a fit of impetuous fury, Louis de Bourbon, Prince de Condé, hastened to Orléans, there to meet in council with Gaspard de Coligny and the Huguenots. He proclaimed himself Protector of the House and Crown of France – implying, by this astonishing title, that he wished no harm to the King or the Queen-mother. It was François de Guise whom he despised, whom he wished to see toppled and broken, whose very presence in the world brought the black bile to his throat.

For two months, negotiations between the Huguenots and the Catholic Triumvirate muddled on. I waited, impotent, in Salon. There was no one to write to, no one to advise. François de Guise was beyond all reach now. The Cardinal de Lorraine had departed for the Council of Trent, attempting to convince the Pope and the College of Cardinals of the urgent and imperative need for Church reform. I busied myself with my work, dreading each night for fear it might bring one of those terrible dreams which heralded disaster. I knew the disaster would come. Yet like any man who loves and dreams, I hoped against hope that some understanding might be achieved.

The Queen-mother, pressured by the Duc de Guise and his party, declared she could not allow more than one form of worship in France. No compromise was possible. The Prince de

Condé and his party declared they would not lay down their arms until the Catholic Triumvirate, led by François de Guise, was overthrown, and liberty of worship was granted the Huguenots. Neither side gave way. Early in July the fighting began.

For the duration of the year, local rebellions and skirmishes and brutal assassinations and tortures were enacted everywhere, as if they were a form of sport. In December, at the siege of Rouen, a Huguenot stronghold, Antoine de Bourbon, King of Navarre, First Prince of the Blood, died of a sword wound. His nine-year-old son, Henri, already staunchly Huguenot, succeeded him as King of Navarre. After the Valois spawn and his uncle, Louis de Bourbon, this youth stood next in line to the French throne.

Shortly after, the real confrontation occurred.

A great battle was fought on the plain of Dreux. The two armies were almost equal in size. After five long hours of bitter combat, the dead numbered seven thousand, Frenchmen slaughtered by Frenchmen, corpses piled upon corpses. The very soil seemed to gape open in anguish and gush torrents of blood. When it was over, the banner of Lorraine flew triumphantly over the field. The Maréchal de St André, one of the Catholic Triumvirs, lay butchered in the blood-slicked grass. The Connêtable de Montmorency had been wounded and taken by the Huguenots. The Prince de Condé, also wounded, had been captured by the Duc de Guise.

All across the country, Catholics lauded the duke as a hero, a champion of the Faith. The young King hastily bestowed upon him the commission of Lieutenant-General of the Kingdom and Commander-in-Chief of the Army. Were it merely power he sought, he possessed it now for the third time, even greater than before – power sanctified by the holy banner under which he campaigned.

The duke remained in the environs of Orléans, preparing to besiege this last bastion of the Huguenot. It was expected that here too, François de Guise would triumph, as at Metz, Calais, Thionville and more recently at Dreux. On the battlefield, some charm seemed to surround him, some impenetrable shield. Although he had suffered many wounds, he appeared to be invincible. Certainly his name was once again a name with which to conjure. Phoenix-like, he had risen above the hatred and disgrace of the last reign. A general relief began to pervade the country. Catholics and Huguenots alike were weary of the incessant and futile bloodshed. Now no one doubted the Huguenots would be beaten. Peace would be restored. In their august clemency, the victors would be merciful and lighten the penalties for heretical worship. The Huguenots would gradually return to the faith which had guided France for nine hundred years. Vain hopes and wishes and dreams . . .

I watched his horoscope. I watched the slow but ineluctable approach of the two malefic planets toward the quadrature of the moon. Sometimes I stared from my observatory window at the inexorable movements of the heavenly bodies through the black, foreboding vault of the sky – the red star that was Mars, lord of war and violence; the yellowish star that was Saturn, lord of sorrow and endings . . .

I tried to prepare myself for the blow. I withdrew into my study and spoke to no one. My wife did not disturb my solitude, for she was used to the spells of dark melancholy that so often seized me. My servants brought up my food and wine and left it outside my door. I avoided Jean-Aimé de Chavigny, refused to see my children. I slept on the hard couch and gazed into the fire hour after hour. But the fire told me nothing. Even my visions had gone. Everything hung suspended, waiting, while I kept silent vigil. I wrote him an urgent letter of warning at his camp outside Orléans. But as the messenger vanished down the street in a flurry of hoofbeats and dust, I knew the message would never reach its goal.

On the night of the seventeenth of February, the anniversary of his birth, I was at last assailed by the dream I had expected and dreaded and in some sense welcomed. At least it heralded the end of the tortuous waiting, though the grief still lay before me.

It is the death of those you love that dogs you . . .

I had gone to bed slightly drunk, which eased the intensifying agony of my gout and the blackness devouring my soul. I must have slept for some hours – the candle stub I habitually kept burning beside my couch had almost exhausted itself. I sat up, or dreamed that I sat up. A draught sifted through the chamber, and the candle flame flickered and danced and guttered and expired. My body was seized with a deadly cold, and a heavy oppression cramped my chest. At first I thought my heart was failing, that it was my own death which lurked imminent in the darkness. For a moment I was relieved.

Then, at the foot of the couch, I saw – or dreamed I saw – François de Guise: a bright but incorporeal figure, a luminous shadow against shadows, faint as mist, illumined by no light I could perceive. He was dressed as he was at St-Germain-en-Laye, in the full regalia of his princely rank and immense wealth, and his jewels smouldered with their own molten flame. I stared in astonishment, for the scar which had disfigured him since his twenty-sixth year had miraculously vanished. His face was as smooth and perfect as when I first met him at Joinville.

At first this apparition claimed my complete attention. Then, dimly at first, I began to perceive that he was not alone. Fainter even than his faint figure, more translucent than mist, I discerned the shadowy shapes of the white-mantled figures, the flicker of steel helmets and chain mail like the glimmer of a fish glimpsed underwater, the bloody glow of the crosses. Remote and unearthly, the silvery sound of a bell wafted through the chamber.

He greeted me with a sad, ironic gaze, and a faint smile upon his lips. His cat-eyes seemed to bore into mine, and there was one soul behind them now. Some message passed between us, though he did not speak and I could not utter a sound.

There was no other way, my friend. The sacrifice had to be made. But I have a son . . .

I closed my eyes, and when I opened them again, he was gone, and his white-mantled host had vanished. I clambered clumsily from bed and frantically lit all the tapers, trembling in every part of my body, my eyes blind. Yes, there was a son. But for the son as well, it was too late.

Word reached Salon two days later. The Duc de Guise had vigorously pushed forward the siege of Orléans. His wife, Anna d'Este, had arrived at a castle near his camp – sent by the Queen-mother to beg mercy, to spare the city the barbaric consequences of assault. He mounted his horse to join her. He did not bother, for so short a ride, to don his cuirass, and was rendered conspicuous by the white plume in his cap. At a crossroads, he was struck by three pistol balls fired from behind a hedge. They passed through him from side to side. He fell forward upon his horse's neck, vainly trying to draw his sword from its scabbard, then fainted. They carried him to the castle. Now, two days later, he still hung uneasily suspended between life and death.

Monseigneur de Santacroce, passing this news on to me, told me the wounds did not appear fatal. François de Guise had inherited the wonderful constitution of his father, with its near-miraculous recuperative power. They had removed the pistol balls. His fever was high, but there was good hope for his survival.

And then Mgr de Santacroce added: 'They say the Queen-mother, in her great concern and anxiety, visits him every day. She prepares possets for him with her own hands.'

I closed my eyes and turned away. I knew now that he was truly lost.

After six days of suffering, François de Lorraine, Duc de Guise, died in the arms of his weeping wife, with his thirteen-year-old son, Henri, kneeling grief-shattered at his side. He received the last sacrament from his brother Louis, Cardinal de Guise. Charles, Cardinal de Lorraine was still immured at the Council of Trent, vainly attempting to resolve, by honeyed diplomacy and golden eloquence, issues no longer capable of resolution save by gunpowder and steel.

I was numb and insensible for many days after. My heart seemed to have been torn from my body, alive and still beating, and flung into the fire. I now understood the true depth of the bond of which Mathias Delvaux had spoken. With its severance, my motivation of twenty years shivered, like a smashed mirror, into a myriad shattered fragments, jagged mimicries of life. I tried to console myself by saying he had himself come to tell me, to offer me hope for a future about which I cared little now that its light had been extinguished. Even that hope was barren. Whenever I thought of young Henri, now Duc de Guise at thirteen years of age, I saw only the slashed lifethread on the polished parquet floor.

I heard later, not without a certain barbaric satisfaction, that the murderer – a petty nobleman named Poltrot – was sentenced to the death of regicides. He was tortured, then drawn and quartered in the Place de Grève, while the angry and embittered populace of Paris hurled insults and offal at him to the end. Under duress, he accused Gaspard de Coligny. M. de Coligny vehemently denied all responsibility for the crime. He admitted, however, that he deemed the murder of François de Guise a blessing to the Huguenots and to the realm. Though the inquiries were thorough and painstaking enough, nothing was ever proved.

I knew, of course, whose hand had paid the assassin – the same pale and gentle hand which so solicitously prepared possets while the duke lay feverish and anguished on his deathbed. Had he won Orléans from the Huguenots, nothing could have impeded his meteoric climb. She struck, therefore, with the snakelike speed of desperation. But who would believe me, when I had only seen it in the horoscopes and in the fire?

The ritual sacrifice of François de Guise brought at least a temporary cessation in the violence. Peace of a kind was concluded at Amboise, on the nineteenth day of March. It seemed that the religious conflagration, having consumed so much of its own fuel, might gutter to a conclusion.

But I knew otherwise. My visions had returned to me. And the worst carnage still lay ahead. I derived a certain solace from the knowledge that I would not see it. By then, I would have joined François de Guise in whatever heaven or hell awaits us all.

XXX

At the beginning of the following year the King, accompanied by his mother, his brother Henri, Duc d'Anjou, eleven-year-old Henri de Navarre, and the entire court, embarked on a royal progress across the lacerated kingdom. This farce was intended to preserve the frail yellowish patina of goodwill diffused by the peace of Amboise. Despite that so-called peace, there were constant uprisings, like erupting boils, while numerous prominent Huguenots were murdered by unnamed and untraceable assassins.

Many Catholics had not forgiven the untimely death of the Duc de Guise. Quietly, they waited for the moment of vengeance to ripen on the tree of fate. Among these were the Cardinal de Lorraine and Henri de Guise who, although just fourteen years of age, had sworn by his father's corpse to have the blood of Gaspard de Coligny. Nevertheless, the young King was determined to make a puerile effort to win the elusive love of his blood-sated people. Thus the royal entourage wriggled forth from Paris and commenced its sluggish crawl, like a great gilded flatworm, through the towns and villages of France.

I learned with bitter irony that the court would visit Salon. It would be ensconced at the Archbishop's spacious palace, so that the Queen-mother might hold audience with her chief astrologer, the celebrated Michel Nostradamus. The royal courier informed me I was requested to wait upon Madame on the seventeenth day of October. I bowed my head, biting my lips to suppress my black laughter. I loathed the woman with ferocious and consuming intensity; I could not imagine how I would face her, let alone dispense the flattery, encouragement and hopeful prognostication she expected. I even contemplated concealing a small dagger beneath my clothes, or perhaps a poisoned pin, offering up what remained of my pointless life in vengeance. But I am not made of heroic stuff. And the habit of twenty years of obedience did not easily release me. My masters had demanded no such sacrifice.

What she longed to know was obvious. How long before her best-beloved son, Henri the Pervert as he was called with sniggers in the inns and alleyways of the town, mounted the throne? I had waited for word from the Cardinal de Lorraine, or some other emissary of the network, amorphous and secret, scattered across France. Yet none came. Well then, I resolved, I shall earn myself a few hundred écus and a glossier reputation, tell the Italian woman what she wishes to hear, and go home.

The Order had apparently lain dormant since the siege of Orléans. Perhaps, I thought hopefully, they had abandoned me, deeming me no longer of use. When I suggested this, Jean-Aimé de Chavigny merely smiled and said nothing. The reflections of the coming event in my own horoscope were ironic. The royal visit would bring great honour to me. Undoubtedly I would receive some title, physician-in-ordinary to the King or some such nonsense, in recognition of my long and faithful service to the house of Valois. I was no longer certain whom I had truly served these twenty years.

Toward mid-September, the entourage began trickling indolently into the town. The great château was frantically refurbished for their stay. Everywhere there was a frenzied bustle, as courtiers, artisans, engineers, builders and magistrates attempted to transform old Salon into a fitting receptacle for the royal presences.

Enormous wood and cloth arches were erected over the town gates. Banners and flags and tapestries were draped from every window and bedecked every shop front. The streets were strewn with sweet-smelling rushes and herbs. The entire countryside was denuded of flowers, that they might perfume the streets and the entry to the château. Massive tubs of blossoms were installed, to divert the royal noses from the stench of the gutters. I purchased for myself a new suit of clothes, with a frivolous white ruff in the latest fashion and a shiny black cap studded with semi-precious stones. And throughout it all, there bubbled within me the same virulent and morbid laughter.

A week before the King's scheduled entry, I at last received a letter from the Cardinal de Lorraine. Returned from the Council of Trent, he had retracted his diplomatic tolerance, devoured by furious hatred of the Huguenots and a murderous thirst for revenge. He was more as if brutally widowed than bereaved. It was whispered that, since the duke's assassination, he had taken to wearing a shirt of chain-mail beneath his robes. Well he might, I thought bitterly, for it was he who should have died. Sometimes I felt I could have done it myself and suffered no disturbance of conscience. In many ways I blamed him for the cankerous fruit his machinations had borne. Yet despite the resentment, I hoped he would summon me. He was the only link I retained with the duke. It was, in the end, the same blood.

He did not mention his brother's death. Unlike most of his missives, the present one was lengthy.

'The Queen-mother worries for this so-called peace, and for the fate of the Duc d'Anjou, her third and vilest son. I have assured her that for a woman bereaved and helpless as she is, with problems of state pressing so heavily upon her poor shoulders, an audience with her most trusted astrologer would be advantageous.

'She must be warned of the danger Henri de Navarre poses to her best-beloved son. I would, of course, never wish you to tell our noble Queen-mother an untruth. But I am led to understand from our counsels in the past that Henri de Navarre is indeed a threat, both to her plans and ours.

'Can you not imagine what a merry game may be played with our three Henris?'

If I prophesied the ascension of the young King of Navarre, the Queen-mother, being what she was, might remove this militant little Huguenot herself. Indefatigable in his schemes, the Cardinal hoped for a circus, the houses of Valois and Bourbon exterminating each other like gladiators in the arena. The path would then be unimpeded for the young scion of Lorraine.

And if this came to pass, the French people would be contented enough. In the young Duc de Guise's veins flowed the blood of St Louis and Louis XII. Although scarcely fourteen, this young Lorraine prince already possessed his father's indomitable courage, his father's fine physique and noble face. When he came to manhood he would be another François de Guise, without a scar. And he had already won the hearts of the Catholic populace.

What I had seen at Blois remained submerged in the pool of my own dark fears and desires. I had written of it obliquely in the *Centuries*, however, though no eyes would see it until after my death.

Paris conjure un grand meurtre commetre
Blois le fera sortir en plein effet . . .

Often I contemplated revealing my vision to Charles de Guise,
for the bitter satisfaction of witnessing his mortification. But I
could not do it. After all that had transpired, he still held me
enchanted by his strange spell.

Because the royal family had come expressly to see their Prophet, I stood with Salon's notables on a dais of white and violet
damask erected before the gateway of St Lazare. The glittering
procession wended its stately way into the town. The young
King, whom I had last seen as a six-year-old child in the royal
nurseries at Blois, rode at the forefront of the cavalcade, on a
grey Arab steed decked with trappings of black velvet and gold.
He was resplendent in a mantle of violet velvet embroidered
with silver, with a double ruff about his neck and a cap thickly
set with diamonds. From a distance, he looked vulnerable and
handsome and romantic, with his striking dark colouring and
endearing boyish dignity. As he drew nearer, one could see the
madness in his eyes.

Behind him, on a magnificent white stallion, rode his brother Henri, Duc d'Anjou, only a year younger. He had obviously been at pains to appear even more sumptuous than his
brother. Yet the contrast between the two was remarkable.
King Charles echoed his father – the same shy, wary, sensitive
gaze. Henri de Valois was purely and utterly his mother's: the
long impenetrable eyes, the feline suppleness, the pendulous
lips, the sloping chin, the pallor that might have been illness
or might have been cosmetic. It was said he was overfond of
dabbling with his mother's beauty pots.

The Queen-mother herself followed in a palanquin draped
with violet velvet and cloth-of-gold. She was shrouded, as
always since her husband's death, in a black gown dripping
with diamonds, so stiff with jewels it encased her stout body
like a sheath of armour. Here was that terrible black spider with
the delicate tracery of scarlet on its belly, and the deadly sting.

Behind this bloated apparition rode Charles de Guise,

Cardinal de Lorraine, poised, polished and sleek as Grecian marble, in a red velvet robe embroidered with a great silver cross, diamonds in his ears and strewn across his fingers like stars. He was seated with graceful dignity on a grey mare, his brilliant eyes narrowed against the afternoon sun, gazing down, as though from a great height, at the crowds swarming along the flower-strewn streets. In his wake followed the dazzling butterflies of the court, the young King Henri de Navarre among them with his tutor at his side. As I studied this youth with the bright sunlight pouring on to his dark shaggy head, I knew he would indeed one day be a King of France.

There followed four companies of men-at-arms, and a company of light horse, and an endless file of guards and lackeys, cooks and grooms, huntsmen and priests, on foot, on horseback, in coaches and in litters – eight hundred of the gentlefolk of France, come to see that peculiar old man who did not sleep in his bed at night like normal folk, but peered at the heavens and pronounced prophecies through his long beard, and foresaw so uncannily the death of King Henri, and the sad passing of pathetic young King François.

The King reached the dais, and the knot of consuls and magistrates bowed and murmured and straightened their robes, attempting to present their youthful master with an edifying picture of humble and devoted service. He waited calmly before them, his sensitive face reflecting a conflict of expressions – the steely schooling which must show no emotion mingled with the flattered and ingenuous pride of the young. The mayor read his complimentary oration, a clumsy potpourri heavily laced with flowery phrases and strained allusions to the young Adonis and the young Theseus. It was as patently boring to His Majesty as every other complimentary oration in every other small and great town through which the weary cavalcade had passed.

The mayor terminated his speech and bowed low. The other magistrates bowed. I managed to lean on my stick and bowed with the rest of them. There was a hush. The King cleared his throat and prepared to speak. The mayor preened himself a little, waiting for praise. He was to be disappointed.

'I came,' said King Charles IX clearly, in his unsteady

fourteen-year-old voice, 'to see Nostradamus.'

A tumult of whispers, gasps, jostlings and shovings seethed upwards like steam. The people craned their necks to see the Prophet so honoured by their King. I kept my head bowed, struggling to restrain my dark laughter. Not long ago, my windows had been shattered by stones, while rude notes and threats were slipped beneath my door.

I stifled the convulsive giggles, the misty ghosts, the snickering shapes that sifted from the dark pool of my bitterness. I fixed my eyes on the white damask beneath my swollen feet.

No one dared gainsay the King. If he esteemed his Prophet, well, then, they would esteem his Prophet too. If nothing else, this royal visit would render bearable my remaining days in Salon. I surveyed the softly carved young face, the shy eyes like some hunted hind, the poignantly dignified bearing. And despite my resentment for his house, I could not suppress a deep ripple of sadness and pity for this poor shadowed scion of Valois, so twisted by a twisted mother, whose life thread would not extend beyond his twenty-fifth year.

I murmured courteous thanks for so signal an honour. But this boy-King who, with a different mother, might have flowered into a gentle and artistic if not valorous ruler, was not interested in ceremony. After all, he had endured many weary weeks of it. He turned to one of his guards.

'Get Maître Nostradamus a horse,' said the King. 'He must ride with us to the palace.'

I protested. I would cherish the honour of his request to the end of my days, I said, but my gout troubled me. I feared I could not manage a mount.

'Nonsense,' said His Most Christian Majesty Charles IX. 'When you are astride your horse, you will not have so much weight on your feet. They will not then pain you.'

With much labour and difficulty, I was hoisted into the saddle of a chestnut mare vacated by an agreeable and amused guard. After some minutes of fussing and shuffling, I managed to regain my dignity, straighten my cap and my furred robe. I turned to find myself confronted by the mocking, glittering, dancing serpent-eyes of the Cardinal de Lorraine. He gave me a courteous nod, and the diamonds in his ears winked like white fire in the sunlight, but he said nothing. To the accompaniment of flutes and drums and cornets, the procession resumed its sluggish progress, winding its way to the central square strewn with roses and fragrant grasses, then up the steep slope to the courtyard of the palace, where the Archbishop of Arles waited with his household guards and retainers.

The ancient edifice swallowed the royal family and the court, while grooms and lackeys and guards and attendants headed for the town's inns and taverns. I was left to make my way home. The townsfolk, who had made my life a misery for seventeen years, parted respectfully as I hobbled past, leaning on my stick.

Early the next morning came the summons from the Queen-mother. I spent some minutes alone, closeted in my observatory, praying to whatever god or demon guided me for strength and sagacity to perform the Cardinal's latest commission. I was escorted at last into the woman's presence, seething with grief and anger and loathing and bitterness, wearing the warmest of smiles plastered to my lips. I met her long, colourless and unfathomable eyes, kept carefully blank through years of torment and rancorous jealousy and humiliation and machination and violent self-restraint. I told her what an immense honour and pleasure it was to see Madame again, and how well she looked, and how she honoured our humble town by the shining gift of her presence.

And my years of schooled dissembling still matched her own, for the hard eyes softened slightly, and the heavy, drooping, once sensual mouth pursed in an almost coquettish moue. She believed me.

'Maître Nostradamus,' she said, her heavily accented voice low, 'you have done me great service, once at St-Germain and once at Blois. You have also done the late King my husband service in your attempt to warn him of his danger. It was Our Lord's will that his time had come. But I have not forgotten your loyalty.'

I bowed my head.

'I would ask you now for another service,' she said, 'which, like the others, must be a secret between us. It is only the poor anxieties of a fond mother over her child. I would not have it bruited about that, weak helpless creature as I am, I am over-protective of my sons.'

Weak, helpless creature, I echoed silently, meeting the bleak grey gaze calmly, observing the struggle between her mistrust of confiding in any human soul and her superstitious fear of my divinatory art. Your own soul is poisoned and blackened by the deaths you have claimed. If I read your horoscope aright, it will be further sullied by the innocent blood of thousands. If there is truly a hell, may you roast in it unto eternity.

'I am happy,' I said, 'to be of assistance to Madame. It is a great honour that you would place your loving motherly concerns in trust with one so humbly your servant.'

'Then let us begin.' She took from the table a familiar parchment. 'Here is the horoscope of Prince Henri, which you made for me at Blois eight years ago.'

She proffered it to me. It was as fresh and unsoiled as if I had just composed it. So, I mused, she is so frightened of me, she has not even handled it since.

She leaned nearer to me, with her old sagging skin, the dark hairs on her upper lip, the pouches of flesh beneath her eyes. And despite my loathing, I could not but pity what had once been a young Catherine, riding from Florence, with a broken heart and a shattered love affair, toward a young and unknown husband whom she dreamed might love her – yet who spurned her until there was nothing left for her but power. She possessed it now. I wondered whether there is truly such a thing as an evil creature, or whether we all carry the seeds of it within us, and, through our brutality to each other, nurture the blossom and fruit.

And then I thought of François de Guise, twisted with the pain of his wound, stoically enduring the merciless probings of useless doctors, his pride and his courage sustaining him with hopes of recovery until the last. And receiving the posset of hot spiced wine from this woman's unctuously kind hand. And knowing, as he drank, that the wine was his own blood, and that in its dregs lay the ruin of his life and his dream.

I studied the horoscope of Prince Henri de Valois, and waited. There was a long silence, troubled only by the wheeze of her heavy breathing beside me.

At last she said, 'At Blois, you told me you saw four crowns. Will he be King?'

I met her eyes again. 'He will be King, Madame.'

She exhaled a long sigh. 'When?'

I swallowed and again stared at the horoscope. 'He must wait a decade, no more.'

'And the King?'

'Will meet a natural death, Madame. As you well know, he does not possess the strongest of constitutions. He has inherited a delicacy similar to that of his brother, the late King François.'

Our eyes met this time for a prolonged and agonising moment. She scanned the blank surface of my face, and fear flickered somewhere in the chill grey depths.

'Is there any danger that threatens the Prince?' she said abruptly.

'The only malefic influence evident is from Saturn. This can mean many things. It is placed in the sign of Aquarius, the Waterbearer, at the Prince's birth. There may be danger to his body through the ankles or the bloodstream, from cold or . . .'

'*Who* is his danger, Maître Nostradamus?' she said sharply.

I gave her a long, sincere, beseeching stare. I allowed my lower lip to quiver slightly, and clasped my hands in alarm.

'Madame,' I said softly, 'you ask me to place myself in extreme difficulty with such a question. I dare not make accusations against any subject of this realm. I fear for my life.'

'You would do well to fear for it if you do not answer me, Maître Nostradamus,' said Catherine de' Medici, and the anger snapped now in her eyes. 'Of whom must I beware?' But her gaze at once softened, and her anxiety conquered her wrath. 'I do not wish to seem so harsh. But I beg you to share your insights with me. It is of the utmost importance. I am deeply concerned for the safety of my son. I know the loyalty you bear me. I am calling on that loyalty now.'

I bowed my head. 'Madame, my loyalty to you is absolute and beyond question. But I cannot make a direct accusation. I must live with my own conscience.'

She smiled slightly, the heavy mouth coquettish again. 'Then you must make an indirect one. I will tell you my own suspicions, and you will reply yes or no. We will play a guessing game. Then your conscience need not trouble you. Have I anything more to fear from the house of Lorraine?'

'The Cardinal de Lorraine,' I said carefully, 'is fallen from power. He cannot harm you or your son.'

'That man,' she hissed, her mouth pinching into a grimace, 'is deadly, and the worst of liars. He is to blame for the state of this poor nation.'

'His career is finished, Madame. It is your hands that have brought peace.'

It would be so easy, I thought, so easy to betray him, to avenge my own wounds, so terribly easy . . . But I could not. Why? I asked myself, and the answer wafted back in the gentle old voice of Mathias Delvaux. *It is a tie of the soul.*

'I shall ask you a different question, Maître Nostradamus. Who will reign when my son Henri is dead?'

I searched her face for some moments, and all the bizarre convoluted past unrolled before me like a series of painted miniatures. We had danced a strange dance, this Italian woman and I. I would not have flinched nor raised a hand in succour had she lain gasping and dying on the floor before me. Yet there was a profound bond here too.

'Navarre,' I said softly.

'Ah,' said Catherine de' Medici.

I shifted to my most pedantic tone, as though the preceding conversation had never occurred. 'You must ensure that the Prince is not subjected to cold or chills,' I said. 'Saturn is in quadrature to Venus in Scorpio. Mars in the sign of the Balance is in quadrature to Jupiter in the Crab. He is an energetic child, and needs much physical exercise. But he must guard his throat and lungs from chills.'

But she looked bored now, having learned what she wished to know. The audience was at an end.

'I am deeply grateful for your assistance, Maître Nostradamus. You have given me most invaluable advice, which eases my anxiety for my son. I will protect the health of the young Prince with my life.'

Would that it could be your life, Madame, I thought, bowing low and kissing her hand. As I hobbled from the royal apartments, I struggled to suppress the ever-present black laughter. I had fulfilled my task. But it meant nothing. Before my eyes flickered the image of Henri de Navarre – stocky, amiable, rough, with merry dark eyes and a goatlike demeanour and the star of his destiny yet unrisen. The opportunity was gone now, and Bourbon, through Navarre, would carry the sceptre and the crown until there was no longer sceptre or crown to carry, until they and the throne itself vanished beneath a river of blood . . . I thought too of young Henri de Guise, with his wonderful lion's mane of golden curls, and the clear, limpid dark blue eyes of his uncle, the Cardinal de Lorraine.

Tough and courageous, determined and cunning, with an already irresistible magnetism, he possessed every quality necessary for kingship. But his fate, inexorable as the stars in their courses, would come to meet him from behind a curtained alcove at Blois.

> Le rang Lorraine fera place à Vendôme,
> Le haut mis bas et le bas mis en haut . . .

Can you not imagine what a merry game may be played with our three Henris?

XXXI

The Cardinal de Lorraine was excessively courteous in his greeting, turning fully upon me the bright beam of his renowned and irresistible charm. But his pale face in the firelight betrayed the recompense exacted of him by time and tragedy. Deep lines were now engraved along the fine nose, and dark hollows sculpted beneath his heavy-lidded eyes. The nutbrown hair and beard were threaded with silver, and his arrogant mouth was bitter.

No wonder, I thought, for it is more than the loss of a brother. With the duke's death were extinguished all his cherished dreams of the papal tiara, which he would never now attain.

For several moments we remained silent. I stared at the ceaselessly shifting dance of the fire. The Cardinal sat motionless in the shadows while the flames flickered wanly against the waxen pallor of his skin, and the scarlet silk of his chasuble, and the dull imprisoned brilliance of his jewels. He scrutinised me from under his somnolent eyelids, probing my thoughts to assess whether my allegiance to him was as firm as it had been to his brother. I observed the restless folding and unfolding of his slender white hands, the heavy bluish shadows of dissipation marked like thumbprints beneath the wise old serpent eyes. Although he was but thirty-nine, his face resembled some fine marble sculpture beginning to corrode, cracking and peeling to reveal some unknown thing beneath. Yet it was still beautiful, even with the stamp of corruption upon it.

'The Queen-mother,' he said at last, 'remarked to me that you had, as always, renewed her faith in the future.' He showed his small white teeth in the most benign of smiles. 'You have a gift of diplomacy, Maître de Notredame. You would have gone far in the Church.'

I said nothing. I hung suspended between the old fascination and my newly acquired reservoir of gall.

'Can it be that you still mourn my brother?' he murmured after a time.

What could I say? If not for your wild schemes and endless spiders' webs, your futile fantasies of foreign conquest, your cruelty, your duplicity, your petty vindictiveness . . . if not for all this, he might have succeeded . . . Yet the horoscope had shown it all from the beginning. And if not for the ruthless brilliance with which this man carved a path for his brother's glory, there would have been no theatre for the duke's heroic role. François de Guise would have remained an attractive but inconsequential German courtier, nameless and lost in the levelling maw of time.

'Perhaps you blame me, Maître de Notredame. But has it never occurred to you that I too loved my brother?'

'I do not blame you, Monseigneur. When we first met at Joinville twenty years ago, I told your father that your brother's horoscope portended a violent death. I believe it to have been his fate. But you must understand the rancour I feel. No doubt it is easy to stand where I do, who have never had to bear such responsibility, and ponder where some different decision, some gentler hand, some more conciliatory action toward the Huguenots, might have effected a different result, and prevented the civil war, and spared his life.'

'I have also done this, Maître de Notredame. I have done it through many a sleepless night, and many a weary morning. Where, I asked myself, did I make the wrong choices, where were my mistakes?'

'Perhaps you did not take sufficient account of human beings,' I said coldly. 'You instigated wars that cost thousands of lives, and bled this country white for the merest ephemeral glimmer of glory.'

The Cardinal replied with his most charming and frivolous smile. 'What does it matter? One should take neither life nor death too seriously. I find I can forgive myself. I see no point in shouldering a burden of guilt for the past. We have a future to shape.'

'Even at the expense of your own blood?'

'All things have their purpose, Maître de Notredame, though they may bring grief. What foolish blindness made my brother take that fatal journey without armour in the midst of a siege? And after both you and others had warned him it was a dangerous time? We can never know, when a man dies, whether it was his fate or his own secret choice. Or perhaps these two are the same thing.'

I could bear him no longer. Like some foul child expelled from a poisonous womb, the words issued unwillingly.

'Do not be so certain of the future, Monseigneur. I have seen a bloody vision of Henri de Guise. He lay in a pitiful and mangled heap on the floor of the King's apartments at Blois, with half a dozen daggers stuck in his body like pins. He will never wear the crown of France. Nor will any of his house.'

A long silence coiled itself about the chamber. The unwelcome yet strangely exhilarating rage coursed through me like new blood. But Charles de Guise merely smiled his bland, gentle smile while the heavy eyes fixed me like those of a bird of prey.

'I do not wish to cheat you of the satisfaction of your hatred, Maître de Notredame,' he said quietly. 'But I saw this long ago in his horoscope. Even François knew it, and told me as much. You have never understood. It is not the goal, but the effort that is required of us. It is the attempt, not the result, which invokes the future.'

I looked away. A morass of desperation and grief pulled me into its mire like an insect caught irrevocably in a silken web. Who are you, I thought, that you have power to turn even this to nothing?

The Cardinal mused for a time, turning his rings over and over on his slender fingers, the sweet mocking smile still curling his lips. *Seduisant* he still was. But cold, so terribly cold.

'With your great insight, Maître de Notredame, perhaps you can tell me something. What was it about my brother that inspired such fanatic love, in you and others of his followers? There have been many brave soldiers in the history of this nation. Yet when he entered Paris after Vassy, the crowds went berserk in a way I have never seen before. I myself inspire fear and hatred, and these content me. They are a surer means to power than love, which is fickle. But I often wonder what his secret was.'

I shrugged and shook my head. 'I do not know, Monseigneur. One cannot ascribe reasons to the heart. Perhaps because he was so fallible. Perhaps for ordinary men like me, who have never performed an action either truly great or truly evil, men like your brother embody our contradictions. In a way which reflects us back to ourselves as what we might have been. Some men have the gift of becoming myth. As though, in being truly men, with all the mad range of human opposites struggling and colliding within them, they are more than human.'

I paused, trying to find words, for this articulation of inchoate things was painful in the extreme. And I marvelled that the Cardinal de Lorraine, toward whom I felt such profound resentment, could yet draw it out of me.

'François de Guise became trapped by his own myth,' I said slowly, 'and so he failed. That too is human. I suppose I loved him because he seemed so noble and so trapped. He seemed in some way to be the epitome of that poor creature we call Man.'

The Cardinal merely watched me with his wise hooded old reptilian eyes. I listened, astonished, to the echoes of what I had just said. I stared dumbly at him.

'I see,' I murmured. 'This is why he had to be sacrificed.'

'They always are,' said the Cardinal de Lorraine, smiling gently. 'François de Guise did not fail. Nor did he become trapped by his myth. He merged with it. What man's mind sees as tragedy may, to the gods and to his own soul, be a matter of tender laughter.'

He invited me to sup with him, for there was at last some peace between us. For twenty years, I had imagined him motivated by the same things that drove other men. Now I glimpsed the vast and ancient wisdom pooled in those cold depths, which no love of any human kind could touch.

Fortified by several cups of wine, I said, 'Is Madame de St Clair still at the court?'

'Madame de St Clair,' he replied, his peculiar gaze veiled and unreadable, 'is dead in childbirth.'

Do you not know the tale, Michel, of the Knight of the Temple, who loved the pure and beautiful virgin Yse? Denied her living body by his vows, he killed her, and disinterred her freshly buried corpse, and beneath the staring white eye of the mocking moon exhausted his distorted passion upon the cold and unyielding flesh. And that night he was visited by a vision, and the beautiful Yse, virgin no longer, appeared to him in smoke and flame and commanded him, in nine months' time, to return to her grave, and gaze again upon her body. At the appointed hour, the Knight kept tryst. And when he had clawed again with torn and bleeding hands into the black earth, and found the casket, and lifted the brazen lid, he looked upon the stinking decaying bones and saw, between the crossed and rotting and worm-infested thighs, the stillborn child . . .

We dined at the great oak table before the fire, on food which had first been tasted by a servant, for the Cardinal was exceedingly wary of poison. It was bruited that he was a coward because of his chain-mail and his poison-tasters. I myself thought it only wisdom.

At last I managed to ask the question which had perplexed me for more than twenty years.

'Monseigneur, I arrived at the abbey of Notre Dame d'Orval when I was thirty-nine years of age. Since then I have served without question an Order whose meaning I have now and then glimpsed, yet whose organisation and goals and structure still remain a mystery to me. I do not even know who stands at the head of it, whose hand has guided its course. I have only done what I understood was its bidding, to the best of my ability.'

He smiled, admiring a large golden ring set with an immense ruby which crowned the index finger of his shapely right hand.

'Why, then,' he said, 'have you remained loyal to it?'

'I have often asked myself that. I have never found an answer. Because of my dreams. Because I felt the hand of fate. Because I loved your brother. I do not know.'

'Have you never asked yourself, then, what we would have done, my brother and I, had we succeeded in our plans?' He looked away, and his gaze abstracted as he withdrew into some private dream of his own. 'François, Duc de Guise as François III, King of France, candidate for the throne of the Holy Roman Empire . . . Charles de Guise, Cardinal de Lorraine as Pope . . . Had I achieved it, I believe I would have chosen the name of Jean. I would have been the twenty-third of that name.'

He suddenly stared directly at me. I felt a silvery chill caressing the back of my neck as those cold brilliant eyes, like chips of lapis, locked on my own.

'Did you know,' he said softly, 'there is an ancient prophecy that the twenty-third Jean to sit on the papal throne will be the Antichrist? Think, Maître de Notredame. Why would we wish for this power, this universal throne?'

'Power is its own vindication. It never occurred to me there was more beyond the rights of the sacred blood and the restoration of the ancient pledge.'

He shook his head. 'You lack imagination, my friend. We already possess power.' His voice had lowered and softened almost to a chant. I seemed to have passed from the chamber and drifted into some dark archaic temple, where the smoke from the fire and the candles wafted white and pollen-like to the ceiling and the ancient, weary eyes imprisoned me.

'It is a very old Order, my friend. Older than you imagine. It was old when the Calabrian monks came to the Forêt de Merlanvaux, to teach young Godefroi de Bouillon. It was old when King Dagobert was slain beneath the sacred oak. It was old in Jerusalem, when Pilate washed his hands, and old when Pythagoras heard the vast machinery of the universe propagating itself in the black void of space. It was old even in Arcadia, where the exiled tribe of Benjamin sought its new homeland. Its shape changed as the old gods changed their shape, according to the currents of the times. But the knowledge is the primordial knowledge of Man, the ground of his being. Did you not know that before the Father there was the Mother? *In the beginning and the end was Notre Dame . . . She existed before the mountains and the seas came into being, or any living thing . . .* Man's destiny is to seek knowledge of himself. But in the end, She is what he knows.'

The Cardinal's voice crept on around and beyond and through me, while his shape grew dim and only his eyes, those strange seawater eyes, remained.

'The Temple was created because power was needed in the world. But their power became expendable. St Bernard created the Cistercian Order because power was needed in the bosom of Holy Church. We have permeated the universities, the government, the military, the clergy, the arts. There will be other subsidiary orders, other masks, other screens. Of whom do you think the derelict on the cross was *truly* an emissary?'

'But why?' I whispered, and my voice seemed to come from a long distance, travelling back to me on the smoke.

'Can you not see?' said Charles de Guise softly. 'For three thousand odd years, God the Father has ruled in heaven. Can you not envisage a world where She is restored to Her rightful place?'

Smoke and silence enfolded me. The mosaic was almost complete. I understood then – it did not matter whether François de Guise was dead. It did not matter whether his son, Henri, fulfilled his task. For there would be sons and more sons, other generations, other branches grafted lovingly on to the great vine spanning time into the dim future, the future I had seen unrolled in fire and smoke and blood, while they waited with the long patience and endurance borne of the wisdom of the womb, the wisdom of night and darkness and birth. Not the bright and brittle intelligence of man, but the eternal phases of the moon waiting and waiting in the womb of time. Vast distances of aeons stretched behind me and ahead of me, and I saw the brilliant glitter of this illustrious house of Guise rise and explode like a great star and vanish into darkness amidst other stars, other planets, other suns, while the great cycle spun on . . .

There was but one thing more. The Cardinal de Lorraine, in his queer way, again intercepted my rushing thoughts.

'You wish to know whose hand guides our design,' he said.

I nodded, bereft of speech by now, only able to stare at him.

'Very well. In your grandfather's time it was the hand of King René d'Anjou that shaped the pattern. When you were born, the pattern was guided by the painter, Sandro Filipepi. When you were a student at Avignon, and my uncle Jean de Lorraine received his Cardinal's *biretta* at the palace of the Popes, the hands of Charles, Connêtable de Bourbon, held the threads.'

His lips curled again in that sweet and mocking smile as he extended his winecup delicately in the gesture of a toast.

'Charles de Bourbon was a great soldier,' he said. 'But greater still was his skill on the lute.'

Perhaps one day I will ask you to look at the horoscope of a poor wandering minstrel who, having lost his honour, has only his lute and his fate . . .

Slow unwanted tears clouded my eyes, transparent wraith-like echoes of that ancient and long-buried sadness.

'When you had lost everything,' the Cardinal said while I strove to meet his gaze, 'and wandered aimlessly through Languedoc and Provence toward Italy, the pattern was ordained by Don Ferrante de Gonzaga, Count of Guastalla, Lieutenant-General of the Peninsula for the house of Habsburg. Failing the throne of the Valois, Maître de Notredame, do not forget that the throne of the Habsburgs still beckons. Can you not imagine a union of Habsburg and Lorraine? Perhaps one day a prince of Lorraine named François will be a German Emperor. The future is very long.'

I strained to follow this tortuous skein. Some of the twisted threads followed the blood. Some must be chosen by their horoscopes. For part of it, of course, my grandfather had lent his wisdom. And there was also Luc Gauricus. I wondered who else had occupied my place before me.

'And now, Monseigneur? Ferrante de Gonzaga disappeared in Flanders seven years ago. He is said to be dead. Who is it I serve now?'

He again gave me his sleepy, mocking serpent's smile, and poured another cup of wine while the candlelight sparked fire from the ruby on his white hand. But he did not answer.

XXXII

A full moon has risen late tonight in the sign of the Goat. Its serene chill light seeps through the open casement window above me, forming a pool of bone whiteness on the floor of my chamber – like an aperture into another world, beckoning me to open the door and move through the glowing portal, beyond the solid matter of my own sick and swollen flesh into the world of dreams. I will hazard that passage soon enough.

Jean-Aimé de Chavigny has paid his customary evening visit to my study, bringing me another batch of letters requesting advice and counsel. I have not bothered to read them. He has given me hot mulled wine and my medicines, and left me a candle stub burning. Anne has bathed my feet and served me my supper. The house is silent now, for the servants and children have gone to bed. I have told Jean-Aimé that he will not see me alive tomorrow. He believes I make this statement in my usual mood of morose melancholy.

I hold in my hands the cup which the Cardinal de Lorraine has given me, that cup carved of solid rock crystal through which the moonlight shines and winks and fragments with a wan whiteness, that cup from which once drank a slaughtered King. I have filled it with wine, for it is the final cup.

This is my blood . . .

I examine once again that inscription which some ancient hand carved into the crystal, to be read by those with unveiled eyes.

> Qui bien beurra
> Dieu voira.
> Qui beurra tout d'une baleine
> Voira Dieu et la Madeleine.

I shall drink it all in a single draught; but what shall I see? The wine in the cup is like blood. When I hold it up to the pale moonlight it turns black, the lees of the lifeblood, the blood of lives which are sacred and lives which are profane. The vessel which holds the lifeblood is cracked now, and the lees flow away. For the line will die, and another branch must take its place.

Do the dead throng to greet us when we cross the threshold? Or shall I awaken and find that I have dreamed a dream about a sick old man who once wanted to be a court gentleman? And wrote a book that no one – not even he himself – understood?

Jean-Aimé de Chavigny has his instructions from the Cardinal de Lorraine. The *Centuries* are finished at last. My will is made. My papers and letters will be consigned to the fire, and all that links me with the house of Lorraine will vanish from the memory and knowledge of man. And Jean-Aimé will be my biographer, my eulogist, my loving and devoted student, my comrade, my disciple. Only through him will the world remember me. And he will leave a legacy which explains nothing, and reveals only shadows against a backdrop of shadows.

Who am I? What have I been? The dancing candle stub suspended before my eyes drips wax on to the parchment and on to my swollen hands. I am a soul of wax, upon which the motion of the world has been imprinted like waves on a sandy beach, ceaselessly changing, littered with footsteps and monuments and sepulchres and bones. Marked with the slow procession of majestic and pathetic figures moving from cradle to power to death: sacrificial kings whose blood fertilises the world, and grim warrior-monks whose solitude conjures the winds on lonely mountaintops, and glittering princes studded with rubies and onyx and jasper whose loins engender wars and plagues, and solemn popes and laughing cardinals whose thin hands caress inverted crucifixes, and spirits of water and fire and earth and air who conjure water into wine in invisible cups. These men I have known, hated and loved: they are themselves and not themselves, noble and ignoble, petty lives intertwined with the dense branches of myth. I was once a man, and then a mouthpiece; but for what? The endless procession dances its dance, and the dance is always the same: light and dark, god and goddess, hubris and humility, life and death. The answer is at last clear to my eyes, extinguished now by the long years of hopes and dreams and struggles and revelations, and human love and grief pitted against inexorable bastions of fate. Long years of visions which have brought death and visions which will bring births and deaths long after my death because I have instructed it to be so. I have written for the past, to enshrine it; for the present, to baffle and bemuse it; and for the future, to portray the pattern, to give hope and take away hope, to offer instruction, to warn, to terrify, to comfort. I am at peace now. Once I thought I had failed. Once I thought they had all failed. For so long, I concealed my knowledge of their tragedy in my belly beside my hopes, strange twins that have at last been born as one child in the hour of my death. I thought it was all to win a throne. I know better now.

There are clocks to tell the hour, and printed books. A new continent has been plundered, and the rock of the Church split open like a rotten fruit, while the heir to the throne of France fornicates with his gentlemen of the bedchamber. It is only the waters that have broken, the first pains, the first spasms. What head will emerge?

The future recedes like a long road spiralling through the mists, and scaling the high mountains, and vanishing in the darkening sky. I have written of fire and blood, pestilence and upheaval, change and war and death, the vicissitudes of cities and nations and men and kings – the long labour of five centuries of the long birth. For whom have I written?

D'un rond, d'un lys, naistra un si grand Prince,
Bientôt et tard venu dans sa Province . . .

The *roi perdu* waits in silence. His moment will not strike for half a millennium. We missed the opportunity. But there never existed any opportunity – only the imperious necessity to create one. Thus we become men, and not blind beasts who swallow their fate unknowing and unstriving. Now will begin the slow disintegration, and the grey bleak landscape of the kingless future, while the second Fish, the dark Fish, thrashes in the depths of the racial soul's fathomless pool. Conquerors and kingdoms will rise and fall, and at the last a great blight, a monstrous darkness, a plague of the spirit that spills out of the soil of Germany and gushes forth in a black stream across the Rhine to poison the world: the shadow of the whole of Europe, bursting the abcess at last with a merciless and pitiful cleansing. And the new world after, when the water pours from the Waterbearer's cup of red stone, and the Great Prince arises and gathers the threads of the united European nations in his hands to begin anew, a fresh cycle, a resurrection. The vine grows strong under the earth, and the blasted branches bear secret sap that will rise with the spring.

I have been a good servant. No one will remember that of me, for those whom I served are all dead but one. What have I served?

Amidst the dance of the fire I have seen his death too, far in the future. I do not know why, but this death above all others is sad and strange, and wrings from me unwilling and final tears. Only a death of fever, a simple death, a kindly death, an innocent death. I see him now surrounded by mist, while the tall and graceful figure in the vivid red robes vanishes, a shadow among shadows.

I must find a way to the bench placed beside the couch to help me into bed. I do not think my dropsical body will carry me even there, for it is terribly weary. Who will I be?

This cup, this *graal* . . .
I have drunk, *tout d'une baleine*.
She has waited for me for a long time.